New Cas

ONE WEEK LOAN

POETRY

WILLIAM BLAKE Edited by David Punter
CHAUCER Edited by Valerie Allen and Aries Axiotis
COLERIDGE, KEATS AND SHELLEY Edited by Peter J. Kitson
JOHN DONNE Edited by Andrew Mousley
SEAMUS HEANEY Edited by Michael Allen

GEORGE ORWELL Edited by Bryan Loughrey
SHELLEY: *Frankenstein* Edited by Fred Botting
STOKER: *Dracula* Edited by Glennis Byron
WOOLF: *Mrs Dalloway* and *To the Lighthouse* Edited by Su Reid

(continued overleaf)

SHEFFIELD HALLAM UNIVERSITY
LEARNING CENTRE
WITHDRAWN FROM STOCK

DRAMA

BECKETT: *Waiting for Godot* and *Endgame* Edited by Steven Connor
APHRA BEHN Edited by Janet Todd
MARLOWE Edited by Avraham Oz
REVENGE TRAGEDY Edited by Stevie Simkin
SHAKESPEARE: *Antony and Cleopatra* Edited by John Drakakis
SHAKESPEARE: *Hamlet* Edited by Martin Coyle
SHAKESPEARE: *Julius Caesar* Edited by Richard Wilson
SHAKESPEARE: *King Lear* Edited by Kiernan Ryan
SHAKESPEARE: *Macbeth* Edited by Alan Sinfield
SHAKESPEARE: *The Merchant of Venice* Edited by Martin Coyle
SHAKESPEARE: *A Midsummer Night's Dream* Edited by Richard Dutton
SHAKESPEARE: *Much Ado About Nothing* and *The Taming of the Shrew* Edited
   by Marion Wynne-Davies
SHAKESPEARE: *Othello* Edited by Lena Cowen Orlin
SHAKESPEARE: *Romeo and Juliet* Edited by R. S. White
SHAKESPEARE: *The Tempest* Edited by R. S. White
SHAKESPEARE: *Twelfth Night* Edited by R. S. White
SHAKESPEARE ON FILM Edited by Robert Shaughnessy
SHAKESPEARE IN PERFORMANCE Edited by Robert Shaughnessy
SHAKESPEARE'S HISTORY PLAYS Edited by Graham Holderness
SHAKESPEARE'S PROBLEM PLAYS Edited by Simon Barker
SHAKESPEARE'S ROMANCES Edited by Alison Thorne
SHAKESPEARE'S TRAGEDIES Edited by Susan Zimmerman
JOHN WEBSTER: *The Duchess of Malfi* Edited by Dympna Callaghan

GENERAL THEMES

FEMINIST THEATRE AND THEORY Edited by Helene Keyssar
POSTCOLONIAL LITERATURES Edited by Michael Parker and
   Roger Starkey

New Casebooks Series
Series Standing Order
ISBN 0-333-71702-3 hardcover
ISBN 0-333-69345-0 paperback
(*outside North America only*)

You can receive future titles in this series as they are published by placing a standing order. Please contact your bookseller or, in case of difficulty, write to us at the address below with your name and address, the title of the series and the ISBN quoted above.

Customer Services Department, Macmillan Distribution Ltd,
Houndmills, Basingstoke, Hampshire RG21 6XS, England

New Casebooks

DUBLINERS

JAMES JOYCE

EDITED BY ANDREW THACKER

Introduction, selection and editorial matter
© Andrew Thacker 2006

All rights reserved. No reproduction, copy or transmission of this publication may be made without written permission.

No paragraph of this publication may be reproduced, copied or transmitted save with written permission or in accordance with the provisions of the Copyright, Designs and Patents Act 1988, or under the terms of any licence permitting limited copying issued by the Copyright Licensing Agency, 90 Tottenham Court Road, London W1T 4LP.

Any person who does any unauthorised act in relation to this publication may be liable to criminal prosecution and civil claims for damages.

The authors have asserted their rights to be identified as the authors of this work in accordance with the Copyright, Designs and Patents Act 1988.

First published 2006 by
PALGRAVE MACMILLAN
Houndmills, Basingstoke, Hampshire RG21 6XS and
175 Fifth Avenue, New York, N. Y. 10010
Companies and representatives throughout the world

PALGRAVE MACMILLAN is the global academic imprint of the Palgrave Macmillan division of St. Martin's Press, LLC and of Palgrave Macmillan Ltd. Macmillan® is a registered trademark in the United States, United Kingdom and other countries. Palgrave is a registered trademark in the European Union and other countries.

ISBN-13: 978 0333-77769-5   hardback
ISBN-10: 0333-77769-7   hardback
ISBN-13: 978 0333-77770-1   paperback
ISBN-10: 0-333-77770-0   paperback

This book is printed on paper suitable for recycling and made from fully managed and sustained forest sources.

A catalogue record for this book is available from the British Library.

Library of Congress Cataloging-in-Publication Data
Dubliners: James Joyce/ edited by Andrew Thacker.
    p. cm. – (New casebooks)
    Includes bibliographical references (p.) and index.
    ISBN 0-333-77769-7 (alk. paper) – ISBN 0-333-77770-0 (pbk.: alk. paper)
    1. Joyce, James, 1882–1941. Dubliners. 2. Dublin (Ireland)–In literature.
I. Thacker, Andrew, 1962– II. New casebooks (Palgrave Macmillan (Firm))
PR6019.O9D86 2005
823'.912–dc22   2005040241

10   9   8   7   6   5   4   3   2   1
15   14 13 12 11 10 09 08 07 06

Printed in China

Contents

Acknowledgements   vii

General Editors' Preface   ix

Introduction: ANDREW THACKER   1

1. A Beginning: Signification, Story, and Discourse in
   Joyce's 'The Sisters'   15
   THOMAS F. STALEY

2. Silences in *Dubliners*   33
   JEAN-MICHEL RABATÉ

3. Through a Cracked Looking-Glass: Desire and
   Frustration in *Dubliners*   52
   SUZETTE A. HENKE

4. Narration Under a Blindfold: Reading Joyce's 'Clay'   76
   MARGOT NORRIS

5. No Cheer for the 'Gratefully Oppressed': Ideology in
   Joyce's *Dubliners*   96
   TREVOR L. WILLIAMS

6. 'An Encounter' Boys' Magazines and the
   Pseudo-Literary   117
   R. B. KERSHNER

7. Uncanny Returns in 'The Dead'   135
   ROBERT SPOO

8. 'Araby': The Exoticised and Orientalised Other   156
   VINCENT J. CHENG

9. The *Dubliners* Epiphony: (Mis)Reading the Book
   of Ourselves   174
   KEVIN J. H. DETTMAR

10. 'Have you no homes to go to?': James Joyce and
    the Politics of Paralysis   196
    LUKE GIBBONS

Further Reading   218

Notes on Contributors   224

Index   227

Acknowledgements

The editor and publishers wish to thank the following for permission to use copyright material:

Vincent J. Cheng, for material from *Joyce, Race and Empire* (1995), pp. 77–9, 88–100, by permission of Cambridge University Press; Kevin J. H. Dettmar, for material from *The Illicit Joyce of Postmodernism: Reading Against the Grain* (1996). Copyright © 1996, by permission of the University of Wisconsin Press; Luke Gibbons, for material from '"Have you no homes to go to?": James Joyce and the Politics of Paralysis' from *Semicolonial Joyce*, ed. Derek Attridge and Majorie Howes (2000), pp. 150–69, by permission of Cambridge University Press; Suzette A. Henke, for material from *James Joyce and the Politics of Desire*, Routledge (1990), pp. 12–24, 42–9, by permission of Taylor & Francis Books Ltd; R. B. Kershner, for material from *Joyce, Bakhtin and Popular Culture: Chronicles of Disorder* (1989), pp. 31–46. Copyright © 1989 by the University of North Carolina Press, by permission of The University of North Carolina Press; Margot Norris, for 'Narration Under a Blindfold: Reading Joyce's "Clay"', *PMLA*, 102:1 (1989), 206–15, by permission of the Modern Language Association of America; Jean-Michel Rabaté, for material from *James Joyce: Authorized Reader* (1991), pp. 20–47, by permission of the Johns Hopkins University Press; Robert Spoo, for 'Uncanny Returns in "The Dead": Ibsenian Intertexts and the Estranged Infant' in *Joyce: The Return of the Repressed*, ed. Susan Stanford Friedman (1993), pp. 89–100, 103, 105–9, 110–13. Copyright © 1993 by Cornell University, by permission of Cornell University Press; Thomas Staley, for 'A Beginning: Signification, Story, and Discourse in Joyce's "The Sisters"', *Genre*, XII (1979), 533–49, by permission of *Genre*; Trevor L. Williams, 'No Cheer for the "Gratefully

Oppressed": Ideology in Joyce's *Dubliners'*, *Style*, 25:3 (1991), 416–17, 419–27, 430–5, by permission of *Style*.

Every effort has been made to trace the copyright holders but if any have been inadvertently overlooked the publishers will be pleased to make the necessary arrangement at the first opportunity.

Quotes from James Joyce, *Dubliners*. Copyright © The Estate of James Joyce.

General Editors' Preface

The purpose of this series of New Casebooks is to reveal some of the ways in which contemporary criticism has changed our understanding of commonly studied texts and writers and, indeed, of the nature of criticism itself. Central to the series is a concern with modern critical theory and its effect on current approaches to the study of literature. Each New Casebook editor has been asked to select a sequence of essays which will introduce the reader to the new critical approaches to the text or texts being discussed in the volume and also illuminate the rich interchange between critical theory and critical practice that characterises so much current writing about literature.

In this focus on modern critical thinking and practice New Casebooks aim not only to inform but also to stimulate, with volumes seeking to reflect both the controversy and the excitement of current criticism. Because much of this criticism is difficult and often employs an unfamiliar critical language, editors have been asked to give the reader as much help as they feel is appropriate, but without simplifying the essays or the issues they raise. Again, editors have been asked to supply a list of further reading which will enable readers to follow up issues raised by the essays in the volume.

The project of New Casebooks, then, is to bring together in an illuminating way those critics who best illustrate the ways in which contemporary criticism has established new methods of analysing texts and who have reinvigorated the important debate about how we 'read' literature. The hope is, of course, that New Casebooks will not only open up this debate to a wider audience, but will also encourage students to extend their own ideas, and think afresh about their responses to the texts they are studying.

John Peck and Martin Coyle
University of Wales, Cardiff

Introduction

ANDREW THACKER

For many years *Dubliners* was the poor relation in the Joyce canon, the major completed book that received the least critical attention. The original Macmillan Casebook of 1973, edited by Morris Beja, combined *Dubliners* with *A Portrait of the Artist as a Young Man* and noted that these works demonstrated 'the achievements of Joyce's young maturity as an artist'.[1] Though the impressive fact that Joyce had completed the stories for *Dubliners* by the time he was in his mid-twenties is acknowledged by Beja's reference to his 'maturity', it still seems that the volume was regarded as the commencement of a career which was only to reach its zenith with the trilogy of novels, *A Portrait (1916)*, *Ulysses (1922)* and *Finnegans Wake (1939)*. The bibliography to Beja's Casebook, for example, lists no monograph devoted solely to *Dubliners*, unlike *A Portrait*.[2] *Ulysses* had already been the subject of numerous critical and exegetical studies, and, because of his reappearance there, the initial drawing of Stephen Dedalus's character in *A Portrait* was regarded as a significant reason for analysing that text.

The relative academic neglect of *Dubliners*, from its publication in 1914 until the first volume of critical essays on the text by Peter Garret in 1968, followed by Clive Hart's collection in 1969, was the result of a number of factors that it is not my intention to rehearse here, given the limitations of space.[3] Two explanations are, however, worth mentioning briefly. First, as a volume of short stories *Dubliners* suffered from the more lowly status possessed by this genre in comparison to the novel.[4] Second, there was perhaps a perception that *Dubliners* is a less stylistically experimental piece of writing, when compared to *Ulysses* or *Finnegans Wake*. Even *A Portrait* shows Joyce employing the 'stream of consciousness' technique throughout, a feature universally noted as typifying the experimental fiction of the early twentieth century. *Dubliners*, read for the first time and without reflection or study, might strike one as discrete from the linguistic pyrotechnics of *Finnegans Wake*: isn't it just a collection of realist or – at a stretch – naturalist stories, similar to those of fellow Irishman George Moore, and clearly displaying the morbid influence of Ibsen? A number of the stories from *Dubliners* had, indeed, first been published in 1904 in a magazine, the *Irish Homestead*, which was the weekly publication of the Irish Agricultural Organisation, a journal dubbed the 'pig's paper' by Stephen Dedalus. The editor, George Russell (known as the writer AE), invited Joyce to contribute something 'simple, rural ... which could be inserted so as not to shock the readers'.[5] This, typically, was advice that Joyce ignored, since the stories in *Dubliners* eschew a 'rural' setting, are often only deceptively 'simple' and clearly caused some 'shock' if we recall Joyce's difficulties in getting certain of the stories published without revision.[6] Even so, we might still view these shocking urban tales as examples of realist prose if we take our cue from Joyce himself. In a letter of 1906, he famously called the style of the stories one of 'scrupulous meanness', in which the people of Ireland could have a 'good look at themselves in my nicely polished looking-glass'.[7] This is an image that has often been interpreted to support a 'realist' reading of *Dubliners*, arguing that Joyce's desire was to 'shock' his readers by revealing what he perceived to be the 'paralysis' of the city.[8]

While none of the critical essays collected in this volume really engages with the devaluation of the short story as a genre, they all share a rejection of the claim that *Dubliners* is not an experimental form of fiction. The multiple approaches of literary and cultural theory over the last thirty years, a variety of which are highlighted in this volume, could all be said to agree upon one thing: that *Dubliners* is a complex and fascinating piece of writing, that it employs stylistic innovations that, while seemingly quieter than those of *Ulysses*, represent a marked development in prose fiction, and that the concerns of the stories mark this work as a modernist rather than realist text.[9] For example, the eminent Joycean critic Derek Attridge notes in an introduction to a collection of his own writings upon Joyce that the aim of one of his essays, a brilliant reading of 'Clay', was to 'question the well-entrenched notions that *Dubliners* is an exercise in careful realism'.[10] It has perhaps taken the heterogeneous insights of contemporary critical theory fully to appreciate and reveal the aesthetic adventures that mark *Dubliners* and make a claim for its central status in the Joyce oeuvre. Another route by which traditional views of *Dubliners* have been revised emerged from critics who read Joyce in reverse, so to speak. Christine van Boheeman noted that 'Reading *Dubliners* with the insights gained from *Finnegans Wake*, we suddenly discover affinities between the two works which reveal a new complexity in the apparent realism of the earliest epiphanies.'[11] This was especially true of those poststructuralist and deconstructive critics who cut their critical teeth by tracing the play of the signifier in the *Wake*.[12]

Over the last thirty years the 'Joyce Industry' has become one of the major scholarly institutions in English and Irish studies in Europe, North America and many other parts of the world.[13] *Dubliners* has received much more attention as part of this general growth in the volume of Joyce criticism. From there being no monograph on *Dubliners* in the early 1970s we can now note, for example, two whole books devoted to Lacanian-derived psychoanalytic interpretations of Joyce's volume.[14] There is now no lack of different interpretations of the stories, using theoretical approaches from just about every perspective possible within literary and cultural studies. In fact, a chronological survey of how *Dubliners* has been read over the last few decades would probably reveal a fairly representative picture of how literary theory itself has developed over this period.[15] From approaches in the late 1970s and early 1980s that used linguistically based theories, such as those drawn from semiotics and structuralism and represented here by Thomas Staley's essay,[16] we notice the emergence in English of a 'poststructuralist Joyce' in the early 1980s, an approach represented here by Rabaté's reading of 'The Sisters'.[17] One prompt for such work was the complex musing of Jacques Derrida upon Joyce, and *Ulysses* in particular.[18] Around this period, too, Joyce began to receive more attention from feminist critics, especially those influenced by the engagement of French feminism with the psychoanalytical work of Jacques Lacan;[19] Henke's contribution (essay 3) in this collection clearly demonstrates this approach. Since the late 1980s the dominantly textual approach of these schools of interpretations has been supplemented by readings that stress the contextual and historical elements of *Dubliners*. The essays here by Kershner, Williams, Cheng and Gibbons all, in diverse fashion, read Joyce through the lens of contemporary Irish social and economic history: putting Dublin back into *Dubliners* might sum up these perspectives.

The essays in this volume follow a rough chronology from the late 1970s to 2000, and attempt to demonstrate some of the multiplicity of theoretical paths to Joyce. The volume also tries to balance between essays that discuss individual stories closely, with ones that attempt a broader consideration of *Dubliners* as a whole. While it would be easy enough to fill a New Casebook with essays that just interpreted 'The Dead' from the point of view of poststructuralism, feminism, New Historicism and other perspectives, the selection here tries to do justice to stories that have traditionally been somewhat overlooked or relegated to the second division of Joyce's work.[20] While 'The Dead' remains a major piece of the Joyce jigsaw, leading into a number of the themes of *Ulysses*, as Richard Ellmann argued,[21] contemporary criticism has been fascinated by the narrative evasions of a story such as 'Clay', or the references to popular culture in 'An Encounter', texts skilfully elucidated in this volume by Norris and Kershner respectively.

Tracing the genealogy of contemporary theory's engagement with Joyce is a problematic, perhaps fruitless, endeavour. However, the publication of Thomas F. Staley's 'A Beginning: Signification, Story, and Discourse in Joyce: "The Sisters" ' in 1979 (essay 1) can be associated with a number of other publications in the same year that offered a new *Dubliners* informed by contemporary narrative theory. Since the early 1970s, structuralist and semiotic modes of interpretation had begun, however grudgingly, to make inroads into English studies. Robert Scholes, author of *Structuralism in Literature*, had offered a structuralist reading of *Ulysses* in 1972, and in 1979 produced a technically rigorous semiotic analysis of 'Eveline', using the theories of Tzvetan Todorov, Gérard Genette and Roland Barthes.[22] Unlike the high structuralist methodology of Scholes, which alarmed many traditional readers of literature with its diagrammatic images of narrative, Staley's essay is a very clear statement of how structuralist and semiotic theories could open up Joyce's texts in fascinating new ways. Staley, a well-known Joycean scholar, uses the work of Barthes, David Lodge and Roman Jakobson to analyse the first story in *Dubliners* as offering a new beginning, not only for Joyce, but for modernist fiction too. The structuralist tenor of Staley's approach is summarised early on, when he notes that although the start of 'The Sisters' does not appear to be massively experimental, it 'places radical emphasis on language and in turn on the text as text. In *Dubliners* Joyce begins to give priority to the word over the world.'[23] Staley sees this stress upon the linguistic construction of the world as part of Joyce's own development as a writer, and as a feature of modernist narratives that reject the realist novel's attempt to produce an imaginary window on the 'real' world. For modernism language was a material phenomenon that shapes our view of the world, and not a transparent textual window upon reality. This is an argument also made by Colin McCabe in his 1979 book, *James Joyce and the Revolution of the Word*, one of the first accounts to insist upon the political implications of the new structuralist attention to language, a dimension not covered by Staley.[24] McCabe compared stories in *Dubliners* such as 'The Sisters' to what he termed the 'classic realist text' of George Eliot in *Middlemarch* and *Daniel Deronda*, infamously suggesting that while Joyce's text was revolutionary in its linguistic undermining of subjectivity, Eliot's text was conservative in the way in which its language worked to confirm a safe, bourgeois reader.

McCabe's provocative claims might be said to herald the emergence of a poststructuralist Joyce, pushing the implications of Staley's claim for the 'radical emphasis upon language' as far as possible. Jean-Michel Rabaté's 'A Portrait of the Reader as a Young Dubliner' (essay 2) was originally published as 'Silences In *Dubliners*', in a book of 'new perspectives' upon Joyce edited by McCabe in 1982.[25] Rabaté's essay – an example of the so-called 'French Joyce'[26] – is an early and classic poststructuralist reading of *Dubliners*, with a considerable focus on silence, puns and linguistic ambiguities in 'The Sisters'. Rabaté's view of this story is in marked contrast to Staley's, and the differences help illuminate the wider shift from structuralism to poststructuralism. For Staley, Joyce's radical emphasis upon the linguistic construction of the world is a kind of confirmation of Joyce's ability as a modernist writer to manipulate words in his view of the world. For Rabaté, Joyce's linguistic 'play' in *Dubliners* is a much more radical questioning of reading and interpretation that always threatens to deconstruct any attempt to neatly understand what the text means. *Dubliners* is 'haunted' by a kind of 'silence of interpretation', shown in the many references to silence in the first story in the volume and elsewhere, and which Rabaté associates with the reader's own silent reading of the text.[27] Rabaté appears to suggest that Joyce's text resists any easy interpretation of what it means, and constantly poses a challenge to the processes of critical exegesis itself. While Staley draws attention to how self-conscious a writer Joyce is, Rabaté presents 'The Sisters' as a story about interpretation, a self-reflexive exploration not of writing, but of reading itself.

Drawing upon the work of Derrida and Lacan, Rabaté's essay also foregrounds another key theme of poststructuralist and deconstructive accounts of Joyce, that of the decentring of subjectivity amidst the infinite play of language. A similar argument is found in

Hélène Cixous's detailed examination of the first paragraph of 'The Sisters' in an essay entitled 'The (R)use of Writing'. Cixous suggests that the halting attempts by the boy in the story to interpret the signs 'paralysis', 'gnomon' and 'simony' show how it 'is impossible for the narrator to constitute himself as an imaginary unity by gaining assurance from a language which escapes mastery, especially since the signifiers from a foreign tongue only make his voice echo'.[28] For Cixous this concern with the slippage of the signifier and the decentring of the subject shows how Joyce's 'revolution of the word' can be perceived even at the commencement of *Dubliners*; it is a strategy that interprets 'The Sisters' not as a realist short story but rather as an embryonic version of *Finnegans Wake*.

In accounts of the development of literary theory Cixous is normally located within the pantheon of French Feminism, that ensemble of thinkers who adopted and adapted poststructuralist insights into the nature of language and subjectivity for the analysis of gender and sexuality. Suzette A. Henke's essay in this volume (essay 3), 'Through a Cracked Looking-Glass: Desire and Frustration in *Dubliners*', is taken from her 1990 book *James Joyce and the Politics of Desire*, which was the first full-length application of French feminist theorists such as Cixous, Julia Kristeva and Luce Irigaray to Joyce.[29] Henke's focus is upon how Joyce became 'a revolutionary writer, forging new psychosexual subject-positions in a controversial discourse of desire'.[30] Despite the fact that Joyce has 'a notoriously ambivalent reputation among feminist scholars', writes Henke, she argues that Joyce's experimental writing 'exhibits a pervasive anti-patriarchal bias ... that challenges the assumptions of traditional culture, including phallocentric authority and logocentric discourse'.[31] Henke's focus upon how Joyce's work undermines patriarchal assumptions draws upon feminist-inflected psychoanalysis, as well as a general poststructuralist argument about the nature of language.

The difference in Henke's approach can be seen if one compares her account of *Dubliners* with that of a slightly earlier essay upon women in *Dubliners* by Florence L. Walzl.[32] Walzl's essay is a good example of an Anglo-American feminist analysis of *Dubliners*. She considers the social history of women's roles in Dublin in the early twentieth century and then focuses upon the different female characters represented in *Dubliners* in order to see how accurately Joyce represents the historical reality of women in Dublin. Broadly we might say that while Walzl studies the historical content of Joyce's

'images of women', Henke focuses upon the psychoanalytic meanings of Joyce's depiction of gender and the formal strategies by
which his writing interrogates the interrelationships of men and
women. For Henke, for example, the multiple references to paralysis in *Dubliners* are to be understood in terms of the psychoanalytic
category of desire: men and women are subject to a kind of psychic
paralysis due to the impossible demands their desire places upon
them to find satisfaction in mythic images of each other. The terror
felt by Gabriel Conroy at the end of 'The Dead', when his wife
Gretta tells of her former love for the dead Michael Furey, is one
such moment of the impossibility of desire finding fulfilment.

Another analysis of the theme of desire is found in Margot
Norris, 'Narration Under a Blindfold: Reading Joyce's "Clay" '
(essay 4).[33] Written by an eminent Joyce critic who was one of the
first to approach *Finnegans Wake* from an overtly theoretical point
of view,[34] this is a classic example of a new narratological reading
of Joyce that uses Lacan and René Girard to show how the reader is
implicated in the self-deceptions of the story's heroine, Maria.
Although Norris's use of theoretical terminology is less prominent
than that of, say, Henke or Cixous, her essay shows how contemporary literary theory has opened up for further discussion a story
that had seemed one of the slighter examples of Joyce's work. The
work of critics influenced by psychoanalysis is also represented in
this volume by Robert Spoo's 'Uncanny Returns in "The Dead" '
(essay 7).[35] This is a very thorough rereading of 'The Dead' from a
Freudian point of view, shifting attention from Gabriel's epiphany
at the end of the story (the dominant critical reading) to elements of
the 'uncanny' found in Gretta Conroy's love for Michael Furey. The
essays by Norris and Spoo both demonstrate perhaps the central
feature of post-Lacanian psychoanalytic criticism; that is, a refusal
to psychoanalyse either the author or the characters in the fiction in
favour of concentrating upon the textual operation of the unconscious in the language of the stories themselves.

Towards the end of the 1980s Joyce criticism, like literary theory
itself, experienced something of a reaction to approaches that took
an overly textual or linguistic focus, even ones with an implied
social dimension such as feminism. The essays by Williams,
Kershner and Cheng below all represent what might be termed a re-
historicisation of Joyce studies, a trend most apparent in Williams's
essay in this volume, ' "No Cheer for the Gratefully Oppressed":
Ideology in Joyce's *Dubliners*' (essay 5). Written by perhaps the

foremost 'traditional' Marxist critic on Joyce, Williams's essay demonstrates how the linguistic style of the text can be linked to questions of ideology and politics. Joyce's work has long been subject to scrutiny, both affirmative and negative, from English-speaking Marxist critics since Alick West's critique of *Ulysses* in the 1930s.[36] More recent eminent Marxists such as Terry Eagleton and Fredric Jameson have also found Joyce's works amenable to analysis.[37] One of the most striking features of *Dubliners* is that it is a text that is deeply embedded within the historical fabric of the Irish capital of the early years of the century. 'Ivy Day in the Committee Room', for example, is set against the background of contemporary Irish politics and the great disgraced leader of nineteenth-century Irish nationalism, Charles Stewart Parnell. Other stories consider social problems of the time such as drunkenness, emigration and the employment prospects of single women. It is, then, no surprise that Marxist and other historicist critics have stressed that the book can only fully be understood when it is inserted into the context of Irish history and politics.[38]

In addition to traditional Marxist accounts, Joyce has also received much interest from critics who have been influenced by Bakhtinian and New Historicist literary approaches. R. B. Kershner's reading (essay 6) of 'An Encounter' is a testimony to this form of 'revisionist' Marxism or 'cultural materialist' approach to Joyce.[39] Kershner's *Joyce, Bakhtin and Popular Culture: Chronicles of Disorder* was the first full-length use of the Russian critic Mikhail Bakhtin in relation to Joyce.[40] Many critics felt that Bakhtin's stress upon the social materiality of language in the novel offered a sophisticated counter to what was perceived as the excessively textual focus of poststructuralist criticism. Kershner's work is also significant for the way in which it reads Joyce through the prism of contemporary popular culture, an approach popularised by the New Historicism. This form of criticism seeks to interpret literary texts through detailed analysis of relevant non-literary texts, in Kershner's case of boys' magazines at the turn of the century. Cheryl Herr outlines a similar strategy in *Joyce's Anatomy of Culture*, demonstrating how Joyce's writing drew upon a meticulous knowledge of Irish newspapers, pantomimes, music hall performances, and even sermons by celebrity preachers, the latter forming the context to the story 'Grace'.[41] Such an approach argues that Joyce's texts do not simply 'reflect' Irish history and society, as classical Marxist criticism might say, but that his writing is shaped by an interactive or, in Bakhtin's terms, dialogic engagement with the cultural institutions and texts of his time. In this model of literary history Joyce is not merely subjected to the dominant structures of power in Irish society, but is able, in Herr's words, to produce 'complex subversions' of the institutions of social power.[42]

This imbrication of culture and power is one of the fundamental features of postcolonial studies, perhaps the major development to emerge in literary studies over recent years. At the time of composition Dublin was, as Joyce noted, the 'second city of the British Empire',[43] and the imperial relationships between Ireland and Britain pervade much of the detail of *Dubliners*. In 'The Dead', for example, Gabriel is discomforted by the nationalist Miss Ivors's accusation that he is a 'West Briton', a pro-British Irish person who refuses to show any interest in speaking Irish or visiting other parts of Ireland. Even the place-names of the streets and sites of Dublin that Joyce was so careful to render accurately in the book contain evidence of the imperial presence of Britain in Ireland: Maria in 'Clay' boards a tram from under Nelson's Pillar, a statue of the English Admiral Horatio Nelson that used to occupy the centre of Dublin's Sackville Street (now O'Connell Street); Gabriel in 'The Dead' recalls a similar image of imperial geography, the monument to another Anglo-Irish hero, the Duke of Wellington, in Dublin's Phoenix Park.

The essays by Vincent Cheng and Luke Gibbons (essays 8 and 10) both take aspects of this imperial history as their focus, displaying how postcolonial criticism combines an interest in the formal properties of literary texts with attention to the historical matters they address. Cheng's analysis of 'Araby' adapts Edward Said's influential concept of Orientalism, and shows how a discourse of 'race' was 'inseparable from the "Irish Question" and issues of Empire and Home Rule'.[44] Irish Orientalism was, as Kershner writes in a collection of articles upon this topic in Joyce, a 'construction of the British Empire but a locally mediated construction: an imperial dream of the East with an Irish accent'.[45] Cheng analyses how in 'Araby' the young boy's desire for the girl is linked to discourses of Orientalism found in the Araby bazaar to which he travels at the close of the story.

Luke Gibbons's ' "Have you no homes to go to?" James Joyce and the Politics of Paralysis' is an excellent example of one of the most recent trends in Joyce criticism, Irish Studies.[46] Energised by the general interest in postcolonialism, recent work in Irish studies has attempted to understand how far concepts drawn from post-colonial studies of non-European literatures can be applied to the relations between Britain and Ireland. In contrast to the essays by Rabaté and Henke, which understand Joyce's theme of 'paralysis' in linguistic and psychoanalytic fashion, Gibbons situates the trope of paralysis within the context of post-famine Irish history. Like Cheng's, Gibbons's account of *Dubliners* is an example of the inter-disciplinary nature of postcolonial studies and of the way in which such an approach is theoretically heterogeneous, borrowing ideas from both Freud and feminist criticism, but based solidly upon a reading of relevant historical material.

Set against the historicist tendencies of postcolonial criticism is the essay by Kevin Dettmar, 'The *Dubliners* Epiphony: (Mis)Reading the Book of Ourselves' (essay 9). This is from his provocative account of a 'postmodern' Joyce that stresses mystery over mastery of the text, and draws upon Barthes and Jean-François Lyotard.[47] For Dettmar, Joyce's writings demonstrate what he terms a 'postmodern stylistics', a form of writing that values 'textual play over high artistic purpose' and emphasises a 'dogged resistance to interpretation' by the critic.[48] Dettmar is aware that Joyce is normally considered a paradigmatically 'modernist' author, but argues for an understanding of postmodernism not as a histori-cal category but rather, as in Lyotard, as a disruptive tendency in aesthetics that can be found in the cultural texts of any period.[49] In particular, Dettmar analyses how the orthodox critical attention to Joyce's famous concept of epiphany misses the point of a story like 'Araby', where the symbols amount only to red herrings for the reader. This analysis offers a sharp contrast to the more politicised reading of 'Araby' by Cheng, while forming a link back to the post-structuralist interpretation of Joyce found in Rabaté.

Modernist or postmodernist, Orientalist or textualist, it seems as if the real strength of *Dubliners* is its ability to bear the weight of these multifarious theoretical categories and still leave much for the reader and critic to debate and enjoy. Often the text that is used to introduce students to the myriad perplexities of Joyce, *Dubliners* is anything but the set of simple rural tales sought from its author by George Russell. The contemporary critical essays collected here hopefully demonstrate an even more complex and exciting side to *Dubliners*, one that might still serve to introduce students to Joyce, but one that will also help them appreciate the unnerving beauty of Joyce's vision of his home city.[50]

Notes

The Joyce Estate has requested that we acknowledge that we are reproducing material from *Dubliners* without their permission, although such permission is not legally required.

1. Morris Beja, 'Introduction', in *James Joyce: 'Dubliners' and 'A Portrait of the Artist as a Young Man'*, A Casebook, ed. Morris Beja (Basingstoke, 1973), p. 16.

2. In fact there was an early monograph devoted to *Dubliners* alone, Warren Beck's Joyce's *Dubliners: Substance, Vision and Art* (Durham, NC, 1969).

3. See Peter K. Garrett (ed.), *Twentieth Century Interpretations of 'Dubliners': A Collection of Critical Essays* (Englewood Cliffs, NJ, 1968); Clive Hart (ed.), *James Joyce's 'Dubliners': Critical Essays* (London, 1969).

4. For a brief discussion of Joyce's place in the history of the short story, see Terence Brown, 'Introduction', James Joyce, *Dubliners*, ed. Terence Brown (Harmondsworth, 1992).

5. *Letters of James Joyce*, vol 2, ed. Richard Ellmann (New York, 1966), p. 43.

6. Two stories in particular were perceived to give offence, 'Ivy Day in the Committee Room' for its reference to King Edward VII, and 'Two Gallants', owing to its subject matter. For a discussion of the publication history of the book, see Hans Walter Gabler, 'Introduction', James Joyce, *Dubliners*, ed. Hans Walter Gabler with Walter Hettche (London, 1993), pp. 1–34.

7. *Letters*, vol 2, p. 134; *Letters*, vol 1, ed. Stuart Gilbert (New York, 1957), p. 64.

8. See Joyce, *Letters*, vol 1, p. 55.

9. The caveat to this is Kevin Dettmar's essay in this collection which reads Joyce as a postmodernist, rather than a modernist.

10. Derek Attridge, *Joyce Effects: On Language, Theory, and History* (Cambridge, 2000), p. xvi.

11. Christine van Boheemen, 'Deconstruction After Joyce', in Bonnie Kime Scott (ed.), *New Alliances in Joyce Studies* (Newark, 1988), p. 35.

12. An early example of this is Stephen Heath's 'Ambiviolences: Notes for Reading Joyce', which first appeared in the important French journal *Tel Quel* (1972) and is reprinted in Derek Attridge and Daniel Ferrer (eds), *Post-Structuralist Joyce: Essays from the French* (Cambridge, 1984). Also see Margot Norris, *The Decentered Universe of 'Finnegans Wake': A Structuralist Analysis* (Baltimore, MD, 1976).

13. Joyce attracts a number of established international conferences and several academic journals devoted to his work, including the important *James Joyce Quarterly*.

14. See Garry M. Leonard, *Reading 'Dubliners' Again: A Lacanian Perspective* (New York, 1993) and Earl G. Ingersoll, *Engendered Trope in Joyce's 'Dubliners'* (Carbondale, IL, 1996).

15. For an overview of theoretical approaches to Joyce up to 1990, see Alan Roughly, *James Joyce and Critical Theory: An Introduction* (Ann Arbor, MI, 1991).

16. Thomas F. Staley, 'A Beginning: Signification, Story, and Discourse in Joyce's "The Sisters" ', *Genre*, 12 (Winter 1979), 533–49.

17. *Post-Structuralist Joyce: Essays from the French* (Cambridge, 1984) was the title of an important collection of essays edited by Derek Attridge and Daniel Ferrer.

18. See Jacques Derrida, 'Two Words for Joyce' in Attridge and Ferrer (eds), *Post-Structuralist Joyce*, and 'Ulysses Gramophone: Hear Say Yes in Joyce', in Jacques Derrida, *Acts of Literature*, ed. Derek Attridge (London, 1992).

19. See, for example, Suzette Henke, *James Joyce and the Politics of Desire* (New York and London, 1990).

20. A volume in the Case Studies in Contemporary Criticism series, *James Joyce: The Dead*, ed. Daniel R. Schwarz (Basingstoke, 1994), uses this story to help introduce students to psychoanalytic, reader-response, New Historicist, feminist and deconstructive criticism.

21. Richard Ellmann, 'The Backgrounds to the Dead', ch. XV of his *James Joyce*, rev. edn (Oxford, 1982).

22. Robert Scholes, *Structuralism in Literature: An Introduction* (New Haven, CT, 1974); '*Ulysses*: A Structuralist Perspective', *James Joyce Quarterly*, 10:1 (1972); 'Semiotic Approaches to a Fictional Text: Joyce's "Eveline" ', *James Joyce Quarterly*, 16:1–2 (1978–9).

23. Staley, 'A Beginning', p. 536.

24. Colin McCabe, *James Joyce and the Revolution of the Word* (Basingstoke, 1979).

25. Colin McCabe (ed.), *James Joyce: New Perspectives* (Brighton, 1982).

26. See Derek Attridge, *Joyce Effects*, pp. 6–8 for a discussion of this development in Joyce studies.

27. Jean-Michel Rabaté, *James Joyce, Authorized Reader* (Baltimore, MD, 1991), p. 21.

28. Hélène Cixous, 'The (R)use of Writing', in *Post-Structuralist Joyce*, ed. Derek Attridge and Daniel Ferrer, p. 26.

29. It is normally understood that Cixous's book, *The Exiles of James Joyce* (New York, 1972), published first in French in 1968, predates her engagement with poststructuralist theory.

30. Henke, *James Joyce and the Politics of Desire*, p. 10.

31. Henke, *James Joyce*, p. 11.

32. Florence L. Walzl, '*Dubliners*: Women in Irish Society', in *Women in Joyce*, ed. Suzette Henke and Elaine Unkeless (Brighton, 1982).

33. Margot Norris, 'Narration Under a Blindfold: Reading Joyce's "Clay" ', *PMLA*, 102:1 (March 1987), 206–15.

34. See Norris, *The Decentered Universe of 'Finnegans Wake'*.

35. Robert Spoo, 'Uncanny Returns in "The Dead": Ibsenian Intertexts and the Estranged Infant', in Susan Stanford Friedman (ed.), *Joyce: The Return of the Repressed* (Ithaca and London, 1993).

36. Alick West, *Crisis and Criticism* (London, 1936).

37. See, for example, Terry Eagleton, *Criticism and Ideology: A Study in Marxist Literary Theory* (London, 1978), and Fredric Jameson, '*Ulysses* in History' in W. J. McCormack and Alistair Stead (eds), *James Joyce and Modern Literature* (London, 1982).

38. For a study of Joyce's own political attitudes, see Dominic Manganiello, *Joyce's Politics* (London, 1980). Two other full-length Marxist interpretations of Joyce are James Fairhall, *James Joyce and the Question of History* (Cambridge, 1993) and Trevor L. Williams, *Reading Joyce Politically* (Gainesville, FL, 1997).

39. The term 'cultural materialism' is often associated with the critic Raymond Williams, and is sometimes used as the British version of the American New Historicism. Primarily it refers to an approach that stresses a more politically committed analysis of the historical content and context of literary and cultural texts. For consideration of both theories see H. Aram Veeser (ed.), *The New Historicism* (London, 1989), Kiernan Ryan (ed.), *New Historicism and Cultural Materialism: A Reader* (London, 1996) and Alan Sinfield, *Faultlines: Cultural Materialism and the Politics of Dissident Reading* (Oxford, 1992).

40. Another Bakhtinian reading of Joyce is that of Keith Booker, *Joyce, Bakhtin and the Literary Tradition* (Ann Arbor, MI, 1995).

41. Cheryl Herr, *Joyce's Anatomy of Culture* (Urbana and Chicago, 1986).

42. Herr, *Anatomy*, p. 14.

43. *Letters*, vol. 2, p. 111.

44. Vincent J. Cheng, *Joyce, Race and Empire* (Cambridge, 1995), p. 15. 'Home Rule' and the 'Irish Question' were phrases used in contemporary political debates to refer to the vexed issue of whether Britain should continue to administer Ireland's affairs, or whether Ireland should have 'Home Rule', that is, independence from Britain.

45. Brandon Kershner, 'Introduction' to 'ReOrienting Joyce' section, *James Joyce Quarterly*, 35:2–3 (Winter/Spring 1998), p. 260.

46. Other examples of this approach include Enda Duffy, *The 'Subaltern' Ulysses* (Minneapolis, 1994), Emer Nolan, *James Joyce and Nationalism* (London, 1995), and *Semicolonial Joyce*, ed. Derek Attridge and Marjorie Howes (Cambridge, 2000).

47. Kevin J. H. Dettmar, *The Illicit Joyce of Postmodernism: Reading Against the Grain* (Wisconsin, 1996). For another reading of Joyce that uses the work of Lyotard see Joseph Valente, *James Joyce and the Problem of Justice: Negotiating Sexual and Colonial Difference* (Cambridge, 1995).

48. Dettmar, *The Illicit Joyce*, p. 10.

49. For this definition of postmodernism, see Jean-François Lyotard, *The Post-Modern Condition: A Report on Knowledge* (Manchester, 1984), pp. 79–81.

50. The selection of materials for this book was originally completed in 2001.

1

A Beginning: Signification, Story, and Discourse in Joyce's 'The Sisters'

THOMAS F. STALEY

I

Just as beginnings in fiction delimit possibilities, they simultaneously awaken expectations; in beginnings the signifying structures
of art and life are surely similar.[1] A number of narrative beginnings
have become signatures in our memories of the literary landscape:
'Mother died today' or 'Happy families are all alike' or 'riverrun,
past Eve and Adam's'. How beginnings become beginnings is an
equally compelling question for life as well as art. It is perhaps arbitrary to call 'The Sisters' a beginning and confine one's discussion
only to the beginning of the story at that, for its composition in its
various stages was not Joyce's initial creative activity. Yet 'The
Sisters' is surely a beginning in Joyce's life-work: in this story in its
final version Joyce's major importance as a writer is initially revealed. Its exploration of the resources of language and its method
of construction and intention also reveal, if only in embryonic form,
the direction not only of Joyce's art but one of the formative stages
in the unfolding of modern literature. 'The Sisters' is important as
the beginning of an entire trajectory of literary accomplishment in
prose from *Dubliners, A Portrait, Ulysses*, and finally to *Finnegans
Wake*; therefore, it is worthwhile to explore more precisely a few
aspects of this beginning.

There are only subtle indications to the contrary that during the planning and in the first published version of 'The Sisters' Joyce was not predominately concerned with his subject matter, both personal and historical – Dublin, Dubliners, and his own personal attitude toward the city and its subjects.[2] His letters reveal that wounds done to him both real and imagined were very much on his mind. It is only in the later stages of the genesis of the stories that we get a strong sense that Joyce shared the modernist aspiration of Flaubert that subject and author be refined out of existence. *Dubliners* was not to be a work of 'almost no subject', 'dependent', as Flaubert said, 'on nothing external, which would be held together by the strength of its style'. Joyce indicated that these stories of Dublin life would be told with 'scrupulous meanness', and written in 'tiny little sentences', phrases which addressed economy of language more than tone, but the subject was of foremost importance. His concern at this stage was primarily with 'moral history', the world of Dublin and its people – Dublin because it 'seemed to be the centre of paralysis'. The title of the stories is itself a 'synecdoche', as David Lodge has pointed out, in 'that the book describes a representative cross-section or sample of the life of the Irish Capital'.[3] There is, in short, little to indicate from Joyce's letters and the first appearance of 'The Sisters' that the work would not fall primarily within the traditions of late nineteenth-century realism.[4] *Dubliners* in its final form, however, while retaining many of the conventions of this tradition, is a work of a different literary order. Like a new species in its evolution, it retains several of the more visible and commonplace characteristics but is essentially different. The various versions of 'The Sisters', and especially the opening paragraph, reflect in their evolution not only the expanding dimensions Joyce gradually conceived for *Dubliners*, but the increasingly mature vision of his art.

Lodge sees *Dubliners* as a transitional work, lying between the metonymic and metaphoric poles of Roman Jakobson's scheme: 'the stories do not quite satisfy the criteria of intelligibility and coherence normally demanded of the classic readerly text.'[5] Lodge's language seems itself schematised, but he is working within an important and cogently rendered argument. He carefully supports and expands his point by citing Barthes' definition from *S/Z* where Barthes contends that in the readerly text, the dominant nineteenth-century model governed by metonymy, 'everything holds together'. As Barthes goes on to explain, 'the readerly is controlled by the principle of non-contradiction, but by multiplying solidarities, by stressing at every opportunity the *compatible* nature of circumstances, by attaching narrated events together with a kind of logical "paste", the discourse carries this principle to the point of obsession.[6] Barthes' own text turns from here to an almost strident argument against the readerly text. Later, this essay will look at several other features of Barthes' arguments, but there is another aspect of this transition to mention and that is the literary-historical context of Joyce's generative process. Herbert Schneidau has made observations similar to Lodge's concerning *Dubliners* as a transitional work within this context of the general development of modernist writing.

> As we all know in Joyce's later writings Dublin, including the associated themes of betrayal and paralysis, remained the 'subject' while the aims of the portrayal were universalised in almost unprecedented ways. Consequently the notion of 'subject' mutates almost beyond recognition; no one had ever used a city in such ways before. In the *Dubliners* stories Joyce had been willing to risk severe attenuation of apprehensible plot, story, action. Obviously he anticipated with some relish complaints that these stories were not 'about' anything. He knew what they were about. But even Joyce's friends were nervous. Ezra Pound felt himself obliged to come to the defence of 'Araby' as 'better' than a story: 'it is a vivid waiting'. In *A Portrait* and *Ulysses*, subjects are specifically much more in evidence, but Joyce is so evasive about climaxes, 'big' scenes, and other standard developments as to make convention-minded readers very uneasy. The hesitant and patronising reader's report on *A Portrait* by Edward Garnett is probably typical.
>
> Joyce is supposed to have said, in later years, that he wrote about Dublin because 'if I can get to the heart of Dublin I can get to the heart of all the cities of the world. In the particular is contained the universal'. This is a highly ingenious statement of a rationale that carries the Western theory of representation as far as it will go, but in some ways it is misleading and fails to reach into the heart of the Modernist strategy of particularisation. For one thing, Joyce was not portraying some essence of *civitas* in his work, though that aspect enters into his ironies. And even though Pound chimed in with a quotation from an unnamed Belgian who said that *A Portrait* was 'as true of my country as of Ireland', Joyce cannot be said to have chosen as subject peculiar parochialisms of modern culture. The reverence of Modernism for precise renderings of particulars demands still further rationalisation.[7]

Somewhere between the original conception of the *Dubliners* stories and their completion, Joyce moved along a path similar to the one that was to transform the manuscript *Stephen Hero*, a prose work in the tradition of late nineteenth-century realism and naturalism, into *A Portrait*, a novel that retains many conventions of the realistic text, such as the Christmas dinner scene, but is dominately a modernist text. *Dubliners* is itself a beginning, and the opening paragraph of the final version of 'The Sisters' makes clear that for Joyce, although preserving the facade of this tradition, the stronger impulse was to take seriously the overture of John's Gospel, 'In the beginning was the word.' (This 'beginning' itself echoes the opening line of Genesis that reveals how God brought an orderly universe out of primordial chaos.) Among other things, the beginning of 'The Sisters', while not rashly innovative, places radical emphasis on language and in turn on the text as text. In *Dubliners* Joyce begins to give priority to the word over the world.

II

There was no hope for him this time: it was the third stroke. Night after night I had passed the house (it was vacation time) and studied the lighted square of window: and night after night I had found it lighted in the same way, faintly and evenly. If he was dead, I thought, I would see the reflection of candles on the darkened blind for I knew that two candles must be set at the head of a corpse. He had often said to me: *I am not long for this world*, and I had thought his words idle. Now I knew they were true. Every night as I gazed up at the window I said softly to myself the word *paralysis*. It had always sounded strangely in my ears, like the word *gnomon* in the Euclid and the word *simony* in the Catechism. But now it sounded to me like the name of some maleficent and sinful being. It filled me with fear, and yet I longed to be nearer to it and look upon its deadly work.

'The Sisters'
(Beginning paragraph, the final version.)

Upon reflection, while attending a Greek Mass in Trieste, the first reader of 'The Sisters' thought its early version 'remarkable'.[8] Once it was finally written, Joyce almost left it at that, content to smile cunningly and pare his fingernails, but not so subsequent readers; by and large those who have written about it affirm the work's imaginative inconsistencies, curious ambiguities, gaps in the discourse, and the general uncertainty it casts on every level from beginning to end. And if the beginning of a text is, as Edward Said has so eloquently told us, 'the entrance to what it offers and the first step in the intentional production of meaning',[9] readers need to explore sufficiently these initial codes, the ensemble of rhetorical markers (the code of connotations), the stylistic codes, the conventional structures – in other words, the full range of the linguistic activity of the text.

The most apparent conclusion, among many, that can be drawn from a study of the evolution of 'The Sisters' in its progressive versions is its movement away from the 'readerly' text. In reworking 'The Sisters' Joyce became increasingly aware of the potential of language itself. This awareness was to change the course of his writing, and, although this point is obvious when we read *Ulysses* and *Finnegans Wake*, his larger assumptions concerning language are clearly visible in *A Portrait*. As Richard Poirier has observed, 'the cultural implications of Stephen's language are from first to last what concerned Joyce'.[10] From Stephen's early preoccupation with words, to his later posturings in the style of Pater, the reader is drawn constantly to a wide range of implications of the language of the text as it calls attention to itself.

Much has been made of the opening paragraph of 'The Sisters' because there is so much to engage and perplex, so much more suggested by the language than the events and circumstances of the text seem to reveal. The first paragraph of 'The Sisters' is more than the narrative event which opens the story; it draws the initial line of a larger narrative enclosure, and is every bit as much the beginning of the first movement in the orchestration of *Dubliners* itself. It has already been noted that the various versions of 'The Sisters' evolved with Joyce's expanding aims, but some were more immediate, such as his desire to integrate the stories thematically as well as chronologically. Following the collective title of the stories is the slightly foregrounded title of the first, 'The Sisters', which he retained throughout all the versions because of its special importance. Initially the title seems ironic in its reference to the vestal virgins Eliza and Nannie, but in the final version it becomes more prominently the first instance of the verbal playfulness of the text in its Elizabeth-Ann, Beth-Annie, Bethany, Lazarus, death associations.[11] There is a persistent self-consciousness in the language of the entire text. The language, too, shadows and alludes to biblical and liturgical references which generate further signification and meaning in the narrative, and these will be discussed later.

Without carrying this first association too far, we can at least see that the title itself offers the first indication of the self-conscious nature of the text. Perhaps it is more obviously so in another way – negatively, for the title is curiously inappropriate for a story that ostensibly narrates the mysterious relationship and the effects of old Father Flynn's death on the young boy narrator. The title signals us away from the traditional slice-of-life, naturalistic sketch that one could expect from the realistic collective title of the stories. Critics who have read 'The Sisters' as a realistic text have had enormous difficulty accounting for the title. Even those who declare it as a signalled break from the realistic mode and a gesture of the story's symbolic portent, find the title awkward and even unsatisfactory. The enigmatic title of the first story conflicts with the precise naturalistic title of the collection. From the start 'The Sisters' begins to reveal meaning in ways that go beyond the consistencies of a readerly text. Further, it is Joyce's intention to combat the assumptions of such a text. He would write in a mode that would reflect the realities of a new century and create what we have come to call the modernist text which depended upon a new set of cultural assumptions and has been open to charges of obscurity. With 'The Sisters' Joyce has just begun a deconstructive process, and the title is the first announcement of a new awareness of the potentiality of language.

To acknowledge the opening paragraph as an overture for the themes, conflicts, and tensions that were to be evoked and stated again and again, not only in the story itself, but throughout all of *Dubliners*, has been critical commonplace.[12] That this final version of the beginning is more than an introduction or overture to the story and the collection has come more slowly to assert itself on the critical consciousness. The virtual nature of the work pointed to so consciously by the text only slowly reduced the certainty and compulsion of critics to assign meanings and thus ultimately abridge the range of possibilities.[13] In these early readings with their rigid and frequently fanciful assignment of symbolic meanings, the potential of the language field itself was abridged, and the fuller range of the text's amplitude was ignored. The asymmetrical activities of the text were excluded, too, in the interest of finding exact correspondences. Much of the criticism of 'The Sisters' in its desire to account for an exact relationship between symbolic and realistic elements fails to construct a grid which allows for the interplay of the various levels of the text, both horizontal and vertical.[14]

Several recent critics of *Dubliners* stories, such as Robert Scholes in his essay on 'Eveline', have attempted to account for the wider potential of the texts by their use of different theoretical models. Scholes's essay, for example, is as much a small-model demonstration of the critical resources in the theories and methods of Todorov, Genette, and Barthes as it is a reading of the story. His application of Barthes' codes is an attempt to demonstrate the deeper and more various levels of the text and their associations both within and outside the text, especially as they relate to language, mode, genre and culture relationships, and assumptions of the author.[15] The present essay avoids Barthes' terminology and does not attempt to apply his codes rigidly to the beginning of 'The Sisters', nor does the writer ascribe to their frequently arbitrary application in *S/Z*. Nevertheless, the reader of Barthes will recognise in this essay an agnostic's imperfect debt along with the measure of doubt: Barthes' work does provide important avenues of adventure in his engagement with a text. And it is Barthes who also cautions us to refrain from structuring a text in large masses and not to delegate a text to a final ensemble, to an ultimate structure.

Given the special importance Joyce assigned to beginnings, the heightened role of the beginning as part of the fundamental boundary and frame in a verbal artistic text, and the beginning as a defining and modelling function, it is worthwhile to confirm this theoretical significance. Jurij Lotman, for example, has assigned crucial importance to the coding function of the beginning of the narrative text:

> When a reader starts reading a book or a spectator watches the beginning of a film or play, he may not know for sure, or may not know at all, into what system the proffered text has been encoded. He is naturally interested in getting a total picture of the text's genre and style and those typical artistic codes which he should activate in his consciousness in order to comprehend the text. On the whole, he derives such information from the beginning.[16]

The beginning paragraph of 'The Sisters' not only propels the reader into the various levels of the text and the special network of codes it generates, but it functions as a model for the entire story; the paradoxical realism, the hint of an extravagant presence of the artifice, the allusive tracery of the architectonics which calls attention to the text as text – all of this as though reality itself were dependent upon artful consciousness – a mode that forecasts an entire avenue of discourse as well as story. The responses to this kind of text have, of course, been varied, but it has been generally agreed

that from this beginning the work hovers between the two fundamental modes of writing, the metaphoric and metonymic.[17] To see
the balance Joyce achieves between these two modes has been the
principal aim of the best criticism of this work. Rather than recon-
cile these two metaphysical orders, it is a more open and far richer
experience to ponder their interplay in Joyce's text. Our response
comes through engagement not conclusiveness – suspension, rather
than closure; suggestion rather than assertion. It comes from situat-
ing itself at a beginning of the crossroads of the two fundamental
modes of writing. As Colin MacCabe has pointed out, from the earliest stages of his career, Joyce gave special attention to the correspondence between word and world, and the many languages or
discourses of the text. MacCabe cites the early paper, 'Drama and
Life', where Joyce draws such distinctions:

> Joyce sets himself against a drama which comes complete with its
> own interpretation and caught within the stereotype of its age, a
> drama which Joyce describes as purveyor supplying plutocrat with a
> 'parody of life which the latter digests medicinally in a darkened
> theatre'. For Joyce, real drama is to be found in works, like those of
> Ibsen, which give us the pleasure 'not of hearing it read out to us but
> of reading it for ourselves, piecing the various parts and going closer
> to see wherever the writing on the parchment is fainter or less
> legible'. The contrast between a text which determines its own
> reading and a text which demands an *activity* of reading was central
> to Joyce from an early age.[18]

The first sentence of 'The Sisters' turns us to the thought of
death: 'There was no hope for him this time: it was the third
stroke.' With its tone of finality and certainty, this opening begins
the circle of death for *Dubliners*, a circle clear enough from the last
lines of the final story, 'The Dead', and clearer still from the pulpit
rhetoric of the priest that closes 'Grace', which at one stage in
Joyce's plan was to be the final story, when he advises his audience
to set right their accounts with God. Besides the emphasis on the
word 'time' in the first half of this sentence, the rhetorical arrangement and the colon give added emphasis to the temporal where
death and dying are in the order of things, and from the beginning
of the story priesthood and death are aligned in some seemingly im-
mutable way.

In the second sentence the boy narrator states that 'night after
night' he had passed the stricken priest's house (we, of course, do

not yet know that the victim and object of his compulsive concentration is a priest; this information is inferred later in the paragraph). The intensity of his gaze narrows his focus to the 'lighted square of window'. The house with its lighted window begins to fill his imagination and memory. As Bachelard tells us, 'in the most interminable of dialectics, the sheltered being gives perceptible limits to his shelter. He experiences the house in its reality and in its virtuality, by means of thought and dreams.'[19] Because of the priest's illness, the narrator is excluded from the house, a house now protected and presided over by the two sisters, where the priest lies dying. A perspective both imaginary and actual begins to take place and will be sustained throughout the text; the levels of discourse are expanded. The antithesis of outside and inside is thus initiated, and it governs certain other textual arrangements and strategies which will be developed. From the outside, the narrator keeps his own vigil and studies the faint and even light from the window to look for a sign, 'the reflection of candles on a darkened blind'. Although we have had the religious foregrounding in the title, the candles and their part in the ritual of death offer the first overt suggestion of a religious element on any level.

Appropriately the religious significance is tied in with death from the first – here the candles would act for the boy, at least, as sentinels for the priest's death – and all forms of religious connotation, object, sacrament, and symbol are clustered and bonded. But equally important is the context of this overt religious association: the narrator says, 'I knew that two candles must be set at the head of a corpse.' The word 'must' alerts us from the first to a world where religious form will be mandatory and religious forms control behaviour. This fact has already penetrated the boy's consciousness – a religion that places form over substance is to become a central theme of the story. Religious practices will be associated with malevolent paralysis, which with its symptom of perversity is an apt metaphor for a religion whose sacraments rather than outward signs of grace seem to have become not only arid rituals, but signs and gestures of a neurotic abandoned people. In rich detail the text plays almost systematically on the perversion of the Church's sacraments and rituals as a sympton of neurosis and haunting fear, but the very decadence of these church rituals and mysteries has drawn the boy compulsively to the priest. And this mysterious conversion of an almost metaphysical order is what attracts the power of the text's language, the force of its signs and meaning. The language associated with the boy and his descriptions of the priest, with its richness of connotation and possibility, stands in bold contrast to the pedestrian dialogue of the other characters.

The narrator also gives special emphasis to the frequency of the boy's visits to the lighted window – visits which seem to take on their own repeated ritual: 'Every night as I gazed up at the window I said softly to myself the word *paralysis*.' Each time he gazes upon this scene his memory and imagination go to the fears and secrets that the priest had evoked and passed on to him. The word 'paralysis' is the first of a cluster of signifiers which begins within the hermeneutic code, whose meanings are not fully clarified either individually or collectively by the text. This signification, however, extends to other levels of the text. Colin MacCabe has observed that 'the reader is introduced to a set of signifiers for which there is no interpretation except strangeness and an undefined evil'.[20] The relationships of the words, 'paralysis', 'simony', and 'gnomon', however, seem to foreground each other, by their arrangements as well as meaning, so that beyond the strangeness and undefined evil, there is also a bonding of religious practice with maleficence and perversion. This triad of words produces in the boy the emotions of fear and longing, and, if as MacCabe contends, the words are part of an opening which displays a 'certain excess of the power of signification,'[21] they also support the inexplicable power over the narrator who is unable to assimilate in his consciousness their meaning or full evocation, only their deadly charm and attraction for him. It is the confluence of meaning, only dimly understood by the boy and the reader, of these three words as much as their individual signification that generates their mystery, a mystery that sets up the mood and tone of the dream sequence which takes the boy 'into some pleasant and vicious region'. Words themselves not only have seductive power over him, but they signal the boy's separation from all of the other characters in the story and his alignment with the priest.

No matter how divergent their conclusion, those who have written about 'The Sisters', and *Dubliners* generally, have sought to codify the various ways in which this first paragraph of the story generates meaning in its introduction of the various codes for the entire story and the collection itself. Primarily the discussions have centred on these three crucial words of the paragraph, 'paralysis', 'simony', and 'gnomon'. Because the words emerge from the boy's consciousness, many of the interpretations have centred their discussion exclusively on the significance of the words for the boy, hence confining their reading to only one level of the text's meaning. But the boy is only the figural medium of the fictional world. Seen only on the one level the words remain incomplete and illusive and in their shadowy significance for the boy they become so for the discourse as well. But beginning from different assumptions there are other possibilities for the reader to explore. It is, of course, in the boy's consciousness that the vague and mysterious connection between 'paralysis', 'simony', and 'gnomon' begins, but their connotations as well as their clustering bring additional semantic elements to the text, thus extending their significations.

The boy murmurs 'paralysis' to himself each night as he gazes up at the window until it becomes almost a part of his nightly ritual, which gives the first clue that the sounds of words are as important to the boy as their semantic connotations and referential meanings. The two latter words are also triggered in his consciousness, initially at least, as much by their sounds as by their strange meaning for him. The word 'gnomon', for example, seems to confirm the eminence of sound, and sound as meaning, for the word has only remote lexigraphical signification for the boy. But because of its remoteness it calls attention to the power of the word as word, and its geometrical meaning establishes another tracery throughout the text, but one independent of the boy's consciousness.

The emphasis on all three as words is enforced syntactically in that each is preceded by the same word, 'word'. But their signification extends to cultural and connotative codes as well as the hermeneutic. We draw them into a relationship by virtue of their syntactical locations as well as through the common strangeness they have for the boy, but more than this we are able from them to begin to 'thematise' the text. Already alerted to the potential playfulness, extended ironies, and the latent verbal resources of this text, we are able to recognise as many critics have, that 'simony' and 'paralysis' when run together, as they are nearly so in the boy's mind, suggest the word 'syphilis' and broaden the associative power of the vague air of corruption that undergirds the entire story and becomes thematic throughout *Dubliners*. Richard Ellmann first offered the hint of this disease, known as it was at the turn of the century as the general paralysis of the insane, and Burton A. Waisbren and Florence L. Walzl have concluded that Joyce deliberately implied that Father Flynn had central nervous system syphilis,[22] which is now described medically as 'paresis'.

Their extreme interpretation takes suggestiveness to finality, but their analysis reveals the persistent strength of the associative possibilities and latent significations that the text renders. Mystery and suspicion are a part of the language itself as well as the narrative it unfolds. Further, and equally important, is the way in which these three words initiate and establish, as the narrative eventually makes clear, a bond between the priest and the boy – a bond of fear and longing but nevertheless a union is initiated. This union lies submerged as well in the narrative and establishes something far more suggestive than the boy's own confused and vague association with the priest.

It can be mentioned at this point that the entire language of the opening paragraph also has a seminal foregrounding function which we realise retrospectively. The passage is immediately followed by the most trivial dialogue between Old Cotter and the boy's uncle as they reveal their vapid imaginations and verbal incapacities in contrast to the careful verbal ordering of the first paragraph, which, among so many other things, displays the boy's rich if puzzled fluency. The richness of language is not displayed again until the boy is alone in his room lying in bed between sleep and dream imagining the priest confessing to him. Richard Poirier, in contrasting the modernism of Frost to Eliot's and Joyce's, makes a broad and an important point about the form of a modernist text and cites this contrast in the language of 'The Sisters' as an example:

> In saying that Joyce and Eliot were compelled by historical conditions while Frost, for the most part, was not, I do not mean that the form of their writings was predetermined by historical circumstances except as they and their readers came to *imagine* that this was the case. Temperamental or psychological alienation played a crucial part, so did a disenchantment with inherited literary forms, but both feelings preceded those broader encounters with historical plights which in the later works seem to be the source and justification for these feelings. 'Modernist' scepticism about 'any small man-made figure of order and concentration' is apparent in the earliest, least historically rooted and least allusive writings of Joyce and Eliot. Joyce's 'The Sisters', in the contrast it establishes between the poetic elegance and balance of the young boy's language when he is alone in his bedroom as against the fracturing banalities of all other conversation in the story, could be a case in point.[23]

The long scene that concludes the story, dominated by the attenuated dialogue between the boy's aunt and Eliza with the latter's account of her brother's strange fate, reflects the same incapacity for language as the earlier dialogue. These sharp linguistic contrasts point not only to the text's emphasis on the language field, but contribute to the meaning of the larger cultural and thematic structure of the story.

The multiple dimensions of this beginning paragraph and the course that it sets for the entire verbal structure of the story derive in part from Joyce's obsessive autobiographical notions regarding the relationship of priesthood and artist, a relationship of central significance in *A Portrait*. Throughout his discussions in *Portrait*, Stephen constantly refers to the artist and his creation in religious and liturgical language and imagery. In a sense art was the performance of the artist of a sacred rite similar to the priest's at Mass. It is more than merely an analogy, it was partially an aesthetic source for what Joyce would come to define as the priesthood of art. The deeply religious and specifically Roman Catholic saturation of Joyce's texts have particular functions on various levels. All of his texts, in a way, are rooted in the assumption that art replaces religion in a fundamental way – not that art dissolves religious constructs, but that it uses them by reconstructing them. Joyce did not want to remove God from the cosmic structure, but he wanted for the artist God's power of creation.

In the same letter to Stanislaus in which he begins by telling his brother about attending the Greek Mass and recalling 'The Sisters', Joyce is referring to the version of the story with the following beginning:

> Three nights in succession I had found myself in Great Britain Street at that hour, as if by providence. Three nights I had raised my eyes to that lighted square of window and speculated. I seemed to understand that it would occur at night. But in spite of the providence which had led my feet and in spite of the reverent curiosity of my eyes I had discovered nothing. Each night the square was lighted in the same way, faintly and evenly. It was not the light of candles so far as I could see. Therefore it had not occurred yet.
>
> On the fourth night at that hour I was in another part of the city. It may have been the same providence that led me there – a whimsical kind of providence – to take me at a disadvantage. As I went home I wondered was that square of window lighted as before or did it reveal the ceremonious candles in the light of which the Christian must take his last sleep. I was not surprised, then, when at supper I found myself a prophet.[24]

In this version the beginning of both story and discourse is much closer to the conventional mode of the realistic text, but the nexus between the boy and the priest is not nearly so clearly drawn. The boy is led to the priest's house by 'providence', but the mystery and attraction that suffuses the language of the final version of the beginning is notably far less intense. A phrase of special interest in this earlier version is 'I found myself a prophet'. It is given an added measure of significance by a revealing passage in this same letter to Stanislaus when Joyce details the actions of the priest at the Greek Mass he was observing that brought his story to mind:

> The altar is not visible but at times the priest opens the gates and shows himself. He opens and shuts them about six times. For the Gospel he comes out of a side gate and comes down into the Chapel and reads out of a book. For the elevation he does the same. At the end when he has blessed the people he shuts the gates: a boy comes running down the side of the chapel with a large tray full of little lumps of bread. The priest comes after him and distributes the lumps to scrambling believers. Damn droll! The Greek priest has been taking a great eyeful out of me: two haruspices.[25]

Whether or not he recalled this experience in the later rewriting of 'The Sisters' we do not know. But the union Joyce draws between himself and the priest in his letter becomes far more pronounced and important in the final version of the text, especially the beginning. It is in the priest's performance of the ritual Greek Mass, a ritual Joyce found exotic and even flamboyant, that Joyce identifies himself with the priest with the word 'haruspices'. The roles of artist and priest are joined in the word which means one who foretells events through observations of natural phenomena, a prophet. As the simple bread through the priest's power becomes the body of Christ and retains the appearance of bread as he offers it to the people, so, too, does the artist transform life to art through language. The priest gives significance to the most mundane, so, too, for Joyce does the artist. Language has the same resources and power of the sacraments such as the Eucharist. Herbert Schneidau has commented that: 'The characteristic Joycean strategy, embodying the sacramentalist ideal, is expansion: a bare nugget or kernel is transformed, by a kind of explosion of the stylistic potentialities latent within it, into a many membered, multilayered construction. Far from collapsing levels of significance, Joyce seeks constantly to add to them.'[26] This strategy of development in Joyce's texts is apparent in the beginning of 'The Sisters', especially in the final version where we begin to see this attempt to create a text of multilayered construction through the emphasis on the resources of language itself. The style of the entire story, for example, not only reinforces the themes, it also discovers and manifests them.

As Hugh Kenner has told us, Joyce's earlier fiction is filled with discarded portraits of himself, portraits he might have been or had the potential to become. The first of these is the boy narrator who is simultaneously enchanted and repelled by the priest and his office, an office in which the priest is a failure, for the priest is the leader of ritual and a community's ritual functions to support and draw it together. For the priest the burden, however, is too heavy; the sacrament becomes a perverse sign of his enfeeblement, his incapacity to perform the rites and rituals of his office. Joyce the artist, the creator of form through the medium of language, views the boy through a retrospective prism which generates not only a figural medium, but an authenticity of focus from which to view the fictional world. Such a perspective, once realised, forged a new beginning for his art and what was to become a dominant art of the century.

The changes that took place in Joyce's progressive versions of 'The Sisters' represent an initial and tentative movement – and it is no more than that when considered in light of *Ulysses* and *Finnegans Wake* – from the metonymic to the metaphoric, from the 'readerly' to the 'writerly', from the realistic/naturalistic to the modernist text, but we are able to see from this development a growing and abiding concern on the part of the author for the nature and potentiality of language itself. Joyce saw language not only as a vehicle but as the informing structure for art in all of its communicative capacities. In 'The Sisters' he was writing language over a dead ritual, a dead communion of people, but, at the same time, he was using the motive power of the sacrament as sign analogously to the power of the word as sign in art. However much the boy in this story is a victim, he has escaped the fate of the adult world and the priest, because he is attuned to the potential and transforming power of the word itself, and this story can be read at one level as the fulfilment of Joyce's own conversion. The beginning of 'The Sisters' is, then, as we noted earlier, an embryonic stage, or maybe only an imperfect impulse, in Joyce's mature development, but it, nevertheless, signals the direction his art would take in its own radical restatement of the nature of art and language. If the reader of *Ulysses* must differentiate constantly between the linguistic possibilities of style and the possible nature of the world, the reader of *Finnegans Wake* is aware from the beginning, wherever the beginning is, that the world has become the word, hence with *Finnegans Wake* the beginning is only in the word.

Notes

[Thomas Staley's essay was first published in 1979. It represents an early attempt to use theories drawn from structuralism and semiotics to analyse the enigmatic first story in *Dubliners*, 'The Sisters'. Staley draws upon ideas found in the structuralist writings of Roland Barthes, Roman Jakobson and David Lodge to analyse the modernism of the story, showing how Joyce developed the story into what Barthes calls a 'writerly' text and away from a 'readerly' one. Staley clearly shows how Joyce's story testifies to a self-conscious interest in the workings of language itself and pays particular attention to the perplexing opening paragraph. A number of notes have been abbreviated or omitted for reasons of space. Ed.]

1. From Tzvetan Todorov and the Russian Formalists, I draw partially my distinctions: *story* comprises a logic of actions and a syntax of characters, and *discourse* comprises the tenses, and aspects and modes of the narrative. These are discussed in much more detail in Todorov's *The Poetics of Prose* (Ithaca, NY, 1977).

2. The most comprehensive discussion of the various versions of 'The Sisters' is in Florence L. Walzl's essay, 'Joyce's "The Sisters": A Development', *James Joyce Quarterly*, 10 (1973), 375–421; see especially p. 376. *The James Joyce Archive* (Garland Press) contains reproductions of the Cornell and Yale manuscripts, as well as a photographic reproduction of the story as it appeared in *The Irish Homestead*. Throughout I will cite from The Viking Critical Library edition of *Dubliners*, ed. Robert Scholes and A. Walton Litz (New York, 1969), when referring to the final version as it appears in *Dubliners*.

3. David Lodge, *The Modes of Modern Writing* (London, 1977), p. 125. I am generally indebted to Lodge's study, and I feel his work is an important bridge between recent European and Anglo-American criticism.

4. The Viking Critical Library Edition conveniently reproduces the first complete manuscript version of 'The Sisters' which is a similar version to the one published in *The Irish Homestead* (Yale ms.).

5. Lodge, *Modes of Modern Writing*, p. 125.

6. Roland Barthes, *S/Z*, trans. Richard Millar (New York, 1974), p. 156.

7. Herbert N. Schneidau, 'Style and Sacrament in Modernist Writing', *The Georgia Review*, 31 (1977), 433–4.

8. Letter to Stanislaus Joyce, 4 April 1905 in *Letters of James Joyce*, Vol. II, ed. Richard Ellmann (New York, 1966), p. 86.

9. Edward Said's brilliant work, *Beginnings* (New York, 1975), has brought the whole idea of literary beginnings to mind with such force and possibility that I have yet to assimilate the work's impact on my thinking, but it is considerable.

10. Richard Poirier, *Robert Frost* (New York, 1977), p. 33.

11. The biblical possibilities of this association were first pointed out by Peter Spielberg in his brief article, ' "The Sisters": No Christ at Bethany', *James Joyce Quarterly*, 3 (1966), 192–5.

12. The most suggestive article on the language of 'The Sisters', and still one of the most provocative generally, is Fritz Senn's ' "He was too Scrupulous Always", Joyce's "The Sisters" ', *James Joyce Quarterly*, 2 (1965), 66–71. His article is based on the conviction 'that even in his earliest published prose Joyce wrote in a most complex, heavily allusive style, different from its later convoluted intricacies in *Ulysses* and *Finnegans Wake* in degree only (p. 66). For articles which discuss the previous criticism see especially: Donald T. Torchiana, 'The Opening of *Dubliners*: A Reconsideration', *Irish University Review*, 1 (1971), 149–60; Bernard Benstock, ' "The Sisters" and the Critics', *James Joyce Quarterly*, 4 (1966), 32–5.

13. Although I am not in full agreement with Wolfgang Iser's views, his discussion of the virtual nature of the literary text I find illuminating; see *The Art of Reading* (Baltimore, MD, 1978).

14. This point obviously needs further development because of the assumptions it makes regarding the nature of the text and the relationship of the reader to the text, but to do so here would require extended discussion. An extreme position on the nature of this relationship can be found in Maria Corti, *An Introduction to Literary Semiotics* (Bloomington and London, 1978).

15. Robert Scholes, 'Semiotic Approaches to a Fictional Text: Joyce's "Eveline" ', *James Joyce Quarterly*, 16 (Fall 78/Winter 79), 65–80. Briefly, Barthes' codes are proairetic, the code of actions; hermeneutic, code of enigmas; cultural, the text's references to things already known; connotative, the location of themes; and symbolic fields.

16. Jurij Lotman, *The Structure of the Artistic Text* (Ann Arbor, MI, 1977), p. 216.

17. For an extended discussion of these two poles of writing, see Lodge, *Modes of Modern Writing*.

18. Colin MacCabe, *James Joyce and the Revolution of the Word* (London, 1975), p. 28.

19. Gaston Bachelard, *The Poetics of Space* (Boston, 1969), p. 5.

20. MacCabe, *James Joyce*, p. 34.

21. Ibid.

22. Burton A. Waisbren and Florence L. Walzl, 'Paresis and the Priest, James Joyce's Symbolic Use of Syphilis in "The Sisters" ', *Annals of Internal Medicine*, 80 (1974), 758–62.

23. Poirier, *Robert Frost*, pp. 40–1.

24. The Viking Critical Edition, pp. 243–4.

25. Joyce, *Letters*, II, pp. 86–7.

26. Schneidau, 'Style and Sacrament in Modernist Writing', p. 441.

2

Silences in *Dubliners*

JEAN-MICHEL RABATÉ

> To keep silent, this is what we all strive for when we write.
> (Maurice Blanchot, *L'Ecriture du désastre*)

Dubliners is a collection of stories haunted by the kind of silence
Maurice Blanchot speaks of,[1] a silence against which the chatter of
urban gossip reveals its hollowness. Meaning is thus only a limit
imposed onto this silence, a border helping to define the diseased
mother, the cancerous womb of Dublin. The silence that many
commentators – including Ezra Pound and Hermann Broch – have
noticed may function like the silence of the analyst or the silence of
the priest at confession, since it lets the symptoms speak of themselves. Silence begs the question of textual hermeneutics, for its disturbing effect is the epiphany of meaning.

The question of the silence of interpretation is built within the
text, prepared and foreseen in the deceptive game it plays with the
reader. This, as I see it, is the primary function of the silences of the
text. For there are different kinds of silences: silence can mean the
inversion of speech, its mirror, that which structures its resonance,
since without silence, speech becomes a mere noise, a meaningless
clatter; silence can reveal a gap, a blank space in the text, that can
be accounted for in terms of the characters who betray themselves
by slips, lapsus, omissions; or in terms of the general economy of
the text, silence can be the void element that ensures displacement,
hence circulation. Silence can finally appear as the end, the limit,
the death of speech, its paralysis. There, silence joins both the mute
symptoms (Eveline's aphasia is a good example of this in *Dubliners*)
and the work of Thanatos inscribed in the production of writing.

The problematics of silence can offer an approach which would go beyond the facile antagonism between the surface realism of the stories and the suggestions, allusions and quasi-symbolist tactics of inferring by cross-references. The only way to gain a broader perspective is to introduce the silent process of reading into the text. Thus one can keep in mind the insistent ethical function of the stories (Joyce knew he was writing a 'chapter of the moral history of my country')[2] and their political relevance, and see these as confronted with the construction of a real Irish capital through literature ('Is it not possible for a few persons of character and culture to make Dublin a capital such as Christiania has become?'),[3] a construction which opposes any capitalistic exploitation. The mirror held up to the Irish may well be nicely polished; it is not dependent on a theory of pure mimesis or of purely symbolist implications. *Dubliners* is not, on the other hand, a direct consequence of Joyce's current theories of aesthetics, such as Stephen expounds them. It is rather the theory itself, in its wider sense, that is mirrored in the text. There, it is coupled with the utmost degree of precision and particularity in the pragmatics of writing that deconstructs the voices of the characters, narrators, commentators, and paves the way toward the constitution of another rhetoric of silences, the silences of the writing being caught up by the silent reading-writing which transforms a collection of short stories into a text.

My question will then become, In what sense does this book offer a theory of its own interpretation, of its reading, of possible metadiscourses about its textuality? In what way is there the temptation of an identification, with what aspects of the text, and to what effects? If, finally, *Dubliners* rules out any final recourse to a metalanguage, what are the consequences for the ethics and the politics of reading?

I shall start with two theoretical or critical preliminaries. For Broch, who wrote a penetrating review of *Ulysses* in 'James Joyce and the Present Time',[4] Joyce, like Hofmannsthal, reveals through his hatred of clichés the traces of what Broch calls a 'Chandos experience', taking this term from Hofmannsthal's fictional letter in which a young and gifted lord tells Bacon that he cannot write any more, nor even speak, after a breakdown of the natural relationship between signifier and signified. Thus, for Hermann Broch, *Dubliners* and *Ulysses* manifest the mutism of a world condemned to silence by the destruction of centred values, in the very hypertrophy of their growth. *Dubliners* marks the reversal from pure indi-

vidual and symptomatic aphasia to the process of recovering the
void; it is to be considered between Lord Chandos's letter (1902)
and Wittgenstein's *Tractatus* (begun in 1911). Ezra Pound, too,
points out the ethical and political import of *Dubliners*, from a different point of view. He praises the clear, hard prose, which
eschews unnecessary detail: 'He carefully avoids telling you a lot
that you don't want to know.'[5] These stories, which are all defined
by the special quality of their 'vivid waiting' for some impossible
escape, render Dublin universal; according to Pound, however,
Joyce has not yet surpassed his Flaubertian model of *Trois contes*.

But the reference to Flaubert is decisive, since it enables the critic
to stress the ideological relevance of the work. Like Flaubert, who
believes that the collapse of France in 1870 might have been
avoided if only people had read his books, Joyce also thinks that his
'diagnosis' might have been useful to his country in turmoil. In
Pound's words, this becomes 'if more people had read *The Portrait*
and certain stories in Mr. Joyce's *Dubliners* there might have been
less recent trouble in Ireland'.[6] I shall have to come back to Joyce's
use of Flaubert and remark on the limitations of Pound's interpretation; it nevertheless throws a double light on the text of *Dubliners*,
which constantly hesitates between the status of a cure, a diagnosis,
and that of a symptom, produced by the same causes it attempts to
heal. Such an oscillation will become apparent if we try to apply the
famous phrase of 'silence, exile, and cunning' to *Dubliners*.[7]

The theme of exile has been the focus of critical attention, while
'silence' seems to have embarrassed everyone. First, the order of the
terms in this well-known triad poses a problem; when Stephen
decides to be an artist, a 'priest of eternal imagination', he selects
these three weapons as the only tools he can use against the en-
croachments of home, fatherland, and church. If the order is
chronological, the initial silence defines his refusal to take part in
the political and linguistic wrangles of Dublin until he exiles himself
and moves to Paris for a start. But then cunning cannot be simply
considered as the third step in this movement towards greater intellectual freedom if this freedom is available elsewhere. Could it be
that Joyce implies a more logical correspondence between the two
triads, silence referring to the family, exile to nationalism, and
cunning to the perverse and religious refusal of religion? I shall, in
fact, suggest strong affinities between silence and paternity, but as
these three 'nets' are constantly overlapping, especially in the
Dublin of *Dubliners*, it must then be that all three concepts or

attitudes work together indissociably and simultaneously. All the dreams of exile to the East in *Dubliners* are part of a ruse that employs silence in different modes of revelation. I shall thus commence by an approach via the silent ruses of interpretation, centred on the notions of perversity, heresy, and orthodoxy, and then move on to an analysis of the exile of 'performance' in the enunciative strategies of the text, until finally everything will appear hinged on the silent name of the capitalised Father.

'The Sisters' offers the real starting-point, for it is more than just the first story in the collection; it also provides an elaborate introduction to the discourses of *Dubliners*. What strikes one from the first page is the deliberate suspension of a number of terms: the identity of the dead priest is disclosed through a series of hesitating, unfinished sentences, and even the 'now' of the initial paragraph is not related to a precise chronology (it is not directly linked to the supper scene which follows). Several signifiers are given, almost too soon, without explanation (paralysis, simony, gnomon), while the real messenger who brings the news of the priest's decease has already made up his mind as to the signification of the event, but deliberately withholds his own conclusions. 'I'll tell you my opinion ...', he says, but he never really affords more than hints of a possible perversion. This continuous suspension of meanings introduces a whole series of unfinished sentences, marked by dots; all of Old Cotter's remarks, except for one (*D*, pp. 7–8); the end of the boy's dream (*D*, p. 12); the aunt's questions (p. 14); and finally the answers given by Eliza ('But still ...') and her conclusion that 'there was something gone wrong with him ...' (pp. 16–17).

We must be aware that the child is not a narrator but an interpreter, who also believes that Old Cotter knows more than he does, while constantly suspecting the validity of his information (he has to read the card pinned on the door to be persuaded that the priest is actually dead). The story begins *in medias res*, so that the child may supply the reader with a figure mirroring his own interpretative process. In this process, the child has to come to terms with hints or allusions (Old Cotter *alludes* to the boy as a child, which angers him), from which he attempts to make sense: 'I puzzled my head to extract meaning from his unfinished sentences' (p. 9). As he imagines that the face of the dead priest follows him in the dark, it becomes obvious that the symbolic realm of interpretation exhibits gaps which are soon filled by imaginary fantasies. These contami-

nate the interpretative process with suggestions of sacrilegious communion. Now the roles of the priest and of the old man appear as
opposite points of view on the very process of reading.

For, in fact, in the child's view, the meaning only hinted at by
Old Cotter through his silences has to be identified with the dream
itself. Indeed, the dream supplies meanings which all develop the
suspended signifiers of the first paragraph. The face wishes to utter
something to the child but fails: 'It began to confess to me in a mur-
muring voice and I wondered why it smiled continually and why
the lips were so moist with spittle. But then I remembered that it
had died of paralysis and I felt that I too was smiling feebly as if to
absolve the simoniac of his sin' (*D*, p. 9). The absence of 'gnomon'
will be accounted for later; what matters here is the exchange of
sacerdotal functions between the boy and the priest. He confesses
the priest, whose voice is heard though not his words, and the perverse enjoyment of the scene in such a 'pleasant and vicious region'
derives from the inversion of the roles and the transmission of the
frozen smile from the priest to the boy. The next time the dream is
mentioned, in a flashback, it again is accompanied by speculations
about Old Cotter's sentences, and the memories are themselves cut
short: '– in Persia, I thought. ... But I could not remember the end
of the dream' (*D*, p. 12).

The strange complicity between the priest and the child, which is
stressed in his recollections of their conversation, enhances two important points: unlike Mr. Cotter, the Reverend Flynn explained to
the boy the *meanings* of different ceremonies, of the sacraments and
institutions. He also obviously got pleasure from these lessons, and
in the parody of the *puer senex* theme, we find the repetition of the
uncanny smile that becomes an obscene leer. So, on the one hand,
we witness a perverse and seductive exchange of sacraments within
an order of faith that appears utterly absurd (until the intricate
questions of the catechism are debunked in 'Grace'); on the other
hand, we find a theory which obstinately refuses to give away its
key: 'I have my own theory about it, he said. I think it was one of
those ... peculiar cases. ... But it's hard to say ...' (p. 8). I would be
tempted to read here the disjunction between *orthodoxy*, defined as
a theory without a meaning, and *perversity*, as a game of signifiers
whose meaning is uncertain.

In order to define this use of the concept of orthodoxy, it might
be helpful to consider the very 'orthodox' approach to the church
by Stephen in a passage of *Ulysses* in which he sees the church

triumphing over all heresies: 'The proud potent titles clanged over Stephen's memory the triumph of their brazen bells: *et unam sanctam catholicam et apostolicam ecclesiam*: the slow growth and change of rite and dogma like his own rare thoughts, a chemistry of stars. ... A horde of heresies fleeing with mitres awry ...'.[8]

Orthodoxy in such a picture is not simply the 'right opinion'; it is concerned with authority in a special, theological sense, linking it with the idea of tradition, blending the voices of the singers in Stephen's image, and also slowly adding rites and dogmas to the canon. Cardinal Newman is probably the best exponent of such a view of orthodoxy; beside the fact that he is highly praised by Joyce as a prose writer, he gives a very consistent definition of orthodoxy in his writings. For Newman, the particularity of heresy is to appeal to the Scriptures alone and to disdain tradition; in this separation of dogma from living faith, the heresiarchs separate themselves from the body of the true church. It is known that Newman began his theological researches with an examination of the heresy of Arius and founded his main conclusions on this case, which figures in Stephen's list of heresies: 'The handful of bishops who supported Arius did not make any appeal to an uninterrupted tradition in their favour. They did but profess to argue from Scripture and from the nature of the case.'[9] Orthodoxy is not dependent on revelation alone or on tradition alone; it is the right authority deriving from an exact balance between Scripture and tradition.

It would then remain to prove that the perversion of such an orthodoxy always stems from a reliance on the written word, or a dismissal of oral tradition. The maternal function of heresy is clearer in *Ulysses* than in *Dubliners*, but I must, for the moment, postpone the articulation of the process of writing with the maternal world. In *Dubliners*, nevertheless, the disjunction between orthodoxy and perversity roughly delimits the world of the absent father and that of the mother's smothering attentions. This can be borne out by a comparison with another passage, from 'A Painful Case'. There is in Mr. Duffy a companion to Mr. Cotter, since he too seems in favour of a separation of the sexes and ages. ('Let a young lad run about and play with young lads of his own age and not be ...', says Mr. Cotter [*D*, p. 8], which appears less drastic than Mr. Duffy's denial of love and friendship, but asserts the same pedagogical repression.) He too has a 'theory', while Mrs. Sinico listens to him, probably as amused by the patter of his aphorisms as the reverend was by the halting answers of the boy: 'Sometimes in return for his theories she gave out some fact of her own life. With almost maternal solicitude she urged him to let his nature open to the full; she became his confessor' (*D*, p. 123).

But when she tries to act out the implications of what he has left unsaid, as she reads in his refusal of intimacy a longing for closer contact, he undercuts such a gross misunderstanding of his own sentences and takes refuge in theoretical equanimity, an enunciated compilation of wisdom without a voice: 'He heard the strange impersonal voice which he recognized as his own, insisting on the soul's incurable loneliness' (p. 124). When Mrs. Sinico presses his hand, he flees, essentially fearing the distortion of an interpretation of his own voice: 'Her interpretation of his words disillusioned him' (p. 124).

The discrepancy between theory and the interpretation of symptoms acquires tragic overtones in this story, while in 'The Sisters' it essentially describes the particular infinity of the process. Such an infinity is mentioned by the child when he adds that he used to enjoy Old Cotter's endless stories before, probably before he had met the priest: the faints and worms can be adequately replaced by the responses of the mass. But what he finally hears during his long silence in the last scene after the visit to the corpse is either the empty gossip of his aunt, or Nannie and Eliza, the ill-fated 'Sisters' of destiny, or the silence of the empty chalice: 'She stopped suddenly as if to listen. I too listened; but there was no sound in the house' (*D*, p. 17). This will be taken up by the final silence that surrounds Mr. Duffy after Mrs. Sinico's death ('He could hear nothing: the night was perfectly silent. He listened again: perfectly silent. He felt that he was alone' [*D*, p. 131]). The endlessness of the other narratives relies on such a victorious silence, and this is the real link between the stories in *Dubliners* and those of *Finnegans Wake*. When Joyce reordered his notes for the *Work in Progress*, he mentioned the 'story of the invalid pensioner' in a context of 'desperate story-telling': 'Arabian nights, serial stories, tales within tales, to be continued, desperate story-telling, one caps another to reproduce a rambling mock-heroic tale.'[10]

While the masculine theory rests on the gnomic utterance of clichés which have no proper conclusions and which in their denunciation of bad 'effects' are akin to the pompous trivialities of a Polonius, the perversity of the dead symbolic father defines the incompleteness of a gnomon, a significant inadequacy. A gnomon is not only the pointer on a sundial, but more specifically 'that part of a parallelogram which remains after a similar parallelogram is taken away from one of its corners', in Euclid. The absent corner hints at the gaping lack revealed not only by the paralysis of the priest, but also by the disjuncture between symptoms and their interpretation. Although the boy is urged by his uncle to 'learn to box his corner' (*D*, pp. 8–9) – which also alludes to the confession box in which the priest has been found laughing silently – this foolish assertion of the subject's autonomy and self-reliance is contradicted by the series of dichotomies the child faces. The 'lighted *square* of window' (italics mine) has not disclosed such a gnomon yet: it would have taken *two* candles set at the head of the corpse to project a shadow visible from the outside. What the child saw in his fascinated gaze was simply the lack of an expected lack, since death has already begun its 'work', but without visible external signs. 'We would see a sign ...' These signs, never ascertainable although working behind the square, are set into motion through the words only.

The words *paralysis, simony*, and *gnomon* become thus inexorably connected through an etymological chain of associations. *Gnomon* implies interpretation and Greek geometry, but is placed curiously beside catechism. Joyce has an illuminating remark in a letter of April 1905: 'While I was attending the Greek mass here last Sunday it seemed to me that my story *The Sisters* was rather remarkable. The Greek mass is strange. The altar is not visible but at times the priest opens the gates and shows himself. ... The Greek priest has been taking a great eyeful out of me: two haruspices'.[11] The connection Joyce implicitly states is striking, suggesting that the very exposure of a sacrament can become the exposure of the person in what can be termed simony. The series of parallel lines intersecting one another can thus describe the figure of the interlocking signifiers. We know, for instance, that Simon Magus, who was the first to try to buy the power to transmit the Holy Ghost from the Apostles, was also a Samaritan prophet, adored as the first God by the members of his sect. They also coupled him with a goddess named Helena, who was said to have been created by his thought. In his teachings can be found the sources of most subsequent heresies spreading Gnosticism through the early Church. He bears witness to the extent to which the messianic Judeo-Christian heresies had been hellenised. Thus, Persia in the boy's dream also calls up the strong Manichean tendencies of the Simonite heresies, while adding another dimension of exoticism to the composite figure of such a 'jewgreek', like Bloom, incestuous and suspected of being homosexual but really in need of a son.

In the same way, *paralysis* eytmologically conveys an idea of dissolution, of an unbinding (*para-lyein*, 'to release, to unbind') which is coupled with an anguishing immobility, while *paresis* means 'to let fall'. The priest's paralysis is both a dropping of some holy vessel (a chalice) in a parapraxis (a slip or lapsus) and the untying of the knots which paradoxically constrict the cramped movements of the protagonists. The fall itself, the *felix culpa* of original sin, links the boy's perverted innocence (it must have been 'the boy's fault' in some version of the incident) to the heresy of the condemned priest. In echo to this, Mr. Duffy laments the ruin of their confessional (the meeting place to which Mrs. Sinico came) and fears another 'collapse' (*D*, p. 124) of his feminine confessor – the first collapse he implicitly alludes to being the gesture of Mrs. Sinico when she kissed his hand!

If Mr. Duffy shrinks away, Old Cotter would prefer to cut off, to lop away the gangrened limbs, appearing thus as a real 'Old cutter'. For the orthodoxy divides in order to anathematise through the particular injunction of lacerated sentences, in a series of performative utterances that stop abruptly before the end. The imitation of Christ is transformed into an apotropaic strategy, such as Stephen practises in the *Portrait* when he tries to become a saint: 'His eyes shunned every encounter with the eyes of women. From time to time also he balked them by a sudden effort of the will, as by lifting them suddenly in the middle of an unfinished sentence and closing the book'.[12] But in *Dubliners*, the maternal tissue of the city, corrupted at its very core by an absent and mute centre (indeed, the priest was never heard in the house 'you wouldn't hear him in the house any more than now' [*D*, p. 15] – 'now' meaning 'now that he is dead'), spreads over, and reforms over the sutured incision, now overgrown with new tissue. This could be why the shop window notice usually reads '*Umbrellas Re-covered*' (*D*, p. 10). The umbrellas are inscribed both in the series of veils, curtains, and clothes such as the greatcoat in which the priest is smothered, priestly vestments which blur the difference, and in the series of parodic phallic substitutes, culminating with O'Madden Burke's gesture as a final law-giver, 'poised upon his umbrella' (*D*, p. 168). In this city of lost property, one cannot recover an absent penis, but the phallus is there as a signifier of the lack to be recovered. The catacombs and the catechism organise a space of echoes (*kata-echein*) which allows for the puns on 'faints' and 'faint', 'not long' and 'I longed', on the first page of 'The

Sisters', since the idle play of the signifiers prepares for the silent and deadly work of Thanatos in the text.[13]

The recovering of the text by itself when it doubles back in this way describes the necessary process of rereading and mirrors the points where it attaches itself inextricably to ambiguous signifiers, which are floating without mooring. One of these is the term 'resignation' used for the priest: 'He was quite resigned. ... He looks quite resigned' (D, p. 14). The signs on his truculent face reveal that this resignation acquires a double edge; the resigned priest has been suspended, so that he is retired and excluded, has resigned his function after his failure to perform his duties. He then assumes the part of the unwilling heretic, perverse precisely because he did not choose to be apart but obeyed the unconscious law of the symptom. The word 'resigned' yields then another hint, pointing towards 'sign'. What this double sign (of the cross) leaves open is the symbolic transference of his attributes to the boy, whose life, too, is 'crossed' by the symptom:

> And then his life was, you might say, crossed.
> – Yes, said my aunt. He was a disappointed man. You could see that.
> A silence took possession of the little room, and, under cover of it I approached the table and tasted my sherry.
>
> (p. 16)

The child who has refused the crackers because he would have made too much noise eating them now indulges in this silent communion. Eliza was 'disappointed' (p. 13) at his refusal, but this devious acceptance of the wine instead of the Eucharist is another 'crossing' of someone's wish. In the first version, the verb used by Joyce to show their first movement when coming into the room was 'We crossed ourselves'; the cross was there as a sign, not the sign of the cross, but the crossing of the sign, through the cancellation of a symbol. The silence of confession, from which the priest has been debarred, superimposes the 'latticed ear of a priest' (P, p. 221) on that of a boy. The priest was 'resigned' because of the crossing between the empty symbol and the transmission of esoteric and perverse powers to someone who is called a 'Rosicrucian' (D, p. 9).

The confession is the process of perverse crossing which breeds a rose on a cross in Dublin. This is why Old Cotter vigorously prohibits the boy's confession ('I wouldn't like children of mine ... to have much to say to a man like that') and utters this unique complete sentence just after he has 'spat rudely into the grate' (*D*, p. 8). The forceful projection of his spittle of course contrasts with the soft oozing of the priest's dribble. The familiar notion of contamination through a poisonous humour can help to explain the curious reversal of the situation of confession. The priest's teaching could have infected the ears of all possible listeners, contaminating by synecdoche the whole of the town. There was a medieval theory of which Joyce was aware which held that heresies could actually poison the atmosphere of a city, as a kind of polluted air (*pestilentia*) penetrating men's viscera.[14] The contagion generated by this infection would surely condemn everyone to excommunication, just as when Henri de Clairvaux found the city of Toulouse so infected with Cathar heresies that no healthy part remained.

[...]

Dubliners can be divided more simply than Joyce suggests with his four-part pre-Viconian scheme of growth from childhood to adolescence, maturity, and the anarchy of public life. The text falls into two main moments. The first one explores the blind alleys of the possible strategies of interpretation, up to 'The Boarding House'; the second part, starting with 'A Little Cloud', hinges on a study of roles and performances, and in fact explores what I would call *enunciation* for short. 'Grace', which was meant to be the conclusion of the book in its first stage, ties all the strands together, as it unites the themes of confession, of interpretation, and of performative utterance. The two significant titles would be 'Encounter' for the first part, an encounter with an Other denied and reduced precisely because it denies and reduces the Other,[15] and 'Counterparts' for the second, the system of balances and oppositions encompassing the blocked gestures of the first part and providing them with an endless circulation within the city of paralysis.

Silence means in the first part a teasing seduction to hermeneutics; the moments of interpretation are generally underlined in the text, as in 'Araby' ('I could interpret these signs' [*D*, p. 34], which foreshadows the final revelation). Lenehan is likewise deliberately ambiguous, since to 'save himself' (p. 55) he leaves his expressions open to several interpretations; he also tries to read signs of reassurance in others' gestures or physique. 'An Encounter' offers the most blatant clues: the narrator fixes a distant aim, the Pigeon House, and is obviously looking for signs, such as the green eyes which his fantasy lends to Norwegian sailors and which he finds in the pervert's face. He has failed to decipher 'the legend' on the boat

(p. 23) and remains unclear about his own motivations ('... for I had some confused notion ...' [p. 23]). The unfinished sentence is similar to the omission of the end of the first boy's dream.

Every time, the interpretation abolishes itself in a moment of silence, either the missing centre of the perverse speech about castigation, this absent secret or mystery never to be disclosed, or the untold action such as the suggested masturbation of the man, which is conveyed by a facile trick of the narration, for the boy has more or less been hypnotised:

> – I say! Look what he's doing!
> As I neither answer nor raised my eyes Mahony exclaimed again:
> – I say. ... He's a queer old josser!
>
> (p. 26)

The plot contrived to achieve some measure of freedom or escape results in a paltry stratagem, when the boys change their names, and an embarrassed silence. The cunning move is similar to the ruse of Ulysses facing the Cyclops, but here it remains insignificant. In the same way, Corley has been 'too hairy' (D, p. 54) to tell his name to the girl he wants to exploit, and this master trickster exhibits the coin of simony in a silent of monstration which gives Lenehan the status of a perverse disciple.

The silence felt in 'Araby' ('I recognised a silence like that which pervades a church after a service' [D, p. 35]) assails the speakers as it invades Dublin: Eveline's speechlessness is formulated in 'silent fervent prayer' (p. 42), and recognition is lost; she cannot even give a 'sign' (p. 43) to Frank. In 'The Boarding House' the complicity between the mother and Polly issues in a 'persistent silence' (p. 68) which cannot be misunderstood; it is the impetus behind the decisive gesture of the end. Mrs. Mooney's moral cleaver will no doubt cut through the hesitation of Bob Doran as it would do through tender meat. What Polly is waiting for in the end is not told, for she herself has forgotten that she was waiting for something: the castrated body of a man ready to accept all the ties of marriage is a direct anticipation of Tom Kernan's fall and is to be followed by Doran's degradation in Ulysses. Both go down the stairs to be met with the loss of some property, be it simply money, freedom and respect, or a corner of the tongue.

Thus, in what I recognise as the second moment, we move towards a definition of failure through the inadequacy of some performance; silence is then constitutive of a discourse, not simply covered or revealed by a discourse. Enunciation refers not simply to direct speech, but assumes the sense of producing meaningful signs in a performance, be it singing or writing. What obviously links the fates of Little Chandler and Farrington is their inability to write. In Chandler's case, the main issue is his blindness to the real process of writing: he cannot think of any mediation between an imaginative mood, a certain psychological state, and the finished product, the idealised book of poems. He accordingly lives in the world of the clichés of romantic bad taste and finally cannot even read the hortatory consolation afforded by Byron's juvenilia.

Farrington, on the other hand, must find substitutes for whatever violence he feels threatening to disrupt his servile copying. It is not a mere accident when he repeats the first name in the contract he has to write out. The repetition of 'Bernard Bernard' (*D*, p. 100) is structurally similar to the repetition of the same verse sung by old Maria (p. 118). Death drives are branched into repetitive parapraxes, until the pure repetition is identified with the silence of death, as we saw in Mr. Duffy's case. Death is then not a voice repeating itself, but the 'laborious drone of the engine reiterating the syllables of her name' (p. 131). The deadly work of the signifiers now seems to undermine the names of the dead, and this appears in 'Ivy Day in the Committee Room'.

It is in this story that the disjuncture between enunciated and enunciation is brought to the fore in a masterwork of political analysis, and it is emphasised by the intricate punctuation that the text develops through its silences. Pauses and silences mark the appearance and disappearance of the characters ('the room was silent again' seems to be a leitmotiv). For silence maps out the presuppositions of the speakers, their unspoken discourses and their modes of expression expose them much more than their empty speeches. Crofton's arrival releases the longer and most sustained speech by Mr. Henchy, and his silence is twofold: 'He was silent for two reasons. The first reason, sufficient in itself, was that he had nothing to say; the second reason was that he considered his companions beneath him' (*D*, p. 146). The void of the enunciated word is not really sufficient, for we have to understand that what matters most is the *a priori* position of superiority he assigns to himself. Enunciation can reveal this position, without any material being spoken. All the while, this empty enunciated word is the object of the competition between the speakers, who all turn to Crofton and try to gain his mute support. Crofton is addressed twice directly by Henchy but refuses to side with him and does not assent either to O'Connor's pleading asides; only the cork popping out of the bottle can give him the cue. And what he adds to the debate is only the term 'gentleman', which will become the object of the derision of 'Grace'.

In the same way, the adverb 'argumentatively' (p. 148), used to qualify the unfinished sentence of Mr. Lyons about the dubious morality of King Edward VII, acquires an ironic significance because the same argument of 'let bygones be bygones' buries it in the silence of betrayal and denial. Denial has to be taken in its religious sense here, for it is such a denial that Joyce betrays, slyly putting perversion to work against itself. The final silences which greet the beginning and the end of the bathetic poem on Parnell culminate in the deflation of Mr. Crofton's final reply. The absence of any standard viewpoint from which to judge this poem leaves the reader teased and speechless, with no discourse at his disposal. The 'clever' piece by Henchy is suspended in a vacuum of political interpretation, since the name of Parnell has been deprived of all political force and turned into a myth, the myth of the dismembered father devoured and mourned by the parricidal sons. Crofton's silence, resting on the assumption of superiority but unable to voice anything more than the void appears then as the only place the text prepares for the reader – after all, the Conservatives had not 'betrayed' Parnell – a place no one can accept.

Names and enunciative strategies are intricately connected in these last stories, but 'Counterparts' provides the example that is easiest to analyse. The first thing the reader witnesses is a violent shout – 'Farrington!' – which sets the dominant tone of aggression. Being called by his name from the outside, Farrington remains 'the man' as a subject of enunciation. But he apparently never utters anything original. We learn that he infuriated Mr. Alleyne by mimicking his Ulster accent, as he will later mimic the flat accent of his terrified son until he finds the felicitous reply which almost escapes his lips. He is then alluded to as the 'consignor' (D, p. 102) when he gains his only real victory, derisory as it is: he pawns his watch for six shillings instead of merely five. From then on, he seems to be the subject of his own speech because he appears capable of narrating the incident, repeating it as he amplifies its nature. He stands the drinks as 'Farrington', for his utterance has transformed a spontaneous witticism which was almost a slip of the tongue ('could he not keep his tongue in his cheek?' [*D*, p. 102]) into a decisive retort, now seeming a 'smart ... thing' (p. 103). What passes unmentioned, of course, is that his answer was the release of an important rage, the first symptom of which was the paralysis of the hand when he could not write. The circle of his downfall is rounded when, in the last part of the story, he is again called 'the man', as he forfeits even his role as a father (p. 109).

But the story 'Grace' affords the real conclusion to the problematics of enunciation: from the slip of the cut or hurt tongue to the divine performative utterance of the pope's proclamation of infallibility, the whole gamut of speech acts is depicted, ascending a ladder that goes from infelicities to 'happy' results. Even such a minor character as Mr. Fogarty helps to define 'grace' in terms of personal appearance and contributes to its connection with utterance: 'He bore himself with a certain grace, complimented little children and spoke with a neat enunciation' (*D*, p. 188), and later: 'He enunciated the word and then drank gravely' (p. 190). The text begins to insist on its own metaphoricity, which is brought to the fore twice. The first 'metaphor', 'we're all going to wash the pot' (p. 184), brings in the theme of confession, while the second, comparing a priest to a 'spiritual accountant' (p. 198), introduces simony. Both are linked with enunciation: 'He uttered the metaphor with a certain homely energy and, encouraged by his own voice, proceeded' (p. 184). The energy of Martin Cunningham's efforts to lead his friend towards salvation is relayed by the 'resonant assurance' of Father Purdon, who asks for permission to use his dominant trope: 'If he might use the metaphor ...' (p. 197). This rhetorical precaution is, of course, superfluous, but it shows that we are invited to difficult readings with possible ruses and tricks, such as the deliberate distortion of the biblical quotation: 'It was one of the most difficult texts in all the Scriptures, he said, to interpret properly' (p. 197). In this devious way, Joyce warns us to read the satire along the lines of Dantean exegesis and progression from Hell to Purgatory and Paradise.

This circular structure links the inverted progress towards a parodic Paradiso for the bankrupt petit bourgeoisie of Dublin to the doomed circularity of confession. The forceful tautology of the doctrine of infallibility ('not one of them ever preached *ex cathedra* a word of false doctrine ... because when the Pope speaks *ex cathedra* ... he is infallible' [p. 191]) stands out as the keystone of the edifice of empty discourse ('until at last the Pope himself stood up and declared infallibility a dogma of the Church *ex cathedra*' [p. 192]). It is Mrs. Kernan's role to underline the feminine transmission of such a doctrine: on the one hand, she refrains from telling the 'gentlemen' that her husband's tongue would not suffer by being shortened (p. 178), while on the other, she feigns 'pity' for the priest who would have to listen to their confession (p. 194). The gap in the tongue signifies the first fall, the inscription of the *gnomon* within the apparatus of enunciation. And the fact that their conversation drifts towards the Council of 1870 reveals that it sets up a trap, with which his friends attempt to get at Kernan through his recanted heresy. John MacHale – who, in Mr. Cunningham's narration, suddenly stands up and shouts '*Credo*' – conveys the hysterical contagion of the performative power of authority and orthodoxy: it is the detail 'with the voice of a lion' (p. 192) that seems so catching here. The other cardinal (Döllinger, in fact) is disqualified, excommunicated: this is a strategy which pushed Mr. Kernan towards the utterance of such a 'Credo'. In order to continue speaking with an equivalent authority, he must utter 'the word of belief and submission' (p. 192) with the others, but also find his marginal freedom; he then adds another performative verb, fetishistically selecting the most trivial item of pomp: 'I bar the candles!' (p. 194). He thus manages to create a similar effect ('conscious of having created an effect on his audience' [p. 194]) which duplicates the unconscious parody of the historical council with its 'farcial gravity'.

The barred tongue opens to the barring of the phallic substitutes. What remains is only the 'retreat business and confession' (p. 194) and their acceptance of a world where business is business. Thus, both the pope and the English king are focal points, helping to expose the undermining of utterance in the void of discourses. The English capital which is demanded by Mr. Henchy and which enables him to condone King Edward's past lapses, and the spiritual accounts which can palliate the most outrageous distortions of the sacred texts and even excuse the aberrations of those 'old popes' who are not precisely 'up to the knocker' (p. 190), both thrive on the same death and prostitution of values. From this point of view, there remains the possibility of ethical judgements. This will disappear with 'The Dead'.

'The Dead' is the supplement to the series of stories of *Dubliners* which, added one year after the completion of the rest, not only mirrors the earlier stories, but modifies them retroactively, pushing them into a new mode of writing. Its function is similar to that of the Penelope chapter in *Ulysses*, with the difference that Gretta's secret has been repressed for so long that it cannot really be voiced, so that her voice only resounds muffled through the memories and desires of her husband.

[...]

The first fourteen stories try to set up the possibility of an ethical discourse criticising the paralysis of Dublin; this is finally left outside the scope of the subject's discourse in 'The Dead', as in *Finnegans Wake*. Like Wittgenstein, Joyce tends to affirm the salvation of ethics through silence, since with the loss of any metalanguage, one can only show, not enunciate, the possibility of direct action or of mythical contemplation.[16] This is why there is a real break and a real loss in the last silence in Anna's final monologue, and not a mere expectancy of the restart for a new beginning.[17] There a certain 'tacebimus' can provide a foundation for the ethics of critical reading. Maurice Blanchot remarks in his introduction to *Lautréamont and Sade* that Heidegger has compared the poems of Hölderlin to a bell held up in a still air, which a soft snow, falling on it, could make vibrate; likewise, the commentary should not be more than a little snow, sounding or ringing this ancient bell.

Finally, the text approaches the region where a supreme silence reigns, returning to the original condition from which it emerges. The space of our reading is suspended between these two blanks, which are necessary to understand our position as subjects of a desire to read, a desire which can be that of losing oneself in the difference of the written signs. This process, indefinitely postponing the absolute loss of the self, manifests itself in fiction as an equivalent of the work of mourning, especially when the text is absorbed by its re-enacting the killing and burial of the dead father, like *Finnegans Wake*. At this point reader and author lose their identities to fuse with the general system of the textual unconscious.

From Jean-Michel Rabaté, *James Joyce, Authorized Reader* (Baltimore, MD, 1991), pp. 20–31; 35–42; 46–7.

Notes

[Rabaté's classically poststructuralist reading of *Dubliners* was originally published in 1982 and marks a considerable shift from the approach demonstrated in Staley's account. It is an example of the 'French Joyce', with Rabaté drawing upon theoretical ideas taken from Jacques Derrida, Jacques Lacan and Maurice Blanchot. Rabaté extends Staley's argument that *Dubliners* demonstrates a keen interest in the word over the world by suggesting that the stories offer a more disruptive and ambiguous theory of discourse than is found in structuralism. By means of a considerable focus upon puns and ambiguities in 'The Sisters' and other stories, Rabaté argues that the various kinds of 'silence' which seem to haunt *Dubliners* represent a challenge to the possibility of any 'metalanguage' or final critical interpretation of the stories. This undermining of meaning by silence is also a threat, argues Rabaté, to subjectivity itself. Ed.]

1. Maurice Blanchot, *L'Ecriture du désastre* (Paris, 1980), p. 187. Also available in English as *The Writing of the Disaster*, trans. Ann Smock (Lincoln, NE, 1986). [All quotations from *Dubliners* are from James Joyce, *Dubliners: The Corrected Text*, ed. Robert Scholes (St Albans, 1977), Ed.]

2. *Letters of James Joyce*, vol. 2, ed. Richard Ellmann (London, 1966), p. 134.

3. *Letters of James Joyce*, vol. 2, p. 105.

4. Hermann Broch, 'James Joyce und die Gegenwart', in *Schriften sur Literatur, I: Kritik* (Frankfurt, 1975), pp. 63–94. See also my article 'Joyce and Broch; or, Who Was the Crocodile?', *Comparative Literature Studies*, 19:2 (1982), 121–33, in which I attempt to describe the theoretical framework in which Broch's reading of *Finnegans Wake* can be understood.

5. *Pound/Joyce: The Letters of Ezra Pound to James Joyce with Pound's Essays on Joyce*, ed. Forrest Read (London, 1968), pp. 27–8.

6. *Pound/Joyce*, p. 90.

7. James Joyce, *A Portrait of the Artist as a Young Man: Text, Criticism, and Notes*, ed. Chester G. Anderson (Harmondsworth and New York, 1977), p. 247. Stephen's 'silence' is thereafter marked by the shift to the mode of the diary instead of direct speech or dialogues.

8. James Joyce, *Ulysses*, ed. and revised by Hans Walter Gabler et al. (New York, 1984), episode I, ll. 650–6. [The Latin phrase is from the Nicene Creed and means 'And in one holy, catholic, and apostolic church'. Ed.]

9. John Henry Newman, *Critical Essays*, 1:128, quoted by Gunter Beimer in *Newman on Tradition*, trans. K. Smith (London, 1967), p. 90.

10. *James Joyce's Scribbledehobble: The Ur-Workbook for 'Finnegans Wake'*, ed. Thomas E. Connolly (Evanston, Illinois, 1961), p. 25.

11. *Letters of James Joyce*, vol. 2, pp. 86–7.

12. Joyce, *A Portrait of the Artist*, p. 150.

13. [Thanatos, the Greek god of death, was the name used by Sigmund Freud to refer to the psychoanalytic concept of the 'death drive'. Ed.]

14. See R. I. Moore's fascinating paper 'Heresy as Disease', in *The Concept of Heresy in the Middle Ages (11th–13th Century)* (The Hague, 1976), pp. 1–11. This conception of heresy as a contagious disease seems to be shared by Mr Tate, the English master in *A Portrait*, when he states his diagnosis of Stephen's paper with the words: 'This fellow has heresy in his essay' (p. 81). Heresy is never far from dogma, in the same way as 'canker' and 'cancer' contribute an ironic epitaph to Wolsey's grave in Leicester Abbey (*A Portrait*, p. 10). See also Annie Tardit's more recent synthesis of the problematics of heresy from a Lacanian point of view, in 'L'appensée, le renard et l'hérésie' in *Joyce avec Lacan*, ed. Jacques Aubert (Paris, 1987), pp. 107–58.

15. By 'Other' I refer to the Lacanian concept of *L'Autre* which has been translated as 'the Big Other' or the 'capitalised Other.' I prefer to leave the term its fluidity, crucial to Lacan's strategies. Nevertheless, it remains very important to distinguish between the 'other' of the imaginary realm and the 'Other' that defines the unconscious as made up of language and determined by the Law and the Name of the Father. What remains untranslatable is the systematic echo introduced by Lacan between *l'object petit à* and the *petit autre* of imaginary identifications.

16. [A reference to the conclusion of Ludwig Wittgenstein's *Tractatus Logico-Philosophicus* (1922), to which Rabaté has earlier compared *Dubliners*. Ed.]

17. [A reference to Anna Livia Plurabelle's monologue in Joyce's *Finnegans Wake* (1939). Ed.]

3

Through a Cracked Looking-Glass: Desire and Frustration in *Dubliners*

SUZETTE A. HENKE

> Virgin veers into Virago. ... No body,
> no belly, no breasts, just tongue.
>> (Hélène Cixous, 'Sorties')

At the time he was composing *Dubliners*, Joyce was fond of envis-
aging himself as an Irish Zola[1] and, in a 1904 letter to Constantine
Curran, declared that his short-story collection would betray the
soul of that hemiplegia or paralysis which many consider a city.[2] It
would hold up to his fellow citizens a 'nicely polished looking-glass'
of moral opprobrium and offer a caustic, multi-dimensional
mimesis of Irish decadence.[3] If one reads Joyce's indictment of
Dublin's 'hemiplegia' from a psychoanalytic perspective, then Irish
paralysis might be diagnosed as a Freudian symptom of psychic
hysteria – the neurotic displacement of aggression, anger, or frustrated libidinal desire played, replayed, and played out in the text of
Dubliners through a pervasive leitmotif of collective repression and
social decentredness. In Joyce's city at the turn of the century, men
and women are continually pitted against one another in patterns of
anxiety and hostility, with each sex perversely demanding mythic
satisfactions of imaginary presence and psychic integration that the
other cannot possibly provide.[4]

Women and children have been relegated to the margins of discourse in a culture that is male centred and woman-avoidant. Barred from communal iteration, they cannot articulate desire, communicate feeling, or valorise emotional need. Males in turn, adopt a speech that strips language of affect and represses erotic expression, until masculine sexuality erupts as a manifestation of phallic urgency – an instinctual yielding to dark, secret, and inarticulate drives. Eros is enacted on a stage of overt danger and covert pleasure, so that the model for heterosexual coupling becomes one of antagonism and conquest – a battle for power won by such gay lotharios as Corley and Gallagher and lost by confused, unimaginative spirits like Little Chandler and Bob Doran. In relationships between the sexes, the central spectre is always envisaged in terms of male desire blocked by the perversities of an arbitrary and tyrannical female will.

Joyce incorporates into the text of *Dubliners* an anatomy of male hysteria over the paralytic fear of being feminised – a terror of Mother Church and Mother Ireland that gives rise to the psychological need for coldness, detachment, and logocentric control. Unconsciously emulating their English masters the Irish assert a specious manhood through blustering claims to patriarchal privilege, making infantile demands that frustrate and feminise those already demeaned by colonial subjugation. The citizens of Dublin are tormented by insatiable desires endlessly replayed on the body of Mother Ireland – a body defiled, raped, and adulterated by British authority. The body of the mother has been usurped by English impostors, but the Irish refuse to enact a national Oedipal rebellion. Kathleen ni Houlihan has been reconstituted in fantasy as an infinitely desirable female, an imaginary presence and centre of psychic integration whose possession is always-already deferred by the intervention of paternal antagonism.

Abject, and cast off from the maternal body, Irish males search for symbols of replacement everywhere in their environment. Mimicking the father, they make themselves into concretised fetishes and identify with the child-phallus that could, in fantasy, satisfy and fully possess the alienated maternal figure. Ireland becomes a text replicating the repressed Gaelic unconscious, and the citizens articulate the letter of the unconscious by inscribing themselves in language as the 'child-phallus who wishes to penetrate his mother's body. ... Exhausted in its course, desire ultimately becomes its own object.'[5]

The beginning of *Dubliners* is oddly sterile and womanless. Joyce depicts a desiccated Garden of Eden inhabited by a fallen race whose imaginary maternal centre has been erased, lost to memory, and eradicated from the mind of the child-narrator who appears in the text as a self-generating character. Maternal separation is the background of his emerging consciousness, the wound or scar of abjection that unmans him even before he has developed a sense of mature individuation. The perpetual gap in the narrative is the unnamed loss of a mother never mentioned – a symbolic absence at the heart of a barren world. It is indicated only in the interstices of the text and evoked, perhaps, by the child's comforting recollection of the familial warmth of Christmas, a pre-Oedipal fantasy that gives refuge from the 'vicious region' of paternal nightmare.

Joyce's inaugural story, 'The Sisters', is dominated by the shadow of a phallic lawgiver whose physical deterioration and mental paralysis were abruptly terminated by a fatal stroke. The boy in the tale has apparently been captivated by the name of the Father, so that his impressionable mind resembles an Aristotelian *tabula rasa* inscribed by an impotent pedagogue. Barred from self-defining utterance, the child writhes in a world of silence and isolation: he does not speak, but ponders with curiosity the contradictory grown-up voices that appropriate the powers of language. Baffled and mute, the enraged boy tries to sublimate passion in futile, animal gestures: 'I crammed my mouth with stirabout for fear I might give utterance to my anger' (*D*, p. 11). Incapable of naming the father who has died and betrayed him, he reverts to a semiotic system of bodily manoeuvres while pondering the ellipses of adult discourse that obscure the identity of a failed Father-God,[6] 'I puzzled my head to extract meaning from his [Cotter's] unfinished sentences' (*D*, p. 11), the boy tells us.

Apparently orphaned (or, like Nora Barnacle, sent out to foster-age with relatives), the child, in search of a paternal surrogate, submits to rigorous training in the kind of logocentric discourse that eventually destroys his tutor, Father Flynn. Yet it is the boy who functions as confessor to the drooling prelate in a dream that identifies the priest as a virtual 'simoniac' guilty of foisting out-moded ecclesiastical offices onto his vulnerable charge. Although the pedagogue can mimic the most august of Catholic theologians, he has evidently lost faith in the Jansenist dogma he preaches. His stance is hypocritical, his tutelage a game. He becomes hebephrenic and hysterical when the womb/chalice of Mother Church cracks and is rent asunder by his own megalomanic and specular gaze. With his faith in sacramental authority shattered. Father Flynn can no longer atone for the religious doubts that finally drive him mad. His desire for faith and spiritual *jouissance* flows back upon itself in frustrated torrents that flood the soul with guilt and deny satisfaction to an unquenchable passion for hermetic power.[7]

As in traditional myth, the impotent patriarch must be killed in order that the young – and the simple – may survive. Joyce calls attention to Father Flynn's sisters in the title of the story, despite their seemingly peripheral role in the narrative. Nannie and Eliza are ignorant and ill-educated, naïve, and somewhat fatuous. They employ malapropisms, talk about 'rheumatic wheels' and the *Freeman's General*, and superstitiously proclaim that James's 'life was, you might say, crossed' (D, p. 17). Although barred from the dominant discourse, they express gentle sympathy for a brother whom they tried to protect from the assaults of a perilous world. 'We wouldn't see him want anything while he was in it' (D, p. 16), they proclaim. In the first version of 'The Sisters', Joyce is more explicit about the priest's phallocratic arrogance: 'He had an egoistic contempt for all women-folk and suffered all their services to him in polite silence' (D, p. 247). It is the sisters, however, who provide an incisive, epigrammatic diagnosis of James's malady: 'He was too scrupulous always' (D, p. 17). Oblivious of the Draconian complexities that tormented their brother, Nannie and Eliza minister to his needs without succumbing to dementia. They respond to the priest's truculence with beef-tea and conversation; and they survive, like Anna Livia in *Finnegans Wake*, to serve a communion of sherry and crackers at his wake.

When females in the story attempt to speak, their words are usually reduced to vacuous gibberish. Unable to master patriarchal discourse, they function as servants to the cultural imperatives that circumscribe their lives. Feminine utterances belong to the little language of social banter and polite conversation – a *parole* that tends to be euphemistic and evasive. Poor deaf Nannie has been 'wore out' from catering to the exigencies of her brother's illness and, like a classical fate or a figure out of Dante, mutely points upwards and beckons to the terrified child. Her mutterings and elocutionary failures veil the reality of death and distract the boy from direct confrontation with the spectral body laid out before him. As he expresses silent contempt for the shabby old woman who summons him to ritual mourning, the child-narrator, mirroring his mentor, already exhibits a dangerous penchant toward intellectual arrogance and self-conscious scrupulosity.

It is significant that the boy's aunt cannot bring herself to utter the word 'die' and cloaks the event in dramatic mystery: 'Did he ... peacefully?' she asks. Death is obscured by euphemistic language until the horror has been sanitised and fades into a static verbal icon. The vocabulary of prettiness and tidiness reduces the priest to an aesthetic object, a decorous and decorative artifact – little more than a 'beautiful corpse' (D, p. 15). St Thomas Aquinas's definition of beauty as 'that which, when seen, pleases', illumines the sisters' repressed emotional relief at their brother's recent demise. Freed from the intrusions of imperious male authority, the survivors celebrate a wake that releases them from deepseated hostility and allows them to admire the priest as a safely crystallised visual spectacle in a non-threatening photographic tableau. The dead – essentialised, objectified and mentally displaced – become the malleable property of the living who mould the memory of the deceased in the image of their own projected fantasies.

If Nannie and Eliza are contemporary versions of the New Testament figures Martha and Mary, their brother is portrayed as a parodic Lazarus with little potential for resurrection. The moribund Father Flynn could hardly be aroused from sedentary torpor and, in the last years of his life, seemed only to respond to the stimulus of *High Toast* snuff. Death comes as a climax to protracted paralysis – a condition that might, ironically, have been symptomatic of tertiary syphilis.[8] At the end of the story Father Flynn's body is exhibited as a stiff phallic rod, a visible sign of masculine authority mentally ossified long before *rigor mortis* sets in. 'There he lay, solemn and copious, vested as for the altar, his large hands loosely retaining a chalice. His face was very truculent, grey and massive; with black cavernous nostrils and circled by a scanty white fur' (D, p. 14). The savage and threatening nostrils, surrounded by tufts of animal hair, possibly suggest an unconscious screen image of the threat of genital invagination.

The verbal puzzles initially announced in 'The Sisters' by the words 'gnomon', 'simony' and 'paralysis' are eventually revealed not as riddles, but as indeterminate symbols that haunt the textual unconscious of the narrative. The priest's potential *siglum* proves to be the incomplete angular or phallic formation of a parallelogram stripped of a diminutive, filial corner. 'Without a doubt', says Cotter in the original version, the 'upper storey ... was gone' (D, p. 244).

Similarly the story (or storey) is rife with examples of both physical and spiritual paralysis, as well as simoniacal practices that barter ecclesiastical offices purchased at too high a price.[9]

Two genuine riddles or aporias in the tale – the mystery of Persia and the mysterious chalice – both evoke repressed symbols of ritual wholeness and imaginary plenitude. In response to Cotter's 'unfinished sentences', the boy recollects a dream set in the sensual ambiance of 'long velvet curtains and a swinging lamp of antique fashion. I felt that I had been very far away, in some land where the customs were strange – in Persia, I thought' (*D*, pp. 13–14). The reference to Persia alludes to an Oriental Other, an exotic vista projected by the fragmented male consciousness and fantasmatically associated with harems, licentiousness, and voluptuous female flesh. The Catholic priest's western asceticism is challenged by the boy's unconscious through inverted images of tantalising desire. The 'grey paralytic' is imaginatively represented as a greedy simoniac eager to exchange ecclesiastical knowledge for a disciple's unwitting troth. The death of this stern father-figure, who lives by the letter of the law, exchanges *règles* for *jeux* in the boy's psychic economy through a movement of carnivalesque pleasure. The child becomes the priest's confessor, and traditional authority is up-ended in magical, exotic charade. When the word-master dies, the narrator acknowledges a sudden surge of psychosomatic release: 'I felt even annoyed at discovering in myself a sensation of freedom as if I had been freed from something by his death' (*D*, p. 12). The boy's unconscious knows what his waking mind cannot admit: that this 'great friend' was guilty of sins of pederastic desire deflected into a demand for psychic appropriation. The older man's 'great wish' for the child was a powerful projection of his own need for psychological mastery – a desire to gain control of the boy under the aegis of pedagogical insemination and to mould this docile disciple into a spiritual replica of himself. It is not surprising, then, that the protagonist confronts his erstwhile guru in a land whose voluptuous topography subverts the older man's pretensions toward asceticism and logocentric control. His indeterminate fantasy lacks both closure and accessible intellectual meaning. 'I could not remember the end of the dream', the narrator confesses (*D*, p. 14).

According to the symbol-system of the Oriental Tarot, the chalice or cup designates a female fertility principle – the womb/body/in-vaginated mother worshipped as pre-Christian goddess. Catholic ritual appropriates the sacred cup for purposes of symbolic couvade in the Mass – a ritual that re-enacts Christ's 'last supper' and his nurturance of the twelve apostles with the bread/host of his own sacrificial body. By virtue of ecclesiastical authority, Father Flynn could mimic the creative function of the mother by pronouncing words that evoke the living presence of Christ in 'body and blood, soul and divinity'. The law and authority of the father supplants the pre-symbolic, uterine magic of the fertilised mother. The body of Christ becomes a maternal, nurturant host, and the words of the priestly father summon the sacramental rebirth of a divine, incarnate Son. The metaphorical rite, however, is suspended over the void by perpetual acts of faith. If belief in the ritual should fail and the body of the surrogate womb/chalice crack, then the priest will be stripped of his theological centre and 'castrated' of the rights/rites of phallic mastery. The demented prelate is powerless to recuperate an integrated image of himself without faith in the specular projections of a mirroring maternal chalice. In compensation for the loss of mystical contact with an imaginary and valorising maternal field, he turns to a young disciple in search of an/Other to replicate his schizophrenically split subjectivity.[10]

The priest attempts to seduce the young boy through Lacanian movements of mesmerising speech. He consigns a fragmented self-image to the care of the other, whose admiring gaze, reflected back in the eyes and consciousness of the subject (*je*), will offer an ideologically unified, if illusory vision of the self (*moi*). It is only through the *regard* of the other (the look, gaze, or mirror of approval) that the fragmented subject is able to construct a fictive self-image – an image which, for all its apparent integrity, is a myth contingent on deliberate misprision. The child performs for the priest a function that the chalice of Mother Church could not. He provides a Lacanian mirror for the debilitated prelate and, by doggedly re-enacting the priest's ecclesiastical obsessions, sutures an implied wound of psychic castration.[11]

Father Flynn, in turn, shields his naïve disciple from acknowledgeing a split in human subjectivity by acting as a psychological mirror that displaces the repressed figure of a pre-Oedipal mother and inscribes (or indoctrinates) the child into the symbolic order and law of the Father. The priest perpetuates a myth of subjective cohesion accessible through complex strategies of intellectual and linguistic mastery. The boy-disciple has recourse to patriarchal assurances of personal initiation into a superior world of masculine knowledge, power, privilege, and satisfaction. In the original story, the child naïvely speculates: 'Of course neither of his sisters was very intelligent. ... Perhaps he found me more intelligent and honoured me with words for that reason' (*D*, p. 247).

The 'queer old josser' of 'An Encounter' casts still another shadow of the menacing patriarch who tries to lure an ingenuous youth to religious or physical perversion. Fired by a 'cowboy and Indian' notion of heroic prowess, the narrator and his friend Mahony go off to seek adventure at the mysterious Dublin Pigeon House, a topography that assumes tropological status as a locus of mysterious desire and forbidden sexual pleasure. Their experiment with adult freedom is frustrated by a disturbing encounter with a would-be pederast. Circling discursively around obsessional fetishes of 'white hands' and 'beautiful soft hair', the man conjures up hypnotic images of virginal nymphettes, then rises to the occasion by going off to masturbate. When he leers at the children and ostensibly exhibits an engorged phallus, the boys witness titillating *machismo* degenerate into homoerotic perversion and the wild sensations of youth give way to the lurid obsessions of senility. At some level, both the narrator and his companion recognise but never fully acknowledge that an aggressive code of masculine prowess can be perverted, by way of frustrated desire, into the emotional chaos of sexual dementia. Libidinous fantasy spins in ever-fixed patterns of deferred homosexual arousal – a physical replica of the need displayed by Father Flynn to penetrate the mind of his child-disciple and implant seminal knowledge spewed forth from ecclesiastical tradition. As Jane Gallop speculates, there is 'a certain pederasty implicit in pedagogy. A greater man penetrates a lesser man with his knowledge'.[12] Both Flynn and the josser take sadistic pleasure in catechetical lessons demonstrative of invidious phallic manipulation.

The adolescent protagonist of 'Araby' turns from the inchoate desires of latency to overtly heterosexual longings. Emotionally, ontogeny recapitulates phylogeny, as the child re-enacts courtship rituals of medieval worship and sacramental obeisance to a distant, unattainable icon. Perched precariously on the brink of erotic expression, he sublimates burgeoning sexual drives to sentimental fantasies of an ideal chivalric love. The boy's *inamorata*, simply identified as 'Mangan's sister', is portrayed as an idolised romantic heroine. Shadowy and elusive, she plays the role of seductive temptress, with swinging dress and a 'soft rope' of hair suggestive of fetishistic entrapment. Her appearance inspires Wordsworthian rapture, though she is little more than the shadow of a dream – a 'brown figure' peered at in specular fashion from behind the blinds of a shabby tenement in North Richmond Street. The young woman becomes a goddess shrouded in mystery, and her adored replica is detached from the real world to be kept safe from mundane defilement. It soon becomes clear that the protagonist is enamoured not of Mangan's sister, but of her sanctified presence as an emblem of psychic integrity, a figure that mirrors back the boy's own inflated dreams of heroic valour. In the tradition of courtly love, this modern-day knight has been entranced by an 'older woman', an eroticised virgin who becomes the focal point of sacerdotal worship. Like Sir Galahad, he cherishes a chaste ideal of masculine gallantry and proudly bears his chalice of platonic devotion 'safely through a throng of foes' (D, p. 31).

In all the ardour and confusion of adolescent attraction, the boy-narrator fails to recognise symptoms of erotic obsession disguised by ritual homage. Shyly, he admits: 'my body was like a harp and her words and gestures were like fingers running upon the wires' (D, p. 31). The musical simile, borrowed from Coleridge's 'Aeolian Harp', represses a veiled but displaced longing for tactile stimulation – for the wires of the boy's newly awakened phallic consciousness to be fondled by the delicate white hands of his beloved. The protagonist yearns for sensuous contact, and his language is saturated with Freudian *double entendre* when he imagines 'fine incessant needles' of rain impinging on the earth's sodden labial beds (D, p. 31). But like a monk struggling for dignity and self-control, he finds ritual solace in a litany of ejaculations repeated like a mantra evocative of his beloved.

When the distant object of his affection finally speaks to him, the protagonist is understandably confused and disoriented. Mangan's sister twists a silver bracelet 'round and round her wrist', unconsciously engaged in gestures of hypnotic seduction. Trained in the body language of feminine flirtation, she unwittingly tempts and taunts her would-be suitor. The boy, in turn, focuses not on her face but on fetishistic projections of her figure – the 'white curve of her neck', her illumined hair, a hand clutching the spike of a railing, and the 'white border of a petticoat' (D, p. 32). Luxuriating in eastern enchantment, he excitedly promises, like a knight of old, to bring back a trophy from the oriental bazaar. As the girl vanishes from sight, she remains perpetually other – a wistful, 'brown-clad figure' inscribed in the young man's consciousness as a fetishistic supplement to male subjectivity.

When Joyce's Arthurian knight, in search of the Holy Grail, finally reaches the Chapel Perilous, he discovers a deserted gallery bereft of eastern splendour. The stall attendant flirting with two English gentlemen exposes the vulgar side of eroticism, and the boy is forced to acknowledge the profane reality of his own emotional infatuation: 'I saw myself as a creature driven and derided by vanity; and my eyes burned with anguish and anger' (*D*, p. 135). The vanity he bemoans evinces a futile desire to appropriate the beloved as an ideal, mystifying centre and dubious mirror-image of coherent subjectivity. Once again, the individual unsuccessfully appeals to an/Other for the psychological reification of a unified, idealised self. Earlier, he had imagined himself an heroic priest of love, secretly bearing his chalice of devotion through a venal, commercialised world. As the lights go out in Araby, the narrator, 'blinded' by infatuation, sees himself clearly for the first time and is shocked by the realisation that he, too, is one of the vulgar. Try as he might, he cannot detach himself from the human comedy of sexual experience, and he chafes at the powerful illusions perpetuated through culturally inscribed romantic myths.

The disillusioned adolescent suddenly understands that he has been socialised into feudal and archaic codes of chivalric behaviour incongruent with the commercial exchange of sexual favours on the nineteenth-century marriage market. Overwhelmed by the veiled mystery of the female body, he sublimates the physical demands of adolescent sexuality to a ritualised discourse of courtly love. Only at the end of the story does he begin to acknowledge, in a moment of epiphany, repressed torrents of sexual desire swirling beneath artificial cultural codes. A tawdry shopgirl reluctantly fends off the advances of two randy Englishmen seeking a bit of fun to enliven their Irish holiday. The boy knows that his own platonic love affair is motivated by a similar agenda. He would like to bed down with Mangan's sister, but is forbidden even to contemplate the satisfactions of erotic contact with a figure as inaccessible as the Virgin Mary. Spiritual obsession has obscured the emotional urgency of his quest and dammed the course of sexual drives rendered futile by the prohibitions of contemporary Catholic mores.

Joyce reverses the narrative of 'Araby' in his tale of Eveline Hill, whose dreams of escape and amorous salvation are imbued with all the exotic trappings characteristic of the kind of popular fiction published in late nineteenth-century ladies' magazines. Eveline sees her suitor Frank as a bronze-faced prince who promises personal redemption and a future of wedded bliss. Caught up in the excitement of 'having a fellow', this Dublin Desdemona floats on illusion until, in her rife imagination, the 'kind, manly, open-hearted Frank' takes on heroic stature. Absorbing the figures of Odysseus and Sir Galahad, he becomes just as unreal as the tales of the 'terrible Patagonians' with which he amuses, and possibly manipulates, his enthralled and exploitable beloved.[13]

If Eveline is bewitched by Frank's stories of adventure, she feels equally moved by 'the pitiful vision of her mother's life', a nightmare that lays its 'spell on the very quick of her being' (D, p. 40). Eveline determines to avoid her mother's battered servitude: 'She would not be treated as her mother had been' (D, p. 37). But those haunting words, 'Derevaun Seraun!', uttered in meaningless madness, call Eveline to a vocation of spectral dissolution. Self-sacrifice to the point of dementia will be the ghost's sole benefice. Wresting a solemn promise from her docile daughter, the dying mother seals Eveline's bonds of incestuous entrapment. The girl, torn between a childhood pledge of filial duty and an exotic fantasy of personal happiness, conducts both sides of a mental debate whose outcome has already been determined. The motif of 'home' resounds like a metronome throughout the story, suggesting the moral compulsions that hypnotise consciousness and preclude the possibility of meaningful change. In this trial of the soul, Eveline serves as both prosecutor and defendant, analyst and spiritual analysand. As she weighs emotion and romantic fantasy against the judgmental voice of conscience, she engages in an exercise of deliberate misprision that sacrifices free will to those Irish gods of hearth and home she has been taught to worship from infancy. Abandoned by her mother and bereft of nurturant care, Eveline succumbs to a compulsive need to *become* the mother sacrificed on the altar of Dublin domesticity. She must fetishise her body and offer herself as sexual and social victim to a demanding patriarch who threatens incestuous entrapment.

Altruism and self-effacement are the edicts inscribed on the young girl's unconscious, and, by the end of the story, she lets her mind switch to automatic pilot. Begging God to show her 'her duty', Eveline reverts to a simple rhetoric of docility and obedience echoing the Virgin Mary's response at the Annunciation: 'Be it done unto me according to thy word.' Resolute in her paralysis, she stares vacantly, almost catatonically, at her departing suitor. Nausea and bodily distress indicate mounting sexual anxiety, as

Use of contrast.

Eveline dimly begins to perceive that elopement with Frank would mean, in realistic terms, a commitment to an intimate physical union that has never come within the purview of her disembodied dreams. The wound of sexual penetration evinces the kind of psychic violation she associates with marriage, servitude, and relentless domestic battering. In a moment of Freudian terror, she imagines replicating her mother's story and drowning in the 'seas of the world', an oceanic symbol that provokes sudden hysteria at the thought of physical defloration. Conflating Frank with the father who 'would drown her', the young woman holds her ground 'like a helpless animal' – trapped, panicked, and frozen in a stance of neurotic immobility. Visions of engulfing seas accost her with uncanny (*unheimlich*, unwombly) resonance, as sex threatens to impinge on a tightly sealed world of romantic illusion. Eveline longs to escape from adult libidinal drives and return to an infantile fantasy of pre-Oedipal bliss, a womb-like passivity in which she would be nurtured and protected by a warm and loving maternal caretaker. But her desire for embryonic security and connection to the body of the mother forces her back into the arms of Mother Church and into lifelong servitude to an unsolicitous male parent who forever prohibits access to the unauthorised phallus of the husband/engenderer.

Bound from childhood to a negative self-image, Eveline can never extricate herself from the web of words woven around the sacrosanct authority of the patriarchal Irish father. In this asphyxiating world of psychic imprisonment, the daughter becomes surrogate spouse to her tyrannical 'Da'. Clearly, Eveline is destined to repeat the sadomasochistic patterns of her mother's life – 'that life of commonplace sacrifices closing in final craziness' (*D*, p. 40). 'Derevaun Seraun' apparently means, in demotic Irish, that 'the end of pleasure is pain'. As Jane Gallop observes, 'the daughter's obligation to reproduce the mother, the mother's story – is a more difficult obstacle than even the Father's law.'[14]

Eveline's catatonic silence at the end of the tale merely confirms the shadowy silence she has always inhabited both at home and in the Stores. She has been inscribed into a male register of need and desire, of authority and irascibility characteristic of Irish parental models. Her exclusion from the dominant discourse is doubled by an enigmatic portrait of another male, the aged priest (now in Melbourne) whose photograph constitutes a specular shrine to absent authority. Unable to question the mysteries of male bonding, Eveline dusts the photo but never demands a fuller portrait of the

Irish prelate who has disappeared 'down under', to the antipodes of geography and consciousness, beyond the reach of concupiscence. His picture serves as a fetishistic reminder of ecclesiastical power – a patriarchal authority contingent on the law of phallic veiling and a self-conscious, ascetic renunciation of women.

As in 'The Sisters', females are excluded from male discourse and consigned to the realm of silence, gibberish, and babble. Once Eveline's mother breaks out of her prison of verbal constraint, she speaks the truth in demented utterances that defer meaning along with linguistic closure. Hysteria, given voice, shrieks in tones of warning and fatuity, casting a lugubrious spell over the perplexed auditors who try to interpret encoded deathbed commands. Babble flows like a turgid excrescence of womb and consciousness, the misshapen effluvia of unbearable oppression. The mother murmurs a private idiolect that bequeathes to her female child the weight of iniquity and misprision. Caught between semiotic dementia and catatonic silence, Eveline predictably chooses the latter.

[...]

In his portrait of Gretta Conroy in 'The Dead', Joyce fashioned for the first time in his fiction the image of a passionate, nurturant, and life-giving woman whose rich, intuitive consciousness was modelled on the confessions of Nora Barnacle. 'The Dead', Richard Ellmann tells us, comprises 'one of Joyce's several tributes to his wife's artless integrity. Nora Barnacle, in spite of her defects of education, was independent, unselfconscious, instinctively right. Gabriel acknowledges the same coherence in his own wife, and he recognises in the west of Ireland, in Michael Furey, a passion he has himself always lacked'.[15]

Gabriel Conroy is, at least in part, a figure of the kind of Irish pedant Joyce might have become had he remained in his native country. A writer of book reviews and after-dinner speeches, Gabriel prides himself on his continental perspective and feels a bit ashamed of the Galway wife his mother once described as 'country cute'. He compulsively protects his family from the hazards of nature by insistent recourse to galoshes, green shades, dumb bells, and stirabout. As a minion of modern civilisation, he betrays a deep-seated, almost neurotic fear of exposure to the perilous fluidity of life symbolised in the ruggedness of a western terrain 'beyond the pale' of urban amenities.

A Joycean surrogate, Conroy takes refuge in a logocentric and dangerously repressive world of verbal mastery cut off from unconscious drives and explosive libidinal desires. With a mixture of nostalgia and condescension, he contemplates pictures of 'the balcony scene in *Romeo and Juliet*' and of the 'murdered princes in the Tower which Aunt Julia had worked in red, blue and brown wools when she was a girl' (*D*, p. 186) as artful embroideries that transform Renaissance tragedy into a casual comedy of the nineteenth-century drawing room. Sanitised, and robbed of cathartic effect, the scenes become part of a Victorian memorial to the necrophiliac eruptions of Shakespearean drama. Though contemptuous of his aunts' naïve and ladylike sensibilities, Gabriel proves just as guilty as they of consigning both subversive heroism and *l'amour fou* to the controlled and static frame of aesthetic appropriation. By framing the ineffable and taming the disruptive agents of love and violence, the artist diminishes their phallic force and castrates the figures, who become specular objects to be devoured by the observer's enveloping gaze.

Similarly, in the register of language and social discourse, Gabriel is intent on constructing a phallocentric fortress of masterful rhetoric to protect his vulnerable ego. Despite the benefits of erudition, training, and intellectual sophistication, he treats every personal encounter as a contest for psychological dominance. Caught between an arrogant cultural pose and hidden feelings of self-doubt, Gabriel makes the social world into a narcissistic stage for dramas of continual self-assertion. Habitually condescending toward women, he dares not 'risk a grandiose phrase' with the annoying Molly Ivors, but challenges her nonetheless with the incendiary remark that 'I'm sick of my own country, sick of it!' (*D*, p. 189). Such a confession might well deserve the charge of 'West Briton' which Gabriel finds egregiously offensive. Instead of expressing his agitation openly, however, and fighting it out with Miss Ivors, he indulges in petty, mean-minded exercises in self-vindication: 'Of course the girl or woman, or whatever she was, was an enthusiast but there was a time for all things. Perhaps he ought not to have answered her like that. But she had no right to call him a West Briton before people, even in joke. She had tried to make him ridiculous before people, heckling him and staring at him with her rabbit's eyes' (*D*, p. 190). In this unconscious appeal to male privilege, Gabriel dismisses his opponent as a childish female whose audacious demeanour has so unsexed her that she seems to belong to a third, unnamable gender. In his mind, the rabid patriot is rhetorically transformed into a heckling rabbit hopping about in irrational frenzy.

Imitating a petulant child, Gabriel saves his final thrust for last. His pedantic postprandial speech tacitly condemns Miss Ivors as a member of the 'new and very serious and hypereducated generation' that betrays traditional Irish hospitality (D, p. 192). 'Very good', he thinks smugly, 'that was one for Miss Ivors. What did he care that his aunts were only two ignorant old women?' (D, p. 192). Gabriel is eager to put down one woman by elevating two others who serve as pawns to balance the scales of masculine indignation and soothe his wounded ego. His indictment of a sceptical and thought-tormented age is largely an act of psychological projection, since Gabriel himself emerges as the most self-conscious figure in the story. Although the speaker mourns the loss of a more spacious era 'gone beyond recall', he is ill-prepared to cherish the memory of an Irishman whose fame his wife Gretta cannot 'willingly let die' (D, p. 203).

Like Torvald Helmer in Ibsen's Doll's House, Gabriel sees his spouse not as an individual with feelings and needs of her own but as a static symbol feeding his creative imagination.[16] 'He asked himself what is a woman standing on the stairs in the shadow, listening to distant music, a symbol of. If he were a painter he would paint her in that attitude. ... Distant Music he would call the picture' (D, p. 210). Shrouded in grace and mystery, Gretta becomes a model of feminine tranquillity, a romantic image of blue and bronze, blurred in a setting of vague nostalgia. Her feelings are framed and appropriated, her passions castrated and erased. Although The Lass of Aughrim has auditory impact on his wife, Gabriel refuses to acknowledge the world of memory and desire stirred by Gretta's response to the Irish ballad. Instead, he translates her meditative mood into a vapid visual impression. Lost in a Whistleresque fantasy, he deliberately distances himself from the emotive qualities of the music and from a tragic sexual narrative rooted in Celtic associations. Like Stephen Dedalus in A Portrait, he freezes the moment of experience and imposes the 'spiritual-heroic refrigerating apparatus of art onto a pallid, sentimental figure constructed by his self-absorbed imagination. To facilitate the project, Gabriel misinterprets Gretta's body language and fails to sense the emotional currents of her silence – of thoughts cast out like lyrical fragments that demand a reading of present nostalgia through a history of love and loss. Framing his wife as a specular object, he ignores the context of smouldering passion that evinces her melancholic posture. Feminine desire is subject to amorous misprision, as the gaps and wounds of Gretta's past experience are replicated in her consciousness by mimetic shapes of idealised longing.

About to project his own desire for a 'yielding mood' onto his wife's vulnerable figure, Gabriel muses: 'She seemed to him so frail that he longed to defend her against something and then to be alone with her. Moments of their secret life together burst like stars upon his memory. ... He longed to recall to her those moments, to make her forget the years of their dull existence together and remember only their moments of ecstasy. For the years, he felt, had not quenched his soul or hers' (*D*, pp. 213–14). Gabriel's surge of conjugal tenderness is entirely focused on private memories filtered through a nostalgic vision of himself as a fiery cavalier. He revels in feelings of spousal possession associated with the couple's dancing earlier that night: 'He had felt proud and happy then, happy that she was his, proud of her grace and wifely carriage (*D*, p. 215). Romantically idealising Gretta's presence, Gabriel constructs an image of her as an exotic mistress whose mysterious demeanour harbours promises of ecstatic flight: 'Under cover of her silence ... he felt that they had escaped from their lives and duties, escaped from home and friends and run away together with wild and radiant hearts to a new adventure' (*D*, p. 215).

Gretta, however, remains mute. It is Gabriel who speaks for her in this emotionally charged fantasy, and it is he who defines their adventure with the same kind of *naïveté* that characterised the futile aspirations of the young boy in 'Araby'. His dream of recapturing the thrill of their honeymoon recollects the first days of conjugal life as a model for the kind of integrity, joy, and emotional satisfaction associated with pre-Oedipal bliss. Bourgeois marriage has meant a fall from paradisal union with the beloved, whose erstwhile desirability acts as a spur to the recrudescence of urgent, if insatiable, erotic need.

Once at the Gresham Hotel, Gabriel's thoughts circle obsessively around male dominance and female submission until, on the brink of sexual frenzy, he feels a keen pang of lust and an overwhelming urge to seize, crush, and 'overmaster' his wife. 'He could have flung his arms about her hips and held her still, for his arms were trembling with desire to seize her and only the stress of his nails against the palms of his hands held the wild impulse of his body in check' (*D*, p. 215). Ironically, he contemplates a kind of emotional (and possibly physical) rape at the very moment when Gretta is most fully absorbed in reminiscences of Michael Furey, a lover whose passion took the form of sacrificial tragedy. This Irish suitor who died for love acted the melodramatic role of a legendary knight who, in good chivalric fashion, laid at the feet of his courtly lady the ultimate gift of his life. By sacrificing all for Gretta, he took permanent possession of her heart. Symbolically, the martyred Furey became a contemporary Christ figure, a mythic hero whose death makes Gretta into an eternal replica of the Virgin Mary as *Pietà*. She is forever an emblem of the *magna mater*, the mother/lover bearing a transfigured godhead in bereft maternal arms.[17]

Lost in a trance of mourning for Michael, Gretta idolises the boy as an always-already-absent object of desire, forever longed for and pined after until the tantalising fact of inaccessibility becomes an aphrodisiac of the spirit. Psychological drives that are dammed and sublimated circle back in rich profusion, as death fetishises the body of the beloved and makes unattainable physical presence a sexual spur in a world of amorous denial. The absent lover torments the dreaming mind until pain piques erotic appetite to the point of libidinal despair. Melodrama prohibits the comedy of physical collusion, the joyous game of 'laugh and lie down' that cannot be played among corpses. Pleasure is masked in self-indulgent longing, physical attraction idealised through tears and sentimental yearning. 'I want' is echoed back as 'I love', Eros disguised in the mimesis of perfect passion for an impotent lover who can no longer touch, threaten, penetrate, wound, or inseminate the female body. The scar of loss, invaginating consciousness, metaphorically reproduces the vaginal gap yearning for prohibited phallic presence. The mind, rent by melancholia, seals up the lover's replica like an embryo in a womb, an encrypted and forever-powerful image of the unattainable lost one. 'I was great with him at that time', says Gretta (*D*, p. 220), recalling a phrase descriptive of pregnancy, as well as of girlish infatuation. Gestating in the heart, the once-beloved object is resuscitated and made real, his absence become a presence through a life-giving process that celebrates the dead son/god/lover resurrected by the mythopoesis of feminine desire.

The ghost of inaccessible *jouissance* flows into the present and reduces Gabriel's dream of sexual possession to a futile, impotent fantasy. Cuckolded by a dead man, the husband is overcome with rage, then assaulted by pitiable confusion. Stripped of the conjugal assumptions that have always sustained an illusory faith in his own integrity, he begins to confront the pettiness of his egocentric vision:

> Gabriel felt humiliated by the failure of his irony and by the evocation of this figure from the dead, a boy in the gasworks. [The irony of his mood soured into sarcasm.] While he had been full of memories of their secret life together, full of tenderness and joy and desire, she had been comparing him in her mind with another. A shameful consciousness of his own person assailed him. He saw himself as a ludicrous figure, acting as a pennyboy for his aunts, a nervous, well-meaning sentimentalist, orating to vulgarians and idealising his own clownish lusts.[18]
>
> (*D*, pp. 219–20)

Humiliated by the ashes of burnt-out lust, Gabriel is shocked to encounter an incontestable opponent – a dead man now elevated to the status of a slain deity whose love once flared with consummate ecstasy. The tale of this meteoric devotion sparks the dying embers of Gabriel's passionate commitment to his wife; and the narrative inaugurates a familiar Joycean pattern of triangulated desire, as Michael becomes the spiritual mediator of Gabriel's affection for Gretta.[19] Longing to appropriate and emotionally fuse with the *imago* of a beneficent mother/wife, Gabriel is forced to acknowledge the utter inaccessibility of an/Other's subjectivity. The opaque and rounded character of an imaginary centre, a knowable and fully illuminated symbol (or symptom) of womanhood, is suddenly shattered by the startling revelation of a secret love perpetually reconstituted through rites of amorous frustration.[20] Unable to reproduce his subjective self-image in the mirror of an/Other, Gabriel is thrust onto the margins of conjugal doubt and forced to re-integrate his ego through splintered reflections of a recollected past, a plethora of emotional fragments that defy mental coherence. Relinquishing his longing for self-valorisation through a totalising vision of the female, he surrenders himself to the unsettling pulsions of a buried, semiotic life that offers the promise of psychic regeneration. By the end of the story, both Gabriel and Michael have been successfully resurrected – one from the paralysis of death-in-life, the other from a legend of life-in-death.

Touched by the spectral presence of Furey, Gabriel begins to cast off his shell of egotistical self-absorption.[21] He feels his identity 'fading out into a grey impalpable world; the solid world itself ... was dissolving and dwindling. ... The time had come for him to set out on his journey westward. ... His soul swooned slowly as he heard the snow falling faintly through the universe and faintly falling, like the descent of their last end, upon all the living and the dead' (D, pp. 223–4). The ending of Joyce's tale is finely ambiguous. We have learned from the author's ironic sensibility in stories such as 'Araby' and 'A Painful Case' to distrust swooning souls and self-deceptive epiphanies – especially when, as in this case, the pre-Raphaelite swoon is embedded in a Christological ambiance of crooked crosses, spears, and 'barren thorns' (D, p. 224). Imitating the Christ-like role of Michael Furey, Gabriel may well be trapped in a self-indulgent replication of romantic asceticism. If so, he has been swept up in the illusory discourse of fealty and courtly love; which Jacques Lacan describes as 'an altogether refined way of making up for the absence of sexual relation by pretending that it is we who put an obstacle to it'.[22]

In Richard Ellmann's view, Gabriel has achieved a genuine sense of maturity and authentic connection with all the living and the dead, a salutary understanding of the 'mutual dependency' and 'interrelationship' that links the whole of humankind.[23] At the conclusion of 'The Dead', the logocentric consciousness of the masculine subject dissolves into a will-less dream of semiotic process where birth and growth are balanced by their binary opposites, decay and death. Gabriel appears to sink into the primitive, repressed world of the unconscious and at last to stand open to those self-effacing dimensions of love and solicitude heretofore denied by a wilful, narcissistic ego.

Gretta Conroy, like Anna Livia Plurabelle, has miraculously resuscitated the shade of a dead man as a living, potent spirit. And like Molly Bloom celebrating her sexual initiation on Howth, she draws the past into the present in the mode of impassioned memory. Revitalising the ghost of her long-dead lover, Gretta gives mythic stature to a man whose life ended in tragic consummation; and, in contrast to the casual comedy enacted by the Dubliners, her act succeeds in endowing Ireland with a kind of legendary grandeur. Through a poetics of absence contingent on desire indefinitely deferred and *inter-dit* (spoken through or between the gaps of frustrated longing), she makes possible the spiritual redemption of Gabriel, whose aesthetic pretensions have degenerated into the fatuities of *l'homme moyen sensuel*. It is, in the end, Gretta who proves to be the true artist of the tale, a woman whose imagination regenerates the past and gives birth to a sustaining narrative that provides a supplement to fading marital affection and inspires the final epiphany of the story. She successfully revitalises the revolutionary and subversive world of love and violence domesticated by her aunts and puritanically refrigerated by her prurient spouse.

By offering a vivid myth of salutary passion, Gretta rejuvenates the moribund spirit of her husband and, as mother and lover to both Michael and Gabriel, emerges as the first of Joyce's extraordinary female characters. Her emotional vitality will inform subsequent portraits of women who usurp the last word of the paternal text and refuse to allow it narrative closure. In touch with the semiotic rhythms of maternal love and erotic bonding, Gretta articulates a spiritually redemptive aesthetics of desire that subverts the logocentric world of patriarchal discourse and presages the future textual victories of Bertha Rowan in *Exiles*, Molly Bloom in *Ulysses*, and Anna Livia Plurabelle at the end (or beginning) of *Finnegans Wake*.

From Suzette A. Henke, *James Joyce and the Politics of Desire* (London, 1990), pp. 12–24; 42–9.

Notes

[This chapter was first published in a 1986 volume of conference proceedings and demonstrates how poststructuralist readings of Joyce began to influence the way in which feminist criticism approached a writer previously somewhat dismissed as another chauvinist male writer. Henke's book was the first full-length application of French feminist theory to Joyce, and draws upon the writings of Julia Kristeva, Luce Irigaray and Hélène Cixous to study the sexual politics of *Dubliners*. Henke's argument clearly shows the impact of the French psychoanalyst Jacques Lacan upon feminist theory in the 1980s. Along with other work by feminists in the 1980s (such as Bonnie Kime Scott's *James Joyce* [Brighton, 1987] and *Joyce and Feminism* [Bloomington, 1984]), Henke's book promoted an interest in gender and sexuality as accepted topics of academic debate for Joyceans. The extract here discusses a number of the early stories in the volume, followed by a more extensive discussion of 'The Dead'. The analysis of 'The Dead' is significant for the way in which Henke stresses the role Gretta Conroy plays in the psychodynamics of desire explored in the story, and for how Gabriel's final 'revelation' represents a shift in the psychic construction of masculine subjectivity. A number of notes have been abbreviated or omitted for reasons of space. Ed.]

1. *Letters of James Joyce*, vol. 2, ed. Richard Ellmann (London, 1966), p. 137. [All quotations to *Dubliners* are from James Joyce, *Dubliners*, ed. Robert Scholes and A. Walton Litz (New York, 1969). Ed.]

2. *Letters of James Joyce*, vol. 1, ed. Stuart Gilbert (New York, 1957; reissued with corrections 1966), p. 55.

3. Engaged in controversy with Grant Richards over the publication of *Dubliners*, Joyce declared: 'My intention was to write a chapter of the moral history of my country and I chose Dublin for the scene because that city seemed to me the centre of paralysis. I have tried to present it to the indifferent public under four of its aspects: childhood, adolescence, maturity and public life. The stories are arranged in this order. I have written it for the most part in a style of scrupulous meanness' (*Letters*, vol. 2, p. 134). 'It is not my fault that the odour of ashpits and old weeds and offal hangs round my stories. I seriously believe that you will retard the course of civilisation in Ireland by preventing the Irish people from having one good look at themselves in my nicely polished looking-glass.' (*Letters*, vol. 1, pp. 63–4).

4. Jacqueline Rose observes: 'Sexuality belongs in this area of instability played out in the register of demand and desire, each sex coming to stand, mythically and exclusively, for that which could satisfy and complete the other' (*Sexuality in the Field of Vision* [London, 1986], p. 53). In '*Dubliners*: Women in Irish Society', in *Women in Joyce*, ed. Suzette Henke and Elaine Unkeless (Urbana, IL, 1982), Florence Walzl examines Joyce's female characters within the context of Dublin culture and analyses gender attributions operative in late-nineteenth-century Ireland. She concludes that 'when Joyce pits men against women in his tales, it can be proved that drastic economic and social pressures actually force Dubliners into such situations of frustrations, deprivation, and hostility. He spares neither sex' (p. 53).

5. Jane Gallop, *Feminism and Psychoanalysis: The Daughter's Seduction* (London, 1982), pp. 173–4. 'The demand for love', writes Lacan, 'can only suffer from a desire whose signifier is alien to it. If the desire of the mother is the phallus, then the child wishes to be the phallus so as to satisfy this desire' (Jacques Lacan, *Feminine Sexuality: Jacques Lacan and the école freudienne*, ed. Juliet Mitchell and Jacqueline Rose, trans. Jacqueline Rose (New York, 1982), p. 83).

6. Philip Herring, in *Joyce's Uncertainty Principle* (Princeton, NJ, 1987), successfully anatomises the 'gnomic nature' of language in 'The Sisters' – a language filled with ellipses, hiatuses, silences, malapropisms, and empty, ritualistic dialogue (pp. 11–18). According to Jean-Michel Rabaté in 'Silence in *Dubliners*' [reprinted in this volume – Ed.] the incomplete figure of the dead or absent father is inscribed in the text of *Dubliners* 'until finally everything will appear hinged on the silent name of the capitalised Father'.

7. [*Jouissance* is a difficult term to translate into English. In the French usage of Lacan and Kristeva it conflates a notion of sexual orgasm, intellectual and emotional pleasure of an ecstatic nature, and a kind of

psychic dissolution of the unified subject that occurs because of this overwhelming sensation. Ed.]

8. See Burton A. Waisbren and Florence L. Walzl, 'Paresis and the Priest: James Joyce's Symbolic Use of Syphilis in "The Sisters" ', *Annals of Internal Medicine*, 80 (1974), 758–62; J. B. Lyons, *James Joyce and Medicine* (New York, 1974), pp. 84–91; and Zack Bowen, 'Joyce's Prophylactic Paralysis: Exposure in *Dubliners*', *James Joyce Quarterly*, 19 (1982), 257–73.

9. In tracing 'Joyce's Revision of "The Sisters": From Epicleti to Modern Fiction', *James Joyce Quarterly*, 24 (1986), 33–54, L. J. Morrissey focuses on the progressive inconclusiveness of Joyce's text and its metamorphosis from a 'readerly' narrative in the first-published *Homestead* version to a 'writerly' offering in *Dubliners*.

10. Juliet Mitchell notes; 'The identity that seems to be that of the subject is in fact a mirage arising when the subject forms an image of itself by identifying with others' perception of it. ... Lacan's human subject is ... a being that can only conceptualise itself when it is mirrored back to itself from the position of another's desire' (Mitchell and Rose [eds], *Feminine Sexuality*, p. 5). In 'Joyce: The (R)use of Writing', in *Post-Structuralist Joyce: Essays from the French*, ed. Derek Attridge and Daniel Ferrer (Cambridge, 1984), Hélène Cixous offers a paradigmatic Freudian reading of 'The Sisters' that concludes: 'Desire (a homosexuality which is only admitted in the dark folds of a confessional) is eclipsed here, so swiftly, almost unnoticed, by the desire to kill' (p. 24).

11. Ellie Ragland-Sullivan, in *Jacques Lacan and the Philosophy of Psychoanalysis* (Urbana, IL, 1986), sees as the fundamental premises of Lacanian theory the 'contention that the human psyche is composed of two different "subjects": an objectlike narcissistic subject of *being*, and a *speaking* subject'. The 'first of the Lacanian subjects (the *moi*) gives rise to and remains perpetually entwined with the second (the *je*) for the duration of all conscious life. ... The Lacanian ego (*moi*) ... is an ideal ego whose elemental form is irretrievable in conscious life, but it is reflected in its chosen identificatory objects (alter egos or ego ideals). The subject of speech (S or *je*) is distinct from the subject of identifications (ego or *moi*), but they interact all the same. The conscious subject, thus viewed, is made up of "inmixed" symbolic chains' (pp. 1–4).

12. Gallop, *Feminism and Psychoanalysis*, p. 64. In *A Scrupulous Meanness* (Urbana, IL, 1971) Edward Brandabur interprets the charge of 'pederasty' literally and concludes that the boy in 'An Encounter', like his predecessor in 'The Sisters', 'is lured by the mystery of initiation into a sadomasochistic system with a degenerate old man' (p. 49). Donald Torchiana, in *Backgrounds for Joyce's 'Dubliners'* (Boston,

1986), provides a more historical interpretation of the encounter, suggesting that 'Joyce presents us with a recrudescence of the sinister Puritanism recalling Cromwell and his sadistic cruelties in Ireland' (p. 45).

13. A number of readers have questioned Frank's sincerity and wondered if his intentions toward Eveline are, in fact, honourable. David Wright reminds us in *Characters of Joyce* (Totowa, NJ, 1983) that 'the word "frank" appears elsewhere in *Dubliners*' in a 'generally ironical' context and that ' "going to Beunos Aires" ' was once a common euphemism for 'becoming a prostitute' (pp. 24–5). In *The Pound Era* (Berkeley and Los Angeles, 1978), Hugh Kenner emphasises the implausibility of Frank's marriage proposal and suggests that this randy sailor 'may have been less than Frank' (p. 34).

14. Gallop, *Feminism and Psychoanalysis*, p. 113. On 'Derevaun Seraun'. William Tindall, in *A Reader's Guide to James Joyce* (New York, 1959), cites Patrick Henchy of Dublin's National Library to suggest that the words are 'corrupt Gaelic for "the end of pleasure is pain" ' (p. 22).

15. Richard Ellmann, *James Joyce* (New York, 1959; revised 1982), p. 249.

16. Unlike Richard Ellmann and Bjorn Tysdael, Bonnie Scott, in *Joyce and Feminism* (Bloomington, 1984), is convinced that Joyce's essays 'Drama and Life' and 'Ibsen's New Drama' manifest a 'distinct interest in women's experience' and illustrate a keen 'admiration for Ibsen's feminism' (p. 47).

17. Without question, Furey has been elevated in Gretta's fantasy life to the status of romantic hero and mystified courtly lover. Lacan asks: 'Indeed, why not acknowledge that if there is no virility which castration does not consecrate, then for the woman it is a castrated lover or a dead man (or even both at the same time) who hides behind the veil where he calls on her adoration (*Feminine Sexuality*, p. 95). See also Ruth Bauerle, 'Date Rape, Mate Rape: A Liturgical Interpretation of "The Dead" ' in *New Alliances in Joyce Studies*, ed. Bonnie Kime Scott (Newark, 1988).

18. Mark Osteen, in 'Gabriel's Sarcasm: A Lost Line in "The Dead" ', *James Joyce Quarterly*, 25 (1988), 259–61, argues for the textual restoration of 'a sentence, present in those late-stage Maunsel proofs but absent from all published versions' of 'The Dead' and here inserted in brackets from *The James Joyce Archive*, ed. Michael Groden et al. (New York and London, 1978), pp. 5; 303.

19. In the passion-vanity dialectic described by René Girard in *Deceit, Desire and the Novel* (Baltimore, 1965), Michael Furey exemplifies the 'passionate person ... distinguished by the emotional autonomy, by the

spontaneity of his desires, by his absolute indifference to the opinion of Others' (p. 19). Gabriel, in contrast, acts as a *vaniteux* whose desire is contingent on both external and internal mediation. Such mediated passion, Girard tells us, 'defines desire *according to Another*' (p. 4), and it is only the other's desire, 'real or presumed, which makes this object infinitely desirable in the eyes of the subject' (p. 7). Michael Furey proves, for Gabriel, to be 'both the instigator of desire and a relentless guardian forbidding its fulfilment' (p. 35).

20. According to Lacan, 'woman is a symptom' for masculine desire (*Feminine Sexuality*, p. 168). 'For the soul to come into being, she, the woman, is differentiated from it, and this has always been the case' (p. 156).

21. Joseph Buttigieg, in *A Portrait of the Artist in Different Perspective* (Athens, OH, 1987), interprets the scene as the sudden eruption of 'involuntary memory' into Gabriel's firmly defended consciousness (p. 38).

22. Jacques Lacan, *Feminine Sexuality*, p. 141.

23. Richard Ellmann, *James Joyce*, p. 252.

4

Narration Under a Blindfold: Reading Joyce's 'Clay'

MARGOT NORRIS

James Joyce's 'Clay' is a 'deceptively' simple little story by design: its narrative self-deception attempts, and fails, to mislead the reader. But as a special case of the blind leading the blind (in a spirit of blindman's buff suited to the centrality of children's games in the story), 'Clay' also offers the multiple insights that come with the restoration of sight: it allows us to see the blind spots in Maria's story and to see ourselves as their cause, if not their instrument. Joyce displays a surprising technical maturity in this early work, whose object is, I believe, to dramatise the powerful workings of desire in human discourse and human lives. The perfect protagonist for this purpose is indeed the 'old maid': a figure who seems to lack everything and therefore embodies total desire, a desire for the recognition and prestige that would let a poor old woman without family, wealth, or social standing maintain her human status in paralytic Dublin and that would let her story be credited by those who hear it. 'Clay' will attempt to mislead the reader, and it fails when we become deaf, as it were, and start seeing.

The narrational manipulations produce a particular style, intended to impress the narratee, that has sometimes ensnared the critic as well. Let me demonstrate. In developing an allegory of Maria as 'the Poor Old Woman or Ireland herself', William York Tindall writes, 'Shopkeepers condescend to her; and when a British colonel is polite to her on the tram, she loses her cake'.[1] A British colonel? The narration tells us only that 'Maria thought he was a colonel-looking gentleman and she reflected how much more polite he was than the young men who simply stared straight before them.' Tindall has risen to the narrative bait and has swallowed Maria's efforts to inflate the bumptious attentions of a garrulous old drunk into the courtly devoirs of a gentleman of rank from the ruling class.[2] Unimportant in itself, this small mistake is symptomatic of a larger impulse in the story's critical history, which, curiously, mirrors Maria's quest. Readers and critics can no more accept the possibility of Maria's insignificance than can Maria herself. The impulse behind the critical treatments of 'Clay', with their heavy emphasis on allegorising Maria in some form – as either Witch or Blessed Virgin, for example – is therefore a collusive response to the story's rhetorical aim of aggrandising Maria. This allegorising tendency extends beyond the boundaries of the story to what Attridge and Ferrer call the 'transcendentalist' approach to Joyce's fiction,[3] which they trace back to T. S. Eliot's influence. Motivated by the need to save modern fiction from charges of triviality, vulgarity, and nihilism, critics assimilate literary works to larger symbolic orders and traditionally sanctioned value systems.

This need to create significance out of pointlessness also shapes the readings that most of my students bring to my classes: specifically, that the meaning of the story depends on interpreting the 'clay' as 'death' – as though this insight produced some sort of punch line, some sort of illumination that makes sense of an otherwise meaningless joke. Death is, of course, a privileged figure in medieval allegory, and, in this interpretation, Maria's failure to perceive its prophetic beckoning through the symbols of the game makes her – all evidence of her sincere Catholic piety to the contrary – a vain and foolish *Jedermann*.[4] But the reading of 'clay' as 'death' is anomalous within the context of the story, for even if Hallow Eve is the night the dead walk abroad in folk tradition, the thought of death is conspicuously absent both from the narration and from its representation of Maria's thoughts.[5] When Joyce does want a story read through a tropology of 'death' (as in 'The Dead' or in 'Hades'), he weaves a complex texture of incident and allusion to guide us to his meaning.

A different way of reading 'Clay' derives from the interpretive backfire that reveals a lack of significance operating at the heart of the desire for it. The critics' need to capitalise Maria, to transform her negative attributes into positive symbols – from poor old woman into Poor Old Woman, from witchlike into Witch, from virginal into Blessed Virgin – betray how little esteem the ungarnished old maid can muster. Joyce, I argue, does not promote the old maid to metaphoric status as much as he explores her need, and her strategies, for promoting herself. These strategies are narrational and rhetorical, as 'Clay' becomes her defence against her interiorisation of all the derision and contempt that has been her traditional portion. To the extent the defence fails, the reader is implicated, functioning as a critical actor in the story. The social consequences and psychological costs of feeling oneself designated as insignificant become a repressive force that splits all the discursive elements of the story in two: the story's subject, its narrative mode, and its reader. Maria divides into two versions of herself (into admirable and pathetic, bourgeois and proletarian, Lady Bountiful and victim), the narration is split into testimonial and exposé, prattle and pantomime, empty language and expressive silence, and the reader is split into gullible narratee and cynical critic, flattered ear and penetrating gaze, consumer of realism and dupe of naturalism. This fractured discourse of 'Clay' is produced by the interplay between the two senses of *significance* working through the text: *significance* as an experience of psychological importance or ontological prestige, and *significance* as the linguistic or semiological meaning produced by modes of signification. The exigencies of the first (Maria's need to be significant) bring about the manipulations of the second, as though the text were trying to control its own meaning because its interpretation mattered to Maria.

Two theoretical points about desire will help to account for the peculiar 'social' function of the narrator of 'Clay' and for the phantasmal narrative voice. Human desire is always born out of an imaginary lack, and desire has another desire, or recognition, as its object.[6] Maria's lacks are imaginary because, like everyone, as an organism she is a plenum, she has everything sufficient for life, and the things she lacks (marriage, wealth, class, beauty) exist only symbolically, in the significance they have for her: a significance itself grounded in their desirability to others. It is in the way sexual attributes become socially codified and significant – the way the difference between male and female, sexually active and celibate, fertile and barren, for example, becomes ontologically as well as semiotically significant within the symbolic order of her society – that Maria, as old maid, is caused especially to suffer. In her social world, being an unmarried, childless, and virginal woman endows her with a negative prestige whose consequences are encoded even in something as trivial as a card game that treats the Old Maid as the nightmare image of undesirability, whose visitation is greeted with dread and disgust as though she could spread her negativity, her status as loser, to all she touches. In fact, Maria plays a different children's game in 'Clay': a game of divination that foretells the future life of young virgins,[7] a future whose state-of-life symbols (ring and prayer book, e.g.) express the semiology of sexually marked and unmarked states. Maria's inappropriate inclusion in the game – she is, after all, an adult and she already has a life – betrays the way a sexually unmarked life, a life negatively marked as virginal, is treated by her society as a life perpetually deferred.

The symptoms the old maid's lacks produce are therefore not solitary brooding and depression but social strategies designed to capture significance by winning the approval of the 'other'. This theoretical background helps explain our sense that, although 'Clay' is narrated in the third person, the speaker is really Maria. I would formulate it this way: narrative speech in 'Clay' is mostly uttered in the language of Maria's desire; it is Maria's desire speaking. And because the narration functions to restore significance to Maria, it preserves the triangular structure of an eavesdropped conversation: the narrative voice of 'Clay' describes Maria as she would like to catch someone speaking about her to someone else. Expressed differently, the narration is putatively directed toward us, to tell us about Maria, but its true beneficiary is Maria herself, whose prestige is certified by being 'recognised' by objective and anonymous 'others'. If we were to construct a 'narrator' from these functions, its personification would be an impossible social hybrid – a creature that is simultaneously Maria's social superior (like the authoritative and eloquent matron) and her metaphysical inferior (as loyally committed to her admiration and protection as the 'vassals and serfs' of her song). This discrepancy undermines the narration on its errand for recognition. It is as though Maria sends us an inadequate signifier to extol her merits: a servant in the penetrable disguise of master. Her paltry stratagem, not the narrator, betrays Maria's ontological plight.

The distinctive features of the story's narration serve the function of gratifying Maria's desire for recognition. The rhetoric is shaped to restore to Maria, discursively, everything that might seem to constitute a 'lack' for her – beauty, husband, children, home, wealth, status – albeit with the qualifications and feints of psychological realism. Restored, these things remain as imaginary as when they were 'lacks', but they allow Maria to feel as if she possessed them, as if she enjoyed the security of wealth ('how much better it was to be independent and to have your own money in your pocket' [p. 102]) and the affection of a family ('he had wanted her to go and live with them' [p. 100]; as if she had emotional, if not biological, children ('but Maria is my proper mother' [p. 100]) and enough attractiveness for her purposes ('she found it a nice tidy little body' [p. 101]). These restorations create a version of Maria's condition that she presumably would like to believe but that the narration does not ultimately succeed in making tenable. According to this version, Maria is a well-bred, middle-class maiden lady living on a small but independent income from a job that earns her the respect of co-workers and superiors. Though unmarried and, of course, childless, she enjoys the affection of a surrogate family that had once employed her more as a governess than as a domestic and that still cherishes her as a favourite sort of godmother who visits them laden with gifts. This version of Maria's life is contradicted by a second, repressed version that is never articulated in the narrative speech but must be read in the narrative silences, ruptures, and evasions that lie between the lines, or in the margins of the text, so to speak, and that constitute the smudged and effaced portions of the 'Clay' palimpsest. According to this second, unconscious version that she 'knows' but does not 'recognise', Maria works long hours for meagre pay as a scullion in a laundry for reformed prostitutes who make her the butt of their jokes. She is ignored and patronised by everyone, including the family whose slavey she once was and from whom she succeeds in extorting only a minimal and ritualised tolerance by manipulating their guilt and pity. These intrinsically related versions are both psychically authored (but not authorised) by Maria. The first, positive version replaces and abolishes the second, whose 'truth' about her insignificance Maria finds intolerable. It fails despite the inestimable advantage of being articulated in speech. Maria's fears can utter the negative version of her life only in silent semiologies: a wince, a blush, a lost object, a moment of forgetfulness, a mistake. The narration becomes a psychological mise-en-scène in which desire is attacked from within.

The drama that transpires within the narrative speech of 'Clay' inevitably triggers a hermeneutical drama that fragments the reader into conflicting roles. Although I reify this reader as 'we' in my discussion, I intend the plural to encompass not only the collectivity of actual readers but also the multiplicity of roles that the 'reader' as a fictional construct of the story embodies: such roles as the gullible narratee, the sceptical critic, the self-reflexive metareader. 'Clay' also uses the extent to which the reader has been historically constructed by novelistic convention. The story's narratee, for example – the putative listener who believes that Maria's life is simple, but good and admirable – embodies the ideology of a docile consumer of nineteenth-century narrative conventions. This interpretation reflects the fiction of Victorian fiction: that mousy governesses and plain dependants, the Jane Eyres and Esther Summersons, can become the heroes of their lives and stories by their everyday acts and virtues. But as discrepancies mount between what is said and what is shown, the reader's docile response is transformed into a critical gaze, hostile to Maria's desire and determined to see Maria not as she wishes to be seen but as she wishes not to be seen. This vision corresponds to the aims and methods of naturalism, as it exposes beneath bourgeois desire and delusion the occluded squalor and humiliation in the lives of the poor. Where the reader as narratee hears the testimonials of Maria's admiring co-workers, for example, the reader as critic sees old prostitutes amuse themselves at her expense. But Joyce subjects even this naturalistic 'truth' to a final interrogative twist that causes the text to reflect the reader's smug superiority like a mirror. The reader's defection from the rhetorical programme is coaxed, then implicitly judged. In the end, the reader of 'Clay' is read by the text.

The reader's collusions with the narrative agenda are partly conditioned by the authority (and its erosion) of the narrative voice. 'Clay' could not be narrated in the first person, by Maria herself, because if Maria is really as insignificant as she (unconsciously) believes, we would undoubtedly dismiss her flattering version of herself as empty boasting or wishful thinking. Furthermore, the narration makes us question whether Maria could speak for herself. She is, after all, quoted directly only in her reactive speech, as affirming or disclaiming the statements of others, '*Yes, my dear*' and '*No, my dear*'. We do not know if her elided 'actual' speech would possess the refinement of accent and diction required to convey the favourable impression that she seeks. It makes sense, therefore, to imagine Maria implicitly inventing, or wishing she could invent, someone who will speak for her (while pretending to speak of her) in the ways she cannot speak for herself. This narrator (the fictitious embodiment of such an invented or wished of narrative voice) must therefore be rendered respectable, and to this end an important strategy in the arsenal of desire is produced: imitation. The narrative voice probably does not speak in the language of Maria's class – whose diction cannot be verified from the text – but uses the idiom of someone mimicking the accents of respectable bourgeois folks, like the matron of the *Dublin by Lamplight* laundry – 'so genteel'. In this respect, the narration of 'Clay' operates on Hugh Kenner's 'Uncle Charles Principle', which 'entails writing about someone much as that someone would choose to be written about'.[8] The word *conservatory*, used to name the place that houses Maria's plants, is borrowed from a social class that lives in mansions and marble halls rather than in laundries. The gentility of Maria's attitudes and opinions – with its optimistic accentuation of the positive ('she found it a nice tidy little body') and its polite circumlocutions ('how easy it was to know a gentleman even when he has a drop taken' [p. 103]) – represents, if not the language of the bourgeoisie, then Maria's notion of both the sentiment and the phrasing of proper middle-class speech.

The narrative voice further buttresses its credibility by producing testimonials from witnesses in all strata of Maria's world to document her prestige. Strategically clustered at the beginning of the narration, in order to create a favourable first impression, these testimonials are curiously self-cancelling because each tribute appears to depend on pushing aside an unpleasant reality in Maria's life. One of the laundry women, for example, inflates Maria's diplomatic skill by setting it in an implied climate of bullying and violence: 'And Ginger Mooney was always saying what she wouldn't do to the dummy who had charge of the irons if it wasn't for Maria' (p. 99). The cook illustrates Maria's domestic skill by replacing with an aesthetic image ('the cook said you could see yourself in the big copper boilers' [p. 99]) the grim visage of Maria's drudgery as she scours the pots to make them shiny. But the most prestigious testimonial comes from a witness in authority whose commendation is quoted verbatim – 'One day the matron had said to her: – Maria, you are a veritable peace-maker!' (p. 99). Maria's peacemaking, the estimation of the matron, and the matron's fine vocabulary – 'veritable' – are all paraded here, and any remaining sceptics are offered additional corroboration: 'And the sub-matron and two of the Board ladies had heard the compliment' (p. 99). But not only does this lavish praise paradoxically draw attention to the chronic quarrelling and dissension that seem to necessitate it; later narrative events sharply dispute these claims for the success of Maria's intervention by dramatising just the opposite. Her meddling into the Donnelly brothers' quarrel nearly kindles a marital fight. We may hear of her peacemaking but we see these efforts prolong and multiply discord.

This complimentary prattle becomes exposed as empty words about the self that fill the space of Maria's insecurities as soon as we confront the censored blanks in the narrative discourse. The first of these occurs when a string of pleasantries about the *Dublin by Lamplight* laundry is punctured by a curious complaint: 'There was one thing she didn't like and that was the tracts on the walls; but the matron was such a nice person to deal with, so genteel' (p. 100). The text creates a series of related enigmas about the laundry: that it has a puzzling religious and institutional orientation rather than a more logical commerical one and that pious Maria is inexplicably offended by a religious text on its walls. This informational gap clearly defines the story's narratee as a naïf, as someone whose ignorance about the true function of *Dublin by Lamplight* can be exploited to Maria's good account. In groping for a way to explain Maria's complaint, the narratee turns from the question of the laundry to the only difference that seems to signify: the difference between Catholic and Protestant. The complaint is interpreted as another of Maria's virtues, a theological virtue, no less, in the form of her Catholic orthodoxy affronted by Protestant Bible thumping. Only the reader armed with the knowledge that *Dublin by Lamplight* was a charitable institution for reformed prostitutes[9] can foil this narrative stratagem and discover what it conceals: that Maria knows the kind of place that is her home, that the tracts on the walls are a constant reminder of that fact – even if she could overlook the vulgarity and the violence of the women – and that anyone who visits her at the laundry finds its status as a laundered whorehouse advertised on its walls. The narrative voice skilfully keeps the true purpose of the laundry a secret, while remarking, but disguising, Maria's discomfort with it.

A closer look at the semiotics of Maria's complaint brings its structure as a censored blank into even clearer focus. The laundry's scandal – the sexual promiscuity whose abolition is its premise – is communicated to us through a series of displaced negations or effacements. The narrator transforms us, in a sense, into a myopic or blind person, confronted by a wall we cannot see that contains writing we cannot read – although we are given to understand that the writing is there. If we could read it (as Reichert, Senn, and Zimmer hypothetically read the motto of *Dublin by Lamplight* laundry: 2 Timothy 2.26, 'they recover themselves from the snare of the devil, to whose will they are held captive' [p. 253]),[10] we would find in the text only the erasure of the vice, the bleaching of the stain, as it were, in the exhortation to reform that is the text's message. But we, as readers, can read all this only through the disapproval in Maria's eye as she gazes at walls we do not see.

The transitional passages that relate her journey from Ballsbridge to Drumcondra reflect an apparent narrational shift to accommodate a changing ontological perspective of Maria. The laundry and the Donnelly home represent sheltered interior spaces in which Maria appears to be socially encoded in flattering and affectionate terms as valued co-worker and dear family friend. But her journey thrusts Maria, anonymously and without credentials, into an outer world of crowded trams and frenetic shoppers in which she must make her way existentially, without the help of flattering testimonials. The narrative voice is obliged to adopt a seemingly existential mode in this section, relying on description as much as on interpretation and reporting action as much as attitude. This shift complicates the manipulation of the reader's favourable response and produces a set of self-correcting narrative manoeuvres. While apparent objectivity lends the narration a particularly credible sound, it exerts itself no less in Maria's service. Whenever the narration cannot prevent us from catching glimpses of unflattering external perceptions of Maria, our attention is quickly diverted from the potentially critical eyes of strangers to Maria's laudable mental apparatus. For example, the determined objectivity of the report 'The tram was full and she had to sit on the little stool at the end of the car, facing all the people, with her toes barely touching the floor' (p. 102) risks implying that the passengers might have found her pathetic sitting there 'facing all the people', like a child on a dunce stool, and that she might have felt her conspicuous shortness ('her toes barely touching the floor') uncomfortably exposed. But the eyes of the strangers are occluded by a deft narrative move into Maria's mind, where we find no painful self-consciousness whatsoever as she busily tends her affairs ('She arranged in her mind all she was going to do'), cheers herself with happy anticipation, and weaves into homespun philosophy her concern over the Donnelly boys' fraternal quarrel: 'but such was life' (p. 102).

It is not until we see Maria hopelessly dithering between two cake shops that we begin to suspect flaws and distractions in her putative mental composure. If on the tram she had already 'arranged in her mind all she was going to do', why does she only now, when she has finished her shopping in Downes's cake shop, tackle her major decision of the evening, what treat to buy the Donnelly parents? Standing outside the shop, she begins her deliberations from scratch: 'Then she thought what else would she buy: she wanted to buy something really nice. They would be sure to have plenty of apples and nuts. It was hard to know what to buy and all she could think of was cake' (p. 102). Of course all she could think of was cake – having just come out of a cake shop after a protracted wait. A series of revisionist questions suggest themselves at this point. Was Maria distracted in her planning on the tram by the critical stare of the other passengers? Is it really the scanty icing on the Downes's plum cakes that prompts her to visit another shop, or is it her embarrassment and annoyance at having to re-enter a shop that had served her rather tardily only moments before? Once she decides on plum cake, why does she vacillate so much in the Henry Street store that she earns a smart prod from the clerk? The narrative voice mentions only the stylish saleslady and Maria in the shop, but it does not say that they are alone. Is the shop crowded with customers who look on testily while Maria takes forever making her decision? I ask these questions to draw attention to the incompleteness and contradictoriness of what is narrated. The narrator's assertion of Maria's composure is often at odds with the depictions of her nervous and disorganised behaviour, and the reader must decide whether to trust the narrative speech or the narrated gestures. However, not withstanding the gaps that invite the investigation of the increasingly sceptical reader, the narrative voice still ably protects Maria from exposure at this point – covering even her self-betraying blush at the clerk's sarcastic wedding-cake reference with an elaborate courtship anecdote as the narration continues on the Drumcondra tram.

If the revisionist reading of the shopping incidents is produced entirely by the critical reader, the narration itself offers an *initial* version of what happened on the Drumcondra tram that is subsequently revised. In this way it exposes the first account, so flattering to Maria, to have functioned as a 'lie'. We may have earlier received the sense – through Maria's defensiveness ('she didn't want any ring or man either' [p. 101]) and the revealing blush at the clerk's offer of wedding cake – that she suffers from a painful and humiliating sense of unmarriageability. The vignette on the tram, however, portrays her not only as pleasing enough to still attract the attentions of a distinguished ('colonel-looking') gentleman but also capable of entertaining his courtesies with perfectly well-bred ease and aplomb: she 'favoured him with demure nods and hems' and 'thanked him and bowed' (p. 103). His tipsiness is mentioned only as a trivial afterthought embedded in an exoneration: 'she thought how easy it was to know a gentleman even when he has a drop taken.' But later, when the forgotten plum cake is missed, we receive a different version of Maria's reaction, one that the narrative voice had, in fact, concealed from us: 'Maria, remembering how confused the gentleman with the greyish moustache had made her, coloured with shame and vexation' (p. 103). This 'confusion', along with the blush of remembrance it evokes, bears witness to a riot of hopeful, painful, uncontrollable feeling that erupts in Maria at every mention of the subject of marriage – a subject one had assumed was long ago serenely settled as outside her realm of plausibilities. We are now invited to recognise that the narrative prose, with its genteel accents, had been giving us the romantic distortions of Maria's desire: the wish to see in a fat flushed old drunk a courtly gentleman, whose military bearing is a metonymic expansion of a gray moustache and whose social imbibing ('when he has a drop taken') a synecdochic contraction of intemperate swilling.

It is important to ask why the narrative voice would tell us the 'truth' about Maria's encounter with the colonel-looking gentleman after having troubled to conceal or censor just that fact in the first place. The answer is that the narration does not technically 'lie' in the sense of deliberately concealing a known fact but rather exhibits the 'blind spot' that is the epistemological consequence of desire. As we look for glorified images of ourselves in the admiring eyes of others, we fail to see ourselves as we are at that moment, as seekers of glorified self-reflections in others' eyes. Maria's narration is doomed to fail in its attempt to direct and control how others see her precisely because it has such a blind spot and cannot, therefore, entirely manipulate the truth about herself – or itself. Her narration cannot see itself as a language of desire, as it were: it cannot see the insecurities and fears that are its source. The forgotten plum cake catches both Maria and her narrative voice off guard and causes the narrative voice, shaken by Maria's discomposure, to blurt out a series of damaging revelations: Maria's hidden excitement on the tram, her urgent need to trade scant resources for goodwill ('At the thought of the failure of her little surprise and of the two and fourpence she had thrown away for nothing she nearly cried out-right' [p. 104]), and her bad manners in moments of stress ('Then she asked all the children had any of them eaten it – by mistake, of course' [p. 103]). Preoccupied as it is with soothing Maria's dis-tress, the narrative voice that earlier said too little now says, perhaps inadvertently, too much: 'the children all said no and looked as if they did not like to eat cakes if they were to be accused of stealing' (p. 103). This important and prescient observation sup-plies the children's motive for their subsequent trick-or-treat-like reprisal against Maria. But the narration obscures the significance of the injured feelings of the children (who receive no apology from Maria and no sympathy from the narrative voice) by immediately turning to the attention lavished on Maria, who is plied with stout, nuts, and entertaining anecdotes – ostensibly to distract her from her loss. The narrative agenda here aims to establish Maria's privi-leged status in the Donnelly household, as it previously established Maria's privileged status in the laundry. The shadowy children – whose largely unspecified number, gender, and names indicate both Maria's and the narrator's lack of interest in them – are repressed like unpleasant thoughts. They behave accordingly, erupting in un-expected places and in devious ways. Although we never clearly see it there, their grievance is behind the disturbance in the game and it causes the narration to falter and nearly fragment. The narration re-covers, however, without exposing Maria: 'Maria understood that it was wrong that time and so she had to do it over again: and this time she got the prayer-book' (p. 105).

The gaps in the narration of the game are so sizeable that the reader is obliged to reconstruct through elaborate inference both a scenario of what happens in the plot and an interpretation of what the events mean. Yet the critic who plunges into this task without interrogating the reason for the gaps or questioning the function they serve risks being manipulated into narrative collusion. For example, Warren Beck, whose excellent reading of 'Clay' I much admire, nonetheless duplicates the narrator's function of protecting Maria in the way he construes the game's disturbance.[11] His recon-struction – that Mrs. Donnelly protects Maria from the shock of re-ceiving the ill omen of 'death within the coming year' – begs many questions. If 'clay' is a traditional symbolic object in the game, then surely previous players have chosen it and survived, and it is neither taken seriously nor feared. Why must Maria, who is well and seemingly unconcerned with her mortality, be protected from the omen on this particular occasion? If the 'clay' is a traditional part of the game, why does Maria not recognise it in the 'soft wet substance' she touches and note, with satisfaction, Mrs. Donnelly's kindness in sparing her its meaning? There is nothing in Beck's explanation that the narrative voice, at least, could not report to us explicitly.

The narrative fracture of this episode makes sense only if there is something to hide, from Maria, and from us if we are to be maintained as appreciative narratees. I believe that the narration suppresses the causal link between the lost plum cake and the sabotaged game, a link in which the maligned children's reprisal takes the form of a trick that is itself an eruption of the 'truth' of the children's true feelings; had it worked, it would have forced further involuntary self-betrayals from Maria. The children are coerced into attesting to Maria's generosity ('Mrs Donnelly said it was too good of her to bring such a big bag of cakes and made all the children say: – Thanks, Maria' [p. 103]) and are prevented from expressing their obvious dislike of her except through the veil of ambiguity. While the narrator nudges us to interpret 'O, here's Maria!' as a joyful welcome, we can, in retrospect, hear in it the inaudible expletives and qualifications of resigned hostility and displeased surprise, as in 'O god, here's Maria already'. The prank with the garden dirt expresses and gratifies the Donnelly children's aggression toward Maria with minimal risk to themselves: it is perpetrated by the older next-door girls (presumably immune to punishment from the Donnelly parents), and it cunningly mitigates the pranksters' blame by manipulating the victim's own imagination in order to inflict shock and repulsion. For it strikes me as curious, if the 'clay' is a symbolic object in the game, that Maria guesses neither what it means nor what it is made of. I believe that Maria is subjected to a much more primitive, conventional, universal childish trick, a trick that depends on making the victim mistake a neutral and benign substance (spaghetti, mushroom soup, Baby Ruth bars, in the game's American versions) for a repulsive, usually excretory material (worms, vomit, turds, etc.). The point of the children's joke is to make prim, 'genteel' Maria recoil in shock and disgust at the sensation of touching 'excrement' – only to reveal to her, on removal of the blindfold, the harmless garden dirt. The embarrassment would be self-inflicted: the victim would be betrayed by her own 'dirty' mind.[12]

The remarkable thing about the trick is not only that it fails, that Maria does not get it, but that a trick, as such, is never mentioned in the story at all, meaning that the narrative voice does not 'get it' either:

> They led her up to the table amid laughing and joking and she put her hand out in the air as she was told to do. She moved her hand about here and there in the air and descended on one of the saucers. She felt a soft wet substance with her fingers and was surprised that nobody spoke or took off her bandage. There was a pause for a few seconds; and then a great deal of scuffling and whispering. Somebody said something about the garden, and at last Mrs Donnelly said something very cross to one of the next-door girls and told her to throw it out at once: that was no play. Maria understood that it was wrong that time and so she had to do it over again: and this time she got the prayer-book.
>
> (p. 105)

This is narration under a blindfold. Like Maria's literal blindfold or 'bandage', the gap in the narration – the narrative voice's failure to explain to us what really happened – represents, metaphorically, the blind spot that marks the site of Maria's psychic wound, her imaginary lacks and fears. For at issue here is more than Maria's failure to make the connection between garden dirt and excrement. She dare not recognise the trick itself, that a trick has been played on her, that she is an object of ridicule, the butt of jokes, a person without sufficient authority to restrain the pranks of malicious youngsters. What is censored by the narration is the significance of what happens, and that significance is the demonstration (once more) of Maria's fear of utter insignificance. What Maria fears is not the touch of excrement on her fingers but the recognition that her only 'family' – like the rest of the world – treats her like shit. This interpretation explains as well why the word *clay* never appears in the story except as the title. The 'soft wet substance' in the narrative is never named, because the very ambiguity of its identity is fraught with such cruel danger to Maria's ego. The naming of the story poses a similar crux, a similar danger; the chosen title, 'Clay', therefore promises an interpretation of Maria's life that preserves complex registers of truth telling and lying. For the narration of 'Clay' is 'clay', in the sense that it is a polite circumlocution that eradicates the dirt and squalor of Maria's life and thereby replicates her own efforts as a slavey. 'Clay' names and exhibits the work of a rhetorical scullion.

Maria's song, her third task in the triadic fairy-tale structure of the story, marks – like her earlier efforts of the gift and the game – an unsuccessful social ritual, a failed attempt to govern her symbolic relationships with others to her better advantage. Once again, there is ambiguity in the request that she sing. We suspect that perhaps the family asks Maria to sing less because her singing gives them pleasure ('Mrs. Donnelly bade the children be quiet and listen to Maria's song' [p. 105]) than because the request is an effective way to get rid of her, to hint that she has overstayed her welcome: 'At last the children grew tired and sleepy and Joe asked Maria would she not sing some little song before she went' (p. 105). Maria responds on two levels to the double meanings of this request. Consciously, she fulfils the conventions of parlour performance by acting like a demure girl, feigning reluctance in order to extort coaxing ('*Do, please, Maria!*' [p. 105]) and delivering her song with blushing modesty. Unconsciously, she answers this extrusion from the Donnelly 'family' with a song of exile – a song written in a language of desire even more explicit than that of 'Clay'. Maria chooses a song from an opera, *The Bohemian Girl*, that is itself a nearly perfect example of the infantile wish fantasy Freud called the 'family romance': the child's fantasy that its parents are really imposters and that its 'true' parents are royalty or aristocrats to whom the child will one day be restored.[13] The prescience of Bunn's princess, abducted in infancy by gypsies but still able to divine her true estate ('I dreamt that I dwelt in marble halls / With vassals and serfs at my side' [p. 106]), nicely mirrors Maria's own implied sense of class displacement, of being trapped in a class below her breeding and sensibility ('she knew that Mooney meant well though, of course, she had the notions of a common woman' [p. 101]). The song, another version of Maria's desire expressed in the borrowed language of the superior class, in such a close analogue to the narration of 'Clay' that Maria's lapsus, her omission of the verse depicting courtship and a marriage proposal, seems almost superfluous. But Joyce uses the specifically romantic content of Maria's repression (suitors, husband, love) to focus carefully the sexual aetiology of her inferiority complex and to emphasise that it is not poverty alone but the negative symbolic value of being an old maid and being unloved that robs her of significance. Because the performance of the song operates on several semiological levels, it requires a complex act of decoding, and it is not clear, from the text, whether Joe listens to the song or to the singer. Does he hear the

pathos of Maria's own plight in her song and weep for Maria, or –
made maudlin by an excess of stout – is he moved to tears by the
pain of the Bohemian girl ('What's Hecuba to him, or he to
Hecuba, / That he should weep for her?' [*Hamlet* 2.2.559–60])
while he remains deaf to Maria's song of exile and longing?

When 'Clay' ends – fittingly, with blindness and lost objects –
what has been accomplished? 'Clay' remains a hypothetical speech
act, Maria's story as no one will ever tell it, as Maria could not
even tell it herself, but as it might be imagined being told. For
Maria, the story, far from remedying her lacks, has multiplied
them, but not until they have passed through the detour of a flattering lie. But is the story, in its residual meaning, merely an exhibition
of a pointless life, or is it the exhibition of the failure of Maria's
denial of its pointlessness? It may seem to come to the same thing,
but in the difference between a judgement (that Maria's life is
pointless) and her failed resistance to that judgement is lodged that
attitudinal half-turn away from Maria and toward the cad who
does the judging. By producing Maria's interpretation, we are implicated in her estimation of herself, offering it as narratee and
withdrawing it as critic, and we thereby contribute to her victimisa-
tion. The naturalistic 'truth' of her poverty and isolation, which we
uncover by seeing 'through' the narrative agenda, makes her life hard
enough. But what disturbs her contentment with her lot and ruins the
efficacy of a kind of Ibsenesque 'life lie' are the insecurities produced
by her fears of the estimation and interpretation of the 'other'. In her
insecurities, in her fears, we should see our own 'evil eye' as readers,
encoded as we are within the story as the washerwomen, the shopkeepers, the young men on the tram, the children, and Society ('with
a big ess', as Gerty MacDowell would say).[14] It is we, as critical and
perceptive readers, who create the pressures that necessitate Maria's
defensive manoeuvres in the way she invents her story.

I was myself prodded to make a self-reflexive turn when some of
my students stubbornly refused to let me get away with an elision
necessary to sustain my naturalistic reading of the story: what
about the narrator's describing Maria (a mythical three times) in
the unmistakably stereotyped features of a witch: 'the tip of her
nose nearly met the tip of her chin' (pp. 101, 105)? This description
is indeed a problem, because surely the narrative voice does not
flatter Maria here. Yet the voice and context in which the narration
delivers these descriptions reveals a necessary concession fronted
with the best possible 'face', as it were, that one finds elsewhere in

the story. Following the initial description of the kitchen – with its flattering signs of Maria's industry in its cleanliness, cosiness, and orderliness – we receive a no-nonsense description of Maria's physical appearance: 'Maria was a very, very small person indeed but she had a very long nose and a very long chin' (p. 99). This blunt and objective sentence is as eloquent in what it does not say as in what it does say. Neither the narrative voice nor any character in the story ever says or is described as thinking that Maria is plain or homely, deformed or grotesque looking, hideous or witchlike. Such interpretations, based strictly on the inferences of the reader, are hermeneutical, not rhetorical, products of the text. Indeed, the rhetoric of the description softens its sense in subtle ways. The description of Maria's stature, while quite emphatic in its 'very, very small ... indeed', nonetheless averts and replaces more evaluative judgements that would interpret her size as an abnormality or deformity and identify Maria as a dwarf or midget. By calling attention to her size and body first, as though they were her salient features, the narration also renders the more damaging information about her facial physiognomy less conspicuous; the curious syntax, with the 'but' serving as a possible qualification, could even be read as a compensatory tribute, as though Maria's childish height were effectively countered by distinctive, well-marked adult features. I am suggesting here only that the narrative voice appears to try to put a good face on Maria's face – not that it succeeds in flattering her.

During the tea (p. 101), Maria twice produces the famous laugh in which 'the tip of her nose nearly met the tip of her chin' – a laugh repeated later, a third time, at the Donnelly house, just as she is blindfolded for the game. Each of these occasions represents a moment of extraordinarily heightened, but uncomfortably ambiguous, attention to Maria: she is told she is sure to get the ring; a toast is drunk to her health with clattering tea mugs; the children insist on blindfolding her for the game. Is Maria being singled out for affectionate tribute, or is she being pressed into service – as dwarves and midgets historically were – as jester and fool? If the latter, does the narrative voice strategically use an uncharacteristically unflattering image of Maria to divert our attention from much more painful revelations? Does this rhetorical manoeuvre turn Maria from tormented buffoon into indulgent good sport ('she knew Mooney meant well, though, of course ...') and mask as jolly heartiness her grimace of pain? Does Lizzie Fleming twit and goad Maria nearly to tears about the ring, obliging the narrative voice gallantly to mask Maria's face at that painful moment with a most genteel turn of phrase – 'when she laughed her grey-green eyes sparkled with disappointed shyness' (p. 101)? The narration has here produced another ambiguous scene whose possible interpretations hold the extremes of estimation for Maria: was the tea fun, was Maria made much of by people who love her, and did she express her pleasure in a grimace of hilarity, or was it a frequent ritual of cruel humiliation in which the aging prostitutes mock Maria's unlosable virginity?

Maria never sees that 'the tip of her nose nearly met the tip of her chin' because the facial expression is, ironically, her most public gesture: her response to uncomfortable moments in the limelight when, perhaps terrified of the extreme exposure, she loses altogether her ability to compose herself. When she later looks at herself in the mirror, in the privacy of her room, she does not see her face at all; she sees only her body, as it looked when it was young and when, perhaps, its size was less conspicuous. She serenely approves what she sees – 'In spite of its years she found it a nice tidy little body.' If the narration shows us only Maria's contented acceptance of her appearance and does not disparage her nose and chin or show any character in the story disparaging them, why would a reader infer she is ugly and witchlike? With such a question the story turns itself on the reader like a mirror, a turn announced in the opening paragraph when 'the cook said you could see yourself in the big copper boilers' (p. 99) and invited us to inspect our own visages in Maria's efforts to scour away the squalor of her life. Why do readers think Maria is ugly? A truthful reply returns an unflattering self-image to readers: that we possess, if our place in the symbolic order of our culture is a safe distance from its margins, a hermeneutical touch as poisonous as that of any witch who ever turned prince into toad. We take minute anatomical deviations – a few inches in height, a few centimetres extra on a nose or a thin – and pouf! we construct a witchlike hag that we expel from possibilities of desirability or estimation. 'Clay' tricks us with the same trick the children try to play on Maria. It offers us a benign, neutral substance – a woman, just a woman – and we recoil with cries, or at least thoughts, of 'witch!' as surely as we would recoil with cries of 'shit!' from the harmless garden soil. 'Clay' reads the reader when it implicitly asks, 'Which is the witch?'

From *PMLA*, 102:2 (March 1987), 206–15.

Notes

[Norris's essay is an excellent example of how new developments in literary theory have made readers see the seemingly minor stories in *Dubliners* in a new light. Norris's theoretical framework demonstrates, as she herself says, an 'impure pedigree' in its use of Lacan's theories of desire, lack, and misrecognition alongside René Girard's narrative theory of desire in the novel. Norris shows how the traditional critic's wish to interpret the story in symbolic terms results in the reader being implicated in the deceptions of the central character of the story, Maria. Maria desires to be someone of significance, and this need is matched in the way that the text itself seems to require the reader to uncover hidden significances in the story, as if, Norris notes, 'the text were trying to control its own meaning because its interpretation mattered to Maria.' Ed.]

1. William York Tindall, *A Reader's Guide to James Joyce* (New York, 1959), p. 30. [All quotations from *Dubliners* are from James Joyce, *Dubliners* (New York, Modern Library–Random, 1969). Ed.]

2. Although I first noticed the error in my own reading of Tindall, I later discovered that Warren Beck had mentioned it in his book, *Joyce's 'Dubliners': Substance, Vision and Art* (Durham, NC, 1969), p. 370.

3. Derek Attridge and Daniel Ferrer, 'Introduction: Highly Continental Evenements', in *Post-Structuralist Joyce*, ed. Attridge and Ferrer (Cambridge, 1984), p. 5.

4. [German for everyone, everybody. Ed.]

5. The definitive study of folkloric motifs in 'Clay' is an unpublished manuscript by Cóilín Owens, a portion of which, titled 'The Folklore of Joyce's "Clay" ', was presented at the Philadelphia James Joyce Symposium in June 1985. [Subsequently published as Cóilín Owens, ' "Clay" (1): Irish Folklore', *James Joyce Quarterly*, 27 (1990), 337–52. Ed.]

6. The impure pedigree of my theoretical assumptions in this essay is, no doubt, recognisable in the uneasy lend of the Girardian politics of desire, which lent me the triangulations, imitation, and master-slave oscillations useful for understanding the social configurations of Maria's desire; and the Lacanian aetiology of desire in the castration complex, which illuminates the sexual source of the *méconnaissance* and scotomas that characterise the story's discourse and that recapitulate the semiological inversions of therapeutic language (e.g. of *parole vide* and *parole pleine*). [See René Girard, *Deceit, Desire and the Novel*, trans. Yvonne Freccero (Baltimore, 1965) and Jacques Lacan, *Écrits*, trans. Alan Sheridan (New York, 1977) and *The Four Fundamental Concepts of Psychoanalysis*, trans. Alan Sheridan (New York, 1978). Ed.]

7. Richard Ellmann, *James Joyce*, 2nd edition (Oxford, 1983), p. 158.

8. Hugh Kenner, *Joyce's Voices* (Berkeley, CA, 1978), p. 21.

9. Warren Beck, *Joyce's 'Dubliners'*, p. 204.

10. Klaus Reichert, Fritz Senn, and Dieter E. Zimmer (eds), *Materialien zu James Joyce's 'Dubliners'* (Frankfurt, 1977), p. 253.

11. Beck, *Joyce's 'Dubliners'*, pp. 212–14.

12. Joyce could readily have got the idea for such a trick as a version of traditional Hallow Eve games and charms from Nora, who played them as a girl in Galway. Mary O'Holleran, Nora's girlhood pal, describes a somewhat similar game and trick: 'We had a party one Holly eve night My father used to make games for us such as cross sticks hanging from the ceiling there would be an apple on one stick soap on the other and a lighted candle on the other stick our eyes would be covered so we could not see and my father would spin the sticks around and we would bite at the apple my father would put the soap in Noras mouth the house would be in roars of laughter while Nora would be getting the soap out of her mouth.' (Richard Ellmann, *James Joyce*, p. 158).

13. Sigmund Freud, 'Family Romances', in *Collected Papers*, vol. 5, ed. James Strachey (New York, 1959). *The Bohemian Girl* is an opera with music composed by Michael Balfe and libretto by Alfred Bunn (see Ruth Bauerle, *The James Joyce Songbook* [New York, 1982] and Bernard Benstock, 'Text, Sub-text, Non-text: Literary and Narrational In/Validities', *James Joyce Quarterly*, 22 [1985] 355–65). The missing verse is:

> I dreamt that suitors besought my hand,
> That knights upon bended knee,
> And with no maiden heart could withstand,
> That they pledged their faith to me.
> And I dreamt that one of this noble host
> Came forth my hand to claim;
> Yet I also dreamt, which charmed me most,
> That you loved me still the same.

14. [A reference to a character in the 'Nausicca' episode of Joyce's *Ulysses*. Ed.]

5

No Cheer for the 'Gratefully Oppressed': Ideology in Joyce's *Dubliners*

TREVOR L. WILLIAMS

This essay examines certain forms of oppression and their effect on consciousness in a few of the stories in Joyce's *Dubliners*.[1] Central to the discussion is the concept of ideology, which I always use with a negative connotation. That is, ideology is not, here, a neutral term describing a set of ideas held by a group or party. Marxists, in voluminous and often abstruse polemics, have so far failed to define the term satisfactorily. Hence, to reduce an extremely complex debate to one paragraph is simplistic but, for present purposes, necessary.

Marx, in *The German Ideology*, seems to argue that ideology is a form of false consciousness, in which people living under capitalism misperceive the economic contradictions of the system and instead invent abstractions (like freedom and equality) that superficially serve to justify the system (one is 'free' to sell one's labour) but that in fact conceal the system's deeper contradictions ('some are more equal than others'). As Ferruccio Rossi-Landi argues in his *Linguistics and Economics* (from which I quote at length later on), one reason why people fail to perceive the oppression they suffer under is that the means of communication, and thus the available subjects for discussion, are controlled by a few monopolistic corporations whose interests are not served by too close a scrutiny of the economic contradictions they embody. The ideological control of the owning class is aided by, as Althusser put it, the 'state apparatuses' (schools, police, the judiciary, the military, churches, and so on), which guarantee the social relations necessary for the reproduction of the state in its present form. Ideology then becomes not so much a particular body of ideas (though it includes that), but the normal, the 'natural' way of perceiving and analysing reality ('common sense' in other words) and at the same time an instrument of oppression. If, however, ideology is so pervasive, guaranteed not only by the state apparatuses but by people's willing complicity in their own self-deception and oppression, how does anyone ever manage to step outside such a system to make it the object of criticism? That 'oppositional' forces exist (outside the state-sanctioned structure of political parties) is obvious, but how individuals escape 'contamination' has not yet been satisfactorily explained. Nor, I hasten to add, does this essay attempt to answer that question.

Even so, Joyce's life and work offer some instructive pointers. His exile from Dublin was precisely a flight from the 'net' of church-state ideology, which so suffused his consciousness but which, from a deracinated European standpoint, he could henceforth criticise. Perhaps his most powerful act of demystification at the personal level was his refusal for twenty-seven years to enter into marriage, a legal apparatus embodying for him both (British) state power and religious repression. But one person's *non serviam* does not solve the general problem of ideological domination, and, apart from a brief flirtation with Italian socialist and anarchist movements, Joyce distanced himself from any political grouping that may have helped solve the problem.[2] Nevertheless, his work always remained preoccupied with the problem of how to escape from that most ideological of instruments, language itself, in particular the language of the English. To become aware of language as such is the beginning of resistance to the ideological power vested within it. In this light *Finnegans Wake* becomes not a new demystified language, an escape from false consciousness, but a practical demonstration of resistance to ideology, especially the oppression imposed by a unitary, monocular, Cyclopean world view. Joyce devoted a quarter of his life to this demonstration, an index of the importance he attached to the depth and persistence of linguistic mystification.

It ought never to be forgotten that the Dublin of Joyce's *Dubliners*, besides being a bastion of Roman Catholic faith, was above all an enclave of the British Empire, a colonial serf of London. In this essay I try to point out some of the psychological consequences of this imperial fact. *Dubliners* remains interesting because the problems it poses of rigid paralysed, mystified thinking and its associated repression and oppression have not gone away. We are still Joyce's Dubliners.

[...]

I

How do church and state manifest themselves in *Dubliners*? First the church: leaving aside 'The Dead' for a moment, what Joyce originally intended as *Dubliners* began and ended with stories in which the power of the church is foregrounded: 'The Sisters' strongly intimates the church's responsibility for paralysis and decay, and 'Grace' develops the notion of simony broached in the first paragraph of 'The Sisters'. In between there is not a single priest who is not somehow morally and intellectually compromised: they are insane (Father Flynn in 'The Sisters'); dead (Father Flynn and the 'former tenant' in 'Araby'); snobbish (Father Butler in 'An Encounter' [p. 20]); 'unfortunate' (like the 'black sheep' Father Keon in 'Ivy Day in the Committee Room' [p. 126]); prurient (the priest confessing Bob Doran in 'The Boarding House' had 'drawn out every ridiculous detail of the affair' with Polly [p. 65]); and above all powerful. In 'Eveline' the yellowing photo of an unidentified priest dominates the room, suggesting appropriately a power that transcends time and space (this priest is 'in Melbourne now' [p. 37]; did Joyce intend the black humour of 'down under' implied here?). And in 'Grace' Father Purdon, the 'spiritual accountant' (p. 174), has the power 'to interpret properly' the Scriptural texts and thus exercises an authority over his businessman congregation virtually indistinguishable in its social effects from that of the civil administration in Dublin.[3] (Coming as it does at the very end of 'Grace', this reference to the interpretation of texts ought to remind us of the terrain on which Joyce the writer was choosing to resist ideological domination: the struggle for a more humane future begins with the 'proper' interpretation of the 'text' of both the present and the past.)

There are in addition scenes in which the manifestation and the effect of the church seem indistinguishable. In 'The Sisters' the chalice, a traditional symbol of the church's power to mediate between god and man, is at best ambivalent. Even when broken it retains the power to paralyse, to suspend all thought, in its function as opiate for 'the masses', but perhaps the text also suggests that paralysis is not a permanent state, that the power of the church can be broken. However, the immediate material effect of the broken chalice, if we are to believe the gossip, is to turn the priest insane. In 'An Encounter' we learn that Joe Dillon's parents 'went to eight-o'clock mass every morning' (p. 19), but alongside this piety the text remorselessly records the boy's actions and utterances and then provides a comment, a kind of 'counterinterpretation' of the church's authority:

> He looked like some kind of an Indian when he capered round the garden, an old tea-cosy on his head, beating a tin with his fist and yelling:
> – Ya! yaka, yaka, yaka!
> Everyone was incredulous when it was reported that he had a vocation for the priesthood. Nevertheless it was true.
>
> (p. 19)

Here is an example of the Joycean narrator paring his fingernails indifferently as he watches his irony unfold: the overall critical stance towards the church within *Dubliners* tells us that 'Ya, yaka' is the language of the church. Thus no one should be 'incredulous' that Joe Dillon has a vocation for the priesthood. In 'Araby' too (p. 31) language is the site of this duality: the boy's love is his 'chalice', and the girl's name springs to his lips in 'strange prayers and praises' (just two terms in a paragraph suffused with religious terminology). This example, in which the adolescent boy reaches naturally for religious language to express romantic love, clearly demonstrates the process of mystification as the frustrated boy tries to hold apart two conceptions of reality against the dominant socioreligious pressure to press them into a false unity.

In 'Clay' and 'A Mother' two exemplars of Catholic piety are described: Maria attends six o'clock mass (p. 101) while Mr. Kearney 'went to the altar every first Friday' (p. 137). We may infer that Maria's piety is one of the means (perhaps the only one) by which she succeeds in remaining unconscious, in keeping the awful reality of her life at bay. Mr. Kearney, much further up the social scale, derives neither spiritual nor social insight from his piety: instead, the concentration on mechanical devotion has prevented him from seeing how the Dublin social system works and must be worked, so that, at a crucial moment in the narrative, this intellectual nullity of a man fails to make the decisive intervention that might have prevented his wife from making such a fool of herself. Both characters are paralysed when put under acute social pressure: when Mr. Holohan appeals to Mr. Kearney to intervene in the argument over the contract, the latter merely 'continued to stroke his beard' (p. 146), his piety helpless to guarantee him either speech or respect. Maria, unable to confront the gap between her own deformed self and the romantic ideal of love held forth in the second stanza of 'I Dreamt that I Dwelt', is forced (so out of her own control seems her consciousness) to sing the first stanza again (p. 106).

Manganiello sees Maria as 'unwittingly a servant of Church and State' and, in her working celibacy, as 'a corporal asset of the State'.[4] A devout Catholic working in a Protestant institution devoted to the reform of 'fallen women', Maria, I would assert, has taken seriously the church's injunction to suppress her sexuality except for the purposes of procreation and thus cannot face even the 'allowable' romance of premarital courtship heavily emphasised in the second stanza of Balfe's song. (Don Gifford notes, I think ironically, that the Donlevy *Cathechism* asks the question, 'who are the peace-makers?' a title accorded Maria [p. 99]. The answer begins: 'Those who subdue their passions ... well'.[5]) More cruelly, however, Maria's unattractive face thoroughly excludes her from the marriage market while her church, which promises so much in the way of ultimate consolation, fails utterly to 'empower' her socially in the face of her hopeless marital prospects.

The church (any church) promises 'empowerment' in the next life, but a social empowerment in this life is frequently implied, too. Alas, just when characters like Maria, Mr. Kearney, and Farrington's son most need to draw on this social power 'guaranteed' by their church, it abandons them as perhaps it must in order to maintain, in Beryl Schlossman's phrase, its 'power *over* the community' (my italics).[6]

It is important to stress that this is not a matter of the passive reception of effects, of a simple base/superstructure relationship between (here) the church and human consciousness. The many biological, social, political, educational, juridical, and other factors that mediate between these two poles must be taken into account as well as the capacity of humans both to reproduce actively and to resist their conditions of existence (though there is not much evidence in *Dubliners* of 'resistance'). A good example of this complex mediating process occurs at the end of 'Counterparts', where it emerges in the last two pages that Farrington lives near the barracks (and thus close to the British presence in Ireland) and that on his return home his wife is 'out at the chapel' (p. 97), having left her five children to the darkness and Farrington. As Farrington prepares to beat his son with the walking stick, the most painful of all the *Dubliners'* endings intervenes, leaving to the reader's imagination the full horror that lies beyond the last ellipse:

> – O, pa! he cried. Don't beat me, pa! And I'll ... I'll say a *Hail Mary* for you ... I'll say a *Hail Mary* for you, pa, if you don't beat me ... I'll say a *Hail Mary...*
>
> (p. 98)

Abstracted from their context, these words appear almost farcical, as if the narrator's main point is to satirise the limits of religious consolation. But of course context is all. The full horror of these words derives from the reader's simultaneous awareness of the social degradation Farrington has endured on this day, a degradation whose political dimension is established early and late: Farrington is in the employ of a 'North of Ireland' man (p. 86); and he lives near the barracks, forever in the shadow of the British soldier. Having failed in the politico-economic world, Farrington (in a well-known reversal) imposes his 'authority' upon his pathetic domestic world. I want to return to this story, but for the moment I would assert that the narrative, in all its complex interweaving between Farrington's inner and outer world, 'accounts for' the ending. The fact remains however that it is the Hail Mary that remains ringing in our ears. We will also have registered that 'Ma' was 'at the chapel' (repeated twice and italicised).

Three points can be made about this focusing upon the church's role: first, the absent mother's complicity in the reproduction of church power is clear, so that it could as well be said of Mrs. Farrington, as it is of Mrs. Kernan in 'Grace', that her 'faith was bounded by her kitchen, but, if she was put to it, she could believe also in the banshee and in the Holy Ghost' (p. 158). Second, the final words demonstrate the endless repetition in Joyce's Dublin of a psychology of dependence. That is, the young boy is searching for the 'correct' discourse that will allow him to survive in these social surroundings just as his father has learned that survival in employment depends upon speaking and writing the language of his 'oppressor' (symbolised in this instance by Mr. Alleyne, his boss). Third, we witness the pervasive contradiction whereby the boy's consciousness, dominated as well as constructed by the church, imbibes the 'power' of the church (the promise of social empowerment again) only to be rendered powerless at a crucial moment in his life.

II

'Counterparts' provides a useful bridge to the consideration of state power, in practice the manifestation of the British presence in Joyce's Dublin. Unlike the church's, the British presence is muted, perhaps reflecting the reality under colonialism of dominated consciousness. This is a paradox: since British power is the ultimately determining factor upon the forms of Irish economic and political life, one might expect this power to be more insistently manifest than in fact it is in Joyce's literary production. Is it that, in some normative process, British power is taken for granted as if this were the only form of government the Irish could know or possibly aspire to? Historical reality of course suggests that the Irish never took the British presence for granted, yet 'historical reality' may mean, for Irish and non-Irish alike, nothing more than our knowledge of important events (like the Easter Rising or the Phoenix Park murders) when the British presence was most acutely manifested and questioned. However, the daily reality for the mass of dominated people under colonialism may be closer to that described in Joyce's work: the colonial power is always 'there' in the background and only occasionally obtrudes itself as in vice-regal cavalcades or in certain people's dependence upon that power for employment.

In 'Counterparts' Farrington's boss is an Ulsterman, the mention of which draws upon the subtext of nineteenth-century Irish history: the uneven economic development of Belfast and Dublin under the aegis of British capitalism. Whatever may be Mr. Alleyne's personal origins, his symbolic function in the story is to remind Dubliners of their dependence upon outside agencies[7] and to mock (since he has all the power) their recourse to a bankrupt discourse (Farrington's 'witty' response [p. 91]) as a mode of resistance. Note how all the modifiers in the opening sentence of this story convey the impression of Alleyne's power, a power confirmed in the 'imperialism' of the imperative mood:

> The bell rang furiously and, when Miss Parker went to the tube, a furious voice called out in a piercing North of Ireland accent:
> – Send Farrington here!
>
> (p. 86)

There is no hope for Farrington. Later in the story, when his money and the mileage he has extracted from his witticism are about to drain away, he suffers two more defeats at the hands of 'outsiders': the woman with 'the London accent' (p. 95) who, he convinces himself, has a 'romantic' interest in him, but who proves to be scarcely aware of his existence;[8] and the English acrobat who beats him (twice) at arm wrestling. (Ironically, when at the end Farrington reproduces in his relationship with his son the power relations between Mr. Alleyne and himself, the adverb 'furiously' reappears: 'The man jumped up furiously and pointed to the fire' [p. 97].)

Few as the manifestations of British presence in *Dubliners* are, they consistently underscore the inequality inscribed within the colonial relationship. For example, Eveline, 'a helpless animal' (p. 41) at the end of that story, lives out the collapse of her romance against a backdrop of milling soldiers leaving for England after completing their tour of garrison duty 'guarding' the likes of Eveline. In 'After the Race', Jimmy, who has been educated at an expensive Catholic college in England, is comprehensively beaten at cards by the Englishman Routh. In 'A Little Cloud', Little Chandler, a pathetic embodiment of literary exhaustion, dreams only of pleasing the English critics, by writing to their expectations of productions that can be labelled 'of the Celtic school' (p. 74). In 'Grace', Mr. Kernan, whose abasement on the floor of the pub urinal neatly sums up the degradation so many of Joyce's Dubliners seem to take for granted, works for an English firm as a tea taster (ironically a job whose very creation bespeaks the expansion of the British Empire),[9] and two of his sons have found work, but in Glasgow and Belfast. Another character in 'Grace' (and this leads to the story's central irony) is Mr. Power, who organises Mr. Kernan's resurrection to social respectability, but whose 'power' derives entirely from his employment in the Royal Irish Constabulary Office in Dublin Castle. In 'Two Gallants', the harp, symbol of Irish nationhood, seems forlorn outside the Kildare Street club, which is redolent of Ascendancy power. All these snapshots are brief but insistent reminders of Irish economic, political, and, above all, psychological dependence, reminders too that the dominated within the colonial relationship are not only exploited but also asked to pay (if only through their psychology of dependence) for the privilege of being exploited. The opening of 'After the Race' describes this process exactly: it is 'the cheer of the gratefully oppressed' (p. 52).[10]

The manifestation of state power is easier to quantify than its effects, though in all the above examples an effect is nearly always implied and is sometimes overt. Most criticism of *Dubliners*, as I have said, takes the fact of 'paralysis' for granted. I would argue that paralysis is ultimately determined by the particular form of government these characters labour under (though all too many characters labour not at all) and that the church, through its pervasive ideological domination, is complicit with the dominating state force, both having a vested interest in controlling the visions of the future available to the people.[11] Thus the 'action' in *Dubliners* (to beg an overwhelming question) is the sum of the effects of these two forces acting in concert. Significantly, character development, an integral part of 'action', has for most Dubliners ceased before the narrative begins. Without the possibility of development, without a future, such characters can only flounder in the narrow space allowed to them, all potentiality displaced into false consciousness, petty snobbery, dreams of escape, and fixation upon the past. Not surprisingly, where human relationships are so alienated, images of decay abound.

Above all, there is paralysis: linguistic, sexual, alcoholic, marital, financial; even history itself seems to have stopped. In the first story the numerous ellipses in the women's conversation draw attention to the inability of some characters to control or 'possess' their own language as if language is owned (not merely derived from) elsewhere.[12] Some characters, like Maria in 'Clay' and the 'queer old josser' in 'An Encounter', are truly on the margins of language, doomed not to progress beyond the low level of linguistic achievement implied in the word 'nice' (which appears eleven times in 'Clay'). Other characters, like Mr. Duffy and Little Chandler, are unable to write, but in the highly verbal 'Ivy Day in the Committee Room' Joe Hynes, with his poem to Parnell, manages to convince his listeners and himself that he has control over the language. The first comment on Hynes's poem after his recitation is the 'Pok!'

(p. 135) of the cork flying from the bottle on the hearth, a reminder that for all the fine sentiment evoked by the poem, most of the characters' conversation leading up to this moment has been shallow and venal, fixated upon a past they scarcely believe in any longer. In a sense Hynes's poem, with its undialectical view of the relationship between past and present, is a fitting climax to all that circular, self-deceptive conversation, an index too of the extent to which characters participate in the reproduction of ideology. To hope that 'Freedom's reign' will arrive at the 'dawning' of some suitable day is a harmless enough activity, so long as the word is taken (as here) for the deed.

Paralysis extends to sexuality and to male-female relationships generally. Sexuality may be repressed (Mr. Duffy) or perversely flaunted (the 'queer old josser' in 'An Encounter') or commodified (Corley's treatment of the girl in 'Two Gallants'). Throughout *Dubliners*, relationships are paralysed at the commodity level, a lugubrious example being Bob Doran's dalliance with Polly, which is transformed by Mrs. Mooney into a very specific economic relationship: marriage equals 'reparation'. If Bob Doran is trapped *into* marriage, Little Chandler is trapped *in* marriage. In 'Araby' and 'Eveline' romance briefly flowers, only to be quickly crowded out by a myriad ideological 'voices'. Alcohol, on the other hand, though paralysing to mind and body, at least has the virtue of easing the pain of moral and political degradation. It may be significant that the alcoholic haze is thickest in those stories ('Counterparts' and 'After the Race') where the narrative pushes the central characters closest to recognition of their economic and political impotence. In 'Counterparts', the narrative immediately stresses Farrington's inferiority (as symbolic 'Dubliner') before northern, and ultimately British, power. From this painful reality he seeks refuge in both alcohol and 'rhetoric' though the latter, an accidental one-line witticism, proves even less effective than alcohol in keeping the pain at bay. 'After the Race' ends in alcoholic stupor, but (or perhaps because) prior to this the narrative has insisted (through the repetition of the word 'money') on Jimmy's utterly parasitic status not only in relation to the rich Europeans, but in relation to his own past and the (British) source of his wealth. Moreover, though Jimmy is 'conscious of the labour latent in money' (p. 44) and is able 'to translate into days' work that lordly car in which he sat' (p. 45), the allusion is to the labour, not of Jimmy, but of his father and his father's employees. Thus, with wealth no longer (as in

Jimmy's case) requiring labour for its generation, history, in the sense of the active reproduction of everyday life or, as Eric Hobsbawm defines it, 'the progressively effective utilisation and transformation of nature by mankind',[13] has ceased for Jimmy's class (the bourgeoisie), even if it ought not to have done for the 'gratefully oppressed' who form the 'channel of poverty and inaction' (p. 42) through which the race passes.[14] But even for them history seems to have stopped, as is demonstrated by the case of Eveline, for whom the voices of an insane past and a brutal present are more potent than any future beckoning across the sea. In 'Ivy Day' too the reference to 'Freedom's reign' one day in Erin sounds a false note coming so soon after the dull compulsion of the characters' present and their mystified view of the past. Jimmy wanted everything to 'stop' (p. 48), and so, in *Dubliners*, it has. Even money (in 'A Mother') has ceased to circulate: the class-conscious Mrs. Kearney, who had treated her daughter's talent and her daughter as commodities, discovers that life itself almost (but certainly her social well-being) depends on the circulation of money. The gold coin shining in Corley's palm at the end of 'Two Gallants' is a fitting tribute to this commodity fetishism which so pervades and paralyses Joyce's Dublin.

A major manifestation of paralysis is the displacement of human potential into inauthentic consciousness, petty snobbery, and so on. I use the adjective 'inauthentic' here rather than 'false' to distinguish those infrequent moments in the text when the narrative demonstrates unequivocally that a character's consciousness is second-hand. At such moments we are briefly reminded of ideology's role in the construction of human consciousness. 'A Painful Case' (one of the stories discussed in some detail below) yields in Mr. Duffy one of those characters who (like Eveline and Maria at the opposite end of the social scale) is prevented even from speaking, so thoroughly deprived is he of authentic subjectivity (he depends on Nietzsche to confirm his existence and lives 'at a little distance from his body' [p. 108]). The reported monologue in 'Clay' ('such was life' [p. 102]; 'even when he has a drop taken' [p. 103]; the repetition of 'nice') suggests that Maria, her mind suffused with cliché, mistaking condescension for kindness, lacks even the most rudimentary intellectual capacity to overcome her near desperate social condition. With Eveline however the text is more specific in implying a source for her inauthenticity. Like Gerty MacDowall's, her consciousness appears to be constructed primarily by the world of women's romance: 'She was about to explore another life with Frank. Frank was very kind, manly, open-hearted ... his hair tumbled forward over a face of bronze. ... Frank would take her in his arms, fold her in his arms. He would save her' (pp. 38–40). Briefer examples of this sudden emerging of inauthentic consciousness into full articulation are Ignatius Gallaher's use of French in 'A Little Cloud' to address an Irish barman, a conscious attempt to ape the ways of a dominant class, and Mrs. Kernan's acceptance of her husband's alcoholism as natural: 'She accepted his frequent intemperance as part of the climate' (p. 156). Bob Doran abandons all hope of authenticity when he allows himself to transform his flirtation with Polly into the (fully mystified) 'sin' (p. 67). And in 'Ivy Day in the Committee Room' the subtext of all the conversation is politics as commodity: whether literally (being paid for canvassing) or metaphorically (the sell-out of Parnell). Perhaps it is especially significant that this story, at once one of the most 'social' in *Dubliners* and one which raises explicitly the question of Ireland's political past and future, should reveal a collective consciousness so thoroughly inauthentic.

Petty snobbery, yet another articulation of false consciousness, also abounds. No age group, no social institution, is uncontaminated. Father Butler's sneers in 'An Encounter' about 'National School boys' (p. 20) are reproduced by the young boy narrator who has always 'despised' (p. 28) his friend Mahony.[15] Bob Doran is offended by Polly's grammar; Little Chandler feels 'superior to the people he passed' (p. 73); Mr. Alleyne calls Farrington an 'impertinent ruffian' (p. 91); Mrs. Kearney's class consciousness is aroused by certain accents (p. 141); Mr. Power is 'surprised' (p. 154) at the manners and accents of Mr. Kernan's children and does not 'relish the use of his Christian name' (p. 160); Crofton considers his companions in the Committee Room 'beneath him' (p. 130). The litany could go on. Even Eveline, low as she is on the social scale, does not escape this particular taint if, as I believe, the phrase 'other people's children' (p. 36) – why not simply 'other children'? – was an attempt by Eveline's family to put some social distance between themselves and their neighbours, an impulse, and this is the common denominator of all these examples, towards reification, the process of fragmentation and objectification both of and between people.

[...]

III

If 'A Painful Case' registers the dominance of the male voice, 'Counterparts' foregrounds language itself.[16] Here it is no longer a question of whether male voices predominate over female (whether quantitatively or qualitatively), but rather a question of the very ownership of language. Rossi-Landi has written persuasively on linguistic 'ownership', a notion he sums up in the following passage:

> The ruling class arrogates to itself the control of programmes 'from a higher social level'. It becomes plausible to define 'ruling class' as *the class which possesses control over the emission and circulation of the verbal and nonverbal messages which are constitutive of a given community*. ... Ideology is a social design; the dominant design is precisely that of the class in power. All behavioural programmes are submitted, on the part of those who hold power in a given historical moment, to a vaster and more fundamental programming which consists in preserving society just as it is, or in reducing change and absorbing it into the existing system as much as possible.[17]

The problem is not simply that language is 'possessed'. Rather the use to which language is put, the subjects that are publicly discussible (what Rossi-Landi calls 'models and programmes'), determines an 'implicit order' to suppress certain topics that the 'competent' speaker, in an act of self-censorship to comply with the dominant code, will obey.

No reader will have difficulty seeing the relevance of this argument to an analysis of the hegemonic forces in Joyce's Dublin. The church and Dublin Castle between them determine the 'dominant codes' and ensure what Herbert Marcuse calls the 'closing of the universe of discourse'.[18] (I have discussed elsewhere[19] the existence of competing or oppositional discourses in *Dubliners*, but they tend to be marginalised. I am thinking of the acts of 'resistance' performed by Lily, Miss Ivors, and Gretta in 'The Dead'.) Nowhere is this subservience to the dominant code more noticeable than in the highly 'verbal' stories 'Ivy Day in the Committee Room' and 'Grace', where conversation either circles and circles as it waits for alcohol to arrive or descends into a kind of *National Inquirer* gossip about the Roman Catholic Church. No amount of low gossip will disturb the power of the church, whereas the efforts of Dubliners to live by a religious code, as Herr argues, 'perpetuate their willed blindness to the economic and political conditions which guarantee the poor quality of their lives'.[20]

One of the less 'verbal' stories in *Dubliners*, 'Counterparts', nevertheless turns on the question of linguistic ownership, and, as I noted earlier, the twin ideological voices of Dublin establish at the beginning (with the 'imperialism' of Mr. Alleyne's 'North of Ireland accent') and at the end (with the repetition of the Hail Mary) such large territorial claims that the individual voice is scarcely heard; hence the story's claustrophobia. When Mr. Alleyne asks Farrington if he takes him for 'an utter fool', Farrington's tongue replies: 'I don't think, sir ... that that's a fair question to put to me' (p. 91). Farrington quickly inflates his slip of the tongue into a fully rounded saloon-bar story, confirmed by a fellow worker Higgins, for which the reward is several rounds of drinks.[21] This gossip, which reveals a remarkable capacity to make a silk purse out of a sow's ear, occupies the middle part of the narrative but fades from memory once the money and the alcohol have run out, thus suggesting its inauthenticity as gossip: it is not sufficient to define personality, to animate, or to confer ownership. Indeed, language constantly 'slips' away from Farrington: he cannot copy even the simplest legal phrase correctly (he writes 'Bernard Bernard' instead of 'Bernard Bodley' [p. 90]). To construct meaning he is forced, in this story of repetitions, to repeat himself (Bernard Bernard, the retold story, the reproduction of Mr. Alleyne's power both in his work – he is a 'copyist' – and at home). He is not allowed to produce his own linguistic 'models' (he has even been caught 'mimicking' [p. 92] Alleyne's Northern Irish accent). Thus Farrington (and his son) are shown using a language which is out of their control, not 'theirs'. The most he can hope to achieve is the cultivation of style, and even that is debased (he makes a 'little cylinder of the coins between his thumb and fingers' [p. 93]). He is helpless before Alleyne's onslaught when the latter adapts Farrington's own words in order to belittle him: ' "*You-know-nothing*. Of course you know nothing" ' (p. 91). This is an accurate statement in the sense that Farrington is so utterly steeped in false consciousness that he cannot construct an accurate picture of reality.

Another obstacle to lucidity is alcohol. More than most stories (the 'political' story 'Ivy Day in the Committee Room' is, perhaps significantly, a serious contender), 'Counterparts' concentrates on alcohol as an obliterator of consciousness and thus of judgement. Like the language Farrington unconsciously manipulates into a temporary rhetorical triumph, alcohol defers the encounter with reality. At the end of the story, Farrington's son, in one of the most poignant moments in Joyce's consistent attack upon the language of Catholic ideology, desperately gropes for the magic language that will spring him from the brutal physical oppression about to descend upon him. But he 'knows nothing': the language of the Hail Mary, far from liberating him, enslaves him. That is, the boy has been educated to see the Hail Mary (rich with its promise of spiritual empowerment) as a form of bargaining chip (do this penance and your sins are forgiven) but instead will find, almost certainly, that the words are spiritually bankrupt, have no exchange value, when used in the 'real' world in an attempt to ward off oppression.

While Mr. Alleyne exercises real power, the precise nature of their comparison or 'counterparting' resides in Farrington's reproduction, in the private sphere, of an ideology of domination and repression. Farrington's defeats on this day are humiliatingly public while his success (extracting an extra shilling from the pawnbroker) is merely private.[22] Any 'success' he has while beating his son will also be private. Farrington's victory over his son reproduces the conditions (the conditions in which his son will come to expect repression as the norm) for the continuing existence of Alleyne's class. Similarly, though he has extracted an extra shilling from the pawnbroker,[23] he acknowledges symbolically what is true actually: time also belongs to the ruling class. In parting with his watch, this vassal of misrule yields up his connection with the world of order and ownership.

IV

The conclusion of 'Araby', where 'English accents' (p. 35) predominate, and the following three stories – 'Eveline', 'After the Race', and 'Two Gallants' – all bring to the surface the subject of Ireland's colonial dependence. Indeed, if those three stories are viewed as a group, they can be seen as the political manifestation of the boy's coming to consciousness in 'Araby': while the story traces the confusions of 'love', its end points to the inferior position of the boy as Irish boy. This break from false consciousness on the boy's part is a move denied to the central characters of the next three stories. In fact the very notion of 'central character' is problematic: Eveline is undoubtedly the main focus of narrative attention in her story though her only 'action' is one of retreat; Jimmy, the centre of attention in 'After the Race', is so effete that his disappearance into an alcoholic haze seems the only appropriate conclusion for so indeterminate a character; and in 'Two Gallants' it is not clear who or what the central character is. Is it Corley or Lenehan or the girl, or is it the coin for which Corley has laboured so parasitically? It is as if, under colonialism, 'character' becomes an irrelevance: for people whose lives are determined outside their own community or country, it is a sham to pretend that they can act freely. Freedom is a luxury (and a contradiction) allowed only to characters in fiction though Joyce's fiction demonstrates that any such freedom is extremely circumscribed either by the 'nightmare of history' or by economic realities. Nowhere does Joyce subscribe to the pernicious myth, so beloved of Hollywood, that the single individual can alone transform society.

'Two Gallants' seems far removed in structure and content from 'Eveline': the first paragraph emphasises movement and process, the free circulation of people within a busy urban environment, while the predominance (compared to 'Eveline') of dialogue, of an 'unceasing murmur' (p. 49), suggests that these people do after all, especially in the mass, have a 'voice'. Yet, as in 'Eveline', contradictions exist. The murmur of the crowd may be 'unceasing', but it is also 'unchanging'. And why should the warm air of an August evening bring, at the height of summer, a 'memory of summer' (p. 49)? Does summer's eagerness to decline into fall reflect the city's own loss of vitality? The air 'circulates', but does it thereby renew itself or merely go round in circles, like Corley's head and Lenehan's aimless wandering?

Moreover, 'Two Gallants' continues, more openly, to hint at a militarised culture. Since Corley is a police informer, this is not surprising. However, the presence of several military metaphors and words with military connotations suggests that the British fettering of Irish consciousness is pervasive. 'Eveline' begins with 'invade'; the following list of words or phrases (my italics) appears only in 'Two Gallants' and nowhere else in *Dubliners*:

> He was a sporting vagrant *armed* with a vast stock of stories, limericks and riddles.
>
> > (p. 50)
>
> The swing of his burly body made his friend *execute* a few light skips from the path to the roadway and back again.
>
> > (p. 51)

> His bulk, his easy pace, and the solid sound of his boots had some-
> thing of the *conqueror* in them. He approached the young woman
> and, without *saluting*, began at once to converse with her. She swung
> her sunshade more quickly and *executed* half turns on her heels.
> Once or twice when he spoke to her *at close quarters* she laughed
> and bent her head.
>
> (p. 55)

In their context, words like 'armed' and 'execute' are innocent
enough: they pass unnoticed as one consumes the text. Yet the italicised words are emphatically there, and there (it bears repeating)
only in 'Two Gallants'. What is interesting about these words is
not so much their actual presence (Corley's military posture and
connections provide sufficient justification) as their role in the ideological process whereby the narrator on behalf of the central
characters (and, crucially, the reader also) accepts them as 'innocent' in the normal course of reading. Within false consciousness,
Lenehan cannot perceive that his only 'armour' against the oppression that he vaguely experiences is the clever joke, the deflection
(as with Farrington) of a potentially political energy into mere
rhetoric. (The contradiction within Lenehan's life is reinforced by
the narrator's ironic, but damagingly realistic, view of the obliga-
tions of friendship: 'his adroitness and eloquence had always prevented his friends from forming any general policy against him'
[p. 50].)

Contradictions proliferate, always underlining the notion of
dependence and paralysis. Lenehan, wearing a yachting cap, his
raincoat slung over his shoulder in 'toreador fashion' (p. 50), pretends to romantic heroism in the midst of a desperate passivity betrayed by his 'ravaged look' (p. 30). He uses 'foreign' speech ('the
recherché biscuit' [p. 50]; 'gay Lothario' [p. 52]) and walks through
streets whose names are predominantly English or foreign.[24] The
relationships between Lenehan, Corley, and the girl are parasitic,
meaningful only in relation to the gold coin, which, epiphanically,
'shows forth' the meaning of life in Dublin: that so much human
labour and ingenuity can be devoted to so servile an end. Perhaps
the most telling moment in this litany of dependence is the scene
with the harpist outside the Kildare Street club, that symbol of the
Protestant Ascendancy. The harpist plays 'Silent, O Moyle', an
example, one of hundreds in Joyce's texts, of his radical historicisation of literary allusion: that is, the reader is forced out of the immediate fiction towards the text alluded to, only to discover that the

latter deals with a specific historical event or with an emotion whose roots can be located in a lived history. The alluded-to text will then almost invariably work ironically, reinforcing the contradictions at the heart of Joyce's texts. Thus, 'Silent, O Moyle' contains the following lines:

> Yet still in her darkness doth Erin lie sleeping,
> Still doth the pale light its dawning delay.
> When will that day-star, mildly springing,
> Warm our isle with peace and love?

As Gifford notes, the pillar of the harp is 'in the figure of a semi-draped woman; i.e., the harp bears another traditional symbol of Ireland, the Poor Old Woman who metamorphoses into a beautiful young woman ("Dark Rosaleen") in the presence of her true lovers, the true patriots'[25] This moment in 'Two Gallants', in all its intertwining of images of Irish 'silence' in the midst of 'strangers', suggests strongly the inescapable fact of unequal relationships both in the fictional and the real Dublin. Lenehan is inferior to Corley; the 'slavey', the lowest class of domestic servant, is inferior to both Lenehan and Corley; the waitress to Lenehan, Lenehan to his usual bar cronies, Corley to his police contacts, and everyone to the shining gold coin.

As in 'Eveline', the political and the personal are seen to be inseparable. If relationships in 'Eveline' are distorted by the nightmare of colonial history, in 'Two Gallants' they are distorted by money itself though money is merely the symbolic expression of all those reified relationships. Until the conclusion one may be led to believe that the elaborate voyeuristic 'delay' in the narrative has to do with Corley's intention to seduce the girl, and indeed it may be that in perpetrating this ambiguity Joyce means to mock the reader's need to consume the text and to participate vicariously in the act of sexual domination. That Corley does intend to seduce the girl seems clear, but the more important point is that the girl must be shown paying for her very own seduction: even the most private personal relationships are invaded by the economic dimension. Corley's position vis à vis the girl is precisely analogous to the political relationship between imperialist power and colonial dependency (Ireland, like other dependencies, it is worth recalling, paid – in taxes, tariffs, and so forth – for the colonial relationship it had not sought), so that 'Two Gallants' reproduces at a deeply internalised level the relationship between Britain and Ireland. Moreover, the story provides one of the clearest demonstrations in Joyce of ideology functioning as the reproduction of a distorted reality.

So distorted is this Dublin reality that, at least in this story, no central character can emerge. Corley is an instrument merely, an instrument of the brutality implicit in the unequal colonial relationship. Lenehan is 'insensitive to all kinds of discourtesy' (p. 50): that is, he has no being of his own. And the girl is nameless, voiceless; the description of her (p. 55) suggests that she is 'beef to the heel', mere fodder, certainly not likely to be metamorphosed into a 'dark Rosaleen', in fact, likely to end up 'on the turf' (p. 53) like another of Corley's conquests. If she has a symbolic function as a woman, clearly there is little hope for Ireland if her young women can so easily be bought and if they are prepared to pay to be bought. These people are so ultimately cut off from the forces of production that they act like automatons within the hideous process of colonialism and its attendant economic exploitation. Relationships are reified; even language itself (in Lenehan's limericks and riddles) becomes objectified, a weapon or commodity to control the behaviour of other people. How appropriate therefore that all these distortions and contradictions should cohere at the last moment in the image of the gold coin, the perfect symbol in history of commodity fetishism and unequal relationships. And, as if to seal these characters' fate, the British sovereign's head, we must assume, nestles comfortably in Corley's palm.

From *Style*, 25:3 (Fall 1991), 416–27; 430–5.

Notes

[Williams's essay is a clear application of Marxism to *Dubliners*, with a particular focus upon how ideology informs the linguistic style of the text. Williams is perhaps the foremost 'traditional' Marxist critic on Joyce and begins the essay with a brief outline of how he understands ideology, drawing upon Marx, Louis Althusser and Ferruccio Rossi-Landi. All of Joyce's work, suggests Williams, is concerned with how to escape or resist the ideologies of the Catholic church and the imperial British state. One particular dimension of this resistance was Joyce's experimentation with language; as Williams suggests, Joyce's work 'always remained preoccupied with the problem of how to escape from that most ideological of instruments, language itself, in particular the language of the English'. Extending this point, Williams uses Rossi-Landi's concept of 'linguistic ownership' to argue that in *Dubliners* Joyce diagnoses the 'paralysing' effects of church and state ideologies upon the inhabitants of his home city. A number of notes have been abbreviated or omitted for reasons of space. Ed.]

1. I have discussed some of the issues in this paper in an earlier essay, Trevor L. Williams, 'Resistance to Paralysis in Dubliners', *Modern Fiction Studies*, 35 (1989), 437–57, where I also suggested that some of the stories in *Dubliners* (especially 'The Dead') show signs of a healthy 'resistance' to the prevailing paralysis. [All references to *Dubliners* are from James Joyce, *Dubliners*, ed. Robert Scholes in consultation with Richard Ellmann (New York, 1967). Ed.].

2. See Dominic Manganiello, *Joyce's Politics* (London, 1980), for a comprehensive discussion of Joyce's early 'socialism'.

3. Of course, the alert reader who knows that Purdon Street was the main street in Dublin's red light district can easily deconstruct Father Purdon's specious 'authority'; see Don Gifford, *Joyce Annotated; Notes for 'Dubliners' and 'A Portrait of the Artist as a Young Man'* (Berkeley, CA, 1982), p. 104.

4. Manganiello, *Joyce's Politics*, p. 97.

5. Gifford, *Joyce Annotated*, p. 79.

6. Beryl Schlossman, *Joyce's Catholic Comedy of Language* (Madison, WI, 1985), p. xviii.

7. In 'Eveline', similarly, we learn that Eveline's neighbourhood has been developed by a Belfast man, one contributory factor in her spiritual impoverishment.

8. This English girl performs the same function as her compatriot at the end of 'Araby': she punctures romantic illusions. Politically, the deflation indicates that the Irish should not look to England, the source of their 'troubles', for help; or, the dream of absorption into English life is a confession of defeat.

9. Cheryl Herr, in *Joyce's Anatomy of Culture* (Urbana, IL, 1986), makes the further point that Mr. Kernan has been 'destroyed not so much by drink as by changes in the economic environment' (p. 241).

10. One further instance of English domination of Irish consciousness is Joe Dillon's adolescent reading matter, '*The Union Jack, Pluck and The Halfpenny Marvel*' (p. 19).

11. Herr, *Joyce's Anatomy of Culture*, makes a similar point when she refers to 'the church's intimate ties to the economic system' (p. 239).

12. For the concept of linguistic ownership, see Ferruccio Rossi-Landi, *Linguistics and Economics* (The Hague, 1977).

13. Eric Hobsbawm, 'Marx and History', *New Left Review*, 143 (1984), 41.

14. Jimmy's father, who grew rich as a butcher and even richer when he secured the police contracts, is referred to as a 'merchant prince' (p. 43). Most the characters in *Dubliners* belong to the petty bourgeoisie, the rest dividing into the solid middle class (insofar as anything in Joyce's Dublin can be said to be 'solid') and the respectable working class. The lines between the three classes are very thin, and a character's class position can sometimes depend as much on his own estimation of himself as on objective factors like ownership or employment, income, property, and so forth. Apart from Jimmy, the bourgeoisie proper include (I would assert): Mr. Duffy ('A Painful Case'); Mrs. Kearney and possibly O' Madden Burke ('A Mother'); possibly Martin Cunningham and Mr. Power ('Grace'); and Gabriel Conroy and his aunts. The respectable working class include Eveline and Maria ('Clay').

15. In 1913 the schoolboys of St Thomas's National School in Lower Rutland Street joined Larkin's strikers during the Dublin Tramway dispute; see Joseph V. O'Brien, *'Dear, Dirty Dublin': A City in Distress, 1899–1916* (Berkeley, CA, 1982), p. 231.

16. [Williams has just been discussing 'A Painful Case' in a section that is omitted here. Ed.]

17. Rossi-Landi, *Linguistics and Economics*, pp. 190–1.

18. Herbert Marcuse, *One-Dimensional Man: Studies in the Ideology of Advanced Industrial Society* (Boston, 1964), p. 84.

19. Williams, 'Resistance to Paralysis in *Dubliners*', pp. 452–7.

20. Herr, Joyce's *Anatomy of Culture*, p. 245.

21. French, in an excellent, thought insufficiently politicised, article, sees Farrington's slip as a conscious impertinence stimulated by the presence of the sexually alluring Miss Delacour; see Marilyn French, 'Missing Pieces in Joyce's *Dubliners*', *Twentieth Century Literature*, 24 (1978), 459.

22. His retort to Alleyne is a public 'success', but its ephemeral nature and the fact that it will almost certainly cost him his job make it a Pyrrhic victory merely.

23. For the prevalence of pawnbroking, see O'Brien, *'Dear, Dirty Dublin'*, p. 162.

24. Terence Brown notes that the names of streets and buildings in 'Two Gallants' 'toll with the inevitability of exclusion'; see Terence Brown, 'The Dublin of *Dubliners*', *James Joyce: An International Perspective*, ed.; Suheil Bushrui and Bernard Benstock (Gerrards Cross, 1982), p. 14.

25. Gifford, *Joyce Annotated*, p. 58.

6

'An Encounter': Boys' Magazines and the Pseudo-Literary

R. B. KERSHNER

The explicit themes of 'An Encounter' are familiar enough: perverse sexuality, transgression, the disappointment of romantic expectations. But, neatly enough, the second story of the collection is also the first of the *Dubliners* tales to be framed intertextually by popular literature. Unlike the boy of 'The Sisters', this protagonist exists in a social context of his peers – a context structured through the ideologies of genres of popular literature, among other elements – and has come to define himself with respect to that context. He sees himself as both one of them and distinct from them; he shares in their ideology, but with a sense of distance that leaves him with the impression that most of his actions are inauthentic; he is play-acting, dramatising, or impersonating the boy he appears to be. He shares this motif of disguise with the boy of the previous story, but without that boy's pervasive sense of the menace surrounding him. This is ironic, for in fact the protagonist of 'An Encounter' is much more directly menaced than is the priest's protégé. Naturally, he shares the younger boy's sense of alienation from adults, but he has the advantage of a social subgroup with whom to share that sense. His playacting is thus less dangerous, because it is less of a private ritual and more of a social one. Acting, in this story, is one of the modes through which the boy attempts to discover his identity, an identity that is posited upon his social situation. He is in the process of determining his individuality and paradoxically finds he must inevitably do so in terms of the ideological formations surrounding him.

The most highly structured source of these ideological formations is the group of boys' magazines shared by the protagonist's peers. Joe Dillon, the future priest, has cemented the bonds among the group of schoolfellows with a library of old numbers of *The Union Jack, Pluck*, and *The Halfpenny Marvel* (*D*, p. 19).[1] The heyday of magazines for children was the late nineteenth and early twentieth century; Sheila Egoff argues that their two main sources were the magazines inspired by the Sunday School movement, whose publication began in the early years of the nineteenth century and continued throughout it, and the boys' 'blood and thunder' magazines (or 'bloods'), which were inaugurated in *The Boys of England* (1866), a magazine of 'Sport, Sensation, Fun and Instruction', and continued to increase in number and popularity until the first World War.[2] The latter group had its origin in the 'penny parts' or 'penny dreadfuls' ostensibly intended for adults and incorporating a strong pseudo-Gothic element and a less literary, more streamlined and repetitive style. The publisher of *Boys of England*, E. J. Brett, can lay some claim to inventing modern mass-market publication practices, in that his magazine was produced cheaply and sold for a penny weekly, while its only competitors sold for sixpence and catered to the 'classes'. In 1869 he issued a halfpenny magazine, *Boys of the World*, thus anticipating the successes of the magazines of the 1890s. Brett also inaugurated the practice of presenting contests with substantial prizes, a promotion scheme that would be crucial to the success of Alfred C. Harmsworth's publications for both children and adults.

The Irish-born Harmsworth's fortune, like that of his rival of the 1890s, George Newnes, was founded on his boys' magazines, of which his Amalgamated Press published more than all other publishers combined.[3] His first effort in this line was *Comic Cuts*, in 1890. *The Halfpenny Marvel Library* began publication in 1893, changed its title to *The Halfpenny Marvel* after three issues, and continued under this title until 1898, when it became simply *The Marvel* (1898–1922).[4] Ironically for a magazine generally regarded as cheaply sensational, it claimed the intent of counteracting the influence of unhealthy sensationalism aimed at children, announcing in the first issue, 'No more penny dreadfuls! These healthy stories of mystery, adventure, etc., will kill them.'[5] Soon *The Marvel* began printing testimonials such as that of the Reverend C.

N. Barham expressing pleasure that the magazine was so 'pure and wholesome in tone'. On the front cover of that issue was a man being tortured, with the caption, 'The gaoler screwed up the horrible machine until the brigand's bones were nearly broken and he shrieked aloud for mercy, though none was shown'.[6] The sadomasochistic element in boys' periodicals was far less visible to the adults of the late nineteenth century than to ourselves; as will become apparent in the discussion of school stories below, it was an accepted, relatively transparent aspect of the ideology of bourgeois schooling.

The *Union Jack Library of High-Class Fiction* lasted from 1894 to 1933, succeeding an earlier, unrelated magazine entitled *The Union Jack*, which was founded in 1880 and ran for three years. Its inaugural issue opened with 'The Silver Arrow'; early issues featured redskins, explorers, prospectors, sailors, and so forth, with only an occasional appearance by the detectives who would later be its mainstay.[7] *Pluck* appeared in 1895, for the first two issues as *Stories of Pluck*, and continued until 1916. It was self-characterised as 'Stories of Pluck – being the daring deeds of plucky sailors, plucky soldiers, plucky railwaymen, plucky boys and plucky girls and all sorts and conditions of British heroes', and asserted unconvincingly that it would contain 'true stories', although sometimes the names of the protagonists would be thinly disguised.[8] Self-characterised as 'a high class weekly library of adventure at home and abroad, on land and sea',[9] one of its favourite themes concerned the adventures of three boys in foreign lands.[10] These were 'Jack, a brave British boy with the adventurous spirit; Sam, a skilled hunter; and Pete, a Negro ventriloquist, who was the real life of the party.'[11] Rather than the straight blood-and-thunder formula, the popular Jack, Sam, and Pete series featured overseas escapades with a strong element of farce. The three boys of 'An Encounter' no doubt imagine themselves such a lucky trio, a miniature paradigm of Empire. They are also, of course, a degenerate version of the Three Musketeers. The protagonist will furnish pluck and inspiration, Mahony the warrior's skills, and Leo Dillon comic relief. Unfortunately, they are Irish and thus awkward representatives of Empire. The protagonist is enough a literalist of the imagination to believe that, as in the magazines, 'real adventures ... must be sought abroad' (*D*, p. 21), and so is sceptical even before the expedition starts. As coup de grace to this early exercise in reader-identification, Leo Dillon fails to show up for the adventure.

All three Harmsworth magazines participated in the new upsurge of romanticism modified by realistic detail that characterised popular literature of the 1880s and 1890s, when Stevenson, Macdonald, Verne, and Barrie blurred the distinction between children's and adults' fiction. All three also were unusual in featuring a heroine, whose part in the stories was negligible – usually consisting in blundering into the clutches of the nearest villain – but who was often, at least in *The Marvel*, given a head-and-shoulders illustration of her own.[12] Thus the girl hovered like a mysterious icon above the male adventures, intimately connected with them in wholly unspecified ways. The 'old josser' quizzing the two boys about their 'totties' at the climax of their day must seem oddly appropriate to the children. They know from their reading that their 'adventure' is about sexuality, although they – like their culture – have no idea why. In both these boys' magazines and the monologue of the old man, the young girl with beautiful hair serves as putative goal and justification for a narrative that in fact demonstrates her irrelevance.

Cheaper variants of more respectable publications such as the famous 'B.O.P', or *Boys' Own Paper* (1879–1946), *Young England* (1880–1935?), and *Boys of the Empire* (1888–89), these adventure magazines of the nineties occupied a dubious middle ground between the penny dreadfuls and truly innocent children's magazines such as *Chatterbox*, whose readers came in time to refer to Harmsworth's magazines as themselves penny dreadfuls. In turn, by the time Joyce was composing the stories of *Dubliners*, Leo Dillon's library was to be supplanted by Amalgamated Press's own *Gem* and *Magnet*, papers whose public-school stories Orwell analysed politically to such devastating effect.[13] Even at the time of the story Dillon's magazines were regarded by adventurous boys as tame, so that even a reader as sheltered as the protagonist-narrator, who attends a Catholic school in Dublin, has a taste for racier American imports such as the 'detective stories which were traversed from time to time by unkempt fierce and beautiful girls' (*D*, p. 20). These would have been easily available to him: E. S. Turner observes that 'the setting up of private detectives was a major literary industry in the "nineties", and that the Aldine Company alone produced over 250 detective titles, many of them American imports.'[14]

Still, *The Halfpenny Marvel* with its green jacket and Wild West stories would be better than nothing; virtuous on the whole, it would nevertheless have the allure of priestly proscription. Perhaps more important, it was among the first thoroughly modern mass-market publications for children, one of the wave of magazines of the 1880s and 1890s that nearly equalled in volume the sum total of those published during the previous eighty years. Harmsworth's magazines helped solidify the genres of story – detective exploration, sea adventure, science fiction, school story, Wild West – into categories that persist today. The popularity of Wild West stories in cultures such as that of middle-class Dublin deserves some analysis in itself.[15] Clearly, the narrator of 'An Encounter' feels it to be somewhat artificial: 'The adventures related in the literature of the Wild West were remote from my nature but, at least, they opened doors of escape.' He is a reluctant participant in the communal fantasy and joins the cowboy-and-Indian games of his fellows out of social fear, because he is 'afraid to seem studious or lacking in robustness' (*D*, p. 20). Appropriately, this fear would be instilled most directly by the ideology of the 'school stories' of those very magazines, stories whose ethics and typologies descended lineally from *Tom Brown's School-Days*.

The boy's fear of appearing overly studious to his classmates is of central significance in the ideological framework of this story. Both of the adults in the story – Father Butler and the 'old josser' – immediately invoke a culturally reified distinction between boys who are active, unthinking, and lower-class and those who are studious, responsible, and upper-middle class. The priest, on discovering Leo Dillon reading 'The Apache Chief' instead of his Roman History, exclaims, 'I'm surprised at boys like you, educated, reading such stuff. I could understand it if you were ... National School boys' (*D*, p. 20). Father Butler's pause indicates that he has trouble finding a suitable circumlocution for 'lower-class', preferably a term that will immediately instil shame in the boys' hearts. During the protagonist's 'miching' expedition, the old man, discovering the protagonist's professed taste for 'literature', says, '– Ah, I can see you are a bookworm like myself. Now, he added, pointing to Mahony who was regarding us with open eyes, he is different; he goes in for games' (*D*, p. 25). The distinction goes back to medieval typologies of the 'active' and 'contemplative' lives, but during the late nineteenth century had begun to take on new social implications.

Raymond Williams points out that the word *culture*, in its modern sense of arts and letters, is seldom encountered before the nineteenth century, and acquires an aura of hostility only in the

closing years of that century, partly as a result of the debate surrounding Arnold's *Culture and Anarchy*.[16] When Old Cotter asserts
that a young lad should run about and play with lads of his own
age rather than study with a priest (*D*, p. 10), he is articulating this
relatively new, class-based hostility to 'culture' – an antagonism ex-
acerbated by the popular Irish identification of 'culture' with the
ruling Protestants. The boy of 'An Encounter' finds himself in a
situation of ideological contradiction, or perhaps at a locus of
conflicting ideologies. He does not want to be thought an unmanly
'swot', or a pretender to cultural (and thus class) distinction, and
yet he has also internalised the public value system represented by
the priest. He is thoroughly aware of the social distinction between
himself and his friends on the one hand and children educated at
public expense on the other. He immediately identifies the boys and
girls he and Mahoney encounter as 'ragged girls' and 'ragged boys'
(*D*, p. 22), tags which signify that they attend one of the 'Ragged
Schools' of Dublin slum areas.[17] Judging from the appearance of
the narrator and Mahony, the 'ragged' children identify them as
better off, and thus Protestants. The narrator feels mingled pride
and shame in the status to which his Jesuit education entitles him
and the further status accrued from his personal identification with
'culture'. The priest's rebuke of Dillon affects him greatly, and the
protagonist believes that 'the confused puffy face of Leo Dillon
awakened one of my consciences' (*D*, p. 20); but then, in reaction,
he is drawn to the 'active' life and hungers for the 'escape which
those chronicles of disorder alone seemed to offer me' (*D*, p. 21).

'Chronicles of disorder' is the key term here. The two boys who
skip school are both enacting popular literary plots, but each has a
different conception of the genre. Mahony is playing Wild West: he
brings a catapult for weapon and 'began to play the Indian as soon
as we were out of public sight' (*D*, p. 22). If, as John Cawelti has
argued, the Wild West dime novel characteristically engages themes
of disguise that include sexual ambiguity, then Mahony's game is
disturbingly appropriate for the story.[18] Indeed, the Western's
divided allegiance between civilisation and pastoral freedom is mirrored in the fact that Joe Dillon, the source of the boys' anarchic
fictions, later becomes a priest. Compared to Mahony, the narrator
has a vaguer and more complex idea of the drama he is engaged in,
but it is probably a romance of the sea. Travel is a necessity,
because 'real adventures ... do not happen to people who remain at
home: they must be sought abroad' (*D*, p. 21). This rather odd

elision of schoolboy drama and sea story in the protagonist's mind was in fact perfectly anticipated by boys' magazines; Jack Harkaway, whose original home was *Boys of England*, immediately leaves for the sea following his school adventures; in fact, he goes on to the Wild West, China, and to various wars, so that the same protagonist could slide easily among genres that later would be strictly segregated.[19]

Watching the ship unloading, the boy 'examined the foreign sailors to see had any of them green eyes for I had some confused notion ...' (*D*, p. 23). The narrator's use of ellipsis here, as in the boy's narration of his dream in 'The Sisters', suggests a turning aside from a realisation best left unconscious, because to put it into words would be to denude it of the mystery upon which the image feeds. More specifically, he is looking for the young, red-haired, green-eyed sailor who is the hero of picaresque adventures in the diluted tradition of Marryat. Mahony has the opportunity to enact his fantasy first, since opportunities for warfare were easily come by; the two boys impersonate Protestants more or less accidentally, and when Mahony chases a crowd of Catholic girls a couple of boys, 'out of chivalry' (*D*, p. 22), decide to retaliate. Mahony and the protagonist then arrange a 'siege', which is a failure because two boys is not enough. The protagonist's fantasy is even more of a failure, since the only green-eyed sailor he can spot is the tall man 'who amused the crowd on the quay by calling out cheerfully every time the planks fell: – All right! All right!' (*D*, p. 23). Far from the folkloric hero who embodies the principles of imagination, sexual regeneration, and anarchy in a necessary opposition to social norms, this quotidian sailor plays to the crowd and gives them back their banal nonsense. Both boys identify with the figure who appears to represent an alternative to the hierarchical, highly ordered aspect of bourgeois ideology: Mahony with the savage Indian, the protagonist with the picaresque sailor. They fail not merely because reality cannot satisfy the desires of the imagination, but also because the 'imagination' they have invoked is as ordered, structured, and predictable as the 'reality' they are attempting to escape. What appear to be 'chronicles of disorder' are merely rituals of a different order, in which the savage Indian and the adventurous sailor must play their endless, assigned roles.

The appearance of the 'queer old josser' marks the division between the boys' pretended adventures and their real one. Instead of an opposing gang of cowboys representing society's order,

Mahony meets a sinister figure who invokes an entirely different 'us-them' distinction: the cultured bookworms versus the ignorant game-players. Instead of a green-eyed sailor, the protagonist meets a man dressed in 'greenish-black' (D, p. 24) with 'bottle-green eyes' (D, p. 27) who walks and speaks in slow, continuous circles, and who takes him on a disturbing voyage of the mind. Unlike Eveline's Frank, who woos her with 'The Bohemian Girl' and popular fantasies of a sailor's adventurous life, this seducer invokes Thomas Moore, Sir Walter Scott, and Lord Lytton. It is nonetheless clearly an attempted seduction, as most commentators have noted: the boy is sitting, holding 'one of those green stems on which girls tell fortunes' (D, p. 24), while the man wields a phallic stick; the boy, repulsed by his advances, pretends to adjust his shoe in a classic ingenue's gesture. For reasons that are not specified, the boy claims to have read every book the old man mentions. Certainly he is proud of the extent of his reading, and he also feels he must choose sides in the dichotomy both the old man and Father Butler have drawn. Rather than be identified with the simple Mahony he risks identification with the literary stranger. He is unaware that the figures the old man mentions were at the time a sort of lowest common denominator of literature, writers who might be more readily identified as popular than as serious. Moore's reputation as poet had been declining since his death in 1852, and by the nineties he survived almost exclusively as a 'parlour poet' and as precursor of sentimentally patriotic versifiers in the tradition of Young Ireland. Less than a decade later even the philistine Bloom feels it to be appropriate that his statue is erected over a urinal.[20] Scott's reputation was near its nadir among literati, although his popularity continued, especially among the older generation. He seems to have been Joyce's particular bête noir, since a taste for him is also assigned to both the dead priest in 'Araby' and to the dwarfish, monkey-faced old 'captain' in Portrait.

Edward George Earle Lytton (1803–73), who styled himself Bulwer-Lytton after he was created a baronet, is a more interesting case, especially in the context of 'An Encounter'. By the 1890s his reputation had also plummeted in critical opinion, although his elevation to the peerage and the self-consciously 'cultured' tone of his books hid their essential vulgarity from many readers. Bulwer-Lytton's ambition, energy, intellect, and ability were disproportionate to the quality of his literary production, so that he came to be regarded as the greatest Victorian example of 'talent betrayed by character'. Disraeli is said to have invoked him as a standard of egotism; the statesman once is supposed to have called Charles Greville 'the most conceited man I ever met, though I have read Cicero and known Bulwer-Lytton'. Perhaps the best-known British inheritor of the romantic tradition of Byron and Goethe in its novelistic form, he was also a successful playwright whose *Lady of Lyons* still played frequently in Dublin during Stephen Dedalus's boyhood. He was even better known for his novels in the 'Silver Fork' tradition of social melodrama in a high-society setting, such as *Pelham*. In books such as these he was able to satisfy the bourgeois taste for images of decadent luxury while simultaneously expressing a bourgeois moral disapprobation of the scene. But despite the explicit moralising of his novels several of them were generally regarded as dangerous, the sort of book you would not want to fall into the hands of women and children – much like some of the classics whose aura he appropriated. The most notorious of these was *The Last Days of Pompeii* (1834), an interminable melodrama of decadent Roman Empire society. Like *Rienzi* (1835), *The Last of the Barons* (1843), and *Harold* (1848), *The Last Days of Pompeii* is packed with carefully researched archaeological information, sometimes integrated into the narrative and sometimes relegated to intrusive footnotes or narrative essays; the Victorian reader would have no doubt that he was receiving valuable instruction even as he was being titillated by the racy story or the extensive descriptions of banquets and decadent entertainments. The style of both dialogue and narrative is mock-classical and slides between the Biblical and the euphuistic. It is a language intended to bear the undeniable signifiers of cultural and social elevation:

> The two friends, seated on a small crag which rose amidst the smooth pebbles, inhaled the voluptuous and cooling breeze, which dancing over the waters, kept music with its invisible feet. There was, perhaps, something in the scene that invited them to silence and reverie. Clodius, shading his eyes from the burning sky, was calculating the gains of the last week; and the Greek, leaning upon his hands, and shrinking not from that sun, – his nation's tutelary deity, – with whose fluent light of poesy, and joy, and love, his own veins were filled, gazed upon the broad expanse, and envied, perhaps, every wind that bent its pinions towards the shores of Greece.
> 'Tell me, Clodius,' said the Greek at last, 'hast thou ever been in love?'
> 'Yes, very often.'

'He who hath loved often,' answered Glaucus, 'has loved never.
There is but one Eros, though there are many counterfeits of him.'[21]

Insofar as the novel can be said to have themes, they are a banal
potpourri of Christian admonition and romantic cliché. Like the
novels of Marie Corelli sixty years later, the book has simple, melodramatic action sequences culminating in tableaus intended to
inspire the reader with awe and pity. Lest the inattentive reader fail
to recognise these moments of frozen passion, at one such tableau
the narrator announces, 'And never, perhaps, since Lucifer and the
Archangel contended for the body of the mighty Lawgiver, was
there a more striking subject for the painter's genius than that scene
exhibited.'[22] The leisurely narrative is frequently interspersed with
Bulwer-Lytton's poetry, usually in the guise of a song performed by
one of the characters. The elevated diction, Roman milieu, and
archaeological references all conspire to suggest to the reader that
he is experiencing the classical Sublime.

Certainly this would be the primary book the 'old josser' has in
mind when he observes that there are some of Lord Lytton's works
that boys could not read (D, p. 25). Marvin Magalaner has observed of Joyce's early reading of Bulwer-Lytton that 'he appropriated those characters and situations within the general story which
might serve as analogues and surrogates, literary substitutes for the
people and scenes of his own projected narratives.'[23] The Last Days
of Pompeii was the only one of Bulwer-Lytton's novels in Joyce's
Trieste library and has considerable significance for 'An Encounter'.
In Bulwer-Lytton's novel the first major plot movement is parallel
to that in The Lady of Lyons: an old, wealthy suitor of a beautiful
young girl is displaced by a young pseudo-prince, and the older
man attempts revenge through the younger. Here the romantic lead
is Glaucus, a Greek-born aristocrat of Pompeii who has good instincts but has been leading a life of mild dissolution. The older
man is Arbaces, an enormously wealthy and powerful Egyptian
who is also known to the initiated as Hermes; he is also a priest of
Isis, a dark goddess with a large number of followers in Pompeii.
Arbaces is given to dark rites and orgies that are dimly known in
the city, but he has such a plausible manner and powerful intellect
that his reputation hardly suffers. He has been made guardian of
the beautiful singer Ione and her brother Apaecides, orphans of
Greek extraction also. Although he stands in loco parentis to the
adolescents, he has begun the seduction of both: Apaecides, a highly

impressionable, religious-minded boy, he has begun to induct into the mysteries of the temple of Isis in order to bind him to his will; Ione, whom he desires, but who regards him as a father, he wishes to seduce by means of the hold he has over her brother.

Arbaces is a sort of emotional vampire who draws the youth from his victims; furthermore, he believes himself genuinely in love for the first time. But Ione has met Glaucus, and the two noble youngsters are fated for each other. Enraged, Arbaces calumniates Glaucus, accusing him of toying with Ione's affection, and takes advantage of her wounded pride to entice her to his house. Meanwhile, her brother, discovering that Isis is a sham and the temple miracles tricks, has been brought near nervous breakdown. Arbaces takes advantage of his instability to bring the boy into the inner sanctum of the priest's house, where he is made drunk and given slave-girls to entertain him while Arbaces looks on delight-edly. At first, he is flattered that the priest 'had deigned to rank him with himself, to set him apart from the laws which bound the vulgar'.[24] Transposed into a melodramatic key, the situation is exactly parallel to that in 'The Sisters' and 'An Encounter': a boy is tempted by an old, somehow disreputable priest-figure who offers initiation into mysteries that combine arcane learning and an undefined element of dark sensuality and that are not accessible to ordinary humanity. Afterward, filled with self-disgust and lassitude, Apaecides encounters a group of early Christians who help him to escape from the evil influence, just in time to join Glaucus in rescuing Ione from the Egyptian's clutches.

Once the girl is in his home, Arbaces presses his suit in slightly disguised form. He urges a sort of Platonic love, although he certainly does not mean to imply that their relationship should not be physical: 'There is a love, beautiful Greek, which is not the love only of the thoughtless and the young – there is a love which sees not with the eyes, which hears not with the ears but in which soul is enamoured of soul. The countryman of thy ancestors, the cave-nursed Plato, dreamed of such a love – his followers have sought to imitate it; but it is a love that is not for the herd to echo. ... Wrinkles do not revolt it – homeliness of feature does not deter; it asks youth, it is true, but it asks it only in the freshness of the emotions.'[25] The narrator stresses Ione's bewilderment and Arbaces's caution: 'He knew that he uttered a language which, if at this day of affected platonisms it would speak unequivocally to the ears of beauty, was at that time strange and unfamiliar.'[26] Like the old josser, Arbaces cannot afford to articulate his desires except through indirection; he also must entice the young with a language they are not ready to understand. But Arbaces eventually makes his intentions clear, while as dramatic counterpoint huge banquets, fountains, and luxurious displays appear before them. When Ione confesses her love for Glaucus, he is overcome with rage and seizes her; she emulates Victorian heroines by fainting away, just as Glaucus and Apaecides burst in to the rescue. Aided by a preparatory tremor from the volcano, the heroes are able to defeat Arbaces and bring the first cycle of the plot – and the only one relevant to 'An Encounter' – to a close.

The coincidence of themes in Bulwer-Lytton's novel and Joyce's story is apparent simply from an outline of the action, but in fact it goes considerably deeper than this. The actual scenes of orgy and seduction in the melodrama are rather mild and go no further than a stolen kiss or a man's head upon a woman's lap; but mingled strains of paedophilia, sodomy, and sadomasochism run just below the surface. Most prominent is the seduction of Ione through her brother, an action barely justified in terms of the plot – there is little evidence that Arbaces's hold over Apaecides gives him any leverage with Ione.

Indeed, far more of the book is devoted to the more elaborate and successful seduction of the boy than to the relatively perfunctory (and unsuccessful) seduction of the girl. Several of the subplots and minor characters encourage such a reading as well. One of Glaucus's companions is described as a man 'in whom Nature seemed twisted and perverted from every natural impulse, and curdled into one dubious thing of effeminacy and art', who spends his happiest hours patting and stroking the shoulders of gladiators with a 'blanched and girlish hand'.[27] Perhaps the book's most shocking scene involves the wife of a retired gladiator, herself a sort of ambiguously sexed monster of brutality, who brawls with young gladiators in her tavern. Glaucus enters to discover her passionately beating a blind young slave-girl with a cord 'already dabbled with blood'.[28] The narrative regularly circles around to such scenes, as if in peripheral and periphrastic commentary upon the relatively straightforward heterosexual romance of the main plot.

The old josser's monologue is a simplified, repetitive version of what might be termed an 'ideology of perversion' couched, like Bulwer-Lytton's narrative, within a framing context of moral disapproval and, curiously enough, within an additional assumed context of superior social status. Steven Marcus has observed that the 'literature of flagellation in Victorian England assumes that its audience had both interest in and connection with the higher gentry and the nobility – that this assumption may itself be laden with fantasies is not at this moment to the point. It further assumes that its audience had the common experience of education at a public school. ... Indeed, for this literature perversity and social privilege are inseparable marks of distinction.'[29] This linkage between high social status and perversity is directly invoked by the old man in 'An Encounter', and in fact helps tie together the story's themes. Further, Marcus notes that although there are two basic scenarios of flagellation, in one of which a boy is beaten by a mother-figure and in the other of which a girl is beaten by an older woman, 'in fact no such distinctions really obtain, on either side of the transaction. In this literature, anybody can be or become anybody else, and the differences between the sexes are blurred and confused.'[30]

The sexual confusion is apparent in *The Last Days of Pompeii*, where it functions as part of the disguise of the underlying perverse narrative. It is also apparent in the old man's narrative, where it functions similarly, as an attempt to disarm his young auditor. Joyce's josser is clearly attracted to boys but disguises this unsuccessfully by continual reference to girls:

> There was nothing he liked, he said, so much as looking at a nice young girl, at her nice white hands and her beautiful soft hair. He gave me the impression that he was repeating something which he had learned by heart or that, magnetised by some words of his own speech, his mind was slowly circling round and round in the same orbit.
>
> (*D*, p. 26)

> And if a boy had a girl for a sweetheart and told lies about it then he would give him such a whipping as no boy ever got in this world. ... He described to me how he would whip such a boy as if he were unfolding some elaborate mystery.
>
> (*D*, p. 27)

The old man's confusion, repetitiousness, and mechanical speech are of course indices of his paralysis, but more specifically they point to the fact that he is a creature of his reading. He recites aloud not only the conventional erotic description of the Victorian girl (to whom he is not attracted) but also the description of a boy being whipped, in which he has considerable psychic investment.

He is a male, pornographic counterpart to Gerty MacDowel:[31] his consciousness is suffused by sadomasochistic, paedophilic narratives, until like some perverse Ancient Mariner he is condemned to recite them to unwilling ears. And like participants in those narratives, he is trapped in an endless, confused round of mechanical repetition of the same scenario: 'His mind, as if magnetised again by his speech, seemed to circle slowly round and round its new centre' (D, p. 27).

Joyce's narrative, which dialogically embraces and interacts with the explicit and implied narratives of popular literature that are its subject, is remarkable in several regards. First it should be noted that the josser is given only two very brief speeches in direct discourse; the vast majority of his talk is presented in indirect discourse, so that it emerges as an amalgam of the boy's and the old man's language – or, more precisely, of the old man's language and the two languages of experience and retrospection embodied in the boy's narration. The major effect of this strange heteroglossia is to make the boy complicit in the old man's speech, to underline his ambivalence in the face of a language that he first accepts, then attempts to reject. The second and last example of direct reported speech of the man is his observation, 'Every boy has a little sweetheart'. The narrator admits that 'In my heart I thought that what he said about boys and sweethearts was reasonable. But I disliked the words in his mouth' (D, p. 25). The old man works upon his listener much as the pornographic text works upon its reader, attempting to establish complicity through an appeal to commonly accepted values (lying merits punishment) and then wrenching the reader into an increasingly perverse realm of experience.

Marcus notes that flagellant literature typically is written from a split perspective: 'The writers of this literature, like some propagandists for homosexuality, need to reassure themselves that their affliction is simultaneously exclusive and universal.'[32] The relationship of the flagellant narrator with the reader of this genre is radically unstable. He is addressed both as one of an elite of sensibility and as a man who shares the unadmitted desires of all men. The old man employs the same unconscious tactic: 'At times he spoke as if he were simply alluding to some fact that everybody knew, and at times he lowered his voice and spoke mysteriously as if he were telling something secret which he did not wish others to overhear' (D, p. 26). Even more than the general run of pornography, flagellant narrative is essentially anecdotal and repetitive; like Bulwer-

Lytton's novel, it exists for the tableau. The indirect reportage of the old man's speech heightens this effect for the reader. Argument and narrative drop away, and we are left with an impression of monotonous, repetitive circularity. The words are subsumed by the voice: 'He repeated his phrases over and over again, varying them and surrounding them with his monotonous voice' (*D*, p. 26). Before this assault the boy has no option but to invoke the strategies of his predecessor in 'The Sisters', silence and disguise. Appropriately for a story that addresses popular fictions, he decides to play 'spy' by plotting with Mahony to give an assumed name if questioned. But even there he does not escape the round of fictions surrounding him, for he assigns Mahony a lower-class, Irish name, 'Murphy', and chooses for himself the higher-status Anglo-Irish name of 'Smith'. Both names, of course, are banal; but that merely emphasises the poverty of the imaginative resources available to him.

Criticism of 'An Encounter' has generally centred on the boy's final appeal to Mahony and his shame at having secretly despised his schoolfellow. Julian Kaye reads the story as the 'symbolic history of the boy narrator's rejection of the authority of father, church, and state as perverted and degenerate and his despairing substitution of the friendship of a contemporary who, although mediocre, can assuage his loneliness.'[33] Less forgivingly, Sidney Feshbach argues that the story is a formal elegy showing the spiritual death of a young boy, and that his 'penitence serves society'.[34] In the perspective of popular fictions, it seems clear that the social distinction the boy-narrator makes a gesture toward abandoning at the end is not his intuitive sense of superiority as artist, but a pernicious fiction enunciated first by the priest and then inadvertently deconstructed by the old josser. What the boy comes intuitively to realise is that fictions like the active/intellectual or the Church School/National School oppositions are not harmlessly free-floating distinctions, but part of complex, embedded ideologies whose ramifications may be baffling or dangerous. If you love Walter Scott you may have to assent to whipping; if you are a bookworm you may wind up mesmerised by a strange and simple text. 'An Encounter' does not recount the defeat of imagination by reality, because the 'imagination' that inspires the outing is mass-produced and the 'reality' the boys encounter is merely another genre of popular fiction.

From R. B. Kershner, *Joyce, Bakhtin and Popular Culture: Chronicles of Disorder* (Chapel Hill, NC, 1989), pp. 31–46.

Notes

[It is useful to contrast Williams's more traditional form of Marxist critique (essay 5) with the cultural materialist perspective employed by Kershner, particularly in their different senses of ideology. Kershner's book analyses the role of references to popular culture in Joyce's text, employing a framework derived from the Russian theorist Mikhail Bakhtin. Bakhtin's work on the subversive power of popular culture – such as the carnival – has been very influential in revising traditional Marxist literary theory, and Joyce's work, with its own blend of the serious and the humorous, lends itself well to Bakthinian insights. Kershner's much cited study was the first full-length use of Bakhtin in relation to Joyce, and in this extract he situates the early *Dubliners* story, 'An Encounter', within the context of popular literature of the time. The young protagonist of the story finds that his own development and self-knowledge are structured by the 'ideological formations surrounding him' and his friends: these formations are the ideologies of masculinity and sexuality found in the boys' magazines and other popular novels read by these group. Kershner's discussion of magazines such as *The Halfpenny Marvel* or the novels of Bulwer-Lytton shows how subtly Joyce drew upon the popular culture of his time when composing *Dubliners*, and also offers a new way to view the central encounter with the 'queer old josser' in the story. Ed.]

1. [All references to *Dubliners* are to James Joyce, *'Dubliners': Text, Criticism, and Notes*, ed. Robert Scholes and A. Walton Litz (New York, 1969). Ed.]

2. Sheila A. Egoff, *Children's Periodicals of the Nineteenth Century* (London, 1951), pp. 3, 16.

3. Ibid., p. 25.

4. *British Library General Catalogue of Printed Books to 1975* (London, 1979).

5. Cited in Marvin Magalaner, *Time of Apprenticeship: The Fiction of Young James Joyce* (London, 1959), p. 149.

6. E. S. Turner, *Boys Will Be Boys* (London, 1948), p. 104.

7. Ibid., pp. 108, 122.

8. Ibid., p. 145. The varying titles of these magazines are no doubt responsible for some confusion among Joyce's annotators regarding them. Don Gifford, *Joyce Annotated: Notes for 'Dubliners' and 'A Portrait of the Artist as a Young Man'*, rev. edn (Berkeley and Los Angeles, 1982), p. 34, agrees with Magalaner, *Time of Apprenticeship* (p. 149), that the *Halfpenny Marvel* began in 1893 and the other two in 1894, while in their edition of *Dubliners* (p. 465) Scholes and Litz have the *Marvel* in 1893, *Union Jack* in 1894, and *Pluck* in 1895. None of these seem aware of the earlier *Union Jack*.

9. *British Library Catalogue.*

10. Magalaner, *Time of Apprenticeship*, p. 149.

11. Turner, *Boys Will Be Boys*, p. 108.

12. Ibid., p. 112.

13. George Orwell, 'Boys' Weeklies', in *The Collected Essays, Journalism and Letters of George Orwell*, ed. Sonia Orwell and Ian Angus, vol. 1 (New York, 1968).

14. Turner, *Boys Will Be Boys*, pp. 143–4.

15. In a novel of which Joyce was fond, *At Swim-Two-Birds* (1939), Flann O'Brien features an Irish writer of cowboy stories and indeed has the writer's characters come to life, staging cattle drives and roundups on the outskirts of Dublin.

16. Raymond Williams, *Keywords: A Vocabulary of Culture and Society*, 2nd edn (New York, 1986), pp. 90–2.

17. Clive Hart (ed.), *James Joyce's 'Dubliners': Critical Essays* (New York, 1969), p. 171.

18. John Cawleti, *Adventure, Mystery and Romance: Formula Stories as Art and Popular Culture* (Chicago, 1976), pp. 212–14.

19. Turner, *Boys Will Be Boys*, p. 80. Note that boys' magazines typically sent a double message. Jack Harkaway's running away to sea is clearly presented as a sign of his heroic character, while the narrator warns, 'We are no advocates for running away; boys who run away from school generally turn out scamps in after life. They show an independence of action and a strong self-will, in which it is very injurious for the young to indulge'; cited in Turner, *Boys*, p. 88.

20. James Joyce, *'Ulysses': The Corrected Text*, ed. Hans Walter Gabler with Wolfhard Steppe and Claus Melchior (New York, 1986), p. 133.

21. Edward Bulwer-Lytton, *The Last Days of Pompeii* (New York, 1903), p. 13.

22. Ibid., p. 369.

23. Magalaner, *Time of Apprenticeship*, p. 46.

24. Bulwer-Lytton, *Last Days of Pompeii*, p. 140.

25. Ibid., p. 143.

26. Ibid., p. 144.

27. Ibid., pp. 124–5.

28. Ibid., p. 128.

29. Steven Marcus, *The Other Victorians: A Study of Sexuality and Pornography in Mid-Nineteenth Century England* (New York, 1974), p. 253.

30. Ibid., p. 257.

31. [A character in the 'Nausicca' episode of Joyce's *Ulysses*. Ed.]

32. Marcus, *The Other Victorians*, p. 255.

33. Julian Kaye, 'The Wings of Dedalus; Two Stories in *Dubliners*', *Modern Fiction Studies*, 4 (Spring 1958), 37.

34. Sidney Feshbach, 'Death in "An Encounter" ', *James Joyce Quarterly*, 2 (Winter 1965), 85.

7

Uncanny Returns in 'The Dead'

ROBERT SPOO

'The Dead' might be described as Joyce's first sustained fictional enigma. The other fourteen *Dubliners* stories, all composed earlier, contain local puzzles and opacities, but these seem integrated and explicable when compared to the persistent unassimilated strangeness of the final story. This element of the 'strange' (a word that echoes throughout 'The Dead') exists on all levels of the text – plot, character, language, imagery, the very act of narrating – and is particularly arresting in that it emerges within the homely context of the Misses Morkan's annual Christmas dance. In this story the uncanny (*das Unheimliche*, or the 'unhomely') makes its home precisely in *das Heimliche*, in that which is familiar and familial, so that the ambivalent etymological journey that Sigmund Freud in his essay 'The "Uncanny" ' (1919) traces for the word *heimlich* – from 'comfortable' and 'homelike' to 'hidden', 'secret', and 'dangerous'[1] – is played out in Gabriel Conroy's relationships with members of his family, in particular with his wife, Gretta.

We are assured in the opening pages of 'The Dead' that the party 'was always a great affair. ... For years and years it had gone off in splendid style as long as anyone could remember'.[2] This investment in a carefully controlled repetition of success sets the stage for ironic appearances of the uncanny and the emergence of unanticipated, ghostly 'wit' at the expense of hyperconscious sociality. This process is repeated at the level of individual psyches, notably in the gradual dismantling of Gabriel's vigilant, self-absorbed aplomb.

Joyce's text generates an uncanniness in which the frightening is not always distinguishable from the comic (as it occasionally is not in E. T. A. Hoffmann's tale 'The Sand-Man', which Freud analyses in 'The "Uncanny" ').[3] This range or instability of affect, representing one of the chief obstacles to determining meaning, gives 'The Dead' dim affinities, haunting in their elusive precocity, with *Finnegans Wake*.

Freud begins 'The "Uncanny" ' with the complaint that neither aesthetic theory nor medico-psychological literature has adequately accounted for the experience of uncanniness. He notes that in 1906 Ernst Jentsch defined the uncanny as a feeling of 'intellectual uncertainty' in the face of the novel and unfamiliar – uncertainty, for example, about whether an animate being is really alive, or, conversely, whether a lifeless object such as a doll or automaton might not be animate (Freud, pp. 226–7). While crediting Jentsch with important insights, Freud contends that uncanny feelings arise primarily from something other than intellectual uncertainty, something less uncertain and far more disturbing. Taking 'The Sand-Man' as a notable instance of the uncanny in literature, Freud asserts that the source of uncanniness in this tale is not the living female doll, Olympia (as Jentsch would have it), but rather the student Nathaniel's castration complex and his struggle with the father imago, a condition represented in the text by 'the theme of the "Sand-Man" who tears out children's eyes' (Freud, p. 227). Freud thus posits repressed infantile complexes, the once-familiar returning in terrifying forms, as the chief source of Nathaniel's uncanny experiences, an interpretive move that reinforces Freud's lengthy lexicographical demonstration that the meaning of the word *heimlich* 'develops in the direction of ambivalence, until it finally coincides with its opposite, *unheimlich*' (Freud, p. 226).

Thus, according to Freud, the uncanny is 'something which is familiar and old-established in the mind and which has become alienated from it only through the process of repression' (Freud, p. 241). He distinguishes between two classes of uncanniness: the resurfacing of primitive religious beliefs that have been 'surmounted' by modern civilisation (such as the belief in the omnipotence of thoughts, secret injurious powers, the return of the dead); and an analogous revival of infantile complexes that have been 'repressed' in the adult (castration complex, womb fantasies, and so forth). Two forms of the uncanny hold a special fascination for Freud: the encounter with a double, which results from a 'dividing and interchanging of the self', a splitting of the ego into observer and observed (Freud, p. 234); and involuntary repetition, 'a "compulsion to repeat" proceeding from the instinctual impulses and probably inherent in the very nature of the instincts – a compulsion powerful enough to overrule the pleasure principle, lending to certain aspects of the mind their daemonic character' (Freud, p. 238).[4]

This brief, necessarily selective summary of 'The "Uncanny" ' provides a starting point for a discussion of 'The Dead' as well as a basis for rethinking aspects of Freud's essay and extending its implicit but largely undeveloped ideas about literary representation. With minimal extrapolation the uncanny might be defined as a mode of psychic and/or textual representation that disguises repressed affects by means of what Freud calls 'estrangement'. The alienated lustre that estrangement lends to these affects appears at the intersection of the familiar and the unfamiliar, the homely and the hidden, giving uncanny events their special quality, at once harrowing and perversely seductive.[5]

'The Dead' is an uncanny narrative the strangeness of which derives in part from a number of such 'estrangements' – seemingly marginal moments in the text where the once-familiar can be fleetingly glimpsed under its incognito. By adopting a flexible psychoanalytic approach and not restricting it to individual characters' psyches or insisting that all estrangements can be traced to the conscious or unconscious mind of the author, I hope to shed light on a variety of textual 'impediments', to use Jacques Lacan's term: discontinuities, bizarre figurations, and flashes of wit that signal the operation of the unconscious.[6] By the 'unconscious' I do not mean some absolute event or psyche immanent in the text but rather a dynamic, problematic convergence of uncanny *experiences* elicited by the act of reading: the experiences of characters in the story, for example, when they encounter such things as doubling and involuntary repetition, as well as the reader's response to analogous phenomena on the level of textual and intertextual play. In the case of intertextual uncanniness, the once-familiar of a prior text is felt to haunt the present text in estranged yet recognisable forms.

It is important to stress that this convergence of experiences is so overdetermined in Joyce's text that the 'sources' of the uncanny cannot easily be traced at any point. Moreover, as Freud himself noted, the uncanny in literature differs from the uncanny in life inasmuch as literature 'contains the whole of the latter and something more besides, something that cannot be found in real life' (Freud, p. 249). This 'something more', this representational excess, points to the unauthored, autogenetic quality of the uncanny as it operates within the peculiar language of literature.[7] The uncanny is itself uncanny when it makes its home in aesthetic discourse.

This broadly textual adaptation of the uncanny seems warranted by Freud himself, who proposes the concept initially as a way of accounting for aesthetic phenomena not amenable to such traditional categories as the sublime and the beautiful (Freud, pp. 219–20). Unfortunately, Freud's scientific and clinical interests lead him to focus almost exclusively on the *content* (what he calls the 'events' or 'particulars') of Hoffmann's tale, reducing its complex texture to a quarry for corroborative instances. As a result, Freud's attention to the formal, aesthetic dimension of the uncanny, and to the rich grammar of representation implied in his own theory of repression and alienated return, gives way to a bustling positivism and an efficient aetiology; *Wahrheit* easily displaces *Dichtung*,[8] authoritatively converting writing into exemplarity, the signifier into the signified.

Even so, Freud offers some promising directions for exploring the relation between the uncanny and textuality. He notes, for example, that fairy tales, while they often contain uncanny elements, produce no feeling of uncanniness because they postulate a world of unreality from the start, whereas writers who set their tales 'in the world of common reality' readily achieve uncanny effects (Freud, p. 250). Although Freud does not develop the point, it might be argued that realism and naturalism represent a 'secularisation' of literature – a sacrifice, in the interests of verifiability and clear-eyed mimesis, of the poetic and the figurative – analogous to the surmounting of primitive beliefs which Freud says paves the way for the return of those beliefs in estranged forms. Thus, the realistic or naturalistic mode – Joyce's fictional mode in *Dubliners* – would seem to be an especially fertile ground for uncanny visitations by virtue of the resolute rationality of its discourse, a discourse in which surmounted or repressed literariness, the excess of the signifier, returns to haunt the reader.

I largely avoid what in many ways continues to be, despite recent revisionary assaults, the standard approach to 'The Dead', which traces Gabriel's progress toward a final epiphany of enlightenment, whether liberating or paralysing.[9] Instead I will focus on marginal elements that have resisted incorporation into this master narrative and as a result have undergone a sort of critical repression, or at least have remained, for the most part, below the threshold of critical articulation. Various uncanny elements will be considered, but the chief enigma involves the figuring of Michael Furey – the boy who died of love for Gretta Conroy when she was a girl – as Gretta's *child*, a mystery the text hints at in various ways but never directly confronts. As a consequence, Gretta's own passion play of repression and return will emerge as one of the deep, driving forces in the text; her experience will be recognised as a problematic 'double' of Gabriel's more conspicuous psychodrama. [...]

Whether the uncanny takes the form of the once-familiar returning in masquerade, or of doubling, or of involuntary patterns and coincidences, the common factor in all cases is the element of repetition. Yet, clearly, repetition alone does not explain the feeling of uncanniness, for even after the repressed element has been extricated from its estranged husk and revealed as the common denominator of a series of psychic and/or textual enigmas (as in Freud's oedipal decoding of 'The Sand-Man'), a residue of the unexplained remains, and this residue continues to haunt. That the aura of the uncanny cannot be wholly exorcised by rational processes points to the abiding mystery surrounding the source or cause of uncanny events, and to the fact that estrangement, as a mode of representation, does not function merely as a mask that can be peeled away and discarded but actually plays a *constitutive* role in the psyche or text.

These two aspects – the sense of a secret or untraceable 'author' of uncanniness and the realisation that the transformations worked by estrangement are ineradicably part of the psyche's development – contribute to the feeling of helplessness that Freud notes in the experience of uncanny repetition (Freud, p. 237). Stephen Dedalus's definition of Aristotelian terror as 'the feeling which arrests the mind in the presence of whatsoever is grave and constant in human sufferings and unites it with the secret cause' is as much about the inscrutability and durability of the uncanny as it is about the tragic emotion.[10]

The foregoing distinctions between kinds of repetition should help us explore the quality of strangeness in 'The Dead'. Not all instances of repetition, even when they contribute to the register of the 'terrifying', qualify as uncanny. For example, certain phrases in the text seem calculated to reinforce the pervasive sense of death: 'My wife here takes three mortal hours to dress herself' (*D*, p. 177);

'Both of them kissed Gabriel's wife, said she must be perished alive' (D, p. 177); 'As the subject had grown lugubrious it was buried in a silence of the table' (D, p. 201). These thematic promptings are not in themselves uncanny, largely because we can see Joyce building up his effect by specific, programmatic repetitions, not unlike his unabashed deployment of rhetorical figures in the 'Aeolus' episode of *Ulysses* to underscore that episode's theme of rhetoric. This kind of repetition is intentionally strained and verges on the compulsive clowning of Joyce's later writings. In 'The Dead' it produces a droll effect of simulated gothic terror. An analogous case might be that of the uncanny in fairy tales, which, as we have seen, Freud regards as devoid of uncanny effect.

Other forms of repetition in 'The Dead' are more haunting and haunted, however. For example, the phrase 'the snow falling faintly through the universe and faintly falling, like the descent of their last end, upon all the living and the dead' (D, p. 224) grows out of at least two earlier moments in the text: at dinner Mary Jane said that the monks have coffins 'to remind them of their last end' (D, p. 201); and later, as the guests are leaving, we learn that 'the sky seemed to be descending' (D, p. 212). The return of these phrases in Gabriel's final meditation produces an effect of uncanniness, in this particular case because he could have heard only one of the phrases (Mary Jane's), but more generally because the swelling rhythmic sonority and expanding perspective render all attempts to assign the final paragraphs to a single consciousness, to find a psychic home for them, as futile as Gabriel's efforts to hold on to his old, stable ego. Here, the uncanny emerges in the space between psyches, in the breakdown of the text's ostensible commitment to a relatively stable psychogenesis and a naturalistic basis for narrative voice, together with the corresponding ideology of the sovereign subject. The 'fading out' of Gabriel's identity both results from and is a precondition for the strange authority of the final paragraphs, an authority that is paradoxically and disconcertingly 'authorless'.[11]

Certain intertextual returns from earlier *Dubliners* stories add to the uncanny quality of 'The Dead' and further erase the boundaries of identity and narrative voice. In the opening story, 'The Sisters', the young boy imagines a terrifying visitation from his recently deceased friend, the old priest (of whom one of the characters remarks that 'there was something uncanny about him' [D, p. 10]): 'I drew the blankets over my head and tried to think of Christmas. But the grey face still followed me. ... I felt my soul receding into some pleasant and vicious region' (*D*, p. 11). The similarities between this passage and the final scene of 'The Dead' are striking: stretching himself 'cautiously along under the sheets', Gabriel begins to be aware of ghostly 'forms'. 'His soul', we are told in a distinct echo of the earlier story, 'had approached that region where dwell the vast hosts of the dead' (*D*, p. 223). Authority for this resonant repetition is impossible to determine, and the problematic nature of narrative voice in 'The Dead' is ironically underscored by the irruption of language from a most definitely 'authored' first-person narrative into this 'authorless' final section. This erasure of the boundary separating the realistic from the fantastic – the rational and narratable from the haunted and unspeakable – produces an uncanny effect of the type noted by Freud in his discussion of realistic fiction in 'The "Uncanny" '. The intertextual 'haunting' in the final paragraphs of 'The Dead' hints at the presence of a dialogism – to be fully realised in *Ulysses* and *Finnegans Wake* – in which the vast hosts of discourses that make up the 'realistic' mode are permitted to have their ghostly say.

Similarly, a passage from 'A Little Cloud' anticipates Gabriel's vision of universal snow:

> He turned often from his tiresome writing to gaze out of the office window. The glow of a late autumn sunset covered the grass plots and walks. It cast a shower of kindly golden dust on the untidy nurses and decrepit old men who drowsed on the benches; it flickered upon all the moving figures – on the children who ran screaming along the gravel paths and on everyone who passed through the gardens. He watched the scene and thought of life; and (as always happened when he thought of life) he became sad.
>
> (*D*, p. 71)

The human panorama, the comprehensive sympathy, the sweeping cadences intimating a soul on the verge of swooning suggest that this scene is an attenuated 'double' of the final passage of 'The Dead', especially if we allow for the substitution of the sunset's 'golden dust' for snow and of Little Chandler's feeble (and pointedly ironised) meditation on life for Gabriel's night thoughts on death. It is important, however, to avoid ascribing these instances of repetition to intentionalistic practices such as Joycean self-parody, pastiche, allusion, prolepsis, cross-reference, or other features of a text conceived of as consciously predetermined and teleological. One reason why the spontaneous, autogenetic quality of such intertextual returns may seem disorienting, especially to readers whose response has been conditioned by the criticism, is that Joyce critics have consistently argued for a text that is infallibly self-conscious, the product of an almost superhuman authorial intention. The concept of an invisible but ubiquitous 'Arranger', which in one form or another has been invoked for most of Joyce's fiction, is limited precisely insofar as it cannot adequately account for a text such as *Finnegans Wake* or for the pervasive strange or 'estranged' quality of 'The Dead'.[12] The doctrine of the Arranger has the further drawback of eliding or masking the role of interpretation in constituting the ingenuity of Joyce's texts, providing a blanket rationale for narcissistic projections of the reading process onto this convenient authorial demiurge. The Arranger is the 'blank check' in the economy of the Joyce industry.

Another range of textual 'impediments' (to recur to Lacan's term) concerns the pervasive military imagery in 'The Dead'. We encounter such phrases as 'an irregular musketry of applause' (*D*, p. 192); 'Freddy Malins acting as officer with his fork on high' (*D*, p. 206); 'Mary Jane led her recruits' (*D*, p. 184); 'Between these rival ends ran parallel lines of side-dishes' (*D*, p. 196); 'three squads of bottles ... drawn up according to the colours of their uniforms' (*D*, p. 197). Although these metaphors can be rationalised as objective correlatives for the putative battle between Gabriel Conroy and his rival Michael Furey, or as symbolic outcroppings of Gabriel's conflict with himself, such readings seem too monotonal and tendentiously thematic to be fully persuasive. I suggest that this imagery represents a resurfacing, with an estranged difference, of the military and quasi-military metaphors of 'Two Gallants', where the cynical insensitivity with which Corley conducts his love affair is linked to what Joyce called 'the moral code of the soldier and (incidentally) of the gallant'.[13] Joyce adopted this equation from his recent reading of the Italian historian and sociologist Guglielmo Ferrero, whose *L'Europa giovane* (1897) and *Il Militarismo* (1898) attacked the militaristic mentality and the related concept of *galanteria*, with its barely submerged agenda of domination and misogyny.[14]

The possibility that Ferrero's writings and 'Two Gallants' are intertexts is further suggested by such phrases as 'Mr Browne ... gallantly escort[ed] Aunt Julia' (*D*, p. 192) and '[Gabriel] raised his glass of port gallantly' (*D*, p. 205). Gabriel's attitude toward Gretta becomes increasingly 'gallant' as the evening progresses; at the end of the party he is feeling 'proud, joyful, tender, valorous' and longs to 'defend her against something and then to be alone with her' (*D*, p. 213). When his aroused chivalry is later checked by her unresponsiveness, he restrains himself from 'brutal language' and desires 'to be master of her strange mood' (*D*, p. 217). In part, no doubt, Gabriel is reincarnating the attitudes Joyce satirised in Corley and Lenehan, but the broad, unstable deployment of military imagery in 'The Dead' (most of it concentrated in the early part, long before Gabriel becomes gallant) cannot be accounted for solely in terms of Gabriel's psyche or Joyce's satirical intent. Military figures occur so randomly and exhibit such a wide range of tone – including the ghostly 'wit' I mentioned earlier – that they overwhelm all attempts to ground them in some specific psychogenesis or intentionality. In this respect the text as a whole mirrors Gretta's homely yet quite *unheimlich* and disconcerting inscrutability; 'The Dead' simply refuses to allow the reader to be master of its strange mood.

The centrality that 'The Dead' gives to the female as impediment to interpretive mastery is focused in a series of social and personal failures that Gabriel experiences in the course of the evening. His suavity and control are baffled in turn by Lily the caretaker's daughter, Molly Ivors (his professional and intellectual equal), and Gretta in a pattern so marked as to raise the possibility that he is in the grip of a repetition compulsion. Gabriel's repetition of error, yet another sign of uncanniness in the story, hints at a 'death drive' on his part that may connect with his later experience of self-dissolution and communion with the dead. It might also be argued that these repetitions, along with the recurrent image of snow in the story, contribute to a structure of delay, and that, as Elizabeth Wright observes of 'The Sand-Man', 'what is delayed is death'.[15]

Gabriel's need for reiterated proofs of control and his aunts' desire for the annual success of their party reflect in different ways an obsession with keeping the unfamiliar from entering the circle of the 'home', be it psychic or social. This industrious staging of homely experience prepares the way for *das Unheimliche*, which in turn will reintroduce *das Heimliche*, the once-familiar, in estranged and threatening guises. Late in the story, when Gabriel is coming to see the futility of his desire for a night of honeymoon passion with Gretta, he passes in front of the cheval glass and sees 'the face whose expression always puzzled him when he saw it in a mirror' (*D*, p. 218). The feeling of uneasiness at encountering one's reflected image – what Freud called the uncanny effect of the

'double' (Freud, p. 248n) – results from an unconscious defamil-
iarising of the familiar, which in Gabriel's case is related to his
intense conscious willing of the familiar, his need for experience
that is predictable and controllable.

The bibulous Freddy Malins, in almost every way the antithesis
of the responsible Gabriel, is nevertheless Gabriel's 'bad' double,
mirroring him in his intense though conflicted relationship to a
dominating mother and even in certain personal habits, such as 'the
mechanical readjustment of his dress' (*D*, p. 185). (Gabriel fusses
with his clothes and pats his tie nervously throughout the evening.)
As Gabriel's double, the docile, unmarried Freddy uncannily embodies Gabriel's buried self (passivity, oedipal dependence, potential for infantile regression), a self that keeps him perpetually
staging or 'scripting' his own experience, as if, for Gabriel, Eros
needed vigilant coaching lest Thanatos supervene in the form of
entropic repetitions of error, as in any case it seems to do. The
attempt to predetermine Gretta's erotic response and the ironic,
leading questions he puts to her about Michael Furey are crucial
examples of his scripting of experience, and they open the way for
the full emergence of the uncanny late in the story.

[...]

'Strange' is a word consistently associated with Gretta Conroy,
especially in the latter part of the story, and with Gabriel's reaction
to her revelations about Michael Furey ('a strange friendly pity for
her entered his soul' [*D*, p. 222]). [...] Gabriel, at the conclusion of
the party, is hypnotised by Gretta as she stands on the stairs in the
shadow, listening to an old ballad being sung in an upstairs room.
As he remains below, straining to hear the air and 'gazing up at his
wife', he notices that there is 'grace and mystery in her attitude as if
she were a symbol of something', and tries to master the strangeness of this spectacle by mentally turning it into a conventional
piece of art, by assigning Gretta to the popular aesthetic category of
the tableau: '*Distant Music* he would call the picture if he were a
painter' (*D*, p. 210).[16]

This painting of the uncanny female is also a sign of repression of
the maternal body. According to Freud the latter is both strange
and familiar, at once a magical cave and a long-lost home: 'This
unheimlich place [the female genitals] ... is the entrance to the
former *Heim* [home] of all human beings, to the place where each
one of us lived once upon a time and in the beginning' (Freud,
p. 245). Gabriel's own struggle with his mother and with the mater-

nal imago – a struggle he consciously casts as resentment of her disapproval of his 'country cute' wife (D, p. 187) – is projected upon
Gretta and her body, which he characterises here in terms of 'grace
and mystery'. Gabriel's reduction of Gretta's uncanny power proves
only temporary, however; her strangeness will reassert itself, and in
a new register, once they reach the hotel room.

[...]

Gretta Conroy [...] is haunted by the past and by a sense of
regret for things done and opportunities missed. At the end of the
party, as Gabriel stands gazing up at her and transforming her into
a tableau, she is listening to the distantly intoned words of a song,
'The Lass of Aughrim', which a boy named Michael Furey used to
sing when she was living in Galway. The song's strange, elusive
lyrics tell of a love affair between Lord Gregory and a peasant girl,
her abandonment by him, and her return one night in the rain with
her child to seek admission at his door. Only a snatch of the song
appears in the text:

> O, the rain falls on my heavy locks
> And the dew wets my skin,
> My babe lies cold ...

(D, p. 210)

Gretta tells Gabriel that when Michael learned that she was leaving
Galway, he left a sickbed and stood below her window in the rain,
and a short while later died. 'I think he died for me', Gretta says
(D, p. 220). Her descriptions of this frail boy – 'a young boy ...
very delicate' (D, p. 219), 'such a gentle boy' (D, p. 221) – are maternal in their tenderness, and the image of Michael shivering
beneath her window suggests a connection with the cold babe lying
in the arms of the peasant mother in the song.[17]

This mother–child relationship is hinted at in other ways, but so
unobtrusively that the surface of the narrative is barely broken by
the emergent figurations. When Gabriel wonders if she had been in
love with Michael, Gretta answers, 'I was great with him at that
time' (D, p. 220). Her West Country dialect is as strange and multivalent as the language of 'The Lass of Aughrim', and the faint
merging here, beneath the literal sense of her words, of the roles of
lover, mother, and unborn infant generates an uncanny music of
otherness that calmly subverts Gabriel's jealous cross-examining.[18]
His questioning of Gretta – a reversal of the catechism he himself
underwent earlier at the hands of Miss Ivors – has the unintended

effect of assisting at the birth of Gretta's long-gestating memory of Michael and her girlhood. Earlier, as they climb the stairs to their hotel room, Gretta is described as being 'bowed in the ascent, her frail shoulders curved as with a burden, her skirt girt tightly about her' (D, p. 215). She is delivered of this burden of the past with the help of Gabriel's unwitting midwifery. (The maieutic method of Socratic dialectic may be a remote analogue here.) After she has fallen asleep, her labour over, Gabriel muses on 'how she who lay beside him had locked in her heart for so many years that image of her lover's eyes when he had told her that he did not wish to live' (D, p. 223).

This image of the past locked away in the womb/heart reappears in *Ulysses* when Stephen is helping his student Sargent, another delicate boy, with his algebra. Stephen finds him 'ugly and futile', but decides that 'someone had loved him, borne him in her arms and in her heart'.[19] Sensing a similarity between Sargent and himself at that age, he thinks of their pasts in terms of repression and return: 'Secrets, silent, stony sit in the dark palaces of both our hearts: secrets weary of their tyranny: tyrants, willing to be dethroned' (U, 2.170–2). Much later, at the end of 'Circe', Bloom's long-dead infant son, Rudy, magically appears to him with 'a delicate mauve face' (U, 15.4965). In this theatrically uncanny finale to an episode in which Bloom gives birth to a brood of dream children, the return of his painful past is figured as a delicate boy, dead for years but re-animated, like Michael Furey, by a series of psychological shocks administered to the parent.[20]

Freud suggests that the uncanny feeling produced by dolls and automata may originate in the childhood belief that dolls are alive or can be brought to life (Freud, p. 233). Marginal, easily ignored images of dolls, infants, and children appear in 'The Dead' long before the hotel room scene. During Mary Jane's piano piece, Gabriel's wandering attention lights on embroidered pictures of 'the balcony scene in *Romeo and Juliet* ... [and] of the two murdered princes in the Tower' (D, p. 186), pictures which combine themes of *Liebestod* and *Kindermord*[21] to the point of overdetermination (suggesting also Gretta's sense of responsibility for Michael Furey's death). Earlier, noticing that Lily has grown into a young woman, Gabriel realises that he 'had known her when she was a child and used to sit on the lowest step nursing a rag doll' (D, p. 177). A few minutes later, stung by Gretta's flippancy about his insistence that she wear 'goloshes', Gabriel retorts, 'It's nothing very wonderful but Gretta thinks it very funny because she says the word reminds her of Christy Minstrels' (*D*, p. 181). By 'Christy Minstrels' Gabriel probably means blackface minstrels in a general sense (for by this period the term no longer referred exclusively to the American troupe of that name), or the phrase may even be a polite circumlocution for 'negro' or 'black'. (Later in the story Freddy Malins praises the singing of the 'negro chieftain' in the pantomime, to the embarrassment of the other dinner guests [*D*, p. 198].) In any case, it is the *word* 'goloshes' that reminds Gretta of black or blackface figures, and the missing verbal link is evidently 'golliwog', the popular term for a grotesque black doll inspired by a series of children's books featuring an animated doll named Golliwogg.[22]

It is interesting that 'golliwog', the vaguely homophonic link with 'goloshes', does not actually emerge into the text but remains beneath the surface, hinted at but never directly indicated. This black doll or dark infant is submerged in the same way that Gretta's relationship with Michael Furey has remained buried for so many years. (Joyce later referred in a poem to the Michael Furey figure as a 'dark lover'.[23] Critics have suggested that the galoshes are a symbol of sterility and prophylaxis; it might be added that what Gabriel is preventing conception *of* is Gretta's relationship to her past. Only fleetingly glimpsed at this point in terms of dolls, her girlhood will come to full term later in the evening in the form of the babe/lover Michael Furey.

The 'impossible' imaging of Michael as Gretta's infant never reaches full articulation in the text, but remains below the threshold of textual consciousness and acquires a good deal of its uncanny power from precisely this occultation. Like other enigmas in 'The Dead', the uncanny babe might be said to be an 'encysted' element, a pocket of repressed material (in this case, Gretta's) resisting assimilation into the text and receiving its particular form through the work of estrangement.

Joyce's notes for *Exiles* shed some light on this repressed material. Written in 1913, seven years after he completed 'The Dead', these notes allowed Joyce to set down memories (chiefly those of his companion, Nora) that might help him with the writing of his semi-autobiographical play. In order to give depth to the character Bertha (the figure based on Nora), Joyce recorded snippets of Nora's early life in Galway, including images of her young admirer, Sonny Bodkin, the original of Michael Furey: 'Graveyard at Rahoon by moonlight where Bodkin's grave is. He lies in the grave.

She sees his tomb (family vault) and weeps. The name is homely. ...
He is dark, unrisen, killed by love and life, young. The earth holds
him' (*E*, p. 152). By 'the earth' Joyce partly means Bertha/Nora
herself (associated, like Molly Bloom, with that element) or, more
specifically, her *womb*. A few lines later, relating Bodkin's grave to
the poet Shelley's in Rome, Joyce writes, 'Shelley whom she has
held in her *womb or grave* rises' (emphasis added). [...]

As intertexts and interconnections multiply, the submerged figure
of the uncanny babe in 'The Dead' begins to take on a more definite
form. The womb/tomb of Bertha/Nora is a later secondary revision
of what Joyce had first figured as Gretta's 'heart', in which she had
'locked ... for so many years that image of her lover's eyes' (*D*,
p. 223). In the notes for *Exiles* Joyce writes further of Sonny
Bodkin that he is 'her buried life, her past', and adds: 'His attendant
images are the trinkets and toys of girlhood (bracelet, cream sweets,
palegreen lily of the valley, the convent garden)' (*E*, p. 152). Just as
Bodkin represents Bertha/Nora's past, so Michael Furey is an estranged figure for Gretta's girlhood, her 'buried life'. Burial was one
of Freud's favourite metaphors for repression, the process 'by which
something in the mind is at once made inaccessible and preserved,
[a] burial of the sort to which Pompeii fell a victim'.[24] Gretta has
had to bury her past in order to become the wife of Gabriel
Conroy, a man who feels ashamed of his wife's simple, rural origins
and unconsciously agrees with his mother's class-based assessment
of her as 'country cute' (*D*, p. 187). Gretta has had to put away her
childhood, to repress it for the sake of her marriage, but it returns
on the evening of the Misses Morkan's party in the form of the
babe/lover Michael Furey. The alienated, intensely charged form in
which this past returns is some measure of how violently Gretta has
had to deny it.

[...]

Discussing Freud's analysis of 'The Sand-Man' and his emphasis
on oedipal themes, Hélène Cixous notes that his 'minimising of [the
female doll] Olympia leads to the focus on Nathaniel'.[25] Similarly,
critics have made much of Gabriel Conroy's 'journey westward'
(*D*, p. 223), but less attention has been paid to the fact that it is
Gretta who travels *back* to her origins in the West, that 'The Dead'
is as much about her journey of reunion as about her husband's
discovery of new psychic terrain. Whatever Gabriel's final swoon
into self-dissolution may mean, whether it is spiritual death that
beckons to him or some other undiscovered country, his wife has

already reached the bourne of the once-familiar, a very specific locale long known to her but in recent years under ban. Gretta's deracination has so thoroughly alienated her from her life in Galway from family and friends, that it has taken years for this 'buried life' to resurface, and when it does, it returns in the weird, estranged form of a boy lover who doubles as her own infant. She was 'great with him at that time', even before she met Gabriel, and the slow, dark birth has taken half a lifetime to reach full term.

It is interesting to compare this uncanny babe/lover with a similar fantasia in H. D.'s *Helen in Egypt*. H. D.'s revisionary epic begins with the countermyth that Helen spent the Trojan War safely hidden away in Egypt while a phantom Helen paced the ramparts of Troy. In this new telling, Helen and Achilles become lovers after the war, and, at one point in her life, Helen concludes that Paris is the child of this union:

> he of the House of the Enemy,
> Troy's last king (this is no easy thing
> to explain, this subtle genealogy)

> is Achilles' son, he is incarnate
> Helen-Achilles' he, my first lover,
> was created by my last.[26]

Paris, Helen's 'first lover', becomes her child, and her last lover, Achilles, the child's father. Helen's relationship to her past, like Gretta Conroy's, is troubled and censored, and this blockage gives rise, in the course of Helen's intense broodings, to uncanny figurations, as in Joyce's text. Just as Achilles has sired his enemy and eventual slayer, so Gabriel is the 'father' of Michael Furey, the 'impalpable and vindictive being' he senses 'coming against him' as Gretta unfolds her past in the hotel room (*D*, p. 220). Gabriel has created Michael in the sense that he is largely responsible for Gretta's renunciation of her origins. But the 'subtle genealogy' that makes Gretta the mother of her own first lover also strangely empowers her in relation to her last one, and by the end of the story it is Gabriel who considers his past futile and negated. The uncanny proliferation of female roles is a sign of Gretta's new-found power and self-knowledge.

Gretta's psychodrama is the dark 'double' of Gabriel's more conspicuous sufferings, partly because hers is the narrative that is most frequently and conveniently ignored by critics, and because the true source of Gabriel's sufferings – his wife's occluded past – lies hidden from him even as it functions deep within his psyche, playing a large part in his self-definition as an Irishman and in his relationship with her. Gretta has already set out for Galway by the time Gabriel reaches his decision to journey westward. [...] Gretta's journey is already fully under way in the strange replies Gabriel elicits from her in the hotel room, his pilgrimage, by comparison, is imitative and of a lesser intensity. Where Gretta already is, Gabriel can only hope to be.

But speculation about the characters' afterlife (in both senses of the word – and such speculation is common in criticism of 'The Dead' – is always a covert attempt to contain the problematic nature of the text. The 'textual energetics' of the story (to use Peter Brooks's phrase),[27] which I have argued arise from the pervasive, multivalent operation of the uncanny, refuse containment and closure, just as they cannot be traced to a single source or set of sources, however construed. I have largely resisted, for example, the text's invitation to an oedipal reading, though Gabriel's mother conflict and the virtual absence of his father in his conscious thoughts might be read as a 'source' of the uncanny babe figuration, making the latter a sort of magic-lantern projection of Gabriel's un-mastered infantile scenario. The oedipal clue might equally be traced to Joyce himself, whose relationship to Nora quickly became infantile and filial in times of stress, as when he wrote her from Dublin in 1909 just after being informed (falsely) of her infidelity: 'O that I could nestle in your womb like a child born of your flesh and blood, be fed by your blood, sleep in the warm secret gloom of your body!' (*Letters*, 2:248). (Curiously, Joyce mentions in the same letter that he has just been to the Gresham Hotel, the setting for Gretta's revelations about Michael Furey.) But the oedipal sce-nario as such, with its male agenda and its limited exegetical power outside Gabriel's (or Joyce's) personal narrative, is unlikely to elicit and at the same time respect the multiform strangeness of this text, which seems in any case to be generated by female scenarios and occlusions of female experience.[28]

Although I have linked the uncanny power of Michael Furey to Gretta's repression of her past, I have not intended this as an ex-haustive psychogenetic explanation of the uncanny in the story. The babe/lover figure – only one 'symptom' of the uncanny among many here – is overdetermined [...]. That the uncanny cannot be 'cured' by critical exegesis points also to what I have called the constitutive role of estrangement. As a mode of representation, estrangement is not merely a mask covering the pain of the once-familiar but is actually fused to the textual-psychic face beneath. In this respect, as in others, 'The Dead' may have more in common with *Finnegans Wake* than with any other work by Joyce.[29] As critics have noted, the bizarre verbal density of *Finnegans Wake* is generated by a kind of dream-work, a process that renders manifest and latent contents inseparable from each other in the same way that estrangement constitutes signification in 'The Dead'. Moreover, both texts are autogenetic and author-less, and refuse, or perpetually absorb, efforts to account for them in terms of sources, authors, Arrangers, or other finite causes of textual effects. Like *Finnegans Wake*, 'The Dead' is incurable and incorrigible.

From *Joyce: The Return of the Repressed*, ed. Susan Stanford Friedman (Ithaca, NY, 1993), pp. 89–100; 103; 105–13.

Notes

[Robert Spoo's essay is a very thorough revision of the most famous story in *Dubliners*, 'The Dead'. Spoo analyses the story from a Freudian point of view, shifting attention from Gabriel's epiphany at the end of the story (the dominant critical reading) to elements of the 'uncanny' found in Gretta Conroy's love for Michael Furey. Spoo interprets Michael Furey as Gretta's symbolic child, a mystery that the text unconsciously hints at but never directly represents. Although Spoo refers to the psychoanalytic ideas of Lacan, as do the essays (2, 3, 4) by Rabaté, Henke, and Norris, it is to Freud's intriguing concept of the 'uncanny' that the essay is mainly indebted. For Spoo the 'uncanny' or 'unhomely' is discovered in the very ordinary family life and home of Gabriel Conroy. Spoo's essay, however, is indebted to the Lacanian revolution in psychoanalysis to the extent that he locates the origin of the 'uncanny' to be within the language of the text of the story, rather than in the psyches of the fictional characters or in that of Joyce the author. Sections of the essay which deal with the story's inter-textual relations to Ibsen have had to be omitted. Ed.]

1. Sigmund Freud, 'The "Uncanny" ' in *The Standard Edition of the Complete Psychological Works*, ed. James Strachey et al. (London, 1955), vol.17; hereafter cited in the text as Freud.

2. James Joyce, *Dubliners*, ed. Robert Scholes, in consultation with Richard Ellmann (New York, 1967), pp. 175–6; hereafter cited in the text as *D*.

3. For a discussion of the relationship between the uncanny and the joke, see Elizabeth Wright, *Psychoanalytic Criticism: Theory in Practice* (London, 1984), pp. 137–50.

4. Freud here alludes to his theory of the repetition compulsion in *Beyond the Pleasure Principle* (1920), a work he drafted in the same year that he completed 'The Uncanny'.

5. I have intentionally blurred the distinction between the uncanny in life and the uncanny in fiction on the grounds that much of psychic life is inaccessible to us except in represented forms (such as accounts of dreams). Wright, in *Psychoanalytic Criticism*, pp. 143–50, argues that Freud makes a positivistic effort to keep this distinction intact in 'The "Uncanny" ' but that the effort fails in a number of 'uncanny' ways.

6. Jacques Lacan, *The Four Fundamental Concepts of Psychoanalysis*, trans. Alan Sheridan (New York, 1981), p. 25.

7. For a parallel use of the term 'autogenesis' to point to the ambiguity of a text's representation of individual minds, see Elizabeth Brunazzi, 'La Narration de l'autogenèse dans *La Tentation de saint Antoine* et dans *Ulysses*' in *'Scribble' 2: Joyce et Flaubert*, ed. Claude Jacquet and André Topia (Paris, 1990), pp. 123–4.

8. [*Wahrheit* and *Dichtung* are German for, respectively, truth and poetry. Ed.]

9. Interpretations that resist the standard reading of 'The Dead' in one way or another include Ruth Bauerle, 'Date Rape, Mate Rape: A Liturgical Interpretation of "The Dead" ', in *New Alliances in Joyce Studies*, ed. Bonnie Kime Scott (Newark, 1988); Ross Chambers, 'Gabriel Conroy Sings for his Supper, or Love Refused', in *Modern Critical Interpretations: James Joyce's 'Dubliners'*, ed. Harold Bloom (New York, 1988); Tilly Eggers, 'What is a Woman ... a Symbol Of?' *James Joyce Quarterly*, 18 (1981), 379–95; R. B. Kershner, ' "The Dead": Women's Speech and Tableau', in *Joyce, Bakhtin, and Popular Literature: Chronicles of Disorder* (Chapel Hill, NC, 1989); Garry Leonard, 'Joyce and Lacan: "The Woman" as a Symptom of "Masculinity" ', in "The Dead" ', *James Joyce Quarterly*, 28 (1991), 451–72; Margot Norris, 'Stifled Back Answers: The Gender Politics of Art in Joyce's "The Dead" ', *Modern Fiction Studies* 35 (1989), 479–503; and Vincent P. Pecora, 'Social Paralysis and the Generosity of the Word: Joyce's "The Dead" ', ch. 6 of *Self and Form in Modern Narrative* (Baltimore, 1989). None of these critics ignores, or fully succeeds in escaping, the traditional focus on Gabriel, and my reading is no exception in this respect. Chambers and Kershner in particular note 'uncanny' elements in 'The Dead',

10. James Joyce, *A Portrait of the Artist as a Young Man*, ed. Chester G. Anderson and Richard Ellmann (New York, 1964), p. 204.

11. The last scene of John Huston's generally successful film adaptation of 'The Dead' (Vestron Pictures, 1987) fails in attempting to convert what I call this strange authority into Gabriel's own first-person voice. The naturalistic premise is simply no longer viable at this point. For different approaches to the question of voice and narrative authority in 'The Dead', see Hugh Kenner, 'The Uncle Charles Principle', ch. 2 of *Joyce's Voices* (Berkeley, CA, 1978); and Janet Egleson Dunleavy, 'The Ectoplasmic Truthtellers of "The Dead" ', *James Joyce Quarterly*, 21 (1984), 307–19.

12. The 'Arranger', a sort of emanation of Joyce himself deduced from the elaborate interconnections in *Ulysses*, was first proposed by David Hayman in *'Ulysses': The Mechanics of Meaning* (Englewood Cliffs, NJ, 1970), and developed ingeniously thereafter by Hugh Kenner in his writings on Joyce.

13. Joyce's letter of May 5, 1906, to Grant Richards, in *Letters of James Joyce*, vol. 2, ed. Richard Ellmann (New York, 1966), p. 133; hereafter cited in the text as *Letters*.

14. For analyses of Ferrero's influence on Joyce, see Edward Brandabur, *A Scrupulous Meanness: A Study of Joyce's Early Work* (Urbana, IL, 1971), pp. 95–8; Dominice Manganiello, *Joyce's Politics* (London, 1980), pp. 46–57; Susan L. Humphreys, 'Ferrero Etc: James Joyce's Debt to Guglielmo Ferrero', *James Joyce Quarterly*, 16 (1979), 239–51; and Robert Spoo, ' "Una Piccola Nuvoletta": Ferrero's *Young Europe* and Joyce's Mature *Dubliners* Stories', *James Joyce Quarterly*, 24 (1987), 401–10.

15. Wright, *Psychoanalytic Criticism*, p. 147.

16. On the tableau and its centrality to Gabriel's erotic imagination, see Kershner, *Joyce, Bakhtin and Popular Literature*, pp. 144–5.

17. Richard Ellmann observes that Gretta is 'a woman with genuine maternal sympathy, which she extends both to the dead boy who loved her and to her inadequate husband', in *James Joyce*, rev. edn (New York, 1982), p. 295.

18. Kershner, *Joyce, Bakhtin and Popular Literature*, p. 150, notes in passing that the 'ambiguities surrounding fathers, mothers, and lovers are echoed faintly in Joyce's story by the suggestions that Michael is a sort of son to Gretta, just as Gabriel is a sort of father.'

19. James Joyce, *Ulysses*, ed. Hans Walter Gabler et al. (New York, 1986), 2:140; hereafter cited in the text as *U*, with episode and line numbers.

20. Images of pregnancy and babies in 'The Dead' may have been influenced by the circumstances of the story's composition. Joyce conceived the idea for the story, or at least its title, in Rome in 1906, but was too overworked and unhappy to begin it. When he did come to

write it almost a year later, he was recovering from rheumatic fever and had to dictate the ending to his brother Stanislaus. The story was finished in September 1907 (see Ellmann, *James Joyce*, pp. 263–4). This long gestation combined with Joyce's illness may have rendered the process of composition itself somewhat uncanny, as it was for T. S. Eliot when he drafted parts of *The Waste Land* almost without conscious thought (or, as he put it, 'in a trance') while recovering from a nervous breakdown. It may also be relevant that Joyce's companion, Nora, was pregnant during this period; their daughter Lucia was born on July 26, 1907.

21. [*Liebestod* is German for a love that results in death, and refers to the conclusion of *Romeo and Juliet*; *Kindermord* is German for child murder. Ed.]

22. The American-born British illustrator Florence Upton (d. 1922) was the originator of the *Golliwogg* series, picture books with simple rhymes written by her mother, Bertha; the first Golliwogg story was published in London in 1895, and a dozen more titles appeared between that time and 1908. The term 'golliwog' was in general use at the turn of the century most often in reference to the golliwog doll. [...] In the 'Nausicca' episode of *Ulysses*, Cissy Caffrey is described as having 'golliwog curls' (*U*, 13: 270). Golliwog dolls, still given to children in Britain and Ireland, are topped with fuzzy shocks of hair.

23. In 'She Weeps over Rahoon', a poem revisiting the Michael Furey theme which Joyce composed in 1912, a female figure mourns her dead 'dark lover' (*Collected Poems* [New York, 1957], p. 50). The phrase also appears in Joyce's notes for *Exiles* (New York, 1951), p. 152; hereafter cited in the text as *E*.

24. Sigmund Freud, *Delusions and Dreams in Jensen's 'Gradiva'*, in *The Standard Edition*, vol. 9, p. 40.

25. Hélène Cixous, 'Fiction and Its Phantoms: A Reading of Freud's *Das Unheimliche* (The "Uncanny")', *New Literary History*, 7 (1976), 535.

26. H. D., *Helen in Egypt* (New York, 1961), pp. 184–5.

27. Peter Brooks, *Reading for the Plot: Design and Intention in Narrative* (New York, 1985), p. 123.

28. Though beyond the scope of this essay, Freud's reading of the female Oedipus complex and its 'resolution' in the birth of a child which symbolically compensates for the absent penis could be related to Gretta and the uncanny babe figuration. See especially Lacan's analysis of this female Oedipal scenario, in *Feminine Sexuality*, ed. Juliet Mitchell and Jacqueline Rose (New York, 1985), pp. 101ff. I am grateful to Joseph A. Kestner for reminding me of this possibility.

29. In *Wandering and Return in 'Finnegans Wake': An Integrative Approach to Joyce's Fictions* (Princeton, NJ, 1991), Kimberly J. Devlin uses Freud's conception of the uncanny to characterise the experience of reading the *Wake*, arguing that Joyce's previous writings return in distorted yet ultimately recognisable forms in his final work.

8

'Araby': The Exoticised and Orientalised Other

VINCENT J. CHENG

Joyce claimed that 'My intention [in *Dubliners*] was to write a chapter of the moral history of my country',[1] and that in so doing 'I have taken the first step towards the spiritual liberation of my country'.[2] If an *intentional/authorial* reading of *Dubliners* thus demands a moral history of the city as 'the centre of paralysis',[3] the stories in *Dubliners* nevertheless provide us with a *symptomatic* reading of the cultural and political histories and tensions of Dublin at the turn of the century – as we shall see repeatedly in looking at these stories. One cultural symptom of the desire for spiritual liberation manifested itself in the various and deeply embedded cultural representations and encodings of such desire within the appropriated images of an exotic Other, especially the Orient; these are the cultural *idées reçues* best depicted by Edward Said's compelling deconstruction of 'Orientalism' as 'the corporate institution for dealing with the Orient … Orientalism as a Western style for dominating, restructuring, and having authority over the Orient'.[4]

A crucial aspect of Orientalism is that the Orient and the exotic other provide for the European self both a *topos* and a *tropos* for 'spiritual liberation', for imagined rebellion, freedom, escape, and licence (even licentiousness) – as a hidden self that was purportedly other, and which resisted the sociopolitical encodings of a known and repressive cultural system and hegemony, allowing for an exploration (both in geographic actuality and in the mind's eye) of the unknown and mysterious heart of darkness: as Said notes further, 'European culture gained in strength and identity by setting itself off against the Orient as a sort of surrogate and even underground self'.[5] As Homi Bhabha points out: '[Orientalism] is, on the one hand, a topic of learning, discovery, practice; on the other, it is the site of dreams, images, fantasies, myths, obsessions and requirements';[6] a discipline of learning and power, on the one hand, but also a fantasy of the Other. The Orient and the racialised exotic Other thus became a culturally constructed repository (what V. G. Kiernan called 'Europe's collective daydream of the Orient)',[7] for the occidental self's drive for difference, mystery, subversion, irrationality, and otherness: 'Orientalism was ultimately a political vision of reality whose structure promoted the difference between the familiar (Europe, the West, "us") and the strange (the Orient, the East, "them")'.[8] Joyce's texts, as we shall see, are at once deeply interwoven with received representations of the romance of the Orient, of the Orient/Other/Exotic as a site of imaginative 'othering' – as well as simultaneously participating in an evolving, genetic scrutiny and critique of such processes of othering and essentialising.

It should be clear at this point that this chapter has introduced a concept of otherness and of the 'other' that varies somewhat from, but is also fundamentally related to and dependent on, the idea of the 'other' explored in the previous chapter. That chapter had analysed the other as the constructed product of an imagined and absolute *difference* from the self, a discursive repository of all that is repugnant to the self, and whose very presence *within* the self is denied and repressed in order to construct the self's own self-image and subjectivity; such a process repeatedly figures the other as primitive, barbaric, bestial, sexually rapacious, stupid, and so on – in the manner in which the English constructed and represented the Irish (as well as other 'races') during the nineteenth century. The current chapter elaborates a somewhat different 'other' – that product of unacknowledged, unauthorised *desire* (beyond the acceptable bounds of the culture's norms): not so much what the self cannot acknowledge as what it cannot have. Thus, for example, the Orientalised Other becomes the imagined locus for the exotic, voluptuousness, *jouissance*, excess, sexual licence, and so on. These two versions of otherness, while obviously differing, are not at all at odds, but merely respond to the various discursive needs of the culture. Since the imagined other is always a construction of the self, it is always *different*, always a result of (and a response to) the specific situation of the imagining subject or self (or culture) that is producing it. Each of these constructions (otherness as difference, otherness as desire) serves different needs within the cultural discourse, but they are not fully distinct from each other; rather, they not only reinforce each other but – both being based on an imagined difference – repeatedly collapse into each other; both are products of a racist ideology and both are central to the discourses of imperialism. Indeed, a main focus in this chapter is to suggest how – in the specific Irish case as represented in *Dubliners* – each of these versions of otherness is always already contaminated by and dependent on the other one. As Said has amply demonstrated, not only had Orientalism 'kept intact the separateness of the Orient, its eccentricity, its backwardness' within the West's 'division of races into advanced and backward ... or European–Aryan and Oriental–African',[9] but, furthermore, such a division of absolute difference went cheek by jowl with the cultural imagining that constructed the Orient as the arena of untold *luxe et volupté*. It is these connections, and their implications, that the current chapter pursues.

[...]

'Araby' begins with the information that 'North Richmond Street, being blind, was a quiet street ... The other houses of the street ... gazed at one another with brown imperturbable faces' (*D*, p. 29).[10] These are the same brown houses which are described in *Stephen Hero* as 'those brown brick houses which seem the very incarnation of Irish paralysis'.[11] While the brown houses 'gaze' at one another imperturbably, their inability to see beyond their own paralysis is suggested in the metonymic invocation of 'blindness' attached to North Richmond Street – and, in fact, in the atmosphere of Joyce's own childhood spent in such paralysis. For in 1894 the Joyces were living at 17 Richmond Street North, in the very house described in the story. During May 14 to May 19 of that year, the 'Araby Bazaar' came to Dublin – an event well and carefully documented by a number of previous studies of *Dubliners* and which I will not recapitulate in detail here.[12] The event had been advertised by a large commercial poster announcing 'Araby in Dublin' (in large, exotic lettering) as a 'Grand Oriental Fete'; the poster pictures an Arab riding a camel, lists the entrance fee as one shilling, and mentions the Jervis Street Hospital (presumably as a charity beneficiary).[13] This is the bazaar referred to in Joyce's story.

This travelling bazaar was a local manifestation of the wide-spread Orientalist interest in 'Araby' prevalent in popular Western culture of the time. For example, a year earlier, the 1893 World Exhibition in Chicago featured something called the 'Midway Plaisance': it was, as Luther Luedtke has documented, 'a teeming bazaar ... out of the *Thousand and One Nights*. When President Grover Cleveland inaugurated the Exhibition on May 1, 1893, it is reported that Algerian and Egyptian belly-dancers dropped their veils along the parade route in tribute. If much was revealed, even more was suggested. The "Street, in Cairo" became famous before the Fair was a week old ...'[14]

The young boy narrating 'Araby' is much like the narrators of the first two stories, a romantic and sensitive boy who likes to read, especially stories of romance and adventure such as *The Abbot* (by Sir Walter Scott), *The Devout Communicant* and *The Memoirs of Vidocq* (*D*, p. 29); his romantic, Gothic tastes are revealed by his admission that he liked the last of these three books best 'because its leaves were yellow' (*D*, p. 29). Yellow leaves also suggest fall; and an impending Fall from grace and loss of Edenic innocence are prefigured by his immediate description, at this point, of 'the wild garden behind the house [which] contained a central apple-tree' (*D*, p. 29).

The object of the boy's romantic obsessions is his friend Mangan's sister, whose sensuality bewitches him: 'Her dress swung as she moved her body and the soft rope of her hair tossed from side to side ... I kept her brown figure always in my eye ... I had never spoken to her, except for a few casual words, and yet her name was like a summons to all my foolish blood' (*D*, p. 30). Mangan's sister induces in the boy a rapturous ecstasy of chivalric romance and religious adoration, as he imagines her even while he wanders through the noise of city streets and markets and 'the shrill litanies of shop-boys':

> Her image accompanied me even in places the most hostile to romance ... These [street] noises converged in a single sensation of life for me: I imagined that I bore my chalice safely through a throng of foes. Her name sprang to my lips at moments in strange prayers and praises which I myself did not understand ...
>
> (*D*, p. 31)

In detailing what the boy calls 'my confused adoration' with a Christian diction involving 'litanies', 'chalice', and 'strange prayers and praises', Joyce partakes in the language of the Holy Grail and of religious quests/crusades to the Holy Land. These mark a convergence between religious adoration of a feminine goddess/Madonna (the sacred cup/chalice/grail as mythical image for the feminine) as the adoration of Our Lady, and the medieval/chivalric courtly tradition of romantic Love as the neo-religious adoration, of one's own Lady. The boy partakes in the female idolisation and deification that is part of both the Romance tradition of courtly love and the Christian essentialising of woman around the desired figure of the Virgin (as one term in the Madonna/Whore binary; more on that later). In so doing, the boy appropriates Mangan's flesh-and-blood sister and objectifies her into an essentialised image of the Madonna, the functional inspiration and Holy Grail ('Her image accompanied me ... [as] I imagined that I bore my chalice safely through a throng of foes') by which the ego images its own desire as a projected and objectified Other; this moment is a prototype for the traditional essentialising of Woman in Western Christian patriarchy.

Appropriately, the adolescent male desire for a feminine Other here is intertwined in the story itself with the exotic and mysterious East: 'When she addressed the first words to me I was so confused that I did not know what to answer. She asked me was I going to *Araby*. I forget whether I answered yes or no. It would be a splendid bazaar, she said; she would love to go' (*D*, p. 31). 'Going to Araby' is precisely the literal as well as figurative curve of the young boy's desire, and the link between Woman and Araby is predetermined in a patriarchal Christian, Western society. For 'Desire', in its broadest sense, can be thought of as a longing for a personal, sexual, or cultural otherness, for difference, for a union with the exotic, the alien, the strange: to get at, to quest and find, to become one with, something outside of the self – that 'pleasant and vicious region' which is the Persia of the mind. Indeed, the 'Orient' (whatever that amorphous word may mean) has always served that function for the Western imagination – which has for centuries pictured the East as the mysterious Other, the inscrutable Orient, a feminised entity to be desired, seduced, explored, and conquered – in what Chandra Mohanty terms the 'Western ideological and political project [of humanism] which involves the necessary recuperation of the "East" and "Woman" as Others'.[15] As Lisa Lowe points out in *Critical Terrains: French and British Orientalisms*: 'Such associations of orientalism with romanticism are not coincidental, for the two situations of desire – the occidental fascination with the Orient and the male lover's passion for his female beloved – are structurally similar. Both depend on a structure that locates an Other – as woman, as oriental scene – as inaccessible, different, beyond.'[16]

In describing his response to what he calls the 'magical name' (*D*, p. 34) of Araby, our young boy almost seems in part aware of the dynamics of such Orientalised 'othering' grafted onto sexual/romantic 'othering' and desire: 'At night in my bedroom and by day in the classroom her image came between me and the page I strove to read. The syllables of the word *Araby* were called to me through the silence in which my soul luxuriated and cast an Eastern enchantment over me ... I had hardly any patience with the serious work of life which ... stood between me and my *desire*' (*D*, p. 32; my emphasis). As with the boy's dream of Persia in 'The Sisters', the fabulous Arabia here is that magical place associated with the exotic, the mysterious, the lush East: the distant lands of untold wealth and unimaginably sensual entertainments, of the *Thousand and One Nights*, of Scheherazade, the Caliph of Baghdad, the *Rubáiyát*, the land of the Phoenix and mysterious rituals, harems, houris, and Grand Oriental Fetes. The bazaar itself probably took its name from a popular song at the time, 'I'll Sing Thee Songs of Araby', which participated in just such exoticisation and othering of the mysterious East.

> I'll sing thee songs of Araby,
> And tales of far Cashmere,
> Wild tales to cheat thee of a sigh,
> Or charm thee to a tear ...
> (*D*, p. 468)

In both religious history and in this boy's personal story, Araby is the site of a 'holy' quest which masks con-quest (and desire) under the guise of religious zeal. Commentators have noted how Joyce puns on the boy's 'beginning to idle' in his idolatry of Mangan's sister. Such is the nature of both Orientalist and feminine 'othering'; Said notes that Orientalism was 'a reconstructed religious impulse, a naturalised supernaturalism'; 'the Orient was a place of pilgrimage' based on 'the Romantic idea of restorative reconstruction (natural supernaturalism)'.[17]

While 'Araby' is a 'magical name' for the boy, Mangan's sister is given no name of her own in the story – for she functions as a female blank page awaiting his male inscription. As Hélène Cixous points out: 'what is called "other" … is the other in a hierarchically organised relationship in which the same [the self] is what rules, *names*, defines, and assigns "its" other … the reduction of a "person" to a "nobody" to the position of "other" – the inexorable plot of racism.'[18] What identity Mangan's sister has is linked with the name of her brother Mangan and, in Joyce's mind, with the Irish poet James Clarence Mangan, a favourite of Joyce's. One of Mangan's best-known poems, and one of Joyce's favourites, is 'Dark Rosaleen', about a young girl who figures for Ireland herself (Dark Rosaleen is a traditional name for Ireland). Thus, Joyce invites us to see Mangan's nameless sister, who is described only as a 'brown figure' (*D*, p. 30), as a cipher or figure for Ireland herself in a nationalised extension of feminine 'othering'.

In 1902 Joyce wrote an essay on 'James Clarence Mangan', which he then reworked in 1907 into a lecture with the same title, delivered at the Università Popolare in Trieste. In the latter, he calls Mangan 'the most significant poet of the modern Celtic world, and one of the most inspired singers that ever used the lyric form in any country' (significantly, he links the dead Mangan with the Irish/English question by suggesting that 'Mangan will be accepted by the Irish as their national poet on the day when the conflict will be decided between my native land and the foreign powers').[19] Mangan was a Romantic poet who claimed that many of his poems were translations from the Arabic (Joyce wrote that 'it appears that he had some knowledge of oriental languages, probably some Sanskrit and Arabic').[20] Significantly, Joyce associates Mangan's Irish romanticism with both the Middle East and with religious-chivalric-romantic questing:

> East and West meet in that personality (we know how), images interweave there like soft, luminous scarves, the words shine and ring like the links in a coat of mail, and whether he sings of Ireland or of Istamboul, his prayer is always the same, that peace may come to her who has lost it, the pearl of his soul, as he calls her, Ameen [a name from Mangan's poem 'The Last Words of Al-Hassan'].
> This figure which he adores recalls the spiritual yearnings and the imaginary loves of the Middle Ages, and Mangan has placed his lady in a world full of melody, of lights and perfumes, a world that grows fatally to frame every face that the eyes of a poet have gazed on with love. There is only one chivalrous idea, only one male devotion, that lights up the faces of Vittoria Colonna, Laura and Beatrice, just as the bitter disillusion and the self-disdain that end the chapter are one

and the same. But the world in which Mangan wishes his lady to dwell ... is a wild world, a world of night in the orient.[21]

In the 1902 version, Joyce had added to the list of Vittoria, Laura, and Beatrice: 'Mona Lisa – [they all] embody one chivalrous idea, which is no mortal thing, bearing it bravely above the accidents of lust and faithlessness and weariness; and she whose white and holy hands have the virtue of enchanted hands, his virgin flower, and flower of flowers, is no less than these an embodiment of that idea.'[22] In these striking and accumulated lines from his two essays on Mangan, Joyce unpacks the medieval–Christian 'othering' of woman as the mysterious virgin Other, the Mona in the Madonna, within the trope of the Orient as Other. Perhaps equally striking is his description of 'the chivalrous idea' as something one 'bear[s] ... bravely above the accidents of lust and faithlessness and weariness' (compare 'bore my chalice through a throng of foes') and which involves 'the bitter disillusion and the self-disdain that end the chapter' – for in these lines Joyce could have equally well been describing his own tale of 'Araby'.

Having boldly promised Mangan's sister (as she turned her silver bracelet around her wrist) that 'If I go ... I will bring you something' (*D*, p. 32), our young narrator awaits impatiently the night of the bazaar. That night he has to contend with his late-returning uncle – unpleasant, selfish, drunk (like so many father-figures in Joyce's texts) – a figure for the paralysis the boy wishes to escape. As the boy is finally allowed to leave, his uncle begins to recite *The Arab's Farewell to his Steed* (more on that later). Clutching 'a florin tightly in my hand' (*D*, p. 34), the boy takes a train ride towards the bazaar. This symbolic journey to Araby is, at once, a desired escape from the labyrinth of Irish paralysis, and a pilgrimage in quest of the feminine and the Oriental Other as the anticipated destination of male desire.

The well-known epiphany which concludes the story involves the boy finding the bazaar nearly deserted, then hearing men 'counting money on a salver' and listening 'to the fall of the coins'; finally, he overhears a banal and mundane conversation, between two young gentlemen and a young lady with English accents – a conversation which illustrates one of Joyce's descriptions of 'epiphany' in *Stephen Hero* as 'the vulgarity of speech'[23] The disappointing reality of the bazaar, its cheap commercialism and drab conversation, seem to cheapen the secret world of dreams and desire the boy had constructed in his mind, deflating the loftiness of his adoration of Mangan's sister. In the final paragraph, the truth of his disillusion 'shines forth' to reveal to him his own blindness and the vanity of his dreams and romantic illusions, in an epiphanic fall from grace and innocence: 'Gazing up into the darkness I saw myself as a creature driven and derided by vanity; and my eyes burned with anguish and anger' (D, p. 35; recall Joyce's discussion of Mangan's chivalry as 'the bitter disillusion and the self-disdain that end the chapter').

On this last page of the story, the word 'fall' occurs twice (both in relation to the 'fall of coins'), for the progress of this story is one of *lapsus*. However, 'the bitter disillusion and the self-disdain that end the chapter' are, in a very problematic sense, always already overdetermined and inevitable – just as the very first paragraph of the story already foreshadows, with its 'yellow leaves' and its image of a 'wild garden' containing 'a central apple-tree' (D, p. 29), the eventual 'fall' into an awareness of vulgarity, materialism, and a debased romanticism. For the story dramatises, from one perspective, the inescapable results and problematics built into the dynamics of 'othering' within a system (Western and Christian) of essentialised/Orientalised binaries, the dynamics of Self and Other.

To begin with, the Orientalising/othering urge essentialises all the heterogeneous manifestations of difference (in nationality, race, ethnicity, culture, and so on) within the notion of a unitary, definable, knowable Other; this voracious concept colonises all alien cultures and ethnicities under the banner of a homogeneous 'Orient' (or, here, 'Araby'). As Said states: 'The actualities of the modern Orient were systematically excluded.'[24] As Lowe argues: 'The binary opposition of Occident and Orient is thus a misleading perception which serves to suppress the specific heterogeneity, inconstancies, and slippages of each individual notion.'[25] For example, the 'Midway Plaisance', the Araby bazaar featured in the 1893 World Exhibition in Chicago, was 'a teeming bazaar of romantic faces, colours, nationalities, and seductions out of the *Thousand and One Nights*' with 'Algerian and Egyptian belly-dancers'; a 'Street in Cairo'; 'a village of Algeria and Tunis, with Arab tents – nearby a Turkish Village and Indian bazaar'; 'in the harem of a Morrish palace barebreasted dancing girls held statuesque poses. Beautiful young women of Algiers, Tunis, Tripoli, Morocco, Egypt, Palestine, Persia, Siam, Burmah, China, and Japan presented themselves somewhat more discreetly' .[26] The totalising exhibition strategy mirrors the Orientalist impulse to equate all 'others' into a single, grand Other.[27] The account by Julian Hawthorne (son of Nathaniel) of the 'Midway Plaisance' both partakes in and describes the exhibition's stereotyping of the mysterious and ineffable Orient: 'a concentration of Oriental gorgeousness, glowing with colour, and such colours as we would not dare to even think of in our own aesthetic moments; and yet nothing is in other than perfect taste and harmony.'[28]

One problem with such an all-encompassing, essentialising discourse is that every term within its extended system of binary oppositions (Self and Other; holy and evil; virgin and whore; and so on) already contains its binary opposite, since the essentialised Other already contains (but cannot recognise or distinguish between) such disparate heterogeneities. As Young puts it, 'There may indeed be other knowledges, but they would take different, multifarious forms – unlike the Western creation of the Orient as a generalised "other" which is constituted as the same everywhere and for all time (there could be no clearer instance, perhaps, of how the other is turned into the same)'; 'the creation of the Orient, if it does not really represent the East, signifies the West's own dislocation from itself, something inside that is presented, narrativised, as being outside'[29] within an ambivalence of desire which Bhabha calls 'that "otherness" which is at once an object of desire and derision'.[30] Thus, the grail-like spirituality of one's desire and questing can all too easily be turned over/into the sensuality of 'fleshpots of Egypt', for both notions are already contained within the essence of an Orientalised Other; what sounds like the muezzin's call in the holy temple is revealed to be the enchanting siren song of harem or houri. As Harry Stone pointed out in a seminal essay on 'Araby', the boy in the story 'makes his journey, but it is a journey to Egypt, to Araby, to the market place, not back to the Holy Land'.[31] As R. B. Kershner points out, 'for the Victorians ... the most important role of the East in the popular imagination was as a locale of sexual license and perversion within a context of sensual wealth – the original arena of *luxe et volupté*'.[32] As Said has thoroughly documented, 'everything about the Orient ... exuded dangerous sex' so that 'in time, "Oriental sex" was as standard a commodity as any other available in the mass culture, with the result that writers and readers could have it, if they wished, without necessarily going to the Orient'.[33] Thus, Julian Hawthorne's cultural raptures inevitably lead him to the 'underbelly' of Orientalism: 'the slender tremulous

scream of the Algerian dancing girls'; 'the female abdomen
execut[ing] such feats as never before entered your wildest and most
unrestrained imagination'; 'a laughing, languishing, roguish glance
from a pair of Oriental eyes, and an invitation from a pair of lips
that are fit to make a Musselman's Paradise'. Luedtke's comment
on the popular commercialisation and material commodification of
the exotic Orient is at one with the substance of the boy's epiphany
in Joyce's story: 'Each Oriental rapture ends, characteristically, with
the clink of coins and price of admission'.[34] As Said notes, finally
'The Orient becomes a living tableau of queerness'.[35] Thus, the
deconstruction of the holy quest as sin and luxury, as sensualist
(and even as materialist and commercialised) indulgence, is already
built into the binary structure of the object-ified essentialism; Desire
as holy quest is also desire as sexual con-quest.

In exact complementarity, the 'othering' of women in Christian
patriarchy results in a similarly binary opposition as the othering of
the Orient. For if, in the scheme of essentialised Woman, Woman is
Madonna, she is also Whore; Our Lady is also the temptress Eve;
the Virgin Mary is also Mary Magdalen (so also Joyce's letters
reveal his tendency to configure Nora as both beatific inspiration
and libidinous motivator, as the essence of all forms of Desire). This
overdetermined encoding within the romantic-religious cult of
female idolatry is suggested in the very nature of the young boy's
reading (both secular and religious), in the very contents of our cultural production: thus his disillusion is already inscribed into his
desire. For, as Stone has pointedly illustrated, Scott's *The Abbot* is a
romance

> with a religious title that obscures the fact that it is the secular cele-
> bration of a worldly queen, Mary Queen of Scots, a queen enshrined
> in history as saint and harlot ... an idolised Catholic queen by the
> name of Mary ... a 'harlot queen', a passionate thrice-married
> woman who was regarded by many of her contemporaries as the
> 'Whore of Babylon', as a murderess who murdered to satisfy her
> lust.[36]

That the boy reads a book by Scott romanticising as an unblem-
ished heroine a Queen Mary who was generally considered a harlot
(the queen as quean; Mary as Magdalen) and associated with
Babylon as a figure of Orientalised luxury, already pre-scribes the
curve of Joyce's story and epiphany and reveals the overdetermined
disillusion that comes with romanticism, the fall lurking behind a

rise. Thus, Stone's nickname for Mangan's sister – the 'Madonna of the Silver Bracelet'[37] – appropriately suggests the disillusion of commercialism and prostitution inscribed into the figure of essentialised Woman. So also, we recall that inscribed into the popular culture's very siren call of desire, that illustrated poster for the Dublin 'Araby Bazaar' in 1894, is already a commodified blend of the lure of the exotic East and blatant commercialism: 'For one shilling, as the programme put it, one could visit "Araby in Dublin" and at the same time aid the Jervis Street Hospital.'[38]

To summarise thus far: our young male narrator projects his personal desire onto a religiously worshipped and feminised icon/idol; he does so, as the patriarchal Christian history of the West has also done, by othering/Orientalising the figure of Woman; as with the West, he figures Woman and Desire by con-figuring them with an essentialised Orient/Araby. Kershner has argued that 'the portrayal of woman as Other in *Ulysses* is in constant dialogical relationship with the portrayal of the Orient as Other';[39] we have seen that this dialogical relationship between female othering and Orientalism is already present in Joyce's works as early as 'Araby'. The analogy may have been inevitable, for (as Said notes) 'Orientalism also encouraged a peculiarly (not to say invidiously) male conception of the world' which figured the Orient as female, with 'its feminine penetrability, its supine malleability'.[40]

Furthermore, Said also argues that 'the scope of Orientalism exactly matched the scope of empire'; after all, 'the whole question of imperialism, as it was debated in the late nineteenth century ... carried forward the binary typology of advanced and backward (or subject) races, cultures, and societies'.[41] This, too, is a relationship that Joyce's 'Araby' excavates, in what is perhaps the story's most striking double-take. At the end, the young boy's epiphany presumably concerns his new awareness of the sordid materiality and vulgar commercialisation behind the stuff of his dreams, that is, the inevitable disillusion behind his romantic othering. But ironically the construction of his epiphany shifts that romanticised othering of the Other into an othering of the Self: for in describing himself as 'a creature driven and derided by vanity' whose 'eyes burned with anguish and anger', the boy is melodramatising his own specific experience into a romanticised and essentialised grand passion. This shift (the self as other) perhaps serves as the transition for what is a possible (and certainly deeply underscored) separate epiphany by the *reader*: the Irish/colonised Self as feminised and Orientalised

Other. Within the complex analogies and dense patterns of figuration woven into this story's texture, especially as they concern Orient and empire, the title of 'Araby' contains a sharp irony: for this is finally a parable about Ireland as much as about an Orientalised Other. Nor should this be surprising: after all, the same binary dynamics of othering and essentialism we have been discussing are also built into the English/Irish relationship.[42]

Nor was this a new concept and cultural premise for Joyce. As Kershner has shown, there was a cultural tradition 'through which the Irish themselves were cast as Orientals, long before Joyce's time':[43] for example, William Collins's 1742 collection of poems titled *Persian Eclogues* was retitled by Collins himself as his 'Irish Eclogues'; Lord Byron, himself an influential Orientalist, wrote in the dedication of Thomas Moore's *The Corsair*: 'Collins, when he denominated his Oriental his Irish Eclogues, was not aware of how true, at least, was a part of his parallel ... wildness, tenderness, and originality, are part of your national claim of oriental descent, to which you have thus far proved your title'; Irish explorer Richard Burton, in writing about the Arabian tales, likened 'imaginative races like the Kelts, and especially Orientals, who imbibe supernaturalism with their mother's milk'; Moore himself wrote *Lalla Rookh*, a book about the Orient, without ever having been to the East, by merely reconfiguring it as another Ireland.[44]

Joyce, in using Mangan's mix of Irish romanticism, medieval romance and chivalry, and Orientalism (Mangan wrote Arabic 'translations' though he was probably quite ignorant of the language), was participating in a similar tactic: for the invocation of Mangan and of a character called 'Mangan's sister', within the popular associations of 'Araby', would likely evoke in Joyce's Irish readers a resonant ambivalence, between Woman as Orient and Woman as Ireland/Dark Rosaleen. Joyce's own vision of Mangan as poet asserts this very conflation within the context of imperial domination and dispossession, for he had earlier written about the works of Mangan, in whom 'East and West meet': 'whether the song is of Ireland or of Istambol it has the same refrain, a prayer that peace may come again to her who has lost her peace, the moonwhite pearl of his soul, Ameen'.[45] Joyce saw Mangan as a national poet ('Mangan is the type of his race'), for 'He, too, cries out, in his life and in his mournful verses, against the injustice of despoilers'.[46]

In Joyce's story the young boy's discovery of the tawdriness of reality in contrast to his idealised romantic dream world occurs in the context of an Ireland presented as a centre of paralysis: where the ineffectiveness of a potentially redeeming religious and spiritual authority is suggested on the opening page by the death of the priest who lived on North Richmond Street (*D*, p. 29), replaced instead by sordid materialism and hucksterism in 'the flaring streets' full of 'drunken men and bargaining women' and 'the shrill litanies of shop-boys who stood on guard by the barrels of pigs' cheeks': this is a commercialised Ireland that has been prostituted to Mammon, peopled by such as Mrs. Mercer (with her mercenary echo), the pawnbroker's wife. The bazaar itself is a tawdry commercial affair in which the narrator's sacred quest is simply to *buy* something. Significantly, he carries a florin as his mode of passage and transaction – the coin of the English invader, a 'silver coin minted by the English with a head of Queen Victoria on one side and the Queen's coat of arms (including the conquered harp of Ireland) on the other' and which Irish Catholics found offensive.[47] Appropriately, the bazaar is exemplified by a shabby stall presided over by vulgar English accents – 'the accents of the ruling race, the foreign conquerors'[48] – supervising a postlapsarian fall, 'the fall of the coins' (*D*, p. 35). All of these details underscore the fact that 'Araby' is but a figure for Ireland (and that Mangan's sister is Dark Rosaleen), an Ireland whose soul and self have been debased and prostituted to political and economic imperialism.

The story's invoked but unquoted poem, *The Arab's Farewell to His Steed*, has a poignant significance in Joyce's scheme, for it too is a story of betrayal and disillusion, in which a beautiful and beloved possession (the Arab's horse) is sold for money to a stranger, in an image that conflates the dark horse of Araby with the image of Ireland as Dark Rosaleen prostituted to the English:

> My beautiful, my beautiful! that standeth meekly by,
> With thy proudly arched and glossy neck, and dark and fiery eye!
> Fret not to roam the desert now with all thy winged speed;
> I may not mount on thee again! – thou'rt sold, my Arab steed!
> The stranger hath thy bridle-rein, thy master hath his gold;
> Fleet-limbed and beautiful, farewell! – thou'rt sold, my steed, thou'rt sold!

Harry Stone has persuasively deciphered the resonant allusiveness and functional appropriateness of Joyce's invocation of this poem, written by Caroline Norton, a vaunted Irish beauty who was sued for divorce by her husband for having committed adultery with Lord Melbourne, the English Prime Minister; the notorious divorce trial then unmasked the scandalous reality that it had been the husband himself who had instigated the adulterous union as a mode of self-advancement. As Stone argues:

> That an Irish woman as beautiful as Caroline Norton should have been sold by her husband for English preferments; that she should have been sold to the man who, in effect, was the English ruler of Ireland; that she, in turn, should have been party to such a sale; that this very woman, writing desperately for money, should compose a sentimental poem celebrating the traitorous sale of a beautiful and supposedly loved creature; and that this poem should later be cherished by the Irish (the uncle's recitation is in character, the poem was a popular recitation piece, it appears in almost every anthology of Irish poetry) – all this is patently and ironically appropriate to what Joyce is saying.[49]

Thus, in Joyce's densely textured story about 'Araby' we have a parallel set of orientalisms: the religious adoration and othering of Our Lady; the romantic idol-isation by the male of his Lady; the quest – in Western history as well as Western romantic literature – for a feminised and essentialised Orient. All these tropes – religious, masculist, racialist – are finally figures for (or mirrors of) Ireland's colonial relation to imperial England – within the always-already corrupted and debased binarity of othering that functions the Other (Ireland) as a debased harlot/houri prostituted to England. Such is the consistent and inevitable logic of essentialist binarism: in which the soul's adoration of the Madonna is degraded into a young seductress with a silver bracelet; in which the chalice of a holy grail is but a cheap porcelain vase the boy almost buys for his Madonna of the Silver Bracelet; and in which the temple of the exotic and idolised Other turns out to be nothing but a cheap marketplace presided over by the English oppressors. Araby and the Persia of the mind, that 'pleasant and vicious region' of one's Desire, are finally tropes for Ireland's relationship to England; in Joyce's vision of a debased and colonised Ireland, Dark Rosaleen is not a Gaelic Madonna but a cheap flirt selling her wares and her self for the coins of strangers.

From Vincent J. Cheng, *Joyce, Race and Empire* (Cambridge, 1995), pp. 77–9; 88–100.

Notes

[Vincent Cheng's analysis of 'Araby' is an excellent example of how post-colonial theory has been used to re-read Joyce's work, and his book was the first full-length study of Joyce from this theoretical point of view. Cheng's essay demonstrates the heterogeneous nature of postcolonial criticism, drawing upon psychoanalytic and feminist theories of the 'other' to unravel the meanings of the 'Araby' bazaar and the boy's longing for Mangan's sister in the story. Cheng draws upon Edward Said's concept of 'orientalism' to understand how the boy's sexual desires are part of a wider discourse of 'race' and imperialism in the story. Orientalism normally refers to the way that the 'Orient' was represented as 'other' to Europe, but here Cheng interprets Ireland as functioning as a kind of orientalised 'other' to England. It is useful to compare this analysis of 'Araby' with that of Dettmar (essay 9). A number of notes have been abbreviated for reasons of space. Ed.]

1. James Joyce, *The Letters of James Joyce*, vol.II, ed. Richard Ellmann (New York, 1966), p. 134.

2. Joyce, *Letters*, vol. I, ed. Stuart Gilbert (New York, 1957), pp. 62–3.

3. *Letters*, vol. II, p. 134.

4. Edward W. Said, *Orientalism* (New York, 1979), p. 3.

5. Ibid.

6. Homi K. Bhabha, 'Difference, Discrimination, and the Discourse of Colonialism', in *The Politics of Theory*, ed. Francis Barker et al. (Colchester, 1983), p. 199.

7. Said, *Orientalism*, p. 52.

8. Ibid., p. 43.

9. Ibid., p. 206.

10. [All references to *Dubliners* are to James Joyce, *Dubliners: Text, Criticism, and Notes*, ed. Robert Scholes and A. Walton Litz (New York, 1969), and given in the text as *D*. Ed.]

11. James Joyce, *Stephen Hero*, ed. John J. Slocum and Herbert Cahoon (Norfolk, CT, 1959), p. 211.

12. See especially Harry Stone, ' "Araby" and the Writings of James Joyce', in *Dubliners: Text, Criticism, and Notes*, ed. Scholes and Litz; Robert M. Adams, *Surface and Symbol: The Consistency of James Joyce's 'Ulysses'* (New York, 1962); Cheryl Herr, *Joyce's Anatomy of Culture* (Urbana, IL, 1986); and R. B. Kershner, *Joyce, Bakhtin, and Popular Literature: Chronicles of Disorder* (Chapel Hill, NC, 1989).

13. For a reproduction of this poster see Richard Ellmann, *James Joyce*, rev. edn (Oxford, 1982), plate 3.

14. Luther Luedkte, 'Julian Hawthorne's Passage to India', unpublished essay, p. 3.

15. Chandra Talpade Mohanty, 'Under Western Eyes: Feminist Scholarship and Colonial Discourses', *Boundary 2*, 12:3–13:1 (1984), 352. Key critics here include Julia Kristeva on Desire and Edward Said on Orientalism.

16. Lisa Lowe, *Critical Terrains: French and British Orientalisms* (Ithaca, NY, 1991), p. 2.

17. Said, *Orientalism*, pp. 127; 168.

18. Hélène Cixous and Catherine Clément, *The Newly Born Woman*, trans. Betsy Wing (Manchester, 1986), pp. 70; 71. My emphasis.

19. James Joyce, *The Critical Writings of James Joyce*, ed. Ellsworth Mason and Richard Ellmann (New York, 1964), p. 179.

20. Ibid., p. 178.

21. Ibid., pp. 182–3.

22. Ibid., p. 79.

23. Joyce, *Stephen Hero*, p. 211.

24. Said, *Orientalism*, p. 177. Said thus concludes forcefully: 'In the system of knowledge about the Orient, the Orient is less a place than a *topos*, a set of references, a congeries of characteristics, that seems to have its origin in a quotation, or a fragment of a text, or a citation from someone's work on the Orient, or some bit of previous imagining, or an amalgam of all these' (p. 177).

25. Lowe, *Critical Terrains*, p. 7.

26. Luedkte, 'Julian Hawthorne's Passage to India', pp. 2; 3.

27. As Lowe points out in *Critical Terrains*, p. 7: 'The [actual, occluded] heterogeneity is borne out most simply in the different meaning of "the Orient" over time. In many eighteenth-century texts the Orient signifies Turkey, the Levant, and the Arabian peninsula occupied by the Ottoman Empire, now known as the Middle East; in nineteenth-century literature the notion of the Orient additionally refers to North Africa, and in the twentieth century more often to Central and Southeast Asia.'

28. Luedkte, 'Julian Hawthorne's Passage to India', p. 6.

29. Robert Young, *White Mythologies: Writing History and the West* (London, 1990), pp. 127; 139.

30. Homi K. Bhabha, 'The Other Question', *Screen*, 24:6 (1983), 19.

31. Stone, ' "Araby" and the Writings of James Joyce', p. 364.

32. R. B. Kershner, '*Ulysses* and the Orient', *James Joyce Quarterly*, 35: 2–3 (1998), 281. So also Oriental bazaars grew to suggest immorality or wrongdoing: in James Joyce, *A Portrait of the Artist as Young Man*, ed. Chester G. Anderson (New York, 1968), p. 76, Heron comments about Stephen, 'Dedalus is a model youth. He doesn't smoke and he doesn't go the bazaars and he doesn't flirt and he doesn't damn anything or damn all.'

33. Said, *Orientalism*, pp. 167; 190.

34. Luedkte, 'Julian Hawthorne's Passage to India', p. 6.

35. Said, *Orientalism*, p. 103.

36. Stone, ' "Araby" and the Writings of James Joyce', p. 350.

37. Ibid., p. 353.

38. Ibid., p. 346.

39. Kershner, '*Ulysses* and the Orient', p. 292.

40. Said, *Orientalism*, pp. 206–8.

41. Ibid., pp. 104; 206.

42. See ch. 2 of Cheng, *Joyce, Race and Empire* (Cambridge, 1995).

43. Kershner, '*Ulysses* and the Orient', p. 284.

44. Ibid., pp. 284–5.

45. Joyce, *Critical Writings*, p. 78.

46. Ibid., p. 81.

47. Stone, ' "Araby" and the Writings of James Joyce', p. 359.

48. Ibid., p. 363.

49. Ibid., p. 358. This is also the first instance of the frequent later usage by Joyce of the image of the 'dark horse' as a symbol for the marginalised Other under British imperial rule (see Cheng, *Joyce, Race and Empire*, ch. 9), as well as for the connection between 'horse' and 'whores' (here, between the dark Arab horse equated with both Dark Rosaleen and Caroline Norton as symbols of Ireland prostituted to the English masters).

9

The *Dubliners* Epiphony: (Mis) Reading the Book of Ourselves

KEVIN J. H. DETTMAR

One of Joyce's strategies for unsettling our reading habits in 'The Sisters' is the liberal use of that detective fiction stock-in-trade, the red herring. False clues proliferate throughout the story, at least one per page, and seemingly in proportion as we look for them. As Hugh Kenner writes, 'Joyce delights in leaving us ... queer things we may misinterpret, as if to keep alive in us an awareness traditional fiction is at pains to lull, the awareness that we *are* interpreting.'[1] A short list would begin with the story's puzzling title; thereafter Joyce throws out curious words, phrases, objects – signs apparently in need of interpretation, signs to which we critics have been only too willing to apply our ingenuity:

> '*paralysis, gnomon,* and *simony*';
> 'faints and worms';
> 'that Rosicrucian';
> 'let him box his corner';
> '*Umbrellas Re-Covered*';
> 'stories about the catacombs and about Napoleon Bonaparte';
> the boy's dream, the ending of which he cannot remember;
> the 'heavy odour in the room – the flowers';
> 'the empty fireplace';
> the breviary 'fallen to the floor';
> 'And then his life was, you might say, crossed';

the 'chalice that he broke';
'they say it was the boy's fault'

Every one of these textual cruxes has elicited its own critical commentary; literary critics, when confronted with such a hoard of
virgin signs, have a field day. The title, for example, has sent critics
off in many different directions trying to explain the apparent discrepancy between the importance accorded the sisters in the title
and their relatively minor role in the story. Edward Brandabur, for
instance, resolves the problem by asserting that 'the title, "The
Sisters", refers not only to Nannie and Eliza, but to an effeminate
relationship between the priest and his disciple'.[2] While clever in its
way, such an explanation in no way enriches our experience of the
story; Brandabur constructs a story parallel to the text we're given,
a story that spells out a good deal that 'The Sisters' leaves unstated.
In the end, we cannot help but feel that he is reading an altogether
different story from the rather impoverished one Joyce wrote.

The story's most famous puzzle is no doubt the three mysteriously linked words *paralysis*, *gnomon*, and *simony*, that the boy
intones in the first paragraph. Colin MacCabe writes that in the
final version of 'The Sisters', 'the theme of paralysis is introduced
and this word together with "gnomon" and "simony" provides a
collection of signifiers which are not determined in their meaning by
the text. ... the reader is introduced to a set of signifiers for which
there is no interpretation except strangeness and an undefined evil.
The opening of the final version of the story displays a certain
excess of the power of signification (the production of a surplus
meaning).'[3] Many elaborate structures have been devised to explain
the thread that connects these three magical words; entire readings
of the story, and indeed of the volume, have subsequently been built
around this hieratic trinity. And yet their relationship is stated explicitly right there on the page, and it seems strangely appropriate
that a man named Herring should be the one to point it out to us:
'No logic binds these three italicised words together – only the
strangeness of their sounds in the boy's ear.'[4] These 'clews' are
related to one another only as signifiers, not as signifieds; in and of
themselves they provide the reader no means of escaping the flat realistic surface of the text.

Phillip Herring's is a scrupulously mean reading, an interpretation that bears in mind Joyce's conviction that 'he is a very bold
man who dares to alter in the presentment, still more to deform,

whatever he has seen and heard'[5] – whatever he has seen and heard and *read*. For the red herrings in 'The Sisters' are just that – what the French call *faux amis*; rather than providing us with a means of transcending the spare surface of the story, these 'reader traps'[6] are instead Joyce's means of reinforcing the story's hermeneutics, and pulling us, kicking and screaming, into a text with which we would prefer to keep a purely professional relationship.

The most common response for critics when they come across a red herring unaware is of course to make a symbol of it. And 'The Sisters' certainly has its share of ostensible symbols, the most glaring of which would be the chalice that Father Flynn has dropped. Over the years the 'symbol' of the chalice has been understood in a number of ways, as standing for the Church, the phallus (male or female), the Grail, and so forth. And yet surely the demise of Father Flynn is meant in part as an allegory of the dangers of overinterpretation that any reader of the story must heed. The chalice itself, as Eliza remarks, was of no real importance – 'they say it was all right, that it contained nothing, I mean' (*D*, p. 17).[7] But Eliza herself, as her locutions show, is not quite so sure ('they say …'); and indeed the incident of the dropped chalice is made the centrepiece of her narrative of the Father's final 'insanity' ('That affected his mind, she said. After that he began to mope by himself, talking to no one and wandering around by himself' [*D*, p. 17]). Of course, we do not know how the incident was interpreted by the priest; but we can see quite plainly that those close to him took the breaking of the chalice, in retrospect at least, as an omen, the chalice itself having been invested by them with too much symbolic importance.

Homer Brown surely has this episode in mind when he writes that 'at least part of the symbolism of *Dubliners* has to do with the failure or inadequacy of the symbol',[8] the chalice in 'The Sisters' is as self-evident a symbol as any reader could hope for, but when its significance is examined, it becomes an antisymbolic object, a 'symbol' that alerts us to the dangers of reading symbolically. Again, Brown remarks that 'in a sense, the symbolism of these stories consists in the failure of the symbolic, the emptiness of the symbol';[9] the chalice is an object so overinvested with meaning that it deconstructs as a symbol and returns to the realm of pure realistic detail, what Barthes calls 'the sumptuous rank of the signifier'.[10] In the same way, the Catholic Church itself is seen in *Dubliners* as a dangerously overvalued symbol, which is liable at any time to crash. The chalice 'contained nothing'; as a result, it is immediately filled with the needs and desires of the characters, and is made a receptacle for all that menaces them.

If this style of reading – the reader as detective – tends unjustifiably to turn objects into symbols, it simultaneously turns characters into the figures of allegory. Tindall sees the figure of the Irish 'Poor Old Woman' (the *Shan Van Vocht*) behind Maria of 'Clay', the slavey of 'Two Gallants', and Mrs. and Kathleen Kearney of 'A Mother'; but of 'The Sisters' he complains: 'Why are there two of them? I should find it easier if there were only one. A poor old woman (the traditional figure) could serve as an image of Ireland. ...'[11] I should find it easier! We should all find Joyce's texts easier would they simply obey the call of our desires; but they resist us, and so we tailor them to the shape of our need as best we can. It's not always a good fit. As Garry Leonard writes, 'Readers do not mind disagreeing on the particulars because all agree she [Maria] means something – and that is the main thing – *that she mean something.* ... And so Maria's tiny shoulders have supported various interpretations that substitute what she "means" for what critics lack.'[12]

The sort of red herring with which Joyce taunts us in 'The Sisters' is a recurring structural feature of *Dubliners*. The second paragraph of 'Araby' is similarly littered with these false clues – *The Abbot, The Devout Communicant*, and *The Memoirs of Vidocq* – and again Herring has resisted the temptation to read these details 'symbolically': 'the titles probably have just enough relevance to encourage readers to inflate them with meaning. (After all, Joyce supplied the pump.) There is no indication that the boy has read them, especially since he views them as physical objects, preferring the one with yellow leaves.'[13] Sometimes, even in Literature, objects are just objects; and for readers trained to read texts as storehouses of symbols, such a scrupulously mean reading requires extreme discipline:

> so much depends
> upon
>
> a red wheel
> barrow

After all, Freud himself is said to have remarked: 'Sometimes a cigar is just a cigar.'

Anyone who has taught *Dubliners* knows that students approach these texts as puzzles; in their estimation, the main task in reading is to figure out what the ending 'means'. Of course, this is only a slightly less sophisticated version of what Joyce's critics have done from the start. Reviewing the French translation of *Dubliners* in 1926, Jacques Chenevière was one of the first critics to praise Joyce for resisting simple conclusions: 'a French novelist – a logician and always, in spite of himself, a moralist even when he considers himself unimpressionable – would begin and end the narrative precisely at the point when even the mysterious would be explicit. Joyce, however, only conducts the reader with a weak hand from which, however, one does not escape. He rarely informs us and does not conclude. ... Sometimes this fog bothers us, accustomed as we are to life, translated literally and appearing logical. How dare art guide us so little and yet remain master of us!'[14] Most early critics, however, were not as sympathetic to Joyce's interest in, as John Cage expresses it, 'keeping things mysterious'.[15] The majority of critics have seen in the conclusion of 'The Sisters', for instance, a moment of terrible, and perhaps incommunicable, insight for the young narrator. In Suzanne Ferguson's reading the story ends in an epiphany for the reader, in which she, in a flash of insight, synthesises the various 'clues' set out in the story and realises that Father Flynn is guilty of a subtle form of simony.[16]

If we are honest, however, for many of us the story ends not in epiphany but in utter muddle. At least part of our confusion stems from Joyce's refusal to state his moral; one contemporary reviewer complained that 'his outlook is self-centred, absorbed in itself rather; he ends his sketch abruptly time after time, satisfied with what he has done, brushing aside any intention of explaining what is set down or supplementing what is omitted'.[17] Joyce's refusal to 'conclude' is understood by this early reader as self-absorption, and it provokes the critic's venom; but at least contemporary reviewers were in a position to see that Joyce had indeed refused to conclude. We are now so used to the institutionalised readings of these stories – 'The Dead' is probably the prime example – that we can no longer even sense their wildness. William Empson's irritated remarks about the inconclusive nature of *Ulysses* are at least as appropriate as a description of *Dubliners*: 'The difficulty about *Ulysses*,' he writes, 'as is obvious if you read the extremely various opinions of critics, is that, whereas most novels tell you what the author expects you to feel, this one not only refuses to tell you the end of the story, it also refuses to tell you what the author thinks would have been a good end to the story.'[18]

If we turn to a poststructuralist critic like MacCabe, however, we can see how Joyce's refusal to conclude in these stories has recently been transvalued – what was described as arrogant convention flaunting in the contemporary reviews is now felt to be an integral component of his genius: 'The text works paratactically, simply placing one event after another, with no ability to draw conclusions from this placing ... The movement of the text is not that of making clear a reference already defined and understood; of fixing the sense of an expression. Instead the text dissolves the simple scenes of Dublin as a city, as a context within which people live their lives, and replaces it with the very text of paralysis.'[19] The close of 'The Sisters' is precisely this 'text of paralysis'; the narrative trails off in ellipses as Eliza begins to repeat yet again the story she has 'written' to explain her brother's death, and Joyce resolutely refuses to come in at the end, even in the person of his narrator, in order to give us any guidance. A postmodern ending is a matter neither of appearance nor of grammar – it has to do, finally, with avoiding 'the sense of an ending' (Kermode).[20] Think, for instance, of the ending of the first part of *Molloy:* 'Molloy could stay, where he happened to be.'[21] Beckett gives us proper grammar, and even a kind of narrative closure, and yet suggests the influence of chance operation, creating an unsettling sense that nothing has been concluded. The postmodern ending is a conclusion ('termination') that reaches no conclusion ('inference').

At the close of 'The Sisters' the narrator appears to us frozen – puzzled and paralysed – and we cannot help but ape his response. Not only do we remain unenlightened; we cannot even decide who, if anyone, in the story has seen the light. But some sort of enlightenment – either for the character, or for the reader – is the traditional goal of a reading of the *Dubliners* story. That famous moment of enlightenment is what Joyce criticism, (mis)taking its clue from Joyce himself, has dubbed the epiphany. Zack Bowen points out, with reference to 'The Sisters', that 'the question of who is having the epiphany is a central issue of the story':

> If the epiphany belongs to the Flynn sisters, then the statement 'So, then, of course, when they saw that, that made them think that there was something gone wrong with him' (*D*, p. 18) constitutes the truth of the story. The priest's laughter is indeed madness. Few of us, however, subscribe to this. The question is really whether the priest,

the boy, or both have an epiphany. ... We are left to our own conclusions about whether the insight was about a senile and decadent way of life which the sisters merely confirmed. Even if that is the substance of the epiphany which presumably we share with the boy, we are still not sure if the priest is a seer of eternal truth or merely a disoriented and demented old man. At any rate, for the purpose of the present discussion, we have at once to ask ourselves where the eternal verities might lie in the case. The answer is that they depend upon the beholder: the sisters' perception is different from Father Flynn's, the boy's, or the readers', who may in themselves differ. Each of us fashions his own truth and sees it as the unalterable law of God.[22]

It is of course extremely difficult to maintain that 'The Sisters' ends in an epiphany – as Bowen wants to do – if readers cannot agree on who has had the epiphany, or of what it might consist. Indeed, even the most cursory glance at the wide variety of readings of 'The Sisters' over the years will suggest at once that we must not only question whether any of the characters have an epiphany, but even doubt that readers share any universal understanding of the mystery of 'The Sisters', which Donald Torchiana calls 'the most controversial piece in *Dubliners*'.[23] Sherlock Holmes, at the end of his cases, relates the logical process by which he came upon his epiphany – the solution to the crime; but, as we have seen, the boy in 'The Sisters' enjoys no such triumph.

Epiphany is Joyce's paleonym that just won't die. Our critical tradition has long privileged authors' pronouncements on their own works over the commentary of any rank 'outsider', and the word epiphany from Joyce's pen has stuck stubbornly to *Dubliners* (even though, as we shall see, he never used the term to describe his short stories). In fact, his earliest impulse was to describe the method of *Dubliners* using the metaphor not of epiphany, but of *epiclesis*; in the oldest surviving reference to his story collection, he calls them 'a series of epicleti – ten – for a paper'.[24] The difference between the two terms is this: an epiphany evidences one's ultimate mastery of a situation, while epiclesis is instead the moment of submission to mystery.[25]

In the Eastern Orthodox Church, epiclesis is the priest's invocation of the Holy Ghost to transmute the elements of the Lord's Supper, a feature of the Mass that had been dropped by the Roman Church before the medieval period. [...] The method of epiclesis is the method of mystery courted and invoked, evoked. When he had

been at work on *Dubliners* for about ten months, Joyce wrote in a
4 April 1905 letter to Stanislaus that 'The Sisters' called to his mind
the Eastern Orthodox mass: 'While I was attending the Greek mass
here [Trieste] last Sunday it seemed to me that my story *The Sisters*
was rather remarkable.' Joyce doesn't bother to spell out the connection between 'The Sisters' and the Mass; the letter, however,
goes on to describe the distinctive elements of the Greek service:
'The Greek mass is strange. The altar is not visible but at times the
priest opens the gates and shows himself. He opens and shuts them
about six times. For the Gospel he comes out of a side gate and
comes down into the chapel and reads out of a book. For the elevation he does the same. At the end when he has blessed the people he
shuts the gates ...'[26] Admittedly, the connection here is tenuous: but
the act of elevation, in the Orthodox service, is accompanied by the
priest's reading of the epiclesis. Thus, one of the elements of the
Greek Mass that seems to have captured Joyce's imagination – and
reminded him of his own short fiction – is the Eastern Church's act
of invocation.[27]

In his memoir *My Brother's Keeper*, Stanislaus Joyce records a
conversation in which Joyce again makes use of the metaphor of the
Eucharist to talk about the method of *Dubliners*: ' "Don't you
think," said he reflectively, choosing his words without haste,
"there is a certain resemblance between the mystery of the Mass
and what I am trying to do? I mean that I am trying in my poems to
give people some kind of intellectual pleasure or spiritual enjoyment
by converting the bread of everyday life into something that has
permanent artistic life of its own ...?" '[28] If Stanislaus has been as
careful in his recording as he says his brother was in his conversation, Joyce here focuses in not simply on the Eucharist itself, but on
the *mystery* of the Eucharist; and once again, that particular
mystery has a name: epiclesis. The method of the epiphany,
however, especially the 'curtain' epiphany that an entire generation
of readers has found the perfect ending to these stories, is a means
for dispelling mystery, for resolving unbearable tensions – providing
a facile closure to that which in reality cannot be neatly tied up.
The stories of *Dubliners* are, as we will explore shortly, militantly
anti-epiphanic. The whole notion of manifestation or self-revelation
is severely undercut in tale after tale; and even the comfortable critical commonplace that the reader, at least, is enlightened is finally an
illusion difficult to maintain. No one, I am persuaded, realises the
full import of these stories upon a first reading; our illumination, if

indeed we experience any, is not a sudden 'Eureka!' but a soft, gradual, hard-won appreciation.

The epiphany has become one of Joyce criticism's most effective methods for mastering the discomforting, uncompromising qualities of these texts – to close them off, to impose closure where in fact none inheres; it is, in other words, a way to fight off the intense disquiet caused by Joyce's 'scrupulous meanness'.[29] Joyce would find no little irony in this situation, for the epiphanic method, as first practised in his notebook of Epiphanies, was a resolutely decontextualising, disorienting, discomforting technique. As MacCabe writes, Joyce's 'earliest prose writings, the *Epiphanies*, lack any appeal to reality which would define what the writing produces. The conversations and situations which make up these brief ten- or twelve-line sketches, lack any accompanying explanation or context. In place of a discourse which attempts to place and situate everything, we have discourses which are determined in their situation by the reader.'[30] Thus in spite of their original spirit, the name epiphany has become one of the Joyce industry's tactics for dealing with these wilful and unruly texts – subjugating them in the name of Joyce the Father, Joyce the Creator.

More has been written about the epiphany than any other stratagem in the Joycean text; and no doubt due to the short, lyric quality of Joyce's stories, epiphany is discussed more often in connection with *Dubliners* than with any other of Joyce's writings. Morris Beja, who has written a study called *Epiphany in the Modern Novel*, writes elsewhere that 'probably no other motif has so pervaded critical discussions of both the volume as a whole and its individual stories';[31] and in a note he goes on to list more than a dozen influential critical investigations of the epiphanies in *Dubliners*. As many have pointed out, Joyce himself never used the word epiphany in reference to *Dubliners*, nor are any of the forty surviving Epiphanies housed at Buffalo and Cornell made use of in the stories. But while none of Joyce's early sketches were incorporated wholesale into the text of *Dubliners*, subsequent critics have nevertheless found Joyce's term a durable one, and the moment of 'manifestation or revelation' it describes central to what Stephen Dedalus would call the *quidditas* of these texts; and teachers and critics have found in Joyce's metaphor a powerful heuristic device.[32]

One primary difficulty with using epiphany as a term for criticism, however, is that it has accrued a fairly wide range of mean-

ings, depending on the purposes of the critic. This is, after all, the
process by which the term first entered the vocabulary of literary
criticism, Joyce putting his own spin on a word brought from Greek
into ecclesiastical English in the fourteenth century. In English,
'Epiphany' originally referred to a feast day, 'the festival commemo-
rating the manifestation of Christ to the Gentiles in the person of
the Magi; observed on January 6th, the 12th day after Christmas'
(*OED*). Given this heritage, it is no doubt ironic that 'The Dead'
takes place on Twelfth Night, the Feast of Epiphany; this is a point
to which we shall have to return. But Joyce's redefinition stripped
epiphany of its festive and religious, if not its mysterious, connotations. In a famous passage in *Stephen Hero*, we are told that the
term as Stephen used it 'meant a sudden spiritual manifestation,
whether in the vulgarity of speech or of gesture or in a memorable
phase of the mind itself. He believed that it was for the man of
letters to record these epiphanies with extreme care, seeing that they
themselves are the most delicate and evanescent of moments'.[33] It is
perhaps not insignificant that Joyce's only explicit treatment of the
doctrine of the epiphany is found in a text kept unpublished during
his lifetime; like the Homeric titles for the chapters of *Ulysses*,
which in spite of Joyce's removing them from the text critics insist
on restoring to the novel, the epiphany is largely a way of writing,
rather than a way of reading. Joyce, in rewriting *Stephen Hero* as *A
Portrait*, omitted Stephen's now-famous disquisition on the
epiphany; we might, for the novelty of it, assume for the time being
that he knew what he was doing.

Joyce's brief discussion suggests two different sorts of epiphany,
according to whether emphasis is placed on the object or event –
the occasion – of the epiphany, or instead on an observer's emotional (or 'spiritual', as Joyce has it) response to that instigating
episode. Hence Joyce's epiphanies, as Scholes and Litz write, 'were
mainly of two kinds ... they recorded "memorable phases" of the
young artist's own mind, or instances of "vulgarity of speech or of
gesture" in the world around him. In practice this resulted in two
quite different *styles* of epiphany: prose poems in which a mental
phase of the artist was narrated, and dramatic notations of vulgarity.'[34] With respect to the archetypal epiphany, the appearance of
Christ to the Magi, a Joycean rendering of the scene could conceiv-
ably capture two distinct epiphanies (and were the nativity a
Dubliners story, both would likely be included): the first, an 'objective', dramatic epiphany, focusing on the infant Christ, the scene in

the manger; and a second, 'subjective', psychological epiphany, focusing on the response of one Magus to the child. What is common to both styles of epiphany is the breaking forth of the mysterious through the dull veneer of the everyday; its emblem is the divine Christ in a Bethlehem stable, what Yeats called 'the uncontrollable mystery on the bestial floor'.

The concluding page of 'Araby' makes a convenient testing ground for any discussion of Joycean epiphany in *Dubliners*, for there we are ostensibly presented [with] two epiphanies, one of each type, in rather close proximity.[35] The first is a dramatic epiphany, very similar in style and content to the specimen Stephen records just previous to the passage from *Stephen Hero* cited above.[36] The snatch of conversation reported in 'Araby' runs this way:

> At the door of the stall a young lady was talking and laughing with two young gentlemen. I remarked their English accents and listed vaguely to their conversation.

> – O, I never said such a thing!
> – O, but you did!
> – O, but I didn't!
> – Didn't she say that?
> – Yes. I heard her.
> – O, there's a … fib!
>
> (*D*, p. 35)

If this is indeed an epiphany – and no critic seems to have argued that it's not – then we might pause for a moment to consider both its message and its audience: what does this epiphany mean, and to whom is it meant to speak?

Critics almost universally agree on the meaning of the epiphany: Bowen for instance writes that 'In "Araby" presumably the boy's epiphany of the absurdity in going to the fair and in his aggrandisement of Mangan's sister is brought home by the shallowness of the conversation in the confessional-gift stand at the fair.'[37] In fact, however, we cannot be certain what the scene has meant to the boy – how he has interpreted or read it. Joyce, through his narrator, refuses to establish a position (explicitly at least) outside the boy, a still point in the text from which we might take our bearings. In this regard, Joyce's procedure is in marked contrast to Virginia Woolf's. She is nearly as famous for her focus on the 'moment of being' as Joyce is for the epiphany; yet Woolf confirms Lily Briscoe's

epiphany at the conclusion of *To the Lighthouse* in a way that
Joyce scrupulously avoids: 'With a sudden intensity, as if she saw it
clear for a second, she drew a line there, in the centre. It was done;
it was finished. Yes, she thought, laying down her brush in extreme
fatigue, I have had my vision.'[38]

Woolf's third-person narrative gives a certain objective distance
on the scene narrated, and we are given no reason to doubt the narrative's assertion. Joyce however gives us no comforting voice from
beyond the text; all we have is the boy's own words – in his retrospective narration of the incident. With that as the only concrete evidence, we're forced to conclude that he hasn't learned his lesson.
The same problem that arises here has been the focus of intense
debate in *A Portrait*; perhaps because of its deceptive simplicity,
however, or perhaps because of Joyce's off-hand description of its
style as 'scrupulously mean', 'Araby' has not been subjected to the
kind of close stylistic scrutiny that *A Portrait* has come in for.

[...]

The closing page of 'Araby' contains a very clear 'dramatic'
epiphany, one in which most critics have found the story's 'moral',
the lesson that our protagonist is intended to learn. As a result the
boy presumably experiences psychological epiphany; but his response to the conversation overheard at the gift stall is so hyper-
bolic as to seem almost a non sequitur: 'Gazing up into the
darkness I saw myself as a creature driven and derided by vanity;
and my eyes burned with anguish and anger' (*D*, p. 35). The boy
sends his gaze into the darkness at the top of the hall, and in that
darkness his mind's eye sees 'reflected' 'a creature driven and
derided by vanity'. Has he then, like Lily Briscoe, 'had his vision'?

The critical consensus is that he has indeed. Clearly, the boy represents himself as having been possessed of a terrible insight; and
yet the form, or better the *style*, of his confession betrays its ostensible revelation. Many commentators have called the boy's self-evalu-
ation too harsh; but it is much more than that. Like Saul of Tarsus,
who goes from thinking himself God's anointed to believing himself
chief among all sinners, the boy in 'Araby' can conceive of himself
only in melodramatic black or white – either chivalric knight in
service of his lady fair or, when that illusion is forcibly wrested
from him, the blackest of sinners. This is a pattern we see played
out in other of the stories, most notably 'The Dead'; Gabriel
Conroy fluctuates wildly between expansive good humour and believing himself 'a ludicrous figure, acting as pennyboy for his aunts,

a nervous well-meaning sentimentalist' (*D*, p. 220). As Yeats's Michael Robartes says in another context, 'there's no human life at the full or the dark';[39] and yet Gabriel and the 'devout communicant' of 'Araby' both carefully avoid having to negotiate that perilous intermediate gray area called life.

This brings us back to the question: What possible criteria do we have for judging the efficacy of the boy's insight at Araby? His revelation might be evaluated in the same way we would a religious conversion, for the language of the closing page is the language of a young man who believes himself to have been spiritually transformed. If in fact he has been transformed, we may reasonably ask whether a new spirit dwells within him, and whether that new spirit has resulted in a new quality of life. For we may state as a working principle that there is no epiphany without efficacy; 'Every good tree', the Lord declared, 'bringeth forth good fruit' (Matt. 7:16–17). It makes no sense to speak of a character's having an epiphany in spite of all evidence to the contrary, just because we readers have seen what she has and believe that we have seen the light. The genuine experience of epiphany cannot remain without effect, in either life or art. Of those to whom more has been revealed, more shall be expected; as Eliot puts it in 'Gerontion', 'After such knowledge, what forgiveness?'[40]

According to the argument put forward by Beja, however, all such considerations are beside the point. What we think about a given character's epiphany is irrelevant; 'What matters is what a given character *feels* about an epiphany or the revelation it provides. An epiphany need not, after all, be "objectively" accurate; as I have argued elsewhere, an epiphany is in its very conception and description a *subjective* phenomenon. So whether Mr. Duffy and the boy at the end of "Araby" are "correct" is much less relevant than how *they* feel about what they have learned.' Following Beja's rubric, then, it is possible to experience an epiphany that is wholly delusional – so that he can say that 'even Eveline' has her epiphany 'before she represses all awareness'.[41] Surely this distorts the term epiphany beyond all usefulness. To begin with, the text proffers absolutely no support for the idea that Eveline has reached any kind of higher self-awareness; indeed, it unrelentingly exposes her process of rationalisation. Frank, for instance, who has been seen as a life preserver, is transformed into a millstone once Eveline realises she cannot leave with him: 'All the seas of the world tumbled about her heart. He was drawing her into them; he would drown her'

(*D*, p. 41). But even if Beja is right – even if Eveline does have a penultimate flash of insight – her ultimate action is to take no action, effectively nullifying any epiphany we might wish to find in her tale. An epiphany is, as Beja insists, by its very nature intensely personal – but that does not mean that it is not available to evaluation by outside criteria.

This is the argument that Bowen makes. 'Epiphanies may be false', he writes, 'because the meaning of experience, when transformed by either the artists' perception or the perception of less gifted characters may in fact be self-delusion.'[42] It is this false epiphany that I am calling epi*phony*. Although the experience of epiphany is always ultimately subjective, the validity – the efficacy – of a character's epiphany *is* available to scrutiny. Two possible avenues for verification are available to us: confirmation from the narrative itself (as in the passage of *To the Lighthouse* discussed above) or the subsequent 'life' of the character. But Joyce consistently refuses explicit narrative comment on the ostensible epiphany's efficacy; nor do the stories present any 'postconversion' life by which we might judge.

The narrator of 'Araby', though, is the story's protagonist at an advanced age. The text of 'Araby' is a product of what *Ulysses* calls 'the retrospective arrangement': 'No longer is Leopold, as he sits there, ruminating, chewing the cud of reminiscence, that staid agent of publicity and holder of a modest substance in the funds. A score of years are blown away. He is young Leopold. There, as in a retrospective arrangement, a mirror within a mirror (hey, presto!), he beholdeth himself'.[43] Does the text that the protagonist of 'Araby' chooses to write give us any reason to believe that he's outgrown this youthful vanity? The boy's closing remark – his artfully rendered epiphany – calls attention to itself for its highly wrought, exquisite style. In his discussion of *A Portrait*, Kenner has identified alliteration and chiasmus as two of the early warning signs that we're reading the free indirect discourse of an immature artist, and not surprisingly, perhaps, we find both symptoms here.[44] The paired adjectives in the first clause – 'driven and derided by vanity' – fabricate an urgent momentum out of all proportion to the motive event; those of the second clause, too – 'my eyes burned with *an*guish *and an*ger' – are chosen on the basis of sound, not sense. This is not the prose of a humbled man, a man whose vain romanticism has been painfully torn from him.

There have been foreshadowings of this decorative, slightly pre-
cious style throughout the story: 'The space of sky above us was the
colour of ever-changing violet and towards it the lamps of the street
lifted their feeble lanterns'; 'I had never spoken to her, except for a
few casual words, and yet her name was like a summons to all my
foolish blood'; 'Through one of the broken panes I heard the rain
impinge upon the earth, the fine incessant needles of water playing
in the sodden beds' (*D*, pp. 30, 31). When used to transform – to
elevate, to 'poeticise' – a landscape, such purple (or 'ever-changing
violet') prose is harmless enough, if somewhat wearying in the long
run. Indeed, one of the 'paper-covered books' the boy finds in 'the
waste room behind the kitchen', Walter Scott's *The Abbot*, could
serve him as a (turgid) stylistic model: 'It was upon the evening of a
sultry summer's day when the sun was half-sunk behind the distant
western mountains of Liddesdale, that the Lady took her solitary
walk on the battlements of a range of buildings, which formed the
front of the castle, where a flat roof of flag-stones presented a broad
and convenient promenade. The level surface of the lake, undis-
turbed except by the occasional dipping of a teal-duck or coot, was
gilded with the beams of the setting luminary, and reflected, as if in
a golden mirror, the hills amongst which it lay enbosomed.'[45]

However, the truth, Ezra Pound was to insist, makes its own
style.[46] While the florid scenic descriptions of a novel like *The
Abbot* or a short story like 'Araby' – wrought in what Pound liked
to call 'licherary langwidg' – transform a landscape, they can only
falsify the self-presentation of a writing subject. Stripped of its lush,
romantic atmosphere, we can imagine 'Araby' ending with another,
more economical, self-exposure: '– I suddenly realised how vain I
was'. To make such a spare confession, however, is clearly not to
the narrator's taste. The Preacher of Ecclesiastes declared simply
'Vanity of vanities – all is vanity'; but such a scrupulously mean
disclosure is not enough for the boy. Like the Apostle Paul, who is
not satisfied to confess himself a sinner but declares instead that
'Christ Jesus came into the world to save sinners – of whom I am
chief' (1 Tim. 1:15), our protagonist is not content simply to
condemn his vanity, but must do it in the most self-important, most
theatrical – the most *vain* – manner imaginable.

In a well-known letter to Grant Richards, Joyce said that he wanted
to give the Irish people – those few who would read *Dubliners* –
'one good look at themselves in my nicely polished looking-

glass.'[47] Such a project is, of course, fraught with danger; writers who set out to change their readers are more often than not ignored, and while some of Joyce's contemporaries may have come to see Dublin, and themselves, in a very different light after reading *Dubliners*, most doubtless remained unshaken. So too, most of his characters at the end of their tales seem unchanged; but then Joyce never promised that his characters would have that 'one good look' he promised his readers. Indeed this is the final epiphany of the most powerful stories in *Dubliners: our* realisation, as readers, that the characters have not had *their* epiphany. Believing that they have transcended, believing themselves finally to be free, characters like the narrator of 'Araby' and Gabriel Conroy pathetically verify their prison – this is perhaps the most bitter paralysis in all of *Dubliners*. [...] Thus, there are at least two contradictory ways to read the last sentence of 'Araby'. It begins, 'Looking up into the darkness, I saw myself. ...' At first blush, we might think the boy is telling us that the blackness at the top of the tent forcibly brought home to him the blackness in his own soul. But instead, his language suggests the gesture of looking at oneself in a mirror, a leitmotif throughout *Dubliners*.[48] The boy pretends that the void, the darkness is a mirror; but we know that if he sees anything at all in that darkness, it can only be a figure projected from his own imagination. Thus the dramatic conclusion of his story is a foregone one, an epigram he's been carrying around for some time and trying to find an occasion to use.

Indeed, while Joyce thought of the stories as looking glasses held up to the reader, the characters in those stories look not into a mirror but into the genial illusions of their own making.

[...]

In the stories of *Dubliners* we read the text of narrative desire; this is the characteristic use to which Joyce puts his free indirect discourse. Norris writes that Joyce's purpose in 'Clay' is 'to dramatise the powerful workings of desire in human discourse and human lives',[49] and that drama is played out not only on the page, but also in the reader. Our mistyreadings,[50] then, are not simply the product of a wilfully perverse writer, nor yet the careless errors of ignorant readers, but instead the result of an intricate pas de deux in which, when we discover our 'errors', we simultaneously find that Joyce has anticipated and cunningly prepared them. The stories of *Dubliners* are Rorschach inkblots wherein we read the text of our desire in the course of (mis)reading the book of ourselves.

Dubliners is a text that implicates us in the deadly work of paralysis, and reveals to us our own paralysis. A 'superiority complex' is either a contributing cause or a symptom of paralysis in many characters in *Dubliners* (for instance the boy in 'An Encounter' – 'I was going to reply indignantly that we were not National School boys to be *whipped*, as he called it' [*D*, p. 27]); and yet we think their problems do not touch us, and therein we too are paralysed. The standard reading of the *Dubliners* stories – that the protagonists of 'An Encounter', 'Araby', 'A Painful Case', 'A Little Cloud', and 'The Dead' all reach a new level of self-awareness by story's end – is powerful evidence of the narrative of desire that runs all through Joyce criticism. When examined closely, however, the texts simply do not support such a reading; these are not stories with happy endings, but stories that resist our desire for closure, for interpretation, for Meaning. *Dubliners*, beginning with 'The Sisters', whispers: Give up the flattering project of interpretation; give in to the mystery which is life.

The stories of *Dubliners* turn us not toward certitude, but toward the void; and while we like to believe ourselves above Joyce's 'poor fledglings', Joyce's texts reveal us to be as wilfully blind, as 'driven and derided by vanity', as any of his characters. Like the sisters in the opening story, we need to believe the paralysis extrinsic to our world. Who, after reading this text, can say '*I* am a Dubliner'? We are quick to point a finger from our superior position and pronounce Corley a paralytic, or Duffy a paralytic. Garry Leonard makes this point early on in his recent book on *Dubliners*: 'Rarely in fiction do characters suffer as exquisitely for the benefit of readers as they do in *Dubliners*, and I propose that readers explore their kinship with the characters' moral paralysis rather than self-righteously suggest various cures for it.'[51] In an interview, Kathy Acker has talked about this phenomenon as characteristic of one class of texts: 'What the reader wants – what the reader's trained to want I should say – is to be at a distance and say, Look at those weird people over there!' Acker goes on to insist, though, that 'I never wanted to say that "over there" '; neither, I am arguing, did Joyce.[52] What these texts force us to confront is that *Dubliners* is *not* a dramatic tableau, but a mirror – and that we, like all of Joyce's Dubliners, steadfastly refuse that one good look *at ourselves* in his nicely polished looking glass. This response was for Jonathan Swift the defining characteristic of satire. He writes in the preface to *The Battle of the Books*: 'Satyr is a sort of Glass, wherein Beholders do generally discover every body's Face but their Own; which is the chief Reason for that kind of Reception it meets with in the World, and that so very few are offended with it.'[53]

From Kevin J.H. Dettmar, *The Illicit Joyce of Postmodernism: Reading Against the Grain* (Wisconsin, 1996).

Notes

[Kevin Dettmar's essay is a provocative account of a 'postmodern' Joyce that stresses the indeterminacy of meaning in the text, and draws theoretically upon Barthes and Jean-François Lyotard. Borrowing from Lyotard, Dettmar understands postmodernism as a kind of style of writing, rather than a specific period in history. Students, notes Dettmar, often approach the stories in *Dubliners* as if they are akin to detective puzzles to be solved. Dettmar believes most criticism of Joyce has followed this pathway and he suggests we reject it for an approach that takes pleasure in the unceasing ambiguities of the text. This extract analyses how the orthodox critical attention to Joyce's concept of epiphany – often understood as the key critical idea utilised by Joyce in his early work – misses the point of a story like 'Araby', where the symbols amount only to red herrings for the reader. Dettmar's account of the story's hesitancies is a good contrast to the more politicised reading of 'Araby' represented by Cheng (essay 8); it is also interesting to consider how far this 'postmodern' approach resembles Rabaté's poststructuralist analysis (essay 2) of *Dubliners*. A number of notes have been abbreviated for reasons of space. Ed.]

1. Hugh Kenner, *The Mechanic Muse* (New York, 1987), p. 77.

2. Edward Brandabur, *A Scrupulous Meanness: A Study of Joyce's Early Work* (Urbana, IL, 1971), p. 42.

3. Colin MacCabe, *James Joyce and the Revolution of the Word* (New York, 1979), p. 34.

4. Phillip Herring, *Joyce's Uncertainty Principle* (Princeton, NJ, 1987), p. 10.

5. James Joyce, *Letters*, vol. 2, ed. Richard Ellmann (New York, 1966), p. 134.

6. Clive Hart uses this term in rather a different sense in his discussion of the 'Wandering Rocks' episode in Clive Hart and David Hayman (eds), *James Joyce's 'Ulysses': Critical Essays* (Berkeley and Los Angeles, 1974).

7. [All references to Dubliners are to James Joyce, *Dubliners: Text, Criticism and Notes*, ed. Robert Scholes and A. Walton Litz (New York, 1976), and are given in the text as *D*. Ed.]

8. Homer Obed Brown, *James Joyce's Early Fiction: The Biography of a Form* (Cleveland, OH, 1972), p. 40.

9. Ibid., p. 48.

10. [Roland Barthes, *The Pleasure of the Text*, trans. Richard Miller (New York, 1975), p. 65. Ed.]

11. William York Tindall, *A Reader's Guide to James Joyce* (New York, 1959), p. 15.

12. Garry M. Leonard, *Reading 'Dubliners' Again: A Lacanian Perspective* (Syracuse, NY, 1993), pp. 203; 204.

13. Herring, *Joyce's Uncertainty Principle*, p. 28. I certainly do not mean to suggest that a careful reading of the popular literature with which Joyce litters his texts, such as Brandy Kershner has performed in *Joyce, Bakhtin, and Popular Literature: Chronicles of Disorder* (Chapel Hill, NC, 1989), is without value. But Kershner is quite clear about what the value of such a source study is; the titles are not symbols or clues that will magically unlock the mysterious texture of the stories.

14. Robert H. Deming (ed.), *James Joyce: The Critical Heritage*, vol. 1 (New York, 1970), p. 71.

15. John Cage, *Conversing with Cage*, ed. Richard Kostelanetz (New York, 1988), p. 208.

16. Suzanne Ferguson, 'A Sherlock at *Dubliners*; Structural and Thematic Analogues in Detective Stories and the Modern Short Story', *James Joyce Quarterly*, 16 (1978–9), 111–21.

17. Deming, *Critical Heritage*, vol. I, pp. 61–2.

18. William Empson, 'The Theme of *Ulysses*', *Kenyon Review*, 18 (Winter 1956), 36.

19. MaCCabe, *James Joyce and the Revolution of the Word*, p. 29.

20. [A reference to Frank Kermode, *The Sense of an Ending: Studies in the Theory of Fiction* (London, 1966). Ed.]

21. Samuel Beckett, *Molloy*, in *Three Novels: 'Molloy', 'Malone Dies', 'The Unnamable'* (New York, 1958), p. 91.

22. Zack Bowen, 'Joyce and the Epiphany Concept: A New Approach', *Journal of Modern Literature*, 9 (1981–2), 106–7.

23. Donald T. Tochiana, *Backgrounds for Joyce's 'Dubliners'* (Boston, 1986), p. 18.

24. Joyce, *Letters*, vol. I, ed. Stuart Gilbert (New York, 1957), p. 55.

25. [See Dettmar, *The Illicit Joyce of Postmodernism*, ch. 3 for further discussion of this idea. Ed.]

26. Joyce, *Letters*, vol. II, p. 86.

27. Thus, clearly, I read this letter rather differently than does Richard Ellmann, *James Joyce*, rev. edn (Oxford, 1982), p. 195, who comments that while living in Trieste Joyce 'often went to the Greek Orthodox Church to compare its ritual, which he considered amateurish, with the Roman'.

28. Stanislaus Joyce, *My Brother's Keeper*, ed. Richard Ellmann (London, 1958), p. 116.

29. While critics have expended considerable time and ink puzzling over exactly what Joyce mean by 'a style of scrupulous meanness', the fact is that we will never know with any certainty. In the face of that uncertainty, I am inclined to believe that 'scrupulous meanness' refers to the surface stylistic poverty of most the volume's narrative – the most noticeable characteristic for *Dubliners*'s first generation of readers. For example, Gerald Gould, writing in the *New Statesman*: 'He has plenty of humour, but it is always the humour of the fact, not of the comment. He dares to let people speak for themselves with the awkward meticulousness, the persistent incompetent repetition, of actual human intercourse. If you have never realised before how direly our daily conversation needs editing, you will realise it from Mr. Joyce's pages. One very powerful story, called "Grace", consists chiefly of lengthy talk so banal, so true to life, that one can scarcely endure it – though one can still less leave off reading it' (Deming, *Critical Heritage*, vol 1, p. 63). Or, more pithily, Ezra Pound: 'I can lay down a good piece of French writing and pick up a piece of writing by Mr. Joyce without feeling as if my head were being stuffed through a cushion' (Deming, vol 1, p. 66).

30. MacCabe, *Revolution of the Word*, p. 28.

31. Morris Beja, 'One Good Look at Themselves: Epiphanies in *Dubliners*', in *Work in Progress: Joyce Centenary Essays*, ed. Richard F. Peterson, Alan M. Cohn, and Edmund L. Epstein (Carbondale, IL, 1983), p. 3.

32. Scholes and Litz write in their edition of *Dubliners* that 'critics have applied the notion of epiphany to that moment in a *Dubliners* story when some sort of revelation takes place. ... "Epiphany" thus comes to mean a moment of revelation or insight such as usually climaxes a *Dubliners* story' (*D*, p. 255).

33. James Joyce, *Stephen Hero*, ed. John J. Slocum and Herbert Cahoon, second edn (New York, 1963), p. 211.

34. *D*, p. 254. Stanislaus Joyce seems to have had only this second type of epiphany in mind in his well-known description of the epiphanies: 'Another experimental form which his literary urge took ... consisted in the noting of what he called "epiphanies" – manifestations or

revelations. Jim always had a contempt for secrecy, and these notes were in the beginning ironical observations of slips, and little errors and gestures – mere straws in the wind – by which people betrayed the very things they were most careful to conceal' (S. Joyce, *My Brother's Keeper*, p. 134).

35. Tindall suggest that this pairing of epiphanies is Joyce's usual procedure in *Dubliners*: 'In most of these stories, there are two epiphanies, similar but not identical: one for the reader, the other for the hero or victim' (Tindall, *Reader's Guide to Joyce*, p. 28).

36. This is the epiphany Stephen records there: 'The Young Lady – (drawling discretely) ... O, yes ... I was ... at the ... cha ... pel ...
The Young Gentleman – (inaudibly) ... I ... (again inaudibly) ... I ...
The Young Lady – (softly) ... O ... but you're ... ve ... ry ... wick ... ed ...' (Joyce, *Stephen Hero*, p. 211).

37. Bowen, 'Joyce and Epiphany Concept', p. 107.

38. Virginia Woolf, *To the Lighthouse* (New York, 1955), p. 310.

39. [W. B. Yeats, 'The Phases of the Moon', in *Yeats's Poems*, ed. A. Norman Jeffares (London, 1989), p. 269. Ed.]

40. [T. S. Eliot, 'Gerontion', in *Collected Poems 1909–1962* (London, 1974), p. 40. Ed.]

41. Beja, 'One Good Look at Themselves', pp. 10; 9.

42. Bowen, 'Joyce and the Epiphany Concept', p. 106.

43. James Joyce, *Ulysses*, ed. Hans Walter Gabler et al. (New York, 1986), p. 337.

44. Hugh Kenner, *Ulysses* (London, 1982).

45. Sir Walter Scott, *The Abbot* (Philadelphia, 1887), pp. 14–15.

46. In a letter to R. W. D. Rouse, 30 December 1934; Ezra Pound, *Selected Letters, 1907–1941*, ed. D. D. Paige (New York, 1971), p. 263.

47. Joyce, *Letters*, vol I, p. 64.

48. Though the instances are too numerous to discuss in any detail here, Joyce systematically undermines the traditional symbolic equation of the mirror with self-awareness throughout *Dubliners*.

49. Margot Norris, *Joyce's Web: The Social Unraveling of Modernism* (Austin, TX, 1992), p. 120.

50. [Dettmar's term for a kind of misreading or interpretation 'in honour of the "generous tears" that fill our eyes, as they do the eyes of Gabriel Conroy and Joe Donnelly at crucial moments in their stories, and

prevent our seeing things quite distinctly' (Dettmar, *The Illicit Joyce of Postmodernism*, p. 100). Ed.]

51. Leonard, *Reading 'Dubliners' Again*, p. 6.

52. Kathy Acker, 'Devoured by Myths: An Interview with Sylvère Lotringer' in *Hannibal Lecter, My Father* (New York, 1991), p. 15.

53. Jonathan Swift, *A Tale of a Tub with Other Early Works 1696–1707*, ed. Herbert Davis (Oxford, 1965), p. 140.

10

'Have you no homes to go to?': James Joyce and the Politics of Paralysis

LUKE GIBBONS

> The vision made him feel keenly the poverty of his own purse and
> spirit ... He would be thirty-one in November. Would he never get a
> good job? Would he never have a home of his own?
>
> 'Two Gallants'
>
> – We were waiting for him to come home with the money. He never
> seems to think he has a home at all.
>
> 'Grace'

Returning from a visit to Ireland in 1903, the novelist Filson
Young commented on the torpor and listlessness that was endemic
to Irish society: 'The sands of national life have run very low in
the glass; the people are physically and mentally exhausted, apa-
thetic, resigned; the very soil of the country itself is starved and
impoverished. So stands Ireland, weak and emaciated, at the
crossroads.'[1] Contrary to de Valera's later comely vision, the view
from this crossroads is not very inspiring, for all traces of enjoyment, or even sobriety and work discipline, have vanished from
the landscape: 'There are no organised amusements; half the
prisons and workhouses are derelict; and only three great tumor-
ous growths stand triumphant and alive – the lunatic asylum, the
public house, and the Catholic chapel; and into these the life of
the remaining population is steadily absorbed.'[2] This bleak vista is

not due to the improving zeal of Puritanism, for Ireland 'never knew that austere and spiritual blend of character that has elsewhere been the legacy of the Puritans'. Instead, it derives from an unstable alliance between the vestiges of a premodern folk culture and the ornamental allure of the Catholic Church: 'For Ireland there can be nothing between paganism and that marvellous superstructure of symbolism which the Roman Catholic faith rears upon an emotional foundation.'[3]

It is worth speculating whether James Joyce knew Filson Young's book, and whether it played any role in introducing the social aspects on the theme of 'paralysis' in *Dubliners*, so notably absent from the earliest publication of the stories. Certainly, the description of the 'dull routine' of Irish life in *Stephen Hero* – 'a life lived in cunning and fear between the shadows of the parish chapel and the asylum' – evokes Young's characterisation above, and echoes of *Ireland at the Crossroads* also appear in *Dubliners*.[4] In any case, the paths of both authors crossed when Joyce sent the manuscript of his stories to Grant Richards, Young's publisher, in 1905.[5] Young was the publisher's reader, and sent a favourable report, on the strength of which Richards signed a contract, ill-fated as it turned out, with Joyce. Young found that Joyce portrayed Dublin 'with sympathy and patience which equal its knowledge of ... its idiom, its people, its streets and its little houses', and, in a turn of phrase echoed in *Ulysses*, praised his 'artistic sincerity [which] has been placed above other cries in the street.'[6] One of the most interesting aspects of Young's own diagnosis of the ills facing Ireland is that it is not poverty alone which is the cause of the problem, but the dysfunctional forms taken by post-Famine modernisation. The restructuring of the economy and the conversion of vast tracts of land into cattle pasture was a recipe for emigration and demoralisation in the outlying areas: 'Along the whole western Irish coast is to be found one great natural influence, unchanging, paralysing, daunting': 'No amenities, no festivities; even the family affection – that great and tragic possession of the Irish – fostered and encouraged, not by community of joy, but by community of misfortune, and too often withered and ended by departure and separation.'[7] Hence the stunted world of *Stephen Hero* and *Dubliners* in which lives are numbed even by the very affections of family and home, the last outposts of intimacy in the disenchanted world of bourgeois private life.

The pathology of post-Famine Ireland

The word 'paralysis' is explicitly introduced in the opening paragraph of 'The Sisters' in *Dubliners*, but as we have noted above, the earliest version of the story, published in the *Irish Homestead* in 1904, did not employ the term.[8] It first appears in essays and letters written by Joyce during this period,[9] and also surfaces in *Stephen Hero* (1904–6) in a context which accords with Filson Young's indictment of Catholicism, but which also evokes morbid images of social plague and pestilence:

> The deadly chill of the atmosphere of the college paralysed Stephen's heart. In a stupour of powerlessness he reviewed the plague of Catholicism. He seemed to see the vermin begotten in the catacombs in an age of sickness and cruelty issuing forth upon the plains and mountains of Europe ... Contempt of [the body] human nature, weakness, nervous tremblings, fear of day and joy, distrust of man and life, hemiplegia of the will, beset the body burdened and disaffected in its members by its black tyrannous lice.[10]

For Stephen's Irish contemporaries, the spectre of disease and pestilence was likely to recall the recent catastrophe of the Great Famine rather than the more distant European past: 'Potato Preservative against Plague and Pestilence, pray for us', intone the 'daughters of Erin' in *Ulysses*, mocking the superstitious trappings of Catholic devotional practices.[11] As Stephen himself drifts through the backstreets of Dublin, the sight of a 'burly black-vested priest taking a stroll of pleasant inspection through these warrens' provokes his anger, and he curses the inhabitants of an island 'who entrust their wills and minds to others that they ensure for themselves a life of spiritual paralysis', while Christ and Caesar 'wax fat upon a starveling rabblement'.[12]

In the eyes of many observers, the devastation wrought upon Irish society both during and after the Famine was such that the entire culture seemed reduced to the kind of enervation associated with hysteria, what became known as 'the great silence'. According to W. Steuart Trench, recounting his own harrowing experiences of Kerry:

> Half Ireland was stunned by the suddenness of the calamity, and Kenmare was completely paralysed ... The local gentry were paralysed, the tradesmen were paralysed, the people were paralysed, and the squatters and cottiers and smallholders ... unable from hunger to

work, and hopeless of any sufficient relief from extraneous sources, sank quietly down, some in their houses, some at the relief works, and died almost without a struggle.[13]

In a sense, the Famine effected in four years what took over four centuries to achieve on the European mainland, namely, the purging of an unruly premodern culture from a newly constituted bourgeois public sphere. As a number of recent scholars have argued, following the pioneering analyses of Norbert Elias and Mikhail Bakhtin, the early modern era witnessed a concerted effort on the part of liberal reformers in Europe to purge popular culture of its festive or carnivalesque elements, and to release prospective citizens and rational subjects from their dependence on what were considered grotesque communal rituals.[14] Through processes of fragmentation, marginalisation, sublimation, and suppression, traditional practices involving bodily excesses such as feasting, violence, drinking, processions, fairs, wakes, superstition, rowdy spectacles, and so on, were brought under scientific observation and subjected to systematic social regulations. These controlling mechanisms sought not so much to eliminate these practices as to sanitise and refine them, in particular redirecting and privatising the sexual energies associated with carnival within the more manageable confines of the home. Much of the animus against superstition and irrationality was directed against the Catholic Church, and the affront presented by its mystique and medievalism to the 'march of intelligence'. It is not surprising, therefore, that the Irish were considered to be in particular need of rational enlightenment, if they were to take their place in the modern world. According to the great historian, W. E. H. Lecky, in a character sketch of the Irish preceded by an image of barely literate priests and monks 'flitting to and fro among the mud hovels':

> In the absence of industrial and intellectual life, and under the constant pressures that draw men to the unseen world, Catholicism acquired an almost undivided empire over the affections and imaginations of the [Irish] people. The type of religion was grossly superstitious. It consecrated that mendicancy which is one of the worst evils of Irish life. Its numerous holidays aggravated the natural idleness of the people. It had no tendency to form those habits of self-reliance, those energetic political and industrial virtues in which the Irish character was and is lamentably deficient; but it filled the imagination with wild and beautiful legends ... and diffused abroad a deep feeling of content and resignation in extreme poverty ...

which has preserved it from at least some of the worst vices that usually accompany social convulsions and great political agitations on the Continent.[15]

It is not too difficult to see in Lecky's diagnosis the elements of quietism and superstition which, as we have noted, characterised Irish responses to the Great Famine in the eyes of both contemporary and later commentators.[16] Lecky, however, was concerned to link this with the historical absence of other kinds of convulsions in Ireland, those having to do with the social hysteria which attended the witch craze in Europe in the previous two centuries. As the author of the highly successful *The History of the Rise and Influence of the Spirit of Rationalism in Europe* (1865),[17] Lecky's ambitious attempt to demonstrate the triumph of reason over irrationality, and to secularise the public sphere, exerted enormous influence on his European contemporaries, not least the young Sigmund Freud. According to William McGrath, it may indeed have been Freud's reading of Lecky which first stimulated his interest in hysteria.[18] Though Freud persisted at one level in construing nervous disorders as the result of purely individual problems, his early psychological researches were part of a general European movement, spearheaded by the great French neurologist Jean-Martin Charcot, which applied scientific, medical explanations to hitherto inexplicable forms of social and religious behaviour. This intellectual trend was aligned to a wider political project which sought to liberalise society by challenging the influence of religion, and particularly the Catholic Church, in schools, hospitals, and other areas of public life.[19] The irony facing social reformers in Ireland, however, was that whereas the Catholic Church was the main target of criticism in metropolitan Europe, the task of modernising Irish society after the Famine devolved on to the Catholic Church itself, and a debilitated middle class coming out from under both the shadow of catastrophe and the legacy of colonial rule.

Though the Famine had dealt a body blow, quite literally, to the carnality of a wayward folk culture, it was unable to displace these energies on to the home, due to the instability of the family, and the frustration of even the limited pleasures provided by the bourgeois privatisation of the erotic, in the post-Famine reorganisation of society. As Clair Wills observes of the actualities of family life in relation to the new emergent ideologies of faith and fatherland,

Given the emphasis in conservative rhetoric on the family as the locus and breeding ground of distinct and traditional values, and on the need to protect it from encroachment by the welfare state, the typically open-ended character of the Irish family until quite recently seems ironic. It is not simply, as [Dympna] McLoughlin has argued, that there were alternative forms of familial and sexual relationship – the pauper family, the gentleman's miss, prostitution – but also that because of the dual institutions of emigration and [domestic] service, the family was not bounded in the way that we conceive of today. In effect, family members were always living in one another's households.[20]

As the incessant campaign against ribald wake amusements shows, the fact that a whole range of popular rituals and practices took place indoors was not sufficient to domesticate them, for they were, like the family structure itself, bound up with communal ties, and with the major festivals and patterns which punctuated the cultural calendar.[21] The most anomalous feature of the disciplinary regimes introduced to curtail the excesses of popular culture in post-Famine Ireland was their ineluctable public dimension, and their inability to fully privatise the communal aspects of culture. Hence, the distinctive character of the 'Devotional Revolution' in the Catholic Church, which sought to counter pre-Famine communal religious practices by an insistence on forms of worship centring on mass attendance, Benediction, devotions, and regular confession, which were of an equally public and 'associative' nature.[22] As Filson Young so graphically puts it, it was as if the tawdry ornamental excesses of the new churches – 'the sickening images, with their gaudy paintings of pink and blue, the wounds gushing crimson paint, the Virgins under their hideous canopies of Reckitt's blue, the prophets in vermilion and purple, the glare and blaze of cheap and hideous decorations that enshrine the mysteries of the Mass',[23] were designed as ersatz compensations for the more earthy sensuality of a once thriving vernacular culture.

For these reasons, the conditions prevailing in other parts of Europe whereby the emotional excesses of carnival and popular customs were 'interiorised' in domestic space, whether in a bourgeois intimate sphere or the more disruptive eroticism of hysteria, did not exist in Ireland. For one thing, the time scale involved in this fundamental transformation of culture was too short and too abrupt. Lecky, Charcot, and Freud were looking at a process which took centuries to evolve, even if the final convulsive spasms were not manifest until the nineteenth century. In Ireland, however, as we have observed, the Famine concentrated in a few years the work of centuries, so that the cultural devastation which ensued did not have the time, the 'long duration', to work its way fully through society. According to Catherine Clément, the hysteric 'whose body is transformed into a theatre for forgotten scenes, relives the past' in a manner akin to the 'sorceress' or 'witch' who 'incarnates the reinscription of the traces of paganism that triumphant Christianity repressed'.[24] Instead of being privatised in the domestic sphere in Ireland, however, these 'forgotten scenes' maintained a liminal or clandestine existence in public space, the spectral traces of the past cohabiting with the modernity that was supposed to abolish it.

It is in this context that we must view the repeated expressions of outrage and bewilderment over the persistence of premodern culture, both in its sinister and carnivalesque forms, in late nineteenth-century Ireland. In his controversial diagnosis of the ills pervading Ireland at the turn of the century, *Five Years in Ireland, 1895–1900*, Michael J. F. McCarthy includes, along with a chapter on 'The Helplessness of the Catholic Peasantry', two further related chapters on 'Belief in Fairies and Witches' and 'Belief in Fairies and Devils and the Tortures of Hell'.[25] These latter chapters deal with a number of gruesome incidents which, the author reminds us, if not exemplary, at least touch on the lives of the thousands of country people 'who, if they do not firmly believe the superstitions which led to such horrible results in these cases, do certainly border on these beliefs'.[26] The most notorious of these took place in County Tipperary in 1895 when a young woman, Bridget Cleary, was tortured and burned to death in her kitchen by her husband, father, and neighbours on the grounds that she may have been a witch or 'possessed by the fairies'. Like the Maamtrasna murders in the west of Ireland a decade earlier, this arrocity became part of a protracted national debate on the state of Ireland at the end of the nineteenth century, coinciding, as Angela Bourke has shown, not only with the arrest and trial of Oscar Wilde, but also with the upsurge of interest in folklore and the occult inspired by the Celtic Twilight and the Literary Revival.[27]

The fashionable craze for the occult in metropolitan Britain represented a retreat from traditional religion and the public world, an attempt to fill a spiritual void through a privatisation of the supernatural in darkened Victorian drawing rooms. By contrast, the link between the occult and folk culture in Ireland allowed a social élite to renew its contact with the wider community, drawing on an alternative clandestine culture to that of the official public sphere: 'I have longed to turn Catholic, that I might be nearer to the people', Lady Gregory confided to Yeats, 'but you have taught me that paganism brings me nearer still'.[28] Yet the brutality of the Bridget Cleary affair was a harsh reminder to those who dreamed of fairyland that their worst nightmares might be confirmed by venturing into the otherworld of rural Ireland.[29] Agitated by the episode, Yeats sought reassurance that when spirits occupy the body, they seek merely to make it uncomfortable for its tenants, but are 'not likely to go too far':

> A man actually did burn his wife to death, in Tipperary a few years ago, and is no doubt still in prison for it. My uncle, George Pollexfen, had an old servant Mary Battle, and when she spoke of the case to me, she described that man as very superstitious. I asked her what she meant by that and she explained that everybody knew that you must only threaten, for whatever injury you did to the changeling the faeries would do to the living person they had carried away ... The Tipperary witch-burner only half knew his own belief.[30]

So far from being a release from the fallen condition of the modern world, not least of the unsettling aspects of this manifestation of the occult was that it did not take place in a hovel, or a remote rural setting, but in a new labourer's cottage beside the public road in Ballyvadlea, County Tipperary. Representatives of the emergent bourgeoisie such as the local medical doctor, the priest, the police, big farmers, and even the market in the form of an egg salesman, coexisted in the story alongside the 'fairy fort' which brought Bridget Cleary to her doom.[31] This relic of an irrational culture, according to McCarthy, exercised a pernicious influence over the inhabitants of the district:

> I am informed that people in Ballyvadlea believe that a person being near this fort at night is liable to be struck with rheumatism, *paralysis* and so forth! Those accursed unlovely and useless remains of barbarism should be levelled to the ground by every man who wishes to see Ireland prosper. I myself know a score of farmers who have these forts on their land: all farmers of the best, comfortable, rational, hospitable, intelligent, keen men of business: yet, not one of them has the courage to remove these nuisances from their holdings, although they continually grumble at the inconvenience they cause.[32]

These events, he continues, took place 'not in darkest Africa, but in Tipperary; not in the ninth or tenth, but at the close of the nineteenth century; not among atheists, but among Catholics, with the Rosary on their lips, and with the priest celebrating mass in their houses.[33] For all the rigours of the 'Devotional Revolution' and the craven pursuit of respectability displayed by the new middle class, the demons of the past had not yet been exorcised.

Joyce and the suburban supernatural

> Out of the material and spiritual battle which has gone so hardly with her, Ireland has emerged with many memories of beliefs ...
> (James Joyce, review of Lady Gregory's *Poets and Dreamers*)

That the liminal forces of the otherworld infiltrated not only the countryside but also the city, unsettling the boundaries of the sedate urban household, is clear from Joyce's description of the long-suffering Mrs. Kernan in 'Grace':

> Her beliefs were not extravagant. She believed steadily in the Sacred Heart as the most generally useful of all Catholic devotions and approved of the sacraments. Her faith was bounded by the kitchen, but, if she was put to it, she could believe also in the banshee and in the Holy Ghost.
>
> (*D*, p. 464)[34]

Though regulated by the tempo and commerce of the modern city, Dublin was subject also to a less frenetic, 'sacred' sense of time, marked characteristically by women and punctuated by Church holy days such as the Epiphany or, even more vestigially, by traces of pagan culture and the old Celtic calendar such as Halloween.[35]

Halloween, of course, was the season in which witches made their appearance, and if the hysteric's body is a secular counterpart, in however muted a form, of the communal suspicion of old, unmarried women which plagued the Middle Ages, then Maria in 'Clay' is indeed one of life's losers. Set on Halloween eve, her physiognomy indicates that all is not well at the outset, as if her body speaks louder than her words, or even her thoughts: 'Maria was a very, very small person indeed, but she had a very long nose and a very long chin. She talked a little through her nose, always soothingly: "*Yes, my dear*," and "*No, my dear*" ' (*D*, p. 110). On this night above all she is conscious of modern urban time, for she carefully estimates how long it will take her to travel on the tram across the city from Ballsbridge where she works, to the home of Joe Donnelly, whom she once nursed, in Drumcondra: 'From Ballsbridge to the Pillar, twenty minutes; from the Pillar to Drumcondra, twenty minutes; and twenty minutes to buy the things. She would be there before eight' (D, p. 110). The Dublin by Lamplight laundry in Ballsbridge where Maria works is an institution for 'fallen women' who, literally, have no homes to go to, but that she is also condemned to this fate by virtue of her lack of marriage prospects is something she can barely contemplate. 'Often,' she muses in relation to Joe, 'he had wanted her to go and live with them; but she would have felt herself in the way (though Joe's wife was ever so nice to her) and she had become accustomed to the life of the laundry' (D, p. 111). When the coarse inmates of the institution tease Maria over getting the ring in the barmbrack at tea, she 'had to laugh and say she didn't want any ring or man either; and when she laughed her grey green eyes sparkled with disappointed shyness ... till the top of her nose nearly met the tip of her chin and till her minute body nearly shook itself asunder' (D, p. 112).

It is striking, as Margot Norris notes in her acute analysis of the story, that the term 'witch' is not actually mentioned in 'Clay', any more than the 'soft wet substance' which Maria touches in the party game is named (apart from the title). But it does not follow from this that the appellation of 'witch' is simply a projection of a witch-hunting proclivity in the reader's ill-disposed imagination, 'a hermeneutical touch as poisonous as that of any witch who ever turned a prince into a toad'.[36] As Norris herself shows, the whole story is structured around such narrative ellipses, and no more so than in the 'semiotic silences', in keeping with the muted condition of the hysteric, which prevents Maria from naming her own experiences. Her repeated involuntary spasms betray rather than express her aching inner life. When she dithers in a shop over buying a plum cake to bring as a present to Joe's house, 'the stylish young lady behind the counter, who was evidently a little annoyed by her, asked her was it wedding cake she wanted to buy. That made Maria blush and smile at the young lady'. (D, pp. 113–14). On the tram, she is so taken aback by a 'colonel-looking gentleman' who strikes up a conversation with her that she forgets the plum cake, and 'remembering how confused the gentleman with the greyish moustache had made her, coloured with shame and vexation and disappointment' (D, p. 115). Her spirits are lifted, however, when the party assembled in Joe's house begin to play Halloween games, of the kind which marked the end of the old Celtic year. As O'Suilleabhain notes, many of these were divinatory in nature, as traditional communities sought to allay the uncertainty of the future.[37] It is one of these which proves Maria's undoing as, blind-folded, her fingers alight not on a prayer book (indicating a reli-gious vocation), water (a sign of emigration), or a wedding ring, but on a portent of death, a saucer of clay substituted as a prank by the children next door. 'She felt a soft wet substance with her fingers and was surprised that nobody spoke or took off her bandage. There was a pause for a few seconds; and then a great deal of scuffling and whispering' (D, p. 117), as those around her tried to shield her from the pain of recognition.

That the truth sinks into her body, however, is clear from her rendering of her party piece, 'I Dreamt that I Dwelt in Marble Halls', in which she suppresses the second verse, with its fantasy of noble suitors lining up for her hand, and involuntarily repeats the first verse. For Maria, dwelling itself is the stuff of dreams, and her forgetting is symptomatic not only of her predicament, but of a whole culture's repression of its family romances through the atrophy of late and loveless marriages. Many Halloween rituals di-rectly addressed the threat of famine, and in this connection, as Donald Torchiana observes, the fact 'that four children of the same family should receive prayer book and water' in the divination game 'suggests the narrowed options in Irish life since the Famine – the church, the marriageless state, and emigration'.[38] All rituals are a form of repetition, but whereas many traditional folk practices perform a constructive role, transforming 'a passive into an active position which results in a mastery over a disturbing, wounding event', destructive repetition is compulsive, based on sameness, stasis, and ultimately (as the clay in the saucer indicates) death.[39] The equation of desiccated ritual with death, and indeed clay, is seen to telling effect in the abject wake which follows Isabel's death in *Stephen Hero*: no one 'can contemplate', muses Stephen, 'the network of falsities and trivialities which make up the funeral of a dead burgher without extreme disgust'.[40] 'The inexpressively mean way in which his sister had been buried' prompts the young Stephen to flout bourgeois propriety by sharing a pint of beer with the grave-diggers rather than the 'small specials' more suited to mourners: 'He was conscious of his startled father and he felt the savour of the bitter clay of the graveyard in his throat.'[41] What we witness in 'Clay' is a similar conversion of enabling rituals into their immobilising opposites, as vestiges of the communal past wither in the emotional sterility of parlour games in bourgeois Dublin. As Kershner describes this process: 'Significantly, the game in which Maria chooses the clay is a traditional one; but the folk tradition, with its possibility of brutal honesty, does not fit the bourgeois household in which everyone conspires to conceal from Maria what she has chosen in her life.'[42]

The fact that the disruptive substance in the parlour game is introduced from the outside (the garden), and indeed by members of the wider community (neighbours) rather than the family, attests to the manner in which the occult hovers in the unresolved regions between the public and private space, in what might be seen as a spectral public sphere. As Bourke contends, part of the underlying animus against Bridget Cleary was that she violated the boundaries between 'inside' and 'outside', between domestic and communal life. Her crime was that she had allegedly taken to straying from the household, and walking alone in a nearby fairy fort, but it is clear that she had also strayed from her crucial role as mother, by not producing any children in six years of marriage: 'Legends of fairy abduction express metaphorically ... the "floating" position of women in the status hierarchy' who were unmarried, or who had failed in the reproductive roles allotted to them in the community.[43] Though veiled in the mystique of the otherworld, Bridget Cleary was, in fact, a victim of a form of domestic violence brought to its ultimate tragic denouement.

The tyranny of home

> The subject of the play is genius breaking out in the home and against the home. You needn't have gone to see it. It's going to happen in your own house.
>
> (James Joyce, on the play *Magda*, 1898)

Domestic violence, albeit of a more understated variety, occurs in 'Eveline' when a young woman attempts to escape the emotional aridity of the home after her mother's death, to escape with her paramour to far-off Buenos Aires. Home in this case signifies not a haven in a heartless world but the lifeless monotony of domestic routines: 'Home! She looked around the room, reviewing all its familiar objects which she had dusted once a week for so many years, wondering where on earth all the dust came from' (*D*, pp. 37–8). The futility of repetition embraces the tragedy of her mother's death, which presides over the story, as evinced by her unintelligible last words: 'saying constantly with foolish insistence "Derevaun Seraun! Derevaun Seraun!" ' (*D*, p. 41). It is significant that Eveline's desire to escape is precipitated not only by her mother's death, but also by her father's domestic violence, which is also construed as repetition:

> She would not be treated as her mother had been. Even now, though she was over nineteen, she sometimes felt herself in danger of her father's violence. She knew it was that that had given her the palpitations. When they were growing up he had never gone for her, like he used to go for Harry and Ernest, because she was a girl; but latterly he had begun to threaten her and say what he would do to her only for her dead mother's sake.
>
> (*D*, p. 38–9).

It may be that Eveline's last-minute change of heart regarding her plans to emigrate is motivated by a deep-seated fear of more domestic violence, for as Katherine Mullin shows in her chapter in another volume, behind the smooth talk of her beau Frank, and his promise of 'a home waiting for her' in Buenos Aires, lies the moral panic of white slavery, with its dismal prospects of seduction, betrayal, and abandonment.[44] In this, as Mullin suggests, 'Eveline' acts as a parody of the kind of uplifting tales on emigration carried by *The Irish Homestead* which contrasted the family romances of idyllic Irish homes with the fleshpots of foreign climes. In one of the canonical homilies on this theme, Revd J. Guinan's *Scenes and Sketches in an Irish Parish, or Priests and People in Doon* (1903), the eve of departure is indeed an American wake, for 'it might truly be said that the parting of many, aye, of most on that [railway] platform, would be the parting of death':

> Many of these rosy-faced, fair young girls, so pure, so innocent, so pious, were exchanging the calm and holy peace of home for an atmosphere of infidelity, scepticism and sin. Alas! some of them, now so like unto the angels, might yet be dragged down to shame and crime, and to an early and dishonoured grave.

And, as if with Eveline's premonition of her own future in mind, it continues:

> If they could only 'forecast the years', how many would choose to live on a dry crust at home rather than emigrate ... One trembled to think of how easily the designing wretches – who, 'tis said, haunt American ports – might deceive and ensnare these poor, sheepish, unsuspecting country girls, who never wandered more than a dozen miles before from the paternal hearth.[45]

In Joyce's story, however, home is not where you escape to, but where you escape from. Though Eveline seeks to reassure herself that 'in her home anyway she had shelter and food' (*D*, p. 38), in fact, due to her father's alcoholism, she 'had hard work to keep the house together and to see that the two young children who had been left to her charge went to school regularly and got their meals regularly' (*D*, p. 39). By the same token, Fr. Guinan inadvertently exposes the shadow of starvation lurking behind the family romance of faith and fatherland through his references to the 'dry crust at home': 'How blessed would have been the lot of that Irish girl, the poor, betrayed victim of hellish agencies of vice, had she remained at home and passed her days in the poverty, aye and wretchedness of a mud wall cabin – a wife and mother mayhap.'[46] Eveline's predicament is that even dreams of 'outside' and faraway places are intercepted by her domestic duties, and bring her back to the stasis of home. As she waits by the window with her farewell letters in her hand, 'inhaling the odour of dusty cretonne':

> Down far in the avenue she could hear a street organ playing. She knew the air. Strange that it should come that very night to remind her of the promise to her mother, her promise to keep the home together as long as she could. She remembered the last night of her mother's illness; she was again in the close dark room at the other side of the hall and outside she heard a melancholy air of Italy. The organ-player had been ordered to go away and given sixpence.
>
> (*D*, p. 41)

As Stephen Dedalus notes in *A Portrait of the Artist*, 'home' is one of the words, along with 'ale' and 'master', that sound different on English and Irish lips,[47] and we may speculate that the latter two words, with their associations of alcohol and colonial domination, are not unrelated to the different resonances of 'home' in Ireland.[48] In *Stephen Hero*, the young Stephen's determination not to be incarcerated within the home gives rise to his restless walks through the streets of Dublin, the wanderings not so much of a modern *flâneur* but of an outcast from a family whose members were strangers to themselves.[49] As Stephen 'promenaded miles of the streets' with his friend Cranly, it is as if the ground he covers distances him from his family, allowing him 'to spread out a few leagues of theory on the subject of the tyranny of home':

> His sister had become almost a stranger to him on account of the way in which she had been brought up. He had hardly spoken a hundred words to her since the time when they had been children together ... She was called his sister as his mother was called his mother but there had never been any proof of that relation offered him in their emotional attitude towards him, or any recognition of it permitted in his emotional attitude towards them.[50]

Such gestures towards intimacy as Stephen experiences take place in public space, as when he caresses Emma's hands on the step on the Rathmines tram,[51] or when she 'leaned appreciably' on his arm as they walk by the courting couples in dusky corners of St. Stephen's Green,[52] or when he tells her that the sight of her 'hips moving inside her waterproof' as she walked 'proudly through the decayed city' filled him with desire: 'I felt that I longed to hold you in my arms – your body. I longed for you to take me in your arms'.[53] As Jules David Law observes of his wider sense of belonging and attachment: 'In Stephen's mind, the integrity of home is preserved ... by a venture outside the home. The external thus supplements, and is perhaps superior to, the internal.'[54]

The meagre enjoyment which Stephen's father draws from life also has its source outside the home, for it was only on his endless social rounds that he 'had been accustomed to regard himself as the centre of a little world, the darling of a little society'. As his alcoholism and profligacy, however, brings increased misery and ruin on his family,

> He consoled and revenged himself by tirades so often prolonged and repeated that he was in danger of becoming a monomaniac. The hearth at night was the sacred witness of these revenges, pondered, muttered, growled and execrated. The exception which his clemency had originally made in favour of his wife was soon out of mind and she began to irritate him by her dutiful symbolism.[55]

Mr. Daedalus could be Eveline's father or, indeed, any of the pathetic figures whose recourse to domestic violence, whether levelled at women or children, runs like a discordant refrain through the pages of *Dubliners*, and, with its attendant chorus of alcoholism and emotional sterility, may be partly responsible for the different sound of 'home' to Irish and English ears. In 'The Boarding House', Mrs. Mooney arranges a separation from a butcher who 'drank, plundered the till, ran headlong into debt' (*D*, p. 166) and fought with her in public, before taking a cleaver to her one night. Mrs. Kernan, in 'Grace', is more stoical with regard to her husband's binges: 'She accepted his frequent intemperance as part of the climate, healed him dutifully whenever he was sick and always tried to make him eat a breakfast. There were worse husbands. He had never been violent since the boys had grown up' (*D*, p. 176). In several other stories – 'A Little Cloud', 'Counterparts', 'Ivy Day at the Committee Room', 'An Encounter' – children are on the receiving end of domestic rage, social frustration, or sexual abuse, not to mention the pervasive corporal punishment in *A Portrait* which was construed, perversely, as a disciplinary corrective to antisocial behaviour.

Some contemporary observers sought to account for the different responses to the idea of 'home' in Ireland and England by arguing that the dysfunctions of the family were greater in Ireland, not on account of a racial pathology, but due to the social and economic consequences of a post-Famine colonial condition. In keeping with Filson Young's analysis quoted above, Michael J. F. McCarthy cites the lack of an urban manufacturing base, and the absence of any vision of social reform in the Catholic Church, as being responsible for the breakdown of national character. In particular, he draws attention to the fact that the notorious Mecklenburgh Street (or 'Monto') area, the 'greatest blot' on public decency in Ireland or Great Britain, was allowed to carry on its immoral traffic in vice in the immediate vicinity of the Catholic Pro-Cathedral. McCarthy links this to the lack of legal protection afforded to women against domestic violence and, in this, both the Catholic Church and the colonial administration were in active collusion. As Elizabeth Steiner-Scott has recently shown, none of the landmark acts in English law, such as the 1853 and 1878 acts giving a wife greater protection against domestic violence, extended to Ireland, nor were the promoters of the sanctity of the home to the forefront of demands for this basic human right.[56] To call into question the integrity of the family was to undermine the foundational fictions of the colonial public sphere, and it was perhaps this porousness between public and private life which led Joyce to proclaim in an early letter to Nora: 'My mind rejects the whole present social order and Christianity – *home*, the recognised virtues, classes of life, and religious doctrines. How could I like the idea of *home?*.'[57]

In his initial plan for *Dubliners*, Joyce made explicit provision for stories dealing with 'public life', but none for private life, as if it had not yet constituted itself as a distinctive affective sphere. Freud's thesis in *Civilization and its Discontents*, that civilisation rests on a restriction of the erotic within the confines of the home, makes little sense when the home itself is drained of sexual passion, even by the standards of Victorian or bourgeois morality. It is this failure to fully interiorise paralysis as an ailment of the individual which accounts for its functioning as a 'cultural-somatic', and not just a psycho-somatic, condition in Ireland. These links between the public and the private survive in the endangered traces of unofficial street or public culture, and it is perhaps from this recalcitrant border zone that Joyce launched his own powerful raids on the inarticulate.[58] Notwithstanding the jingle in *Ulysses*, more than Plumtree's Potted Meat is required to make a home complete, or 'an abode of bliss', in the emotional void of Joyce's Dublin.

From *Semicolonial Joyce*, ed. Derek Attridge and Marjorie Howes (Cambridge, 2000), pp. 150–69.

Notes

[Luke Gibbons' essay is an excellent example of one of the most recent trends in Joyce criticism, Irish Studies. While many earlier critics have noted the importance of Joyce's Irish heritage to an understanding of his writing, it is only recently that Irish critics themselves, such as Gibbons, have read his work in close relation to the historical and political complexities of Ireland. Gibbons situates Joyce's central image of 'paralysis' in *Dubliners* within the context of Irish history in the years after the disasters of the famine in the mid-nineteenth century. In particular, Gibbons shows how the historical pressures of post-famine Ireland produced a complex and traumatic sense of what 'home' represented to Joyce, evident in 'Eveline', a story of potential emigration. The essay is a good example of the state of much contemporary theoretical work in literary studies: it is interdisciplinary in using Freud and feminist criticism, but based upon detailed historical work. It is useful to compare this version of postcolonial criticism to that employed by Cheng (essay 8) in this volume. A number of notes have been abbreviated for reasons of space. Ed.]

1. Filson Young, *Ireland at the Crossroads: An Essay in Explanation* (London, 1903), pp. 15–16. Young (1876–1938) was born in Ballyeaston, County Antrim, and spent most of his life as a novelist, critic, and journalist in London.

2. Young, *Ireland at the Crossroads*, pp. 5–6.

3. Ibid., p. 31.

4. See, for example, Young's discussion of the monks' sleeping practices in Mount Melleray, which is similar to that which recurs during the dinner conversation in 'The Dead': the monks, Young informs us, 'sleep in their habits, in cubicles partitioned off in the great dormitory; the cubicles are as big as an ordinary grave, and their furniture is simply a raised wooden platform with a mattress laid upon it' (*Ireland at the Crossroads*, p. 99).

5. Grant Richards wrote to Joyce on 10 May 1906: 'The man who read your stories for us was a man whose work you are likely to know, Filson Young (James Joyce, *Letters*, vol. II, ed. Richard Ellmann [New York, 1966], p. 135). Young's novel, *The Sands of Pleasure* (1905), was among the books in Joyce's Trieste library, and, as Kershner suggests in *Joyce, Bakhtin and Popular Literature: Chronicles of Disorder* (Chapel Hill, NC, 1989), pp. 272–7, its Ibsenite approach to sexuality and Parisian 'low-life' must have appealed to Joyce.

6. Cited in Marvin Magalaner and Richard M. Kain, *Joyce: The Man, the Work, the Reputation* (New York, 1962), p. 65. Young also discerned 'an order and symmetrical connection between the stories making them one book'. Though Richards claimed that Young agreed with this reservations about printing the book, the fact that Joyce valued his comments is clear from attempts to get him to write an introduction for the eventual publication of *Dubliners* in 1914. Young, however, did not accede to the request, for reasons that are not clear (Richard Ellmann, *James Joyce*, rev. edn [Oxford, 1982], p. 353).

7. Young, *Ireland at the Crossroads*, pp. 53; 52–3.

8. For the introduction of the theme of paralysis, and its sexual connotations, in the early fiction, see Burton A. Waisbren and Florence L. Walzl, 'Paresis and the Priest: James Joyce's Symbolic Use of Syphilis in "The Sisters" ', *Annals of Internal Medicine*, 80 (June 1974), 758–62.

9. For the most often cited formulations, see the description of the artist 'amid the general paralysis of an insane society' in Joyce's early essay, 'A Portrait of the Artist', *Poems and Shorter Writings*, ed. Richard Ellmann, A. Walton Litz and John Whittier-Ferguson (London, 1991);

Joyce's letter to Constantine Curran, July (?) 1904, in which he first proposes a collection of stories entitled *Dubliners*: 'I call the series Dubliners to betray the soul of that hemiplegia or paralysis which many consider a city' (*Letters*, vol. I, ed. Stuart Gilbert [New York, 1957), p. 55); and the well-known letter to Grant Richards, 5 May 1906: 'My intention was to write a chapter in the moral history of my country and I chose Dublin for the scene because that city seemed to me the centre of paralysis' (*Letters*, II, p. 134).

10. James Joyce, *Stephen Hero* (London, 1991), pp. 198–9.

11. As Ellmann, *James Joyce*, p. 79, notes, one of Joyce's earliest literary efforts, a play entitled *A Brilliant Career*, was described by William Archer as a 'huge fable of politics and pestilence'. For a particularly insightful account of the impact of the Great Famine on Joyce's writings, see Mary Lowe-Evans, *Crimes Against Fecundity: Joyce and Population Control* (Syracuse, NY, 1989), pp. 5–31.

12. Joyce, *Stephen Hero*, pp. 150–1. See also Stephen's description of bourgeois suburbia as 'those brown brick houses which seem the very incarnation of Irish paralysis' (p. 216).

13. W. Steuart Trench, *Realities of Irish Life* (London, 1868), pp. 113; 115.

14. See M. M. Bakhtin, *Rabelais and his World*, trans. H. Iswolski (Cambridge, MA, 1968) and Norbert Elias, *The Civilizing Process*, trans. E. Jephcott, 2 vols (New York, 1978, 1982).

15. W. E. H. Lecky, *Ireland in the Eighteenth Century*, vol. I (London, 1892), pp. 407–8.

16. It is ironical that as the author of four volumes on the turbulent 1790s in Ireland, Lecky persisted in seeing Ireland as missing the great political agitations which convulsed the Continent during this period.

17. Lecky's remarkably successful book went into eighteen editions and was translated into several languages. See Donal McCartney, *W. E. H. Lecky, Historian and Politician, 1838–1903* (Dublin, 1994), p. 34. The discussions of modernity and tradition in *Stephen Hero* (p. 154) bear the hallmarks of Lecky, and, indeed, Stephen comes across Moyhihan in the National Library, preparing for his inaugural address at the Literary and Historical Society, with 'some bulky volumes of Lecky at his side'.

18. William McGrath, *Freud's Discovery of Psychoanalysis: The Politics of Hysteria* (Ithaca, NY, 1986), p. 79.

19. See Jan Goldstein, 'The Hysteria Diagnosis and the Politics of Anticlericalism in Late Nineteenth-century France', *Journal of Modern History*, 54 (June 1982), 209–39.

20. Clair Wills, 'Rocking the Cradle? – Women's Studies and the Family in Twentieth-century Ireland', *Bullán*, 1:2 (1994), 102–3.

21. For the relationship between unruly conduct at wakes and wider communal concerns bound up with faction fighting and agrarian secret societies, see Sean O'Suilleabhain, *Irish Folk Custom and Belief* (Dublin, 1967), pp. 71–2.

22. It is difficult not to suspect that the undue importance subsequently attached to the family rosary, and to the Virgin Mary, was an attempt to bring religion into the household, the Catholic equivalent to reading the Bible. Even then, however, it was still 'public' in the sense that it involved a shared, participative ritual.

23. Young, *Ireland at the Crossroads*, p. 73.

24. Hélène Cixous and Catherine Clément, *The Newly Born Woman*, trans. Betsy Wing (Manchester, 1986), p. 5.

25. It is highly likely that Joyce was acquainted with McCarthy's anticlerical works, though he would not have sympathised with his imperial leanings. Joyce owned a copy of MacCarthy's *The Irish Revolution*, and Stanislaus Joyce, in *My Brother's Keeper* (London, 1958), records his own reading of MacCarthy's best known work, *Priests and People in Ireland* (1902).

26. Michael J. F. McCarthy, *Five Years in Ireland, 1895–1900* (London, 1902), pp. 141–2.

27. See Angela Bourke, 'Reading a Woman's Death: Colonial Text and Oral Tradition in Nineteenth-century Ireland', *Feminist Studies*, 21:3 (1995), 553–86, and *The Burning of Bridget Cleary* (London, 1999).

28. Cited in R. F. Foster, *W. B. Yeats: A Life*, vol. I, *The Apprentice Mage* (Oxford, 1997), p. 170.

29. I develop this point in ' "Some Hysterical Hatred": History, Hysteria and the Literary Revival, *Irish University Review*, 27:1 (1997), 7–23.

30. W. B. Yeats, 'Two Essays and Notes', in Lady Augusta Gregory, *Visions and Beliefs in the West of Ireland* (Gerrard's Cross, 1979), p. 360.

31. Bourke notes that 'All indications are that the Clearys were a modern couple, much more upwardly mobile in socio-economic terms than their neighbours or Bridget's relatives', 'Reading a Woman's Death', pp. 575–6.

32. McCarthy, *Five Years in Ireland*, p. 159. My italics.

33. Ibid., p. 173. As Bourke notes, citing the coroner's verdict that 'amongst Hottentots one would not expect to hear of such an occurrence', such comparisons with Africa were integral to colonial

attempts to primitivise subaltern culture, which, in the particular case of Ireland at the turn of the century, meant it could not be entrusted with Home Rule ('Reading a Woman's Death', pp. 558–60).

34. [All references to *Dubliners* are to James Joyce, *Dubliners* (London, 1991) and given in the text as *D*. Ed.].

35. See Mary Francis Cusack, *Women's Work in Modern Society* (Kenmare, 1975), p. 282.

36. Margot Norris, 'Narration Under a Blindfold: Reading Joyce's "Clay" ', *PMLA*, 102 (1987), 215. [Reprinted in this volume – Ed.]

37. That the spectre of death and famine loomed large at this particular time of year is clear from O'Suilleabhain's observation that Halloween was believed to be a time when 'fairy forts' were opened, and the dead might reappear. People stayed indoors 'and many games were played, and divinatory acts performed afterwards. The food supply for the winter being very important, hunger and famine were symbolically banished by throwing a cake of bread against the door' (*Irish Folk Custom and Belief*, p. 70). By losing the plum cake, Maria is, in effect, leaving the inner sanctum of the home at the mercy of the 'otherworld'. Stanislaus Joyce notes how James was not immune to a version of this custom, throwing a loaf of bread in through the front door of their house in Cabra on one New Year's Eve.

38. Donald T. Torchiana, *Backgrounds for Joyce's 'Dubliners'* (Boston, 1986), p. 157.

39. See Shlomith Rimmon-Kennan, 'The Paradoxical Status of Repetition', *Poetics Today*, I (1980), cited in Elizabeth Bronfen, *Over Her Dead Body: Death, Femininity and the Aesthetic* (Manchester, 1992), p. 325.

40. Joyce, *Stephen Hero*, p. 173.

41. Ibid.

42. Kershner, *Joyce, Bakhtin and Popular Literature*, p. 108.

43. Bourke, 'Reading a Woman's Death', p. 574.

44. [See Katherine Mullin, 'Don't Cry for Me, Argentina: "Eveline" and the Seductions of Emigration Propaganda', in *Semi-colonial Joyce*, ed. Derek Attridge and Marjorie Howes (Cambridge, 2000). Ed.]

45. Revd J. Canon Guinan ('A Country Curate'), *Scenes and Sketches in an Irish Parish, or Priests and People in Doon* (Dublin, 1925), pp. 43–4.

46. Ibid., p. 45.

47. James Joyce, *A Portrait of the Artist as a Young Man* (Harmondsworth, 1992), p. 205.

48. For an insightful discussion of Stephen's rejection of home, see Stephen Watt, *Joyce, O'Casey and the Irish Popular Theatre* (Syracuse, NY, 1991), pp. 93–112.

49. The cultural specificity of the *flâneur* in Joyce's Dublin is the subject of Enda Duffy, *The Subaltern 'Ulysses'* (Minneapolis, 1994), ch. 2.

50. Joyce, *Stephen Hero*, pp. 130; 131.

51. Ibid., p. 72.

52. Ibid., p. 158.

53. Ibid., pp. 202–3.

54. Jules David Law, 'Joyce's "Delicate Siamese" Equation: The Dialectic of Home in *Ulysses*', *PMLA*, 102 (1987), 203.

55. Joyce, *Stephen Hero*, p. 115.

56. Elizabeth Steiner-Scott. ' "To Bounce a Boot off her Now and Then": Domestic Violence in Post-Famine Ireland', *Women and Irish History*, ed. Maryann Giallancella Valiulis and Mary O'Dowd (Dublin, 1997).

57. Joyce, *Letters*, II, p. 48; italics mine.

58. I deal with this in relation to other works of Joyce in Luke Gibbons, ' "Where Wolfe Tone's Statue Was Not": Joyce, Monuments and Mourning in Irish Culture', paper delivered at Classic Joyce conference, Rome, June 1998.

Further Reading

Editions and Other Works

Dubliners, ed. Jeri Johnson, Oxford World's Classics (Oxford: Oxford University Press, 2000).

Dubliners, ed. Hans Walter Gabler and Walter Hettche (London: Garland, 1993).

Dubliners: An Annotated Edition, ed. John Wyse Jackson and Bernard McGinley (London: Sinclair-Stevenson, 1993).

Dubliners, ed. Terence Brown (Harmondsworth: Penguin, 1992).

Dubliners, ed. Joseph McMinn (Stroud: Sutton, 1992).

The James Joyce Archive, ed. Michael Groden (63 vols; New York and London: Garland, 1977–80), vols 4–6: *Dubliners* materials.

Dubliners, ed. Robert Scholes and A. Walton Litz, Viking Critical Library Edition, includes explanatory notes and critical essays (New York: Viking, 1969).

The Critical Writings of James Joyce, ed. Ellsworth Mason and Richard Ellmann (New York: Viking Press, 1973).

James Joyce: Occasional, Critical, and Political Writing, ed. Kevin Barry, Oxford World's Classics (Oxford: Oxford University Press, 2000).

Letters of James Joyce, 3 vols: vol. 1 ed. Stuart Gilbert; vols 2 and 3 ed. Richard Ellmann (New York: Viking, 1957, 1966).

Selected Letters, ed. Richard Ellmann (London: Faber, 1975).

Poems and Shorter Writings, ed. Richard Ellmann, A. Walton Litz, and John Whittier-Ferguson (London: Faber, 1991).

Biography

Richard Ellmann, *James Joyce* (1959; rev. edn 1982; Oxford: Oxford University Press, 1982).

Stanislaus Joyce, *My Brother's Keeper: James Joyce's Early Years*, ed. Richard Ellmann (1958; New York: Viking, 1969).

Arthur Power, *Conversations with James Joyce* (1974; Dublin: Lilliput Press, 1999).

Brenda Maddox, *Nora: A Biography of Nora Joyce* (London: Hamish Hamilton, 1988).

Bibliography

Robert H. Deming (ed.), *A Bibliography of James Joyce Studies*, 2nd edn (Boston: Hall, 1977).
Thomas Jackson Rice, *James Joyce: A Guide to Research* (New York and London: Garland, 1982).
John J. Slocum and Herbert Cahoon, *A Bibliography of James Joyce* (1954; Westport, CT: Greenwood Press, 1971).
James Joyce Quarterly. This periodical publishes lists of primary and secondary material on Joyce under the title 'Current James Joyce Checklist'. It also contains the most contemporary critical articles on Joyce.
Website: http://www.cohums.ohio-state.edu/english/organizations/ijjf/ – site for the International James Joyce Foundation; good links to the many Joyce sites worldwide.

Selected General Criticism of Joyce

[These studies of Joyce all contain useful discussions of *Dubliners*. I have concentrated mainly upon criticism informed by contemporary literary theory since the 1970s. Ed.]
Derek Attridge (ed.), *The Cambridge Companion to James Joyce* (Cambridge: Cambridge University Press, 1990).
Derek Attridge and Daniel Ferrer (eds), *Post-Structuralist Joyce: Essays from the French* (Cambridge: Cambridge University Press, 1984).
Derek Attridge and Marjorie Howes (eds), *Semicolonial Joyce* (Cambridge: Cambridge University Press, 2000).
Morris Beja et al. (eds), *James Joyce: The Centennial Symposium* (Urbana: University of Illinois Press, 1986).
Bernard Benstock (ed.), *The Augmented Ninth: Papers from the Ninth James Joyce Symposium* (Syracuse: Syracuse University Press, 1988).
Shari Benstock and Bernard Benstock, *Who's He When He's at Home: A James Joyce Directory* (Urbana: University of Illinois Press, 1980).
Keith Booker, *Joyce, Bakhtin and the Literary Tradition* (Ann Arbor: University of Michigan Press, 1995).
Zack Bowen and James F. Carens (eds), *A Companion to Joyce Studies* (Westport, CT: Greenwood Press, 1984).
John Brannigan, Geoff Ward and Julian Wolfreys (eds), *Re: Joyce: Text, Culture, Politics* (Basingstoke: Macmillan – now Palgrave Macmillan, 1998).
Sheldon Brivic, *The Veil of Signs: Joyce, Lacan, and Perception* (Champaign: University of Illinois Press, 1991).
Richard Brown, *James Joyce and Sexuality* (Cambridge: Cambridge University Press, 1985).
Vincent J. Cheng, *Joyce, Race and Empire* (Cambridge: Cambridge University Press, 1995).
Hélène Cixous, *The Exiles of James* (1968), trans. Sally A. J. Purcell (New York: David Lewis, 1972).
Steven Connor, *James Joyce*, Writers and their Work Series (Plymouth: Northcote House/British Council, 1996).

Robert H. Deming (ed.), *James Joyce: The Critical Heritage*, 2 vols (London: Routledge and Kegan Paul, 1970).

Kevin J. H. Dettmar, *The Illicit Joyce of Postmodernism* (Madison: University of Wisconsin Press, 1996).

James Fairhall, *James Joyce and the Question of History* (Cambridge: Cambridge University Press, 1993).

Ruth Frehner and Ursula Zellers (eds), *A Collideorscape of Joyce: Festschrift for Fritz Senn* (Dublin: Lilliput Press, 1998).

Susan Stanford Friedman (ed.), *Joyce: The Return of the Repressed* (Ithaca and London: Cornell University Press, 1993).

Vivien Heller, *Joyce, Decadence, and Emancipation* (Urbana: University of Illinois Press, 1995).

Suzette A. Henke, *James Joyce and the Politics of Desire* (New York/London: Routledge, 1990).

Cheryl Herr, *Joyce's Anatomy of Culture* (Urbana: University of Illinois Press, 1986).

Hugh Kenner, *Joyce's Voices* (Berkeley: University of California Press, 1978).

R. B. Kershner, *Joyce, Bakhtin and Popular Culture: Chronicles of Disorder* (Chapel Hill: University of North Carolina Press, 1989).

Colin MacCabe, *James Joyce and the Revolution of the Word* (Basingstoke: Macmillan, 1979).

Vicki Mahaffey, *Reauthorizing Joyce* (Cambridge: Cambridge University Press, 1988).

Dominic Manganiello, *Joyce's Politics* (London: Routledge, 1980).

Augustine Martin (ed.), *James Joyce: The Artist and the Labyrinth* (London: Ryan, 1990).

W. J. McCormack and Alistair Stead (eds), *James Joyce and Modern Literature* (London: Routledge, 1982).

Emer Nolan, *James Joyce and Nationalism* (London: Routledge, 1995).

Margot Norris, *Joyce's Web: The Social Unraveling of Modernism* (Austin: University of Texas Press, 1992).

Patrick Parrinder, *James Joyce* (Cambridge: Cambridge University Press, 1984).

Jean-Michel Rabaté, *James Joyce: Authorized Reader* (Baltimore: John's Hopkins University Press, 1991).

John Paul Riquelme, *Teller and Tale in Joyce's Fiction* (Baltimore: John's Hopkins University Press, 1983).

Alan Roughly, *James Joyce and Critical Theory: An Introduction* (Ann Arbor: University of Michigan Press, 1991).

Bonnie Kime Scott, *James Joyce*, Feminist Readings Series (Brighton: Harvester, 1987).

Bonnie Kime Scott, *Joyce and Feminism* (Bloomington: Indiana University Press, 1984).

Bonnie Kime Scott (ed.), *New Alliances in Joyce Studies* (Newark: University of Delaware Press, 1988).

Joseph Valente, *James Joyce and the Problem of Justice: Negotiating Sexual and Colonial Difference* (Cambridge: Cambridge University Press, 1995).

Joseph Valente (ed.), *Quare Joyce* (Ann Arbor: University of Michigan Press, 1998).
Katie Wales, *The Language of James Joyce* (Basingstoke: Macmillan – now Palgrave Macmillan, 1992).
Trevor L. Williams, *Reading Joyce Politically* (Gainesville: University of Florida Press, 1997).

Guides and Concordances to *Dubliners*

Donald T. Torchiana, *Backgrounds for Joyce's 'Dubliners'* (Boston: Allen and Unwin, 1986).
Don Gifford, *Joyce Annotated: Notes for 'Dubliners' and 'A Portrait of the Artist as a Young Man'*, 2nd edn (Berkeley: University of California Press, 1982).
Bruce Bidwell and Linda Heffer, *The Joycean Way: A Topographic Guide to 'Dubliners' and 'A Portrait of the Artist as a Young Man'* (Dublin: Wolfhound Press; Baltimore: Johns Hopkins University Press, 1982).
Wilhelm Füger (ed.), *Concordance to James Joyce's 'Dubliners'* (Hildesheim and New York: Georg Olms, 1980).

Selected Criticism of *Dubliners*

[I have concentrated mainly upon criticism informed by contemporary literary theory since the 1970s. Ed.]
Derek Attridge, 'Touching "Clay": Reference and Reality in *Dubliners*' in *Joyce Effects: On Language, Theory, and History* (Cambridge: Cambridge University Press, 2000).
Bruce Avery, 'Distant Music: Sound and the Dialogics of Satire in "The Dead" ', *James Joyce Quarterly*, 28:2 (1991), 473–83.
Ruth Bauerle, 'Date Rape, Mate Rape: A Liturgical Interpretation of "The Dead" ', in Bonnie Kime Scott (ed.), *New Alliances in Joyce Studies*.
Morris Beja (ed.), *'Dubliners' and 'A Portrait of the Artist as a Young Man': A Casebook* (Basingstoke: Macmillan, 1973).
Morris Beja, 'One Good Look at Themselves: Epiphanies in *Dubliners*' In *Work in Progress: Joyce Centenary Essays*, ed. Richard Petersen, A. Cohn, E. Epstein (Carbondale: Southern Illinois University Press, 1983).
Bernard Benstock, *Narrative Con/Texts in 'Dubliners'* (Basingstoke: Macmillan – now Palgrave Macmillan, 1994).
Alain Blayac, ' "After the Race": A Study in Epiphanies', *Les Cahiers de la Nouvelle: Journal of the Short Story in English*, 2 (1984), 115–27.
Harold Bloom (ed.), *Modern Critical Interpretations: James Joyce's 'Dubliners'* (New York, Chelsea House, 1988).
Rosa M. Bolleltieri Bosinelli and Harold F. Mosher Jr. (eds), *ReJoycing: New Readings of 'Dubliners'* (Lexington: University Press of Kentucky, 1998).
Zack Bowen, 'Joyce and the Epiphany Concept: A New Approach', *Journal of Modern Literature*, 9 (1981–2), 106–7.
Zack Bowen, 'Joyce's Prophylactic Paralysis: Exposure in *Dubliners*', *James Joyce Quarterly*, 19 (1982), 257–73.

Edward Brandabur, *A Scrupulous Meanness: A Study of Joyce's Early Work* (Urbana: University of Illinois Press, 1971).

Ross Chambers, 'Gabriel Conroy Sings for his Supper, or Love Refused' in *Modern Critical Interpretations: James Joyce's 'Dubliners'*, ed. Harold Bloom (New York, 1988).

Hélène Cixous, 'Joyce: The (R)use of Writing', in Derek Attridge and Daniel Ferrer, (eds), *Post-Structuralist Joyce: Essays from the French*.

Seamus Deane, 'Dead Ends: Joyce's Finest Moments', in Derek Attridge and Marjorie Howes (eds), *Semicolonial Joyce*.

Edward Duffy, ' "The Sisters" as the Introduction to *Dubliners*', *Papers on Language and Literature*, 22:4 (1986), 417–28.

Heyward Ehrlich, ' "Araby" in Context: The "Splendid Bazaar", Irish Orientalism, and James Clarence Mangan', *James Joyce Quarterly*, 35:2–3 (1998), 309–31.

Marilyn French, 'Missing Pieces in Joyce's *Dubliners*', *Twentieth Century Literature*, 24:4 (Winter 1978), 443–72.

Marilyn French, 'Women in Joyce's Dublin', in Bernard Benstock (ed.), *James Joyce: The Augmented Ninth*.

Sherrill E. Grace, 'Rediscovering Mrs. Kearney: An Other Reading of "A Mother" ', in Bernard Benstock (ed.), *James Joyce: The Augmented Ninth*.

Clive Hart (ed.), *James Joyce's 'Dubliners': Critical Essays* (London: Faber, 1969).

Clive Hart, 'Joyce, Huston, and the Making of "The Dead" ', Lecture given at Princess Grace Library Monaco (Gerrard's Cross: Colin Smyth, 1988).

Cheryl Herr, 'The Sermon as "Mass Product" ', ch. 6 of *Joyce's Anatomy of Culture* (Urbana: University of Illinois Press, 1986).

Earl G. Ingersoll, *Engendered Trope in Joyce's 'Dubliners'* (Carbondale: Southern Illinois Press, 1996).

James Joyce Quarterly: Dubliners Issue, 28:2 (Winter 1991).

Garry M. Leonard, *Reading 'Dubliners' Again: A Lacanian Perspective* (New York: Syracuse University Press, 1993).

David Lloyd, ' "Counterparts": *Dubliners*, Masculinity and Temperance Nationalism' in Attridge and Howes (eds), *Semicolonial Joyce*.

Rod Mengham, 'Military Occupation in "The Dead" ' in John Brannigan, Geoff Ward and Julian Wolfreys (eds), *Re: Joyce: Text, Culture, Politics*.

L. J. Morrissey, 'Joyce's Revision of "The Sisters": From Epicleti to Modern Fiction', *James Joyce Quarterly*, 24 (1986), 33–54.

Katherin Mullin, 'Don't Cry for Me, Argentina: "Eveline" and the Seductions of Emigration Propaganda', in Attridge and Howes (eds), *Semicolonial Joyce*.

Margot Norris, 'A Walk on the Wild(e) Side: The Doubled Reading of "An Encounter" ', in Joseph Valente (ed.), *Quare Joyce* (Ann Arbor: University of Michigan Press, 1998).

Margot Norris, 'Stifled Back Answers: The Gender Politics of Art in Joyce's "The Dead" ', *Modern Fiction Studies*, 35:3 (1989), 479–503.

Cóilín Owens, 'Clay: Irish Folklore', *James Joyce Quarterly*, 27 (1990), 337–52.

Vincent Pecora, 'Social Paralysis and the Generosity of the Word: Joyce's "The Dead" ', ch. 6 of *Self and Form in Modern Narrative* (Baltimore: John's Hopkins University Press, 1989).

Mary Power and Ulrich Schneider (eds), *New Perspectives on 'Dubliners'* (Amsterdam: Rodopi, 1997).

J. P. Riquelme, 'Joyce's "The Dead": The Dissolution of the Self and the Police', *Style*, 25:3 (1991), 489–505.

Robert Scholes, ' "Counterparts" and the Method of *Dubliners*', in *James Joyce, Dubliners*, ed. Robert Scholes and A. Walton Litz (Harmondsworth: Penguin, 1976).

Robert Scholes, 'Semiotic Approaches to a Fictional Text: Joyce's "Eveline" ', in his *Semiotics and Interpretation* (New Haven: Yale University Press, 1982).

Daniel R. Schwarz, *James Joyce: 'The Dead'*, Case Studies in Contemporary Criticism (Basingstoke: Macmillan – now Palgrave Macmillan, 1994).

Fritz Senn, ' "The Boarding House" Seen as a Tale of Misdirection', *James Joyce Quarterly*, 23:4 (1986), 405–13.

Robert Spoo, ' "Una Piccola Nuvoletta": Ferrero's *Young Europe* and Joyce's Mature *Dubliners* Stories', *James Joyce Quarterly*, 24:4 (1987), 401–10.

Joseph Valente, 'Joyce's Sexual Differend: An Example from *Dubliners*', ch. 2 of his *James Joyce and the Problem of Justice: Negotiating Sexual and Colonial Difference*.

Burton A. Waisbren and Florence L. Walzl, 'Paresis and the Priest: James Joyce's Symbolic Use of Sphilis in "The Sisters" ', *Annals of Internal Medicine*, 80 (1974), 758–62.

Florence L. Walzl, '*Dubliners*: Women in Irish Society' in Suzette Henke and Elaine Unkeless (eds), *Women in Joyce* (Brighton: Harvester Press, 1982).

Florence L. Walzl, 'Joyce's "The Sisters": A Development', *James Joyce Quarterly*, 10 (1973), 375–421.

Craig Hauser Werner, '*Dubliners': A Pluralistic World* (Boston: Twayne, 1988).

Hana Wirth-Nesher, 'Reading Joyce's City: Public Space, Self and Gender in *Dubliners*', in Benstock (ed.), *James Joyce: The Augmented Ninth*.

Notes on Contributors

Vincent J. Cheng is the author of *Inauthentic: The Anxiety over Culture and Identity* (2004), *Joyce, Race and Empire* (1995), *Shakespeare and Joyce: A Study of 'Finnegans Wake'* (1984), and *'Le Cid': A Translation in Rhymed Couplets* (1987), as well as many articles on modern literature; and co-editor of *Joyce in Context* (1992) and *Joycean Cultures* (1998). He is Shirley Sutton Thomas Professor of English at the University of Utah.

Kevin Dettmar is Professor and Chair of the Department of English at Southern Illinois University, Carbondale. He is the author of *The Illicit Joyce of Postmodernism: Reading Against the Grain* (1996), and editor or co-editor of two volumes on modernism, *Rereading the New: A Backward Glance at Modernism* (1992) and *Marketing Modernisms: Canonization, Self-Promotion, Rereading* (1996) and one on contemporary music, *Reading Rock & Roll: Authenticity, Appropriation, Aesthetics* (1999). He is also editor, with Jennifer Wicke, of the twentieth-century materials for the *Longman Anthology of British Literature*, and served as Vice-President of the Modernist Studies Association.

Luke Gibbons is Keough Family Chair in Irish Studies and the Director of Graduate Studies for Keough Institute, at the University of Notre Dame. He is the author of *Edmund Burke and Ireland: Aesthetics, Politics and the Colonial Sublime 1750–1850* (2003), *The Quiet Man* (2002), *Transformation in Irish Culture* (1996), co-author of *Cinema in Ireland* (1988), and a contributing editor to the *Field Day Anthology of Irish Writing* (ed. Seamus Deane, 1991). He is also co-editor (with Peadar Kirby and Michael Cronin) of *Reinventing Ireland: Culture, Society and the Global Economy* (2002) and (with Dudley Andrew) of *The Theatre of Irish Cinema* (2002). He is a member of the Board of Trustees of the International James Joyce Foundation.

Suzette Henke is Thurston B. Morton, Sr Professor of Literary Studies at the University of Louisville. She is the author of *Joyce's Moraculous Sindbook: A Study of 'Ulysses'* and *James Joyce and the Politics of Desire*, and co-editor, with Elaine Unkeless, of *Women in Joyce*. She has published numerous essays in the field of modern literature and women's studies on authors such as Virginia Woolf, Dorothy Richardson, Doris

Lessing, Anais Nin, Samuel Beckett, and Janet Frame. Her most recent book is *Shattered Subjects: Trauma and Testimony in Women's Life-Writing* (1998).

R. Brandon Kershner is Alumni Professor of English at the University of Florida and is working on a book on *Ulysses*. He has published widely on modern British and Irish writers and has edited *Joyce and Popular Culture* (1996), *Cultural Studies of Joyce* (2003), and co-edited an issue of the *James Joyce Quarterly* entitled 'ReOrienting Joyce'. He is presently a member of the Board of Trustees of the International James Joyce Foundation.

Margot Norris is Professor of English and Comparative Literature at the University of California, Irvine, where she teaches modern literature and modern intellectual history. She is the author of *The Decentered Universe of 'Finnegans Wake'* (1976), *Beasts of the Modern Imagination: Darwin, Nietzsche, Kafka, Ernst, and Lawrence* (1985), *Joyce's Web: The Social Unraveling of Modernism* (1992) and *Writing War in the Twentieth Century* (2000), *Suspicious Readings of Joyce's 'Dubliners'* (2003) and *Ulysses* (2004), a study of Joseph Strick's film of Joyce's *Ulysses*.

Jean-Michel Rabaté is Professor of English and Comparative Literature at the University of Pennsylvania and has published and edited some fifteen books on various topics including Beckett, Bernhard, Pound, Joyce and literary theory. His most recent books are *The Ghosts of Modernity* (1996), *Joyce and the Politics of Egoism* (2001) and *Jacques Lacan and Literature* (2001). He has recently edited three collections of essays, *Writing the Image after Roland Barthes* (1997), *Jacques Lacan in America* (2000), and *The Cambridge Companion to Jacques Lacan* (2002).

Robert Spoo was, until 2000, editor of the *James Joyce Quarterly* at the University of Tulsa. He is the author or co-author of numerous books and articles, including *James Joyce and the Language of History: Dedalus's Nightmare* (1994) and *Ezra and Dorothy Pound: Letters in Captivity, 1945–6* (1999). He has also written widely on legal subjects including 'Copyright Protectionism and its Discontents: The Case of James Joyce's *Ulysses* in America', *Yale Law Journal*, 108:3 (1998). After working as an attorney in the intellectual property group of a New York legal office he is currently a lawyer in private practice in Tulsa. He also serves as Copyrights Editor for the *Journal of Modern Literature* and the *James Joyce Quarterly*, and as External Advisor to the *Modernist Journals Project* (Brown University and University of Tulsa).

Thomas F. Staley is Director of the Harry Ransom Humanities Research Center at the University of Texas at Austin, where he is also Professor of English, holding The Harry Huntt Ransom Chair in Liberal Arts. He has written or edited thirteen books on James Joyce, Italo Svevo, modern British women novelists including Jean Rhys and Dorothy Richardson, and on modern literature in general. His most recent books are *An Annotated Critical Bibliography of James Joyce* (1989), *Writing the*

Lives of Writers (1998) and an edited edition of *The Paris Diaries of Stuart Gilbert* (1993). He has been the chairman or co-chairman for four international James Joyce symposia in Dublin and Trieste, and is a board member and former president of the James Joyce Foundation. He was a Fulbright Scholar at the University of Trieste in 1966 and 1971. Staley is the founding editor of the *James Joyce Quarterly*, which he edited for 26 years, and also initiated the *Joyce Studies Annual*.

Trevor L. Williams is Professor of English at the University of Victoria, BC, Canada. He was born in Llangollen, North Wales, and is presently engaged in writing a novel entitled (provisionally) *Sweets of Sin*. He has published *Reading Joyce Politically* (1997) and was a guest lecturer at the Joyce Summer School in Dublin, 1999.

Index

Acker, Kathy, 190
'After the Race', 103, 104, 105–6,
    111
Althusser, Louis, 97
Aquinas, St Thomas, 56
'Araby', 9, 43, 44, 59–61, 98, 99,
    105, 110, 115n, 158–70, 177,
    184–9
Attridge, Derek, 2, 77

Bachelard, Gaston, 23
Bakhtin, Mikhail, 8, 132n, 199
Barnacle, Nora, 54, 64, 147–8,
    150, 166
Barthes, Roland, 16–17, 21, 30n,
    31n, 176, 191n
Beckett, Samuel, 179
Belfast, 102
Beja, Morris, 1, 182, 186–7
Bhabha, Homi, 157, 165
Blanchot, Maurice, 33, 49
'The Boarding House', 43, 44, 98,
    211
Boheeman, Christine van, 2–3
The Bohemian Girl, 90–1, 124
Bourke, Angela, 202, 207
Bowen, Zack, 179–80, 184, 187
The Boys of England, 118
Boys' Own Paper, 120
Brandabur, Edward, 175
Brett, E.J., 118
Broch, Hermann, 34
Brooks, Peter, 150
Brown, Homer, 176
Byron, Lord, 168

Cage, John, 178
Cawelti, John, 122
Chandos, Lord, 34–5
Chenevière, Jacques, 178
Cheng, Vincent, 9
Cixous, Hélène, 6, 13n, 52, 73n,
    148, 162
'Clay', 2, 4, 7, 76–93, 99, 104,
    106, 189, 204–7
Clément, Catherine, 202
colonialism, 53, 102–14
Collins, William, 168
'Counterparts', 43, 45, 46–7,
    101–3, 105, 108, 109–10
cultural materialism, 13n, 117–31,
    132n
Curran, Constantine, 52

'The Dead', 4, 7, 9, 48–9, 64–71,
    108, 135–51, 185–6
Dedalus, Stephen, 2
Derrida, Jacques, 3, 12n, 50n
Dettmar, Kevin, 10
Doolittle, Hilda ('H.D.'), 149
Dublin, 9, 34, 52, 97–8, 102, 158

Eagleton, Terry, 8
Elias, Norbert, 199
Eliot, George, 5
Eliot, T.S., 186
Ellmann, Richard, 4, 25, 64, 70
Empson, William, 178–9
'An Encounter', 4, 43–4, 59, 73n,
    98, 99, 104, 107, 117–31, 190
epiclesis, 180–1

227

epiphany, 163–4, 179–91, 193–4n
'Eveline', 44, 61–4, 74n, 98, 105,
    106–7, 111, 115n, 186–7,
    207–9, 212n

feminism, and feminist criticism,
    6–7, 52–71, 212n
Ferguson, Suzanne, 178
Ferrero, Guglielmo, 142
Feshbach, Sidney, 131
Flaubert, Gustave, 35
Freud, Sigmund, 90, 136–41,
    143–6, 148, 177, 200, 212
    family romance, 90
    the uncanny, 63, 135–51

Gallop, Jane, 59, 63
gender, 52–71, 159–70
Gibbons, Luke, 9–10
Gifford, Don, 100, 113
Girard, René, 74–5n, 94n
'Grace', 8, 43, 47–8, 98, 101, 103,
    108, 204, 211
Greek Mass, 27–8, 40, 181
Guinan, Revd J., 208–9

Harmsworth, Alfred C., 118, 120
Hawthorne, Julian, 165
Heath, Stephen, 11n,
Henke, Suzette A., 6
Herr, Cheryl, 8–9, 108
Herring, Phillip, 175, 177
Hoffmann, E.T.A., 'The Sand-Man',
    136, 139, 143
Home Rule, 14n
Ibsen, Henrik, 74n
    A Doll's House, 66
The Irish Famine, 197, 198–204,
    206
Irish Homestead, 2, 198
Irish Studies, 9–10, 196–212
'Ivy Day in the Committee Room',
    8, 11n, 45–6, 98, 104, 106,
    107, 108

Jakobson, Roman, on metaphor
    and metonymy, 16
Jameson, Fredric, 8
jouissance, 72–3n

Joyce, James
    comments on Dubliners, 2, 16,
        17, 27, 34, 52, 72n, 156,
        180–1, 188–9, 193n, 212,
        214n
    'Drama and Life', 22
    Dubliners, see entries for
        individual stories
    Exiles, 71, 147–8
    Finnegans Wake, 29–30, 39, 49,
        55, 71, 97, 142, 151
    'James Clarence Mangan', 162–3
    A Portrait of the Artist as a
        Young Man, 18, 27, 41, 66,
        185, 187, 209–10
    Stephen Hero, 18, 158, 163, 183,
        184, 197, 206, 210–11
    Ulysses, 29–30, 34, 37–8, 44, 49,
        71, 140, 146, 187, 198, 212
Joyce, Stanislaus, 216n
    My Brother's Keeper, 181

Kaye, Julian, 131
Kenner, Hugh, 29, 82, 174, 187
Kershner, R.B., 8, 165, 167, 168,
    192n, 207
Kiernan, V.G., 157

Lacan, Jacques, 3, 50n, 51n, 58,
    70, 72–3n, 94n, 137
The Lass of Aughrim, 66, 145
Law, Jules David, 210
Lecky, W. E. H., 199–200, 214n
Leonard, Garry, 177, 190
'A Little Cloud', 43, 103, 107, 141
Lodge, David, 16
Lotman, Jurij, 21
Lowe, Lisa, 160–1, 164, 172n
Luedtke, Luther, 166
Lyotard, Jean-François, 10, 191
Lytton, Edward George Earle
    ('Bulwer-Lytton'), 124–31
    The Last Days of Pompeii,
        125–9

Magalaner, Marvin, 126
magazine publishing, 117–31
Mangan, James Clarence, 162
    'Dark Rosaleen', 162–3